MEMORY IN DEATH

MEMORY IN DEATH

J. D. ROBB

DOUBLEDAY LARGE PRINT
HOME LIBRARY EDITION

G. P. PUTNAM'S SONS
NEW YORK

This Large Print Edition, prepared especially for Doubleday Large Print Home Library, contains the complete, unabridged text of the original Publisher's Edition.

G. P. PUTNAM'S SONS
Publishers Since 1838
Published by the Penguin Group
Penguin Group (USA) Inc., 375 Hudson Street, New York, New York 10014, USA • Penguin Group (Canada), 90 Eglinton Avenue East, Suite 700, Toronto, Ontario M4P 2Y3, Canada (a division of Pearson Penguin Canada Inc.) • Penguin Books Ltd, 80 Strand, London WC2R 0RL, England • Penguin Ireland, 25 St Stephen's Green, Dublin 2, Ireland (a division of Penguin Books Ltd) • Penguin Group (Australia), 250 Camberwell Road, Camberwell, Victoria 3124, Australia (a division of Pearson Australia Group Pty Ltd) • Penguin Books India Pvt Ltd, 11 Community Centre, Panchsheel Park, New Delhi–110 017, India • Penguin Group (NZ), Cnr Airborne and Rosedale Roads, Albany, Auckland 1310, New Zealand (a division of Pearson New Zealand Ltd) • Penguin Books (South Africa) (Pty) Ltd, 24 Sturdee Avenue, Rosebank, Johannesburg 2196, South Africa

Penguin Books Ltd, Registered Offices: 80 Strand, London WC2R 0RL, England

ISBN 0-7394-6397-7

Printed in the United States of America

This is a work of fiction. Names, characters, places, and incidents either are the product of the author's imagination or are used fictitiously, and any resemblance to actual persons, living or dead, businesses, companies, events, or locales is entirely coincidental.

While the author has made every effort to provide accurate telephone numbers and Internet addresses at the time of publication, neither the publisher nor the author assumes any responsibility for errors, or for changes that occur after publication. Further, the publisher does not have any control over and does not assume any responsibility for author or third-party websites or their content.

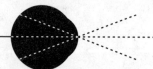

This Large Print Book carries the Seal of Approval of N.A.V.H.

There was an old woman
who lived in a shoe,
She had so many children
she didn't know what to do;
She gave them some broth
without any bread;
She whipped them all soundly
and put them to bed.
—NURSERY RHYME

Memory, the warder of the brain.
—WILLIAM SHAKESPEARE

MEMORY IN DEATH

I

Death was not taking a holiday. New York may have been decked out in its glitter and glamour, madly festooned in December of 2059, but Santa Claus was dead. And a couple of his elves weren't looking so good.

Lieutenant Eve Dallas stood on the sidewalk with the insanity of Times Square screaming around her and studied what was left of St. Nick. A couple of kids, still young enough to believe that a fat guy in a red suit would wiggle down the chimney to bring them presents instead of murdering them in their sleep, were shrieking at a decibel designed to puncture eardrums. She wondered why whoever was in charge of them didn't haul them away.

Not her job, she thought. Thank God. She preferred the bloody mess at her feet.

She looked up, way up. Dropped down from the thirty-sixth floor of the Broadway View Hotel. So the first officer on-scene had reported. Shouting, "Ho, ho, ho"—according to witnesses—until he'd gone *splat,* and had taken out some hapless son of a bitch who'd been strolling through the endless party.

The task of separating the two smashed bodies would be an unpleasant one, she imagined.

Two other victims had escaped with minor injuries—one had simply dropped like a tree and cracked her head on the sidewalk in shock when the nasty spatter of blood, gore, and brain matter had splashed all over her. Dallas would leave them to the medical techs for the moment, and get statements when, hopefully, they were more coherent.

She already knew what had happened here. She could see it in the glassy eyes of Santa's little helpers.

She started toward them in a boot-length black leather coat that swirled in the chilly air. Her hair was short and brown around a lean face. Her eyes were the color of good, aged whiskey and were long like the rest of her. And like the rest of her, they were all cop.

"Guy in the Santa gig's your buddy?"

"Oh, man. Tubbs. Oh, man."

One was black, one was white, but they were both faintly green at the moment. She couldn't much blame them. She gauged them as late twenties, and their upscale partywear indicated they were probably junior execs at the firm that had had its holiday bash rudely interrupted.

"I'm going to arrange to have you both escorted downtown where you'll give your statements. I'd like you to voluntarily agree to illegals testing. If you don't . . ." She waited a beat, smiled thinly. "We'll do it the hard way."

"Oh, man, oh, shit. Tubbs. He's dead. He's dead, right?"

"That's official," Eve said and turned to signal to her partner.

Detective Peabody, her dark hair currently worn in sporty waves, straightened from her crouch by the tangle of body parts. She was mildly green herself, Eve noted, but holding steady.

"Got ID on both victims," she announced. "Santa's Lawrence, Max, age twenty-eight,

Midtown address. Guy who—ha-ha—broke his fall's Jacobs, Leo, age thirty-three. Queens."

"I'm going to arrange to have these two taken into holding, get a test for illegals, get their statements when we finish here. I assume you want to go up, look at the scene, speak with the other witnesses."

"I . . ."

"You're primary on this one."

"Right." Peabody took a deep breath. "Did you talk to them at all?"

"Leaving that for you. You want to take a poke at them here?"

"Well . . ." Peabody searched Eve's face, obviously looking for the right answer. Eve didn't give it to her. "They're pretty shaken up, and it's chaos out here, but . . . We might get more out of them here and now, before they settle down and start thinking about how much trouble they might be in."

"Which one do you want?"

"Um. I'll take the black guy."

Eve nodded, walked back. "You." She pointed. "Name?"

"Steiner. Ron Steiner."

"We're going to take a little walk, Mr. Steiner."

"I feel sick."

"I bet." She gestured for him to rise, took his arm, and walked a few paces away. "You and Tubbs worked together?"

"Yeah. Yeah. Tyro Communications. We—we hung out."

"Big guy, huh?"

"Who, Tubbs? Yeah, yeah." Steiner wiped sweat from his brow. "Came in about two-fifty, I guess. So we figured it'd be a gag to have him rent the Santa suit for the party."

"What kind of toys and goodies did Tubbs have in his sack today, Ron?"

"Oh, man." He covered his face with his hands. "Oh, Jesus."

"We're not on record yet, Ron. We will be, but right now just tell me what went down. Your friend's dead, and so is some poor schmuck who was just walking on the side-walk."

He spoke through his hands. "Bosses set up this lunch buffet deal for the office party. Wouldn't even spring for some brew, you know?" Ron shivered twice, hard, then dropped his arms to his sides. "So a bunch of us got together, and we pooled to rent the suite for the whole day. After the brass left, we brought out the booze and the . . . the recreational chemicals. So to speak."

"Such as?"

He swallowed, then finally met her eyes. "You know, a little Exotica, some Push and Jazz."

"Zeus?"

"I don't mess with that. I'll take the test, you'll see. All I did was a few tokes of Jazz." When Eve said nothing, merely stared into his eyes, he welled up. "He never used heavy stuff. Not Tubbs, man, I *swear*. I'd've known. But I think he had some today, maybe laced some of the Push with it, or somebody did. Asshole," he said as tears spilled down his cheeks. "He was juiced up, I can tell you that. But man, it was a *party*. We were just having fun. People were laughing and dancing. Then Tubbs, he opens the window."

His hands were everywhere now. His face, his throat, his hair. "Oh, God, oh, God. I fig- ured it was because it was getting smokey. Next thing you know, he's climbing up, he's got this big, stupid grin on his face. He shouts, 'Merry Christmas to all, and to all a good night.' Then he fucking dived out. Head first. Jesus Christ, he was just gone.

Nobody even thought to grab for him. It happened so fast, so damn fast. People started screaming and running, and I ran to the window and looked."

He mopped at his face with his hands, shuddered again. "And I yelled for somebody to call nine-one-one, and Ben and I ran down. I don't know why. We were his friends, and we ran down."

"Where'd he get the stuff, Ron?"

"Man, this is fucked up." He looked away, over her head, out to the street. Fighting, Eve knew, the standard little war between ratting out and standing up.

"He must've gotten it from Zero. A bunch of us chipped in so we could get a party pack. Nothing heavy, I swear."

"Where does Zero operate?"

"He runs a data club, Broadway and Twenty-ninth. Zero's. Sells recreationals under the counter. Tubbs, man, he was harmless. He was just a big stupid guy."

The big stupid guy and the poor schmuck he landed on were being scraped off the sidewalk when Eve walked into party central. It looked as she'd expected it would look: an unholy mess of abandoned clothes, spilled booze, dropped food. The window remained open, which was fortunate as the stench of smoke, puke, and sex still permeated.

Witnesses who hadn't run like rabbits had given statements in adjoining rooms, then had been released.

"What's your take?" Eve asked Peabody as she crossed the minefield of plates and glasses scattered on the carpet.

"Other than Tubbs won't make it home for Christmas? Poor idiot got himself hyped, probably figured Rudolph was hovering outside with the rest of the reindeer and the sled. He jumped, in clear view of more than a dozen witnesses. Death by Extreme Stupidity."

When Eve said nothing, only continued to look out the open window, Peabody stopped bagging pills she found on the floor. "You've got another take?"

"Nobody pushed him, but he had help getting extremely stupid." Absently, she rubbed her hip that still ached a bit now and then from a healing wound. "There's going to be something in his tox screen other than happy pills or something to give him his three-hour woody."

"Nothing in the statements to indicate that anyone had anything against the guy. He was just a schmoe. And he's the one who brought the illegals in."

"That's right."

"You want to go after the pusher?"

"Illegals killed him. The guy who sold them held the weapon." She caught herself rubbing her hip, stopped, and turned around. "What did you get from the witnesses regarding this guy's illegals habit?"

"He didn't really have one. Just played around a little now and then at parties." Peabody paused a moment. "And one of the ways pushers increase their business is to spice the deal here and there. Okay. I'll see if Illegals has anything on this Zero, then we'll go have a talk with him."

She let Peabody run the show and spent her time getting the data on the next of kin. Tubbs had no spouse or cohab, but he had a mother in Brooklyn. Jacobs had a wife and a kid. As it was unlikely any investigation would be necessary into either victim's life, she contacted a departmental grief counselor. Informing next of kin was always tough, but the holidays added layers.

Back on the sidewalk, she stood looking at the police barricades, the throngs behind them, the ugly smears left behind on the pavement. It had been stupid, and plain bad luck, and had too many elements of farce to be overlooked.

But two men who'd been alive that morning were now in bags on their way to the morgue.

"Hey, lady! Hey, lady! *Hey, lady!*"

On the third call, Eve glanced around and spotted the kid who'd scooted under the police line. He carried a battered suitcase nearly as big as he was.

"You talking to me? Do I *look* like a lady?"

"Got good stuff." As she watched, more impressed than surprised, he flipped the latch on the case. A three-legged stand popped out of the bottom, and the case folded out and became a table loaded with mufflers and scarves. "Good stuff. Hundred percent cashmere."

The kid had skin the color of good black coffee, and eyes of impossible green. There was an airboard hanging on a strap at his back, and the board was painted in hot reds, yellows, and oranges to simulate flames.

Even as he grinned at her, his nimble fingers were pulling up various scarves. "Nice color for you, lady."

"Jesus, kid, I'm a cop."

"Cops know good stuff."

She waved off a uniform hot-footing it in their direction. "I've got a couple of dead guys to deal with here."

"They gone now."

"Did you see the leaper?"

"Nah." He shook his head in obvious disgust. "Missed it, but I heard. Get a good crowd when somebody goes and jumps out the window, so I pulled up and came over. Doing good business. How 'bout this red one here. Look fine with that bad-ass coat."

She had to appreciate his balls, but kept her face stern. "I wear a bad-ass coat because I am a bad-ass, and if these are cashmere, I'll eat the whole trunk of them."

"Label says cashmere; that's what counts." He smiled again, winningly. "You'd look fine in this red one. Make you a good deal."

She shook her head, but there was a checked one, black and green, that caught her eye. She knew someone who'd wear it. Probably. "How much?" She picked up the checked scarf, found it softer than she'd have guessed.

"Seventy-five. Cheap as dirt."

She dropped it again, and gave him a look he'd understand. "I've got plenty of dirt."

"Sixty-five."

"Fifty, flat." She pulled out credits, made the exchange. "Now get behind the line before I run you in for being short."

"Take the red one, too. Come on, lady. Half price. Good deal."

"No. And if I find out you've got your fingers in any pockets, I'll find you. Beat it."

He only smiled again, flipped the latch, and folded up. "No sweat, no big. Merry Christmas and all that shit."

"Back at you." She turned, spotted Peabody heading her way, and with some haste stuffed the scarf in her pocket.

"You bought something. You shopped!"

"I didn't shop. I purchased what is likely stolen merchandise, or gray-market goods. It's potential evidence."

"My ass." Peabody got her fingers on the tip of the scarf, rubbed. "It's nice. How

much? Maybe I wanted one. I haven't finished Christmas shopping yet. Where'd he
go?"

"Peabody."

"Damn it. Okay, okay. Illegals has a sheet
on Gant, Martin, aka Zero. I wrangled
around with a Detective Piers, but our two
dead guys outweigh his ongoing investigation. We'll go bring him in for Interview."

As they started toward their vehicle,
Peabody looked over her shoulder. "Did he
have any red ones?"

The club was open for business, as clubs in
this sector tended to be, twenty-four hours
a day, seven days a week. Zero's was a slick
step up from a joint, with a circular revolving
bar, privacy cubes, a lot of silver and black
that would appeal to the young professional
crowd. At the moment the music was tame
and recorded, with wall screens filled with a
homely male face, fortunately half-hidden
by a lot of lank purple hair. He sang mo-
rosely of the futility of life.

Eve could have told him that for Tubbs
Lawrence and Leo Jacobs the alternative
probably seemed a lot more futile.

The bouncer was big as a maxibus, and his tunic jacket proved that black wasn't necessarily slimming. He made them as cops the minute they stepped in. Eve saw the flicker in his eyes, the important rolling back of his shoulders.

The floor didn't actually vibrate when he crossed the room, but she wouldn't have called him light on his feet.

He gave them both a hard look out of nut-brown eyes, and showed his teeth.

"You got a problem?"

Peabody was a little late with the answer, habitually waiting for Eve to take the lead. "Depends. We'd like to talk to your boss."

"Zero's busy."

"Gosh, then I guess we'll have to wait." Peabody took a long look around. "While we're waiting we might as well take a look at your licenses." Now she showed her teeth as well. "I like busywork. Maybe we'll chat up some of your clientele. Community relations, and all that."

As she spoke, she pulled out her badge. "Meanwhile you can tell him Detective Peabody, and my partner, Lieutenant Dallas, are waiting."

Peabody strolled over to a table where a

man in a business suit and a woman—who looked unlikely to be his wife due to the amount of breast spilling out of her pink spangled top—were huddled. "Good afternoon, sir!" She greeted him with an enthusiastic smile, and all the blood drained out of his face. "And what brings you into this fine establishment this afternoon?"

He got quickly to his feet, mumbled about having an appointment. As he rabbited, the woman rose. As she was about six inches taller than Peabody, she pushed those impressive breasts in Peabody's face. "I'm doing business here! I'm doing business here!"

Still smiling, Peabody took out a memo book. "Name, please?"

"What the fuck!"

"Ms. What-the-Fuck, I'd like to see your license."

"Bull!"

"No, really. Just a spotcheck."

"Bull." She spun herself and those breasts toward the bouncer. "This cop ran off my john."

"I'm sorry, I'd like to see your companion license. If everything's in order, I'll let you get back to work."

Bull—and it seemed the day for people to

have names appropriate to their bodies—
flanked Peabody, who now looked, Eve
thought, like a slight yet sturdy filling between two bulky pieces of bread.

Eve rolled to her toes, just in case.

"You got no right coming in here rousting
customers."

"I'm just using my time wisely while we
wait to speak with Mr. Gant. Lieutenant, I
don't believe Mr. Bull appreciates police officers."

"I got better use for women."

Eve rolled onto her toes again, and her
tone was cool as the December breeze.
"Want to try to use me? Bull."

She saw the movement out of the corner
of her eye, the flash of color on the narrow,
spiral stairs that led to the second level.
"Looks like your boss has time after all."

Another appearance-appropriate name,
she decided. The man was barely five feet in
height and couldn't have weighed a hundred pounds. He used the short guy's compensation swagger and wore a bright blue
suit with a florid pink shirt. His hair was
short, straight, reminding her of pictures of
Julius Caesar.

It was ink black, like his eyes.

A silver eyetooth winked as he offered a smile.

"Something I can do for you, Officers?"

"Mr. Gant?"

He spread his hands, nodded at Peabody. "Just call me Zero."

"I'm afraid we've had a complaint. We're going to need you to come downtown and answer some questions."

"What sort of complaint?"

"It involves the sale of illegal substances." Peabody glanced to one of the privacy cubes. "Such as the ones currently being ingested by some of your clientele."

"Privacy booths." This time he raised his spread hands in a shrug. "Hard to keep your eye on everyone. But I'll certainly have those people removed. I run a class establishment."

"We'll talk about that downtown."

"Am I under arrest?"

Peabody lifted her eyebrows. "Do you want to be?"

The good humor in Zero's eyes hardened into something much less pleasant. "Bull, contact Fienes, have him meet me . . ."

"Cop Central," Peabody supplied. "With Detective Peabody."

Zero got his coat, a long white number that probably was one hundred percent cashmere. As they stepped outside, Eve looked down at him.

"You got an idiot on your door, Zero."

Zero lifted his shoulders. "He has his uses."

Eve took a winding route through Central, giving Zero a bored glance. "Holidays," she said vaguely as they mobbed onto another people glide. "Everybody's scrambling to clear their desks so they can sit around and do nothing. Lucky to book an interview room for an hour the way things are."

"Waste of time."

"Come on, Zero, you know how it goes. You get a complaint, you do the dance."

"I know most of the Illegals cops." He narrowed his eyes at her. "I don't know you, but there's something . . ."

"People get transferred, don't they?"

Off the glide, she led the way to one of the smaller interview rooms. "Have a seat," she invited, gesturing to one of the two chairs at a little table. "You want something? Coffee, whatever?"

"Just my lawyer."

"I'll go check on that. Detective? Can I have a minute?"

She stepped out, closed the door behind Peabody. "I was about to check my pockets for bread crumbs," Peabody commented. "Why did we circle around?"

"No point letting him know we're Homicide unless he asks. Far as he knows, this is a straight Illegals inquiry. He knows the ropes, knows how to grease them. He's not worried about us taking a little poke there. Figures if we've got a solid complaint, he'll fob it off, pay a fine, go back to business as usual."

"Cocky little son of a bitch," Peabody muttered.

"Yeah, so use it. Fumble around some. We're not going to get him on murder. But we establish his connection to Tubbs, let him think one of his customers is trying to screw with him. Work him so we're just trying to put this into the file. Tubbs hurt somebody, and now he's trying to foist it off on Zero. Trying to make a deal so he gets off on the possession."

"I got it, piss him off. We don't give a damn either way." Peabody rubbed her palms on her thighs. "I'll go Miranda him, see if I can establish a rapport."

"I'll see about his lawyer. You know, I bet he goes to Illegals instead of Homicide." Eve smiled, strolled off.

Outside the interview room, Peabody steadied herself, then inspired, slapped and pinched her cheeks pink. When she walked in, her eyes were down and her color was up.

"I . . . I'm going to turn on the record, Mr. Gant, and read you your rights. My . . . The lieutenant is going to check to see if your attorney's arrived."

His smile was smug as she cleared her throat, engaged the record, and recited the Revised Miranda. "Um, do you understand your rights and obligations, Mr. Gant?"

"Sure. She give you some grief?"

"Not my fault she wants to go home early today, and this got dumped on us. Anyway, we have information that indicates illegal substances have been bought and sold on the premises owned by . . . Shoot, I'm supposed to wait for the lawyer. Sorry."

"No sweat." He tipped back now, obviously a man in charge, and gave her a go-ahead wave. "Why don't you just run it through for me, save us all time."

"Well, okay. An individual has filed a complaint, stating that illegals were purchased from you, by him."

"What? He complain I overcharge? If I did sell illegals, which I don't, why does he go to the cops? Better Business Bureau, maybe."

Peabody returned his grin, though she made hers a little forced. "The situation is, this individual injured another individual while under the influence of the illegals allegedly purchased through you."

Zero rolled his eyes to the ceiling, a gesture of impatient disgust. "So he gets himself juiced, then he wants to push the fact he was an asshole onto the guy who sold him the juice. What a world."

"That's nutshelling it, I guess."

"Not saying I had any juice to sell, but a guy can't go whining about the vendor, get me?"

"Mr. Lawrence claims—"

"How'm I supposed to know some guy named Lawrence? You know how many people I see every day?"

"Well, they call him Tubbs, but—"

"Tubbs? *Tubbs* went narc on me? That fat son of a bitch?"

Eve wound her way back, figuring she'd confused things enough that the lawyer would be hunting for them for a good twenty minutes. Rather than go into Interview, she slipped into Observation. The first thing she heard was Zero's curse as he came halfway out of his chair.

It made her smile.

Peabody looked both alarmed and embarrassed, Eve noted. Good touch—the right touch.

"Please, Mr. Gant—"

"I want to talk to that bastard. I want him to look me in the face."

"We really can't arrange that right now. But—"

"That tub of shit in trouble?"

"Well, you could say that. Yes, you could say . . . um."

"Good. And you can tell him for me, he'd better not come back to my place." Zero stabbed a finger on her, setting his trio of rings glittering angrily. "I don't want to see him or those asshole suits he runs with in my place again. He'll get another kick for buying and possession, right?"

"Actually, he didn't have any illegals on his person at the time of the incident. We're doing a tox screen, so we can get him for use."

"He tries to fuck with me, I'll fuck with him." Secure in his world, Zero sat back, folded his arms. "Say I happened to pass some juice—personal use, not for resale. We're talking the usual fine, community service."

"That's the norm, yes, sir."

"Why don't you bring Piers in here. I've worked with Piers before."

"Oh, I think Detective Piers is off duty."

"You bring him in on this. He'll take care of the details."

"Absolutely."

"Dumbass comes into my place. He *solicits* illegals from me. Fat slob's always nickel-and-diming me, you get it? Mostly Push—and not worth my time. But I'm going to do him a favor since he and his buddies are regulars. Just a favor for a customer. He wants a party pack, so I go out of my way to do him this favor—at cost! No profit. That keeps the fine down," he reminded her.

"Yes, sir."

"Even gave him a separate stash, customized just for him."

"Customized?"

"Holiday gift. Didn't charge him for it. No exchange of funds. I ought to be able to sue him. I ought to be able to sue that rat bastard for my time and emotional distress. I'm going to ask my lawyer about that."

"You can ask your lawyer, Mr. Gant, but it's going to be tough to sue Mr. Lawrence, seeing as he's dead."

"What do you mean, dead?"

"Apparently the customized juice didn't agree with him." The harried and uncertain Peabody was gone, and in her place was a stone-cold cop. "He's dead, and he took an innocent bystander with him."

"What the hell is this?"

"This is me—oh, and I'm Homicide, by the way, not Illegals—arresting you. Martin Gant, you're under arrest for the murder of Max Lawrence and Leo Jacobs. For trafficking in illegal substances, for owning and operating an entertainment venue that distributes illegal substances."

She turned as Eve opened the door. "All done here?" Eve said brightly. "I have these two nice officers ready to escort our guest down to booking. Oh, your lawyer appears to be wandering around the facility. We'll make sure he finds you."

"I'll have your badges."

Eve took one of his arms, and Peabody the other, as they hauled him to his feet. "Not in this lifetime," Eve said, and passed him to the uniforms, watched him walk out the door. "Nice job, Detective."

"I think I got lucky. Really lucky. And I think he's greasing palms in Illegals."

"Yeah, going to have to have a chat with Piers. Let's go write it up."

"He won't go down for murder. You said."

"No." As they walked, Eve shook her head. "Maybe Man Two. Maybe. But he'll do time. He'll do some time, and they'll pull his operating license. Fines and legal fees will cost him big. He'll pay. Best we get."

"Best they get," Peabody corrected. "Tubbs and Jacobs."

They swung into the bull pen as Officer Troy Trueheart stepped out. He was tall, and he was built, and he was as fresh as a peach with the fuzz still on it.

"Oh, Lieutenant, there's a woman here to see you."

"About what?"

"She said it was personal." He glanced around, frowned. "I don't see her. I don't think she left. I just got her some coffee a few minutes ago."

"Name?"

"Lombard. Mrs. Lombard."

"Well, if you round her up, let me know."

"Dallas? I'll write up the report. I'd like to," Peabody added. "Feels like taking it all the way through."

"I'll remind you of that when this goes to court."

Eve walked through the bull pen and to her office.

It was a stingy room with barely any space for the desk, a spare chair, and the skinny pane of glass masquerading as a window. She didn't have any problem spotting the woman.

She sat in the spare chair, sipping coffee from a recyclable cup. Her hair was reddish blond, worn in a cap that had apparently exploded into curls. Her skin was very white, except for the pink on her cheeks, the pink on her lips. Her eyes were grass green.

Middle fifties, Eve judged, filing it all away in a fingersnap. A big-boned body in a green dress with black collar and cuffs. Black heels, and the requisite enormous black purse sitting neatly on the floor by her feet.

She squeaked when Eve came in, nearly spilled the coffee, then hastily set it aside.

"*There* you are!"

She leaped up, the pink in her face deepening, her eyes going bright. There was a twang to her voice, and something in it set Eve's nerves on edge.

"Mrs. Lombard? You're not allowed to wander around the offices."

"I just wanted to see where you worked. Why, honey, just *look* at you." She rushed forward, and would have had Eve in an embrace if Eve's reflexes weren't so quick.

"Hold it. Who are you? What do you want?"

Those green eyes widened, went swimming. "Why, honey, don't you know me? I'm your mama!"

2

Cold rimed her belly, frosted its way up to her throat. She couldn't breathe through the ice of it. The woman's arms were around her now; she was powerless to stop them. She was smothered by them, by the overwhelming scent of roses. And the teary voice—Texas, Texas twang—pounded in her head like vicious fists.

Through it she could hear her desk 'link beep. She could hear the chatter from the bull pen. She hadn't closed the door. God, the door was open, and anyone could . . .

Then it was all noise, a buzzing hive of hornets in her head. They stung at her chest and brought back the heat, a breathless roll of it that washed through her and grayed her vision.

No, you're not. No, you're not. You're not.

Was that her voice? It was so small, a child's voice. Were the words outside her head, or just buzzing there like the bees?

She got her hands up, somehow she got them up and pushed at the soft, plump arms that clamped around her. "Let go of me. Let go."

She stumbled back, very nearly ran. "I don't know you." She stared at the face, but she couldn't make out the features any longer. It was a blur, just color and shape. "I *don't* know you."

"Eve, honey, it's Trudy! Oh, look at me crying like I had to water the cats." She sniffled, pulled a wide pink handkerchief out of some pocket, dabbed. "Silly, just silly old me. I figured you'd know me the second you saw me, just the way I did you. 'Course it has been more than twenty years, between us girls." She gave Eve a watery smile. "I expect I show a few of them."

"I don't know you," Eve repeated, very carefully. "You're not my mother."

Trudy's lashes fluttered. There was something behind them, something in those eyes, but Eve couldn't quite focus.

"Sugar pie, you really don't remember? You and me and Bobby in our sweet little house in Summervale? Just north of Lufkin?"

There was a dull buzz of memory, just on the corner of her mind. But it was making her ill to search for it. "After . . ."

"You were such a quiet little thing, no bigger than two cents' worth of soap. Of course, you'd had a horrible time of it, hadn't you, honey? Poor little lamb. I said I could be a good mama to that poor little lamb, and I took you right on home with me."

"Foster care." Her lips felt bruised, swollen by the words. "After."

"You *do* remember!" Trudy's hands fluttered up to her cheeks. "I swear, hardly a day's gone by in all these years I haven't thought of you and wondered how you'd turned out. And just look! A policewoman, living in New York City. Married, too. No babies of your own yet, though?"

Sickness roiling in her belly. Fear scratching at her throat. "What do you want?"

"Why, to catch up with my girl." The voice was a trill, almost a song. "Bobby's with me. He's married now, and Zana's the sweetest thing on two legs. We came up from Texas to see the sights, and find our little girl. We have to have ourselves a real reunion.

Bobby'll take the whole bunch of us out to dinner."

She sat back in the chair again, smoothed at her skirts while she studied Eve's face. "My, my, you grew up tall, didn't you? Still skinny as a snake, but it looks good on you. God knows I'm forever trying to shake off a few pounds. Bobby now, he's got his daddy's build—which is just about the only thing that no-account ever gave him, or me, for that matter. Just wait till he sees you!"

Eve stayed on her feet. "How did you find me?"

"Well, it's the damnedest thing, excuse my French. There I was puttering around my kitchen. You'll remember I set store by a clean kitchen. I had the screen on for company, and they were talking about those doctors who got murdered, and that cloning. Sin against God and humanity, you ask me, and I was about to switch to something else, but it was so *interesting* somehow. Why, the teeth nearly dropped out of my head when I saw you talking on there. They had your name, too, right there. Lieutenant Eve Dallas, New York City Police and Security Department. You're a heroine, that's what they said. And you'd been wounded, too. Poor little lamb. But you look to be fit now. You're looking very fit."

There was a woman sitting in her visitor's chair. Red hair, green eyes, lips curved in a smile of sweet sentiment. Eve saw a monster, fanged and clawed. One that didn't need to wait for the dark.

"You need to go. You have to go now."

"You must be busy as a one-armed paper hanger, and here I am just babbling on. You just tell me where you want to have dinner, and I'll get on, have Bobby make some reservations."

"No. No. I remember you." A little, some. It was easy to let it haze. It was *necessary*. "I'm not interested. I don't want to see you."

"What a thing to say." The voice registered hurt, but the eyes were hard now. "What a way to be. I took you into my home. I was a mama to you."

"No, you weren't." Dark rooms, so dark. Cold water. *I set store by a clean kitchen.*

No. Don't think now. Don't remember now.

"You're going to want to go now, right now. Quietly. I'm not a helpless child anymore. So you're going to want to go, and keep going."

"Now, Eve, honey—"

"Get out, get out. Now." Her hands were shaking so that she balled them into fists to hide the tremors. "Or I'll put you in a fucking cage. You'll be the one in a cage, I swear it."

Trudy picked up her purse, and a black coat she'd hung over the back of the chair. "Shame on you."

Her eyes as she walked by Eve were wet with tears. And hard as stone.

Eve started to close the door, to lock it. But the room was overwhelmed with the scent of roses. Her stomach clenched, so she braced her hands on her desk until the worst of the nausea passed.

"Sir, the woman who was . . . Lieutenant? Sir, are you all right?"

She shook her head at Trueheart's voice, waved him back. Digging for control, she straightened. She had to hold on, hold onto herself, until she got out. Got away. "Tell Detective Peabody something's come up. I have to go."

"Lieutenant, if there's anything I can do—"

"I just told you what to do." Because she couldn't bear the concern on his face, she left her desk, the unanswered 'link, the messages, the paperwork, arrowed straight through the bull pen, ignoring the hails.

She had to get out, outside. Away. Sweat was sliding down her back as she jumped on the first glide down. She could swear she felt her own bones trembling, and the cartilage in her knees sloshing, but she kept going. Even when she heard Peabody call her name, she kept going.

"Wait, wait! Whoa. What's the matter? What happened?"

"I have to go. You'll have to handle Zero, the PA. Next of kin of the victims may be calling in for more answers. They usually do. You have to deal with them. I have to go."

"Wait. Jesus, did something happen to Roarke?"

"No."

"Will you wait one damn minute!"

Instead, feeling her stomach revolt, Eve sprinted into the closest bathroom. She let the sickness come—what choice did she have? She let it come, the bitter bile of it, pouring through the fear and panic and memory, until she was empty.

"Okay. Okay." She was shaking, and her face ran with sweat. But there were no tears. There wouldn't be tears to add to the humiliation.

"Here. Here you go." Peabody pushed

dampened tissues into her hand. "It's all I've got. I'll get some water."

"No." Eve let her head fall back on the wall of the stall. "No. Anything goes in now is just going to come up again. I'm okay."

"My ass. Morris has guests in the morgue that look better than you."

"I just need to go."

"Tell me what happened."

"I just need to go. I'm taking the rest of the day, comp time. You can handle the case, you're up to it." *I'm not*, she thought. *I'm just not.* "Any problems, just . . . just stall 'til tomorrow."

"Screw the case. Look, I'll get you home. You're in no shape to—"

"Peabody, if you're my friend, back off. Let me be. Just do the job," Eve said as she got shakily to her feet. "And let me be."

Peabody let her go, but she pulled out her pocket 'link as she headed back up to Homicide. Maybe she had to back off, but she knew someone who didn't.

And wouldn't.

Eve's first thought was to set her vehicle on auto. But it was better to be in control, bet-

ter to concentrate on navigating the trip uptown. Better, she thought, to deal with the
traffic, the snags, the time, the sheer bad
temper of New York than her own misery.

Going home, that was the object. She'd
be okay once she was home.

Maybe her stomach was raw and her
head pounding, but she'd been sick before,
and unhappy before. The first eight years of
her life had been a slow ride through hell,
and the ones following it hadn't been a
damn picnic at the beach.

She'd gotten through, she'd gotten by.

She'd get through, she'd get by again.

She wasn't going to be sucked back in.
She wasn't going to be a *victim* because
some voice from the past panicked her.

But her hands shook on the wheel
nonetheless, and she kept all the windows
down to the harsh air, the city smells.

Soy dogs smoking on a glide-cart, the
sour belch of a maxibus, a curbside recycler
that hadn't been serviced in recent memory.
She could take the stench of all that, and the
sheer weight of aromas layering the air from
the mass of humanity that thronged the
streets and glides.

She could take the noise, the blats and

the beeps that thumbed their collective noses at noise pollution laws. The tidal wave of voices rolled toward her, through her, past her. Thousands crammed the streets, the natives clipping along, tourists gawking and getting in the way. People juggling and hauling boxes and shopping bags.

Christmas was coming. Don't be late.

She'd bought a scarf off the street from a smart-ass kid she'd enjoyed. Green and black checks, for Dr. Mira's husband. What would Mira have to say about her reaction to today's ugly flashback?

Plenty. The criminal profiler and psychiatrist would have plenty to say in her classy and concerned way.

Eve didn't give a rat's bony ass.

She wanted home.

Her eyes blurred when the gates opened for her. Blurred with weariness and relief. The great, grand lawn flowed, acres of peace and beauty in the center of the chaos of the city she'd made hers.

Roarke had the vision, and the power, to create this haven for himself, and for her the sanctuary she hadn't known she'd wanted.

It looked like an elegant fortress, but it

was home. Just home, for all its size and fierce beauty. Behind those walls, that stone and glass, was the life they'd created together. Their lives, their memories, spilled out into all those vast rooms.

He'd given her home, she needed to remember that. And to remember that no one could take it from her, no one could rip her back to when she'd had nothing, had been nothing.

No one could do that but Eve herself.

But she was cold, so cold, and the headache was tearing through her skull like demon claws.

She dragged herself out of the car, swayed on a hip that now ached horribly. Then she put one foot in front of the other until she'd made it up the steps, through the door.

She barely registered Summerset, Roarke's majordomo, glide into the foyer. She didn't have the energy to spar with him, hoped she had enough to get up the stairs.

"Don't talk to me." She gripped the newel post, and the cold sweat on her palms made it slick. She pulled herself up the stairs, one tread at a time.

The effort had her breath coming short.

Her chest was so tight, so tight it felt as if someone had banded steel around it.

In the bedroom, she pulled off her coat, let it fall, dragged off her clothes as she aimed for the bathroom.

"Jets on," she ordered. "Full. One hundred and one degrees."

Naked, she stepped under the spray, into the heat. And exhausted, lowered herself to the shower floor, curled up, and let the heat and force of the water battle the cold.

That's where he found her, curled on the wet tiles with water beating over her. Steam hung like a curtain.

It ripped at his heart to see her.

He grabbed a bath sheet. "Jets off," Roarke ordered, and crouched down to bundle her up.

"No. Don't." She slapped out at him, automatic defense without any sting. "Just leave me alone."

"Not in this lifetime. Stop it!" His voice was sharp, and the Irish in it had a bite. "You'll have boiled your bones in another minute." He hauled her up, lifting her off her feet and into his arms when she tried to curl up again. "Just hush now. Ssh. I've got you."

She closed her eyes. Shutting him out, he knew well enough. But he carried her into the bedroom, over to the platform that held their bed, and sitting with her on his lap rubbed the towel over her.

"I'm going to get you a robe, and a soother."

"I don't want—"

"Didn't ask what you wanted, did I?" He lifted her chin with his hand, traced his thumb down its shallow dent. "Eve, look at me. Look at me now." There was resentment as well as fatigue in her eyes—and it nearly made him smile. "You're too sick to argue with me, and we both know it. Whatever's hurt you . . . well, you'll tell me about it, then we'll see what's to be done." He touched his lips to her forehead, her cheeks, her lips.

"I've already taken care of it. Nothing has to be done."

"Well, that'll save us some time, won't it?" He shifted her, then rose to get her a warm robe.

She'd gotten his suit wet, she noted. Damn suit probably cost more than the tailor made in two years. Now the shoulders and sleeves were damp. She watched in silence as he shrugged out of the jacket, laid it over the back of a chair in the sitting area.

Graceful as a cat, she thought, and a lot more dangerous. He'd probably been in one of his hundreds of weekly meetings, making plans to buy a freaking solar system. Now he was here, flipping through the closet for a robe. Long and lean, a body of elegant and disciplined muscles, the face of a young Irish god who could seduce with one look out of those Celtic blue eyes.

She didn't want him here. Didn't want anyone here.

"I want to be alone."

He arched an eyebrow, cocked his head a little so that silky mane of midnight flowed around his face. "To suffer and brood, is it? You'd have a better time fighting with me. Here, put this on."

"I don't want to fight."

He laid the robe beside her, bent so their eyes were level. "If I have the opportunity, I'll take whoever put that look on your face, my darling Eve, and peel the skin from their bones. One thin layer at a time. Now put on your robe."

"She shouldn't have called you." Her

voice hitched before she could steady it, and added another tear to humiliation. "Peabody contacted you, I know it. She should've left it alone. I'd've been all right in a little while. I'd be fine."

"Bollocks. You don't go down easy. I know it, and so does she." He crossed to the AutoChef, programmed for a soother. "This will take the edge off that headache, settle your stomach. No tranqs," he added, glancing back at her. "I promise."

"It's stupid. I let it get to me, and it's stupid. It's not worth all this." She pushed at her hair. "It just caught me off guard, that's all." When she got to her feet, her legs felt loose and ungainly. "I just needed to come home for a while."

"Do you think I'm going to settle for that?"

"No." Though she wanted to crawl into the bed, pull the covers over her head for an hour, she sat, met his eyes as he brought her the soother. "No. I left Peabody with a mess. I let her take primary, and she did good, but right at the sticking point I left her to deal with it by herself. Stupid. Irresponsible."

"Why did you?"

Because it was drink the damn soother or have him pour it into her, she drank it in three gulps. "There was a woman waiting for me in my office. I didn't recognize her, not at first. Not at first." She set the empty glass aside. "She said she was my mother. She wasn't," Eve said quickly. "She wasn't, and I knew it, but having her say it knocked me. She's probably about the right age, and there was something familiar, so it knocked me hard."

He took her hand, held it tight. "Who was she?"

"Her name's Lombard. Trudy Lombard. After they . . . When I got out of the hospital in Dallas, I went into the system. No ID, no memory, trauma, sexual assault. I know how it works now, but then, I didn't know what was happening, what was going to happen. He told me, before, my father, that if the cops or the social workers ever got me, they'd put me in a hole, they'd lock me in the dark. They didn't, but . . ."

"Sometimes the places they put you aren't much better."

"Yeah." He'd know, she thought. He'd understand. "I was in a state home for a while. Few weeks, maybe. It's sketchy. I guess they were looking for parents or guardians, trying to track where I'd come from, what had happened. Then they put me in a foster home. That was supposed to help mainstream me. They gave me to Lombard. Someplace in east Texas. She had a house, and a son a couple years older than me."

"She hurt you."

It wasn't a question. He would know that, too. He would understand that. "She never hit me, not like he did. She never left a mark."

He swore, with a quiet viciousness that eased the tension balled in her more than the soother.

"Yeah, it's easier to cope with a direct punch than subtle little tortures. They didn't know what to do with me." She pushed at her wet hair, and now her fingers were steady. "I wasn't giving them anything. I didn't have anything to give. They probably figured I'd do better in a house with no male authority figure, because of the rape."

He said nothing, simply drew her toward him to brush his lips over her temple.

"She never yelled at me, and she never hit me—no more than a few slaps. She saw to it I was clean, that I had decent clothes. I know the pathology now, but I wasn't even nine. When she told me I was filthy and made me wash in cold water every morning, every night, I didn't understand. She always looked so sad, so disappointed. If she locked me in the dark, she said it was only to teach me to behave. Every day there were punishments. If I didn't eat everything on my plate, or I ate it too fast, too slow, I'd have to scrub the kitchen with a toothbrush. Something like that."

I set store by a clean kitchen.

"She didn't have domestics. She had me. I was always too slow, too stupid, too ungrateful, too something. She'd tell me I was pathetic, or I was evil, and always in this soft, kindly voice with this look of puzzled disappointment on her face. I was still nothing. Worse than nothing."

"She should never have passed the screening."

"It happens. Worse than her happens. I was lucky it wasn't worse. I had nightmares. I had nightmares all the time, almost every night back then. And she'd . . . oh, God, she'd come in and she'd say I'd never get healthy and strong if I didn't get a good night's sleep."

Because she could, she reached for his hand, let it anchor her in the now while she took herself back. "She'd turn off the lights and lock the door. She'd lock me in the dark. If I cried, it was worse. They'd take me back, put me in a cage for mental defectives. That's what they did to girls who wouldn't behave. And Bobby, her boy, she'd use me there, too. She'd tell him to look at me, and remember what happened to bad children, to children without a real mother to take care of them."

He was touching her now, rubbing her back, smoothing her hair. "They did home checks?"

"Yeah. Sure." She dashed a tear away—tears were useless, then and now. "It all looked nice and clean on the surface. Tidy house, pretty yard. I had my own room, clothes. What would I have told them? She said I was evil. I'd wake up from a nightmare where I was covered with blood, so I must've been evil. When she told me someone had hurt me, thrown me away with the garbage because I was bad, I believed her."

"Eve." He took both her hands, brought them to his lips. He wanted to gather her up, cover her in something soft, something beautiful. He wanted to hold her until every horrid memory was washed away. "What you are is a miracle."

"She was a vicious, sadistic woman. Just another predator. I know that now." Had to remember that now, Eve thought as she drew a deep breath. "But then all I knew was that she was in charge. I ran away. But this was a small town, not Dallas, and they found me. I planned it better when I ran the second time, and I got over into Oklahoma, and when they found me, I fought them."

"Damn right you did."

He said it with such a combination of pride and anger, she heard herself laugh. "Bloodied one of the social workers' noses." And that memory, she realized, wasn't so bad. "Ended up in juvie for a while, but it was better than her. I put it away, Roarke. I put it aside. Then there she was, sitting in my office, and I was back to being scared."

He wished she'd bloodied goddamn Trudy Lombard's nose, gotten some little bit of her own back. She'd have been better for that. "She'll never hurt you again."

Eve faced him now, eye to eye. "I fell apart. Disintegrated. I'm feeling just steady enough now for that to piss me off. The Icove case."

"What?"

She lowered her head to her hands, rubbed them hard over her face before she lifted it again. "She said she'd seen me giving an interview about the Icove murders, the Quiet Birth fiasco. I asked how she'd found me, and she said she'd heard about the case."

He rolled his healing shoulder out of habit. "I doubt there's anyone in the known universe who hasn't by now. She came here, specifically, to see you?"

"Said she wanted to catch up, see how I'd turned out. Wanted a nice reunion." She was recovered enough that her tone was sour and cynical. It was music to Roarke's ears.

"She's got her son and his wife with her, apparently. I kicked her out. At least I had enough left to do that. She gave me that look, that puzzled disappointment—with the nasty edge just under it."

"You'll want to make sure she goes away, stays away. I can—"

"No, I don't." She shoved back, stood up. "No, I don't, and I don't want you touching it. I want to forget this, forget her. Whatever jollies she thought she might get by taking me down some memory lane she's swept and polished, she won't get them. If Peabody had kept her nose out, I'd've been straightened out when you got home. We wouldn't be having this discussion."

He waited a long minute, then rose as well. "And that's how you'd have handled this? By telling me nothing?"

"This one, yeah. It's done, it's over. It's my problem. I let it twist me around. Now I'm untwisted. It doesn't apply to us. I don't want it to apply to us. If you want to help me out here, you'll let it fade."

He started to speak, thought better of it, then shrugged. "All right, then."

But he took her shoulders, rubbed. He drew her in, and felt her body relax against his.

She was more twisted up than she real-ized, he thought, if she believed the woman had tracked her across the country, across the years, for no real purpose.

It was only a matter of time before that purpose became clear.

"It's going dark," he murmured. "Holiday lights, on."

She turned her head on his shoulder, and

together they studied the huge live pine in the window as the festive lights flashed on.

"You always go overboard," she said quietly.

"I don't think you can with Christmas, especially if you're us, and had so many thin ones. Besides, it's tradition for us now, isn't it? A tree in the bedroom at Christmas."

"You've got a tree in nearly every room in the house."

He grinned at that. "I do, don't I? I'm a slave to sentiment." He kissed her, softly, then circled his arms around her again. "What do you say to a quiet meal up here? With no work for either of us. We'll watch some screen, drink some wine. Make love."

She tightened her arms around him. She'd needed home, she thought, and here it was. "I'd say, 'Thanks.' "

And when she was asleep, he left her, briefly, for his private office. He crossed the tiles, laid his hand on the palm print.

"Roarke," he said. "Power up."

As the console hummed, flickered with light, he used the house 'link to contact Summerset.

"If anyone by the name of Lombard attempts to reach Eve here, put them through to me. Wherever I might be."

"Of course. Is the lieutenant all right?"

"She is, yes. Thanks." He clicked off, then ordered a search. It would take a bit of time to pinpoint where this Lombard was staying while in New York. But it was best, always best, to know the location of an adversary.

He doubted it would be much longer before he knew just what the woman wanted—though he was dead certain he already knew.

3

Normal, Eve thought, when she strapped on her weapon harness. She felt normal again. Maybe those whiners who were forever talking about expressing your feelings were onto something.

God, she hoped not. If they were, she'd end up neck deep in mangled bodies.

Regardless, she felt steady—steady enough to scowl at the nasty weather whirling outside the bedroom window.

"What exactly do they call that business?" Roarke asked as he stepped beside her. "It's not snow, not rain, not even really sleet. It must be—"

"Crap," she said. "It's cold, wet, crap."

"Ah." He nodded, rubbed the back of his knuckles absently up and down her spine.

"Of course. Maybe it'll keep people indoors and you'll have a quiet day."

"People kill each other inside, too," she reminded him. "Especially when they get fed up looking out the window at crap." Because she sounded just like the woman he adored, he gave her a friendly pat on the shoulder.

"Well, it's off to work for you, then. I'll be handling 'link conferences here for another hour or so before I have to go out in this." He turned her, gripped the lapels of her jacket, kissed her quick and hard. "Be safe."

She reached for her coat, started to swing it on, and felt the slight bulge in the pocket. "Oh, I picked this up for Dennis Mira. Just a, you know, Christmas token thing."

"Looks like him." Roarke nodded at the scarf she held, even as his eyes laughed at her. "Aren't you the clever shopper?"

"I didn't shop. I picked it up. Do you think there's any way it could get wrapped?"

With a half smile, Roarke held out his hand for it. "I'll notify the elves. And I'll have it put with the antique teapot you bought for

Mira—which you didn't shop for either, but, as I recall, came across."

"That'd be good, smart ass. See you later."

"Lieutenant? You haven't forgotten our Christmas party?"

She spun around. "Christmas party? That's not tonight. Is it? It's not."

It was small of him, he could admit it. But he loved seeing that quick panic on her face as she tried to remember which day was which. "Tomorrow. So if you've anything you need or want to come across to pick up beforehand, it should be today."

"Sure. Right. No problem." Shit, she thought as she headed downstairs. Was there anything else? Why were there all these people who had to be crossed off her pick-up-something list? Was she actually going to have to start *making* a list?

If it came to that it might be best to move away altogether and start over.

She could dump the whole business on Roarke, of course. He actually liked to come across stuff to pick up. The man *shopped*—something she avoided at all possible costs. But if you were going to end up with all these people in your life, it seemed you should at

least spend a half a minute picking something up, personally. Plus, she thought it was
another kind of rule.

Relationships were lousy with rules, that
much she'd learned. It was just her bad luck
that she usually tried to play by them.

One of the rules she enjoyed was verbally
bitch-slapping Summerset on her way in or
out the door. He was there—of course he
was there, the skeleton in a black suit—in
the foyer.

"My vehicle better be right where I left it,
Nancy."

His lips thinned. "You'll find the object
you call a vehicle currently embarrassing
the front of this house. I require any and all
additions or adjustments to your personal
guest list for tomorrow's gathering by two
this afternoon."

"Yeah? Well, check with my social secre-
tary. I'll be a little busy serving and protecting the city for lists."

She strolled out, then hissed. List? She
was supposed to have a list for this, too?
What was wrong with just running into
someone and telling them to come on by?

She hunched against the nasty, freezing
rain, slid into her car. The heater was al-

ready running. Summerset's work, probably, which would have to go on the list of reasons not to strangle him in his sleep.

At least that was a short one.

She started down the drive, engaged the dash 'link and tagged Roarke.

"Miss me already?"

"Every second without you is a personal hell. Listen, am I supposed to have a list? Like a guest list for this deal tomorrow?"

"Do you want one?"

"No. No, I don't want a damn list, but—"

"It's taken care of, Eve."

"Okay, good then. Fine." Another thought wandered into her brain. "I probably have an entire outfit, down to the underwear, all picked out, too, don't I?"

"Showing exquisite taste—with underwear optional."

It made her laugh. "I never miss a trick. Later."

Peabody was already at her desk when Eve walked into Central. It added another little pinch of guilt. She crossed over, waited until Peabody glanced up from her paperwork.

"Would you mind coming into my office for a minute?"

There was a blink of surprise. "Sure. Right behind you."

With a nod, Eve headed into her office, programmed two coffees—one light and sweet for Peabody. That got her another blink of surprise when Peabody stepped in.

"Shut the door, will you?"

"Sure. Um, I have the report on . . . thanks," she added when Eve handed her the coffee. "On Zero. The PA went in hard, Second Degree, two counts, using the illegals sale as a deadly weapon in the act of committing, with—"

"Sit down."

"Jeez, am I being transferred to Long Island or something?"

"No." Eve sat herself, waiting, watched Peabody warily take a seat. "I'm going to apologize for walking out on you yesterday, for not doing my job, and leaving you to deal with it."

"We were all but wrapped, and you were sick."

"It wasn't wrapped, and if I was sick, it was my problem. I made it yours. You called Roarke."

Eve waited a beat while Peabody got busy looking at the wall and drinking coffee. "I was going to slap you good for that," she said when Peabody opened her mouth. "But it was probably the sort of thing a partner should do."

"You were in bad shape. I didn't know what else *to* do. Okay now?"

"Fine." She studied her coffee a moment. Partnership was another thing with rules. "There was a woman in my office when we got back yesterday. Someone I knew a long time ago. It gave me a knock. A big one. She was my first foster mother—loose term on the mother. It was a rough patch, and having her come in like that, after all this time, it . . . I couldn't—"

No, Eve thought, you always could.

"I didn't handle it," she corrected. "So I ditched. You handled the case, Peabody, and largely alone. You did a good job."

"What did she want?"

"I don't know, don't care. I got her out. Door's closed. If she wheedles her way through it again, she won't be taking me by surprise. And I *will* handle it."

Rising, she went to her window, shoved it up. Cold and wet spilled in as she leaned out and tore free the evidence bag she'd fixed to the outside wall. In it were four unopened candy bars.

"You have chocolate bars sealed and taped outside the window," Peabody said with a mixture of awe and puzzlement.

"I did have," Eve corrected. She was giving up the best hiding place she'd devised from the nefarious candy thief. She unsealed the bag, handed the speechless Peabody a bar. "They'll be somewhere else after you leave and I lock the door and find a new spot for my cache."

"Okay. I'm putting it in my pocket before I tell you we didn't get Murder Two."

"Didn't figure you did."

Not one to take chances with chocolate, Peabody shoved the bar into her pocket anyway. "PA told me we wouldn't before we went in to pitch the deal. He wanted Zero bad, more than me, I think. Zero's slipped through his fingers plenty, and the PA wanted to nail him."

Eve leaned against her desk. "I like a PA with an agenda."

"It helps," Peabody agreed. "We spooked them with talk of two consecutive life sentences, off planet penal colony, made noises about eye witnesses."

Peabody tapped her fingers on her pocket as if to reassure herself the candy was still there. "We got ourselves a search and seize, and popped some illegals from the club and Zero's residence. Petty stuff, really, and the claim they were for personal use might have been true, but we just kept piling it up. By the time we'd finished, Zero and his lawyer were looking at Man Two as a gift from the Higher Powers. Five to ten, and he probably won't serve the full minimum, but—"

"You got him in a cage, and that's a check in the win column. He loses his license, he pays out the butt in fees and fines, his club will likely go tits up. You keep the chocolate."

"It was great." And since the candy in her pocket was currently screaming her name, Peabody gave in, took it out, and unwrapped enough to break off a knuckle's worth. "It was a rush to push it through," she said with her happy mouth full. "I'm sorry you missed it."

"So am I. Thanks for covering."

"No problem. You can put the bag back

outside. It'll be safe from me." At the narrowed, speculative look in Eve's eye, she rushed on. "Ah, not that it wouldn't be safe from me anywhere you put it. I'm not saying that I've ever had any part in taking any candy of any sort from this office."

Eve flattened the look—cop interrogating suspect. "And if we did a quick little truth test on that?"

"What?" Peabody put a hand to her ear. "Did you hear that? Someone's calling me from the bull pen. There may be crimes being committed even now while we lollygag. Gotta go."

Eyes still narrowed, Eve walked to the door, shut and locked it. Lollygag? What the hell kind of word was lollygag? A guilty one if she was any judge.

She gave the bag a shake as she considered where her next candy vault might be.

Between a meeting with the senior staff of one of his manufacturing arms and a lunch he had scheduled in his executive dining room with investors, Roarke's interoffice 'link beeped.

"Yes, Caro." His brow winged up when he noted she'd engaged privacy mode.

"The individual you mentioned this morning is downstairs, lobby level, and requesting a moment of your time."

He'd bet himself a half mil she'd contact him before noon. Now he went double or nothing she'd show her hand before he booted her out again.

"Is she alone?"

"Apparently."

"Keep her waiting down there another ten minutes, then escort her up. Not personally. Send an assistant, please, Caro—a young one. Keep her cooling out there until I buzz you."

"I'll take care of it. Would you like me to buzz you again a few minutes after she's in your office?"

"No." He smiled, and it wasn't pleasant. "I'll get rid of her personally."

He was looking forward to it.

After checking the time, he rose, walked to the wall of glass that opened his office to the spires and towers of the city. It was just rain now, he noted. Dreary and gray and dull, shitting down on the streets from an ugly sky.

Well, he and Eve knew all about being shit on. Life hadn't dealt either of them a pretty hand, and had given them no stake to play it. What they'd done—each in his own way—was make a win out of it. Bluffing, bulling, and at least in his case, cheating their way to the pot at the end of the day.

But there was always another game to be played, always another player willing to do all manner of nasty things to take a share. Or take it all.

Well, come on, then, he thought. He wasn't just willing, but more than able to do all manner of nasty things himself.

He couldn't go back, more's the pity, and beat her bastard of a father into a gibbering, bloody pulp. He couldn't make the dead suffer, as Eve suffered still. But here, fate had dropped a pale substitute right into his hands.

A live one. Plump and pink and prime for skinning.

Trudy Lombard was in for a very unpleasant surprise.

He imagined the last thing that would be on her mind when she crawled out again would be to slither her way around Eve.

He turned, glanced around his office.

He'd made it what it was. Needed to. He knew what she would see when she came in, out of the cold and the gray. She'd see power and wealth, space and luxury. She'd scent the money, though if she wasn't brainless, she'd have some idea of the pot on his table.

An idea that would be considerably short, come to that, he mused. He may have been legal now, but that didn't mean he felt the need to make public what was in all his pockets.

He kept books in his private office at home, updating quarterly. Eve had access to them, should she ever have any interest. Which she wouldn't, he thought with a faint smile. She was easier with his money than she'd once been, but he was still a faint em-barrassment to her.

He wished he knew the name of the gods who'd looked down on him the day he'd met her. If he could stack everything he owned, had done, had accomplished, on one side of a scale, it still wouldn't outweigh the gift of her.

As he waited for time to pass, he slid a hand into his pocket, rubbed the button he carried, one that had fallen off her suit jacket the first time he'd met her.

And as he thought of her, he wondered how soon her mind would clear and snap back. How soon she'd realize why she'd encountered this ghost from her past.

Once she did, he mused, and closed his hand over the button, she was going to be right pissed.

Judging the time was right, he walked back to his desk, sat, buzzed his admin.

"Caro, you can bring her in now."

"Yes, sir."

While he waited those last moments, he chained up what was inside him. What wanted the taste of blood and bone.

She was what he'd expected from his research of her. What in some circles was called a handsome woman—big and bony, her hair freshly done, her face not unattractive and carefully enhanced.

She wore a purple suit with bright gold buttons and a knee-length skirt. Good, sensible heels. Her scent was strong and rosy.

He got to his feet, and though he remained in a position of power behind his desk, he offered a polite smile and his hand.

"Ms. Lombard." Smooth, he thought

when her hand was in his. Soft and smooth, but he wouldn't have said weak.

"I so appreciate you taking a few minutes out of what I know must be a very busy schedule."

"Not at all. I'm always interested in meeting one of my wife's . . . connections? Thank you, Caro."

He knew the brisk tone told his admin not to offer refreshment. She simply inclined her head, backed out. Shut the doors.

"Please, have a seat."

"Thank you. Thank you so much." Her voice and her eyes were bright. "I wasn't sure if little Eve—sorry, I still think of her that way—if Eve had mentioned me."

"Did you think she wouldn't?"

"Well, you see, I feel *terrible*, just terrible, about the way I handled things yesterday." She pressed a hand to her heart.

Her nails, he noted, were long, well manicured, and painted boldly red. There was a ring on her right hand, a thick gold band around a sizable amethyst.

Matching earrings, he observed, to make a well-put-together if unimaginative ensemble.

"And how did you handle things yesterday?" he asked her.

"Well, poorly, I confess. I realized I should have contacted her first, and instead I just jumped in head first, a habit of mine. I'm just too impulsive, especially when my feelings are engaged. Eve had such a hard, hard time back then, and seeing me, out of the blue, no warning at all, it must've taken her right back. I upset her."

Now she pressed that hand to her lips, and her eyes shimmered. "You have no idea what that poor, sweet child was like when she came to me. Like a little ghost in my house, hardly casting a shadow, and scared of even that just the same."

"Yes, I imagine so."

"And I blame myself for not thinking it through first, because I understand now that seeing me again just made her remember those terrible days before she was safe again."

"So, you've come to see me so I can pass your apologies along. I'm happy to do so. Though I think you've overestimated your impact on my wife."

He sat back, swiveled the chair lazily. "I believe she was a bit irritated by the unexpected visit. But upset? It isn't the word I'd choose. So, please, rest your mind, Ms. Lombard. I hope you'll enjoy your time in the city, however brief, before you return home."

It was a dismissal, flat and pleasant. A busy man idly brushing a speck of lint off his jacket pocket.

He saw it register, saw that quick flick, like a snake's tongue, flash in her eyes.

And there she is, he thought. There's the viper under the conservative dress and sugary accent.

"Oh, oh, but I *couldn't* go back to Texas without seeing my little Eve, without making personal amends, and being sure she's all right."

"I can assure you, she's fine."

"And Bobby? Why my Bobby's fretting to see her. He was like a brother to her."

"Really? How odd then she's never mentioned him."

Her smile was indulgent now, and just a little sly. "I think she had just a tiny little crush on him. I expect she doesn't want you to be jealous."

His laugh was quick, rich and long. "Please. Now, if you'd like, you can certainly leave your name and address with my administrative assistant. If the lieutenant wants to contact you, she will. Otherwise . . ."

"Now this just won't do. This won't do at all." Trudy sat up straighter, and her tone took on a little lash. "I took care of that girl for over six months, took her into my home out of the goodness of my heart. And believe me when I say she wasn't easy. I think I deserve more than this."

"Do you? And what do you think you deserve?"

"All right now." She shifted in her chair into what he assumed was her bargaining pose. "If you think that seeing me and my boy isn't the right thing, then—and I know I'm talking to a businessman here—I think I should be compensated. Not only for the time and the effort, and the trouble I went to for that girl all those years back when nobody wanted to take her in, but for all the inconvenience and expense it's taken for me to come here, just to see how she's doing."

"I see. And do you have a measure of this compensation in mind?"

"This has taken me by surprise, I have to admit." Her fingers fussed with her hair, red against red. "I don't know how you can put a price on what I gave that child, or what it's costing me to turn away from her now."

"But you'll manage to do so, I'm sure."

It was temper he saw deepen the color in her cheeks, not embarrassment. He merely kept that mildly interested look on his face.

"I'd think a man in your position can afford to be generous with someone in mine. That girl would likely be in jail instead of putting people in one if it wasn't for me. And she wouldn't even *speak* to me when I went to see her yesterday."

She looked away, blinking at tears he noted she could call up at will.

"I think we're past that now." He allowed a sliver of impatience to come into his voice. "What's your price?"

"I think two million dollars wouldn't be unreasonable."

"And for two million dollars . . . that's U.S. dollars?"

"Of course it is." Faint irritation took the place of tears. "What would I want with foreign money?"

"For that, you and your Bobby will happily go back to where you came from and leave my wife alone."

"She doesn't want to see us?" She raised her hands as if in defeat. "We won't be seen."

"And if I find that measure of compensation a bit too dear?"

"For a man of your means, I can't imagine, but . . . I'd be forced to mention the possibility of my—being upset by all this—discussing the situation with someone. Maybe a reporter."

He swiveled lazily again. "And that would concern me, because . . ."

"Being a sentimental woman, I kept files on every one of the children I was in charge of. I have histories, details—and some of those might be difficult, even embarrassing for you and for Eve. Did you know, for instance, that she'd had sexual relations repeatedly, and all before she was nine years old?"

"And do you equate rape with sexual relations?" His tone was mild as milk, even as his blood boiled. "That's quite unenlightened of you, Ms. Lombard."

"Regardless of what you call it, I think some people might feel a woman with that kind of thing in her makeup isn't the sort who should be a lieutenant of the police department. I'm not sure of that myself," she added. "Maybe it's my civic duty to talk to the media, maybe her superiors at the police station."

"But two million—that's USD—would outweigh your civic duty."

"I just want what's coming to me. Did you know she had blood on her when she was found? She . . . or someone else . . . washed most of it off, but they did tests."

Her eyes were brighter now, as bold and as sharp as her long red nails. "And not all the blood was hers.

"She used to have nightmares," Trudy continued. "And it seemed to me that she was stabbing somebody to death in those nightmares. I wonder what people would make of that, if I was upset and said something. I bet people'd pay good money for a story like that, considering who she is now. And who she's married to."

"They might," Roarke agreed. "People often enjoy wallowing in another's pain and misery."

"So I don't think the compensation I mentioned is too dear. I'll just take it and go back to Texas. Eve won't have to think about me again, even after all I did for her."

"You've misspoken. It was *to* her, not *for* her. Now then, what you don't understand, Ms. Lombard, is I'm compensating you right now."

"You'd better think before—"

"I'm compensating you," he interrupted, "by not getting up, coming over there, and twisting your head off your neck with my bare hands."

She gasped, theatrically. "You're threatening me?"

"Indeed, I'm not," he continued in the same easy tone. "I'm explaining to you how you're being compensated for walking away from this. I'm telling you what's not happening to you, and believe me, it's costing me dearly not to put my hands on you for what you did to my wife when she was defenseless."

He rose, slowly. There wasn't a gasp this time, and no theatrics. She simply froze as all the blood drained out of her face. Finally, he decided, she saw what was under his own shell, under the sophistication, the style, the manners money had bought him.

Even a viper hadn't a prayer against it.

With his eyes on hers, he came around the desk, then leaned back against it. Close enough that he heard her breath shudder out.

"Do you know what could be done, what I could do like that?" He snapped his fingers. "I could kill you, here and now, without a flinch. I could have as many people as I deemed appropriate swear you'd left this office hale and hearty. I could have security discs altered to prove it. They'd never find your body—what was left of it when I was done with you. So consider your life—which I assume is worth a considerable amount to you—your compensation."

"You must be crazy." She shrank back in her chair. "You must be out of your mind."

"Consider that if you ever think of bargaining with me again . . . If you consider lining your pockets by speaking of a child's torture and nightmare for money . . . If you ever attempt to contact my wife again . . . Think of that, and be afraid. Be afraid," he repeated, leaning toward her a bit, "because restraining myself from carving pieces of you away, slowly, one at a time, is irritating. I dislike being irritated."

He took one step toward her, had her scrambling to her feet and backing toward the door. "Oh, and you may want to pass the message on to your son, should he feel inclined to try my patience."

When she reached the door, fumbled behind her for it, he spoke softly. "There's nowhere in or off this world you could hide from me if you do anything more to hurt my wife. Nowhere I wouldn't go to settle with you for it." He waited a beat, smiled, and said: "Run."

She ran, and he heard a thin scream, like a wheezing breath as her footsteps pounded away. He dipped his hands in his pockets, closed one over Eve's button again as he walked back to study the dank gloom of the December sky.

"Sir?"

He didn't turn as his admin stepped into his office. "Yes, Caro."

"Did you want Security to monitor Ms. Lombard's exit?"

"That won't be necessary."

"She seemed to be in a hurry."

He watched the ghost of his reflection smile a little. "She had a sudden change of plans." He turned now, glanced at his wrist unit. "Well, it's time for lunch, isn't it? I'll go up, greet our guests. I have quite the appetite this afternoon."

"I imagine," Caro murmured.

"Oh, and Caro?" he said as he strolled toward his private elevator. "Would you notify Security that neither Ms. Lombard nor her son—I'll see they have an ID print of him—should be given access to this building?"

"I'll take care of it right away."

"One more thing? They're staying at the West Side Hotel, over on Tenth. I'd like to know when they check out."

"I'll see to that, sir."

He glanced back as the elevator opened. "You're a treasure, Caro."

She thought, as the door closed behind him, that at moments like this she was pleased he thought so.

4

To keep her mind busy, Eve concentrated on paperwork and follow-ups. Dealing with the drone work had the added benefit of getting her desk reasonably clear before the holidays snuck up and bit her in the ass.

She was making considerable headway when Peabody came to her office door.

"Tubbs's tox came back positive for traces of Zeus, and various others. Other vic was clean. The bodies, such as they are, will be released to next of kin tomorrow."

"Good job."

"Dallas?"

"Mmm. I'm sending the squad's expense chits up. Most of them," she said with a sneer. "Baxter and I are going to have a little chat."

"Dallas." Eve glanced up, saw Peabody's face. "What?"

"I've got to go to court. Celina."

Eve got to her feet. "We've already given our testimony."

"Prosecution called me separately, remember? As one of the victims."

"Yeah, but . . . I thought you weren't coming up for that yet, not for another week or two anyway. With the holidays . . ."

"It's moving along pretty fast. I need to go in."

"When?"

"Sort of now. It shouldn't take long, but . . . You're going with me?" Peabody asked as Eve grabbed her coat.

"What do you think?"

On a long breath, Peabody closed her eyes. "Thanks. Thanks. McNab's going to meet me there. He's out in the field, and he's going to try to . . . Thanks."

On the way out, Eve stopped at one of the vending units. "Get yourself some water," she told Peabody. "Get me the cold caffeine."

"Good idea. My throat's already dry. I'm prepped," Peabody continued as she entered her code, made her choices. "The prosecution team drilled me good. And it's not like it's the first time I've testified in court."

"It's the first time you've testified as a victim. It's different. You know it's different."

She passed Eve a tube of Pepsi, and took a long pull from the water as they walked. "It wasn't even Celina who hurt me. I don't know why I'm so spooked."

"She was part of it. She had foreknowledge and did nothing. She's charged with accessory for a reason, Peabody. You go in, you lay out what happened, you don't let the defense shake you. Then you walk away from it."

You could walk away from it, Eve thought, but you never really got away. Peabody would remember every moment of that attack. She'd remember the pain and the fear. Justice might be served, but even justice couldn't wipe away the memories.

She went out the main doors. However crappy the day, the short walk would settle Peabody down. "You're a cop," she began, "and you took a hard hit in the line. That matters to juries. You're a woman." Eve slid her hands into her pockets, out of the cold rain. "Whether or not it should apply, that matters to juries, too. The fact that this big, crazy son of a bitch—one who'd killed and mutilated multiple women—kicked you around . . . it matters big time."

"He's sewed up." And that was a huge relief. "Too damn crazy to stand trial. He'll be locked up in an institution for the mentally defective, violence sector, 'til he croaks."

"Your job here is to make what Celina *didn't* do matter. To help the prosecution prove she was responsible."

"They'll get her cold on Annalisa Sommers's murder, the one she did herself. She'll go up for that. Maybe it's enough."

"Enough for you?"

Peabody stared straight ahead, chugged more water. "I'm working on it being enough."

"Then you're doing better than I am. You made it through, others didn't. She watched. Every one of the dead after she linked psychically with John Blue is on her. Every minute you spent in the hospital, in recovery. Every bad moment you've had about it is on her, too. I damn well want her to pay."

As they walked up the courthouse steps,

Peabody swallowed hard. "Hands are shaking."

"Toughen up" was all Eve said.

Once they were through security, she could have badged her way into the courtroom. Instead she waited with Peabody while APA Cher Reo made her way over.

"We've got a short recess," Reo began. "You'll testify next."

"How's it going in there?" Eve asked.

"She's got good lawyers." Reo glanced back toward the double doors. She was pretty and blonde, with perky blue eyes and a faint Southern drawl. She was also tough as titanium. "We're both playing the psychic card, in different ways. Their stand is that the images Celina received—the murders, the violence—resulted in trauma, diminished capacity. They've got their experts swearing to it, and as a result they're trying to hang all the responsibility on Blue. He's crazy, he invaded her mind, and there you go."

"Bullshit."

"Well, yes." Reo fluffed at her hair. "On our end we have her snuggled up safe in bed at home, watching Blue torture and mutilate and kill, which gave her the bright

idea to do the same, with his MO, to her former lover's fiancée. Under the guise of
working with the cops, she held back while
women were murdered, and while a NYPSD
detective was critically injured. A decorated
officer, who courageously fought back and
was intimately involved in closing the case."

Reo put a hand on Peabody's arm, gave
it a little rub in what Eve recognized as a
woman-to-woman support gesture. "You
want to go over it again? We've got a few
more minutes."

"Maybe. Okay, maybe." Peabody turned
to Eve. Her eyes were a little too bright, her
smile a little too tight. "You can go on in. I'll
get one more briefing from Reo, then I might
want to throw up. I'd do that better alone."

Eve waited until Reo took Peabody into a
conference room, then she pulled out her
communicator and tagged McNab. "Where
are you?"

"On my way." His pretty face and the long
blond tail he wore bobbed on her screen.
"Three blocks south. I had to hoof it. Who
the hell let all these people out on the
street?"

"There's a recess, nearly over. You've got

a few minutes. I'll be in the back. Save you a seat."

She clicked off, walked in, and sat, as she had countless times in the course of her career. Halls of justice, she thought as she studied the bench, the gallery, the reporters and those who piled in out of curiosity. Sometimes—she liked to think most times—justice was served here.

She wanted it for Peabody.

They'd dunked the ball of the case in the net for the arrest, for the indictment. Now the ball was passed to the lawyers, to the judge, and to the twelve citizens who sat on the jury.

She studied them when they filed in.

A moment later, Celina Sanchez was led in with her legal team.

Their eyes met, held with that quick, buzzing connection between hunter and prey. It all came back, all the bodies, all the blood, the waste, and the cruelty.

For love, Celina had said at the end of it. She'd done it all for love.

And that, Eve thought, was the biggest bullshit of all.

Celina took her seat, faced front. Her luxurious hair was worn back and up—sleek and almost prim. Instead of her preferred bold colors, there was a staid gray suit.

Just packaging, Eve noted. She knew what was inside it. Unless the jury was dirt stupid, they knew, too.

Reo stepped in, leaned down briefly. "She's going to be fine. It's good you're here." Then she walked to the front to take her place with the State's team.

As the bailiff called for the court to rise, McNab bolted through the doors. His face was pink from cold and exertion, but was still a few shades calmer than the puce shirt he wore under a jacket with a blue and pink zigzag pattern so bright and busy it stung the eyes. On matching puce airboots, he nipped in beside Eve, spoke in a breathless whisper.

"Didn't want me to sit with her—needed a minute. We thought we had 'til Monday. Damn it."

"She knows how to handle herself."

There was no point telling him her stomach was tying itself into greasy knots. No point in telling him she knew what he saw in his head as they took their seats and the PA called Peabody.

He'd see himself running, with his heart

slamming in his throat, hear himself shouting, "Officer down!" into his communicator
as he flew down the steps of the apartment
building to get to her.

Eve hadn't been there, but she saw it,
too. She hadn't been there to see Peabody
broken and bloody and crumpled on the
street. But she could see.

She wanted every member of the jury to
see it, too.

As directed, Peabody gave her name, her
rank, her badge number. The PA was brisk
with her—good strategy, in Eve's mind.
Treat her like a cop. He reviewed with her
some of the testimony already given, and he
and the lead for the defense did their little
lawyer dance.

When she was asked to take them
through the evening of the attack, she
started out strong. The timing, the steps,
the way she'd contacted her cohab partner,
Detective Ian McNab, as she'd walked
home from the subway. So when her voice
broke, the jury heard it, they saw it. And
they saw a woman's struggle to stay alive, a
cop's fight to survive.

"I was able to deploy my weapon."

"You were severely injured, and in a life-

or-death struggle with a man who was considerably bigger than you, but you were
able to reach your weapon?"

"Yes, sir. I got one off. He threw me, was
throwing me. I remember being airborne,
and firing. Then I hit the ground, and I don't
remember anything until I woke in the hospital."

"I have here a list of the injuries you sustained, Detective. With the court's permission, I'll read them off for your verification."

As it began, McNab's hand groped for
Eve's.

She let him hold it through the recitation,
through the verification, the objections, the
questions. She said nothing when the defense began their cross, and McNab's fingers tightened like thin wires on hers.

Peabody was shaky now, and the defense played on that. But that might be a
mistake, Eve thought. Screwing with the
victim, the only survivor in a series of
hideous murders.

"According to your own testimony, Detective, and the statements and testimony of
other witnesses to the attack, John Joseph
Blue was alone when he assaulted you."

"That's correct."

"Ms. Sanchez was not there at the time you were injured."

"No, sir. Not physically."

"According to prior testimony, Ms. Sanchez had never met or spoken with or had contact with the man who attacked you, with John Joseph Blue."

"That's not accurate. She had contact with John Blue. Psychically."

"I would qualify the word *contact*. Ms. Sanchez had observed, through her gift, violent murders committed by one John Joseph Blue, to which he has confessed. Isn't it true that Ms. Sanchez came to you voluntarily to offer her assistance in your investigation?"

"No, sir, it's not."

"Detective, I have reports in evidence that clearly state Ms. Sanchez volunteered her help, without any fee, to the investigating officers, and that her assistance was accepted. That, in fact, she was instrumental in identifying Blue, and thereby stopping him."

While he'd spoken, Peabody lifted a water glass, drank deep. Her voice was steady again, a cop's again when she continued. "No, sir, she did not give the investigative team or the department, or the victims or the city assistance. She, in fact, hindered the investigation by holding back key information in order to kill Annalisa Sommers, which was her primary objective."

"Your Honor, I ask that this witness's speculative and inflammatory statement be stricken from the record."

"Objection." The PA was on his feet. "This witness is a trained police officer, one of the key members of the investigative team."

The dance continued, but Eve could see Peabody relax into it now. She'd found her rhythm.

"You've got two seconds to let go of my hand before I use the other to punch you," Eve said mildly.

"Oh. Sorry." McNab released her, gave a nervy little laugh. "She's okay, don't you think?"

"She's fine."

There was more, then re-cross. When she stepped down, Peabody was a little pale, but Eve was pleased to see her turn her head, look directly at Celina.

She'd remember that, too, Eve decided. She'd remember she'd stood up, and she'd looked.

"That's my girl," McNab said the minute they were outside the courtroom. His arms went around her. "She-Body, you rocked!"

"More like I was rocky, but I think I came around. And Jesus, I'm glad it's over." She rubbed a hand over her belly, mustered up a genuine smile. "Thanks for sticking," she said to Eve.

"No problem." Eve checked the time. "Tour's over in two. Take off, take the personal."

"I'm okay, I—"

"Nothing's shaking anyway." She spotted Nadine Furst, Channel 75's on-air ace, clicking her way over the tiles in her skinny-heeled boots, her camera in her wake. "At least, nothing official."

"There she is. How'd it go, Peabody?"

"Okay. I think it went good."

"You up for a quick one-on-one?"

Eve started to object on principle, then stopped herself. It would probably be good for Peabody to have her say outside the courtroom. And she could trust Nadine.

"I guess. Sure. I can do that."

"It's lousy out, but it'd make better screen if we did it on the steps. Give up your girl a minute, McNab."

"Nope, but you can borrow her."

"Dallas, looking forward to tomorrow." They headed for the doors. "I could use a quick one from you, too. The sober, flat-eyed, 'justice is being served' kind of thing."

"No. It's Peabody's show. Take the personal," Eve said to Peabody, and took a look up at the sky before she started down the steps.

At the bottom, she turned, looked back. Nadine was right, it would make good screen—Peabody, damp in the drizzle, on the steps of the courthouse. It'd be something Peabody would want her family to see, how she'd stood there and talked of the job and justice.

Since she liked seeing it herself, she watched a few moments. She turned away again, just in time to see the shove, grab, and go.

"My purse! My purse!"

"Oh, shit," Eve muttered. She blew out a breath, and gave chase.

Halfway down the steps, Nadine risked a broken neck by rushing. "Get on her!" she shouted to her camera. "Stay on her. Look at her go!" When Peabody and McNab whizzed by, Nadine all but danced on the courthouse steps. "Don't lose them, for God's sake."

The snatcher was about six foot, Eve judged, and looked a solid one-ninety. Most of his height was legs, and he was using them. He bowled people over like pins, leaving her to leap over the piles.

Her coat streamed back, leather snapping in the wind.

She didn't waste her breath shouting for him to stop, identifying herself as the police. His eyes had met hers—as Celina's had—and they'd recognized the hunt.

He grabbed a glide-cart on the corner—operator and all—and shoved it. Soy dogs skidded onto the ground, drink tubes splatted and burst.

She jigged away from a pedestrian he all but threw at her, then jagged from another. Judging the distance, she pumped her legs, shoved off. Her tackle took him down, sheered them both across the wet sidewalk an inch from the curb, where the brakes of a maxibus screamed like a woman.

Her healing hip cried like a baby at the jolt.

He managed to get one in while she was avoiding being crunched under skidding wheels. She tasted blood when the elbow jammed her jaw.

"Now that was stupid." She yanked his arms back, slapped on restraints. "That was bone stupid. Now you've got assaulting an officer on your tab."

"Never said cop. How'm I supposed to know? 'Sides, you were chasing me, you nearly threw me in front of a bus. Police brutality!" He shouted it, humping his body as he struggled to look for some sympathetic bystander. "I'm minding my own and you try to kill me."

"Minding your own." Eve turned her head, spat out blood. At least her throbbing jaw took her mind off her hip.

She tugged, pulled out the purse—and another three, along with assorted wallets. "Pretty good haul," she commented.

He sat up, shrugged, philosophical now. "Holidays. People come out, whatever the hell. Don't slap the assault on, okay? Come on, cut me one, will ya? It was reflex."

Eve wiggled her jaw. "You've got good ones."

"You're fucking fast, gotta admire it."

She shoved at her wet hair as Peabody and McNab ran up. "Disperse this crowd, will you? And get a black-and-white down here to haul this guy in. Multiple counts, robbery. Seeing as it's this close to Christmas, I'll give you a pass on the assault."

"Appreciate it."

"Let's get—get that camera out of my face," Eve snapped.

McNab busied himself gathering the bags and wallets. "Your lip's bleeding, Lieutenant."

"Nah." She swiped a hand over it. "Bit my own damn tongue."

"Car's on its way, sir," Peabody reported. "Nice pedestrian-hurdling, by the way."

Eve crouched down to have another word with the snatcher. "If you'd run the other way, we'd be at Central, out of this damn cold drizzle."

"Yeah, like I'd be that stupid."

"Stupid enough to do the grab right in front of the courthouse."

He gave her a sorrowful look. "I couldn't stop myself. The woman's swinging the damn purse around, gabbing to the woman walking with her. She practically *gave* it to me."

"Right. Tell it to your PD."

"Lieutenant Dallas?" Nadine, huffing a little, stepped up. She had a hand clamped over the arm of a woman with huge brown eyes. "This is Leeanne Petrie, whose property you've just recovered."

"Ma'am. I just don't know how to thank you."

"Start by not calling me ma'am. We'll need you to come down to Central, Ms. Petrie, to make a statement and sign for your property."

"I've never had so much excitement. Why, that man just shoved me right down on the ground! I'm from a little place called White Springs—just south of Wichita, Kansas. I've never had so much excitement."

It had to be said. "You're not in Kansas anymore."

Because she pulled rank and ordered Peabody home, straightening out the mugging mess kept her at Central until after shift. Dark had the temperatures dropping, and the incessant drizzle turned into sleet. The now tricky streets turned the drive home into a marathon of annoyance.

Stuck in it, she sipped on ice water to soothe her sore tongue, and let her mind drift. She was a handful of blocks from home when it drifted to Trudy Lombard, and the light went off.

"Not me. Jesus, it's not about me. Why would it be? Damn it, damn it, damn it."

She flicked on sirens, shot into vertical. Cursing herself and the snarls that made the maneuver all but suicidal, she engaged her dash 'link.

"Roarke," she snapped when Summerset came on. "Is he there yet? Put him on."

"He's just come through the gates, hasn't yet reached the house. If there's an emergency—"

"Tell him I'll be there in ten. I need to talk to him. If anyone named Lombard contacts the house, don't put her through to him. You got that? Don't put her through."

She flicked off, whipped her wheel, and nipped back down to the street to narrowly miss a trio of fenders.

Son of a bitch! What else would she be

after but money? Big, shiny piles of it. And who in the known universe had the biggest piles?

She wasn't getting away with it. And if he even *thought* of paying her off to make her go away, Eve vowed she'd personally skin him.

She fishtailed, and roared through the gates of home. Roarke opened the door himself as she braked in front of the house.

"Am I under arrest?" he called out, and circled a finger in the air. "Sirens, Lieutenant."

She called them off, slammed the door. "I'm so stupid! I'm a goddamn idiot."

"If you're going to talk that way about the woman I love, I'm not going to offer you a drink."

"It's you. It was never me. If I hadn't let her turn me inside out, I'd've known it from the get. Lombard."

"All right. And what's this?" He skimmed a finger gently over the faint bruise on her jaw.

"Nothing." Anger had smothered any lingering pain. "Are you listening to me? I know her. I know the type. She doesn't do anything without a purpose. Maybe the purpose is jollies, but she didn't go to all the trouble and expense to come here just to bust my balls. It's about you."

"You need to calm down. In the parlor." He took her arm. "There's a nice fire. You'll have some wine."

"Will you *stop*." She slapped his hand off, but he simply shifted and tugged off her wet coat.

"Take a minute, catch your breath," he advised. "You may not be wanting a drink, but I am. Filthy weather."

She did take a breath, pressed her hands to her face to steady herself. "I couldn't think, that was the trouble. Didn't think. Just reacted. And I know better. She must've figured she'd come see me, try to play the reunion card. I was just a kid, and messed up with it. So maybe she banked that I didn't remember what it had been like with her. Then she can be the long-lost mother, angel of mercy, whatever, grease those wheels so when she tapped me for money, I'd ask you to give it to her."

"Underestimated you. Here." He handed her a glass of wine.

"Backup plan." She took the wine, paced to the hearth with its snapping fire, back again. "Someone like her has one. I'm not receptive, she'll have a way to go straight to the source. Right to you. Try for sympathy, some hard-luck story. Move to threats if that doesn't shake the money tree. She'd want a nice fat lump sum, come back for more later, but get a juicy bite right off . . ."

She took a moment to study his face. "And none of this is news to you."

"As you said, you'd have come to it yourself right away if you hadn't been so twisted up." He lowered his head enough to brush his lips over her jaw. "Come, sit by the fire."

"Wait, wait." She grabbed his sleeve. "You didn't go warn her off. You didn't go see her."

"I had and have no intention of going to her. Unless she continues to harass and upset you. Do you know she had eleven other children put in her care over the years? I wonder how many of them she tormented as she did you."

"You ran her? Of course you ran her." She turned away. "I'm really slow on this one."

"It's taken care of, Eve. Put it out of your mind."

She kept her back to him, took a slow sip of the wine. "How is it taken care of?"

"She came to my office today. I made it clear that it would be best for all concerned if she went back to Texas and didn't attempt to contact you again."

"You spoke to her?" She squeezed her eyes shut against the helpless anger. "You knew who she was, what she was, but you let her in your office."

"I've had worse in there. What did you expect me to do?"

"I expected you'd leave this to me. That you'd understand this is my problem. This is for me to handle."

"It's not your problem, but ours—or was. And it was for us to handle. Now it's done."

"I don't want you dealing with my problems, my business." She whirled around and before either of them knew she intended it, she let the glass fly. Wine and glass splatted and shattered. "This was my personal business."

"You don't have personal business from me any longer, any more than I do from you."

"I don't need to be shielded, I *won't* be shielded. I won't be tended to."

"Oh, I see." His voice softened, a dangerous sign. "So it's perfectly fine, we'll say, for me to see to those pesky little details. Can this get wrapped, for instance. But the things that matter, I'm to keep my nose out?"

"It's not the same. I'm a lousy wife, I get that." Her throat was clogging up, and her voice thickening as the words fought their way through. "I don't remember to do things—don't know how and don't give a rat's ass about finding out. But—"

"You're not a lousy wife, and I'd be the one to judge that. But you are, Eve, an extremely difficult woman. She came to me, she tried to shake me down, and she won't try it again. I have every right to protect you, and my own interests. So if you want to have one of your snits about it, you'll have to have it alone."

"Don't you walk away from me." Her fingers actually itched to pick up something precious to throw at him as he started for the doorway. But that was too female, and too foolish. "Don't you walk away and flick off my feelings."

He stopped, looked back at her with eyes searing with temper. "Darling Eve, if your feelings weren't so important to me, we wouldn't be having this conversation. If and when I walk away from you, it's to prevent myself from taking the alternative, which at the moment would be to beat your head against some hard object until a little sense rattles into it again."

"Were you even going to tell me?"

"I don't know. There were good reasons on both sides of that, and I was still weighing them. She hurt you, and I won't have it. That's simple. For God's sake, Eve, when I found out about my mother, and went into a spin, didn't you knock it out of me? Didn't you tend to me, even stand in front of me?"

"It's not the same." Her stomach burned, and the acid of it spewed into words. "What did you get, Roarke? What did you fall into but people who love and accept you? Good, decent people. And what do they want from you? Not a damn thing. Yeah, you had it rough. Your father killed your mother. But what else did you find out? She loved you. She was a young, innocent girl who loved you. It's not the same for me. Nobody loved me. Nobody and nothing I came from was decent or innocent or good."

Her voice hitched, but she bore down, let the rest spew out. "So yeah, you took a hard and nasty slap, and it sent you reeling.

But what did you fall into? Right into gold. What else is new?"

He didn't stop her when she strode from the room. Didn't go after her when she charged up the steps. At that moment, he couldn't think of a single reason why he should.

5

The gym seemed the obvious place for him to work off steam, and he had plenty of it. His shoulder was still weak from wounds he'd incurred a few weeks before, helping his infuriating wife on the job.

It was all right, apparently, for him to risk his bloody life, but not—according to the Book of Eve—to get rid of a fucking blackmailer.

Bollocks to that, he thought. He wasn't going to stew about it.

It was time, he decided, to punish his body back into shape.

He went for weights rather than one of the holomachines, and programmed a brutal session of reps and sets.

Her solution, he knew, had she headed downstairs rather than up, would have been to activate one of the sparring droids. Then beat the bleeding hell out of it.

To each his own.

Knowing her, she'd be pacing her office, kicking whatever was handy, and cursing his name. She'd have to get over it. Never in his life, he thought as he pumped his way through bench presses, had he known such a rational woman who could flip so quickly and so *stupidly* into irrational behavior.

What the bloody, buggering hell had she expected him to do? Give her a shout and ask her to pinch that ridiculous Texas fly off his neck for him?

Well, she'd married the wrong man for that, hadn't she? Too bad for her.

She didn't want to be protected when she damn well needed protection, didn't want to be looked after when she was blind with grief and stress? That was too fucking bad for her as well, wasn't it?

He ripped through the session, taking dark satisfaction in the burn of his muscles, the ache of the healing wounds, and the drip of his own sweat.

• • •

She was exactly where he'd assumed she'd be, doing precisely what he'd assumed she'd be doing. She stopped pacing long enough to give her desk three hard kicks.

And the hip she'd injured battling beside Roarke protested.

"Damn him. Damn him! Can't he stay out of anything?"

The fat cat, Galahad, padded in, plopped down in the doorway of the kitchen as if prepared to enjoy the show.

"Do you see this?" she demanded of the cat, and slapped a hand on her sidearm. "You know why they gave me this? Because I can handle myself. I don't need some—some *man* charging in to tidy up my mess."

The cat angled his head, blinked his dual-colored eyes, then shot a leg in the air to wash it.

"Yeah, you're probably on his side." Absently, she rubbed her sore hip. "Male of the fricking species. Do I look like some wilting, helpless *female*?"

Okay, maybe she had, she admitted as she resumed pacing. For a couple of minutes. But he knew her, didn't he? He knew she'd pull it together.

Just like he'd known Lombard would come sniffing around him.

"But did he say anything?" She threw her hands up. "Did he say: 'Well now, Eve, I think perhaps the sadistic bitch from your past will likely be paying me a visit?' No, no, he did not. It's all that damn money, that's what it is. It's what I get for getting hooked up with a guy who owns most of the world, and a good chunk of its satellites. What the hell was I thinking?"

Since she'd exhausted a good portion of her energy with her anger, she flopped into her sleep chair. Scowled at nothing in particular.

Hadn't been thinking, she admitted as the worst of the blind, red rage faded. But she was thinking now.

It was his money. He had a right to protect himself from poachers. She sure as hell hadn't stepped up to do it.

She sat up, dropped her head in her hands. No, she'd been too busy wallowing and whining and, screw it, wilting.

And she'd attacked the one person who fully understood her, who knew everything she kept bottled inside. Attacked him because of that, she realized. Mira would probably give her a big gold star for reaching that unhappy conclusion.

So, she was a bitch. It wasn't as if she hadn't made full disclosure before the I do's. He'd known what he was getting, damn it. She wasn't going to apologize for it.

But she sat, drumming her fingers on her knee, and the scene in the parlor began to play back in her head. She closed her eyes as her stomach sank, and twisted.

"Oh God, what have I done?"

Roarke swiped sweat off his face, reached for a bottle of water. He considered programming another session, maybe a good, strong run. He hadn't quite worked off all the mad, and hadn't so much as started on the resentment.

He took another chug, debated whether to sluice it off in the pool instead. And she walked in.

His back went up, he swore he could feel it rise, one vertebra at a time.

"You want a workout you'll have to wait. I'm not done, and don't care for the company."

She wanted to say he was pushing himself too hard, physically. That his body hadn't healed well enough as yet. But he'd snap her neck like a twig for that one. Deservedly so.

"I just need a minute to say I'm sorry. So sorry. I don't know where it came from, I didn't know that was in me. I'm ashamed that it was." Her voice shook, but she'd finish it out, and she wouldn't finish it with tears. "Your family. I'm glad you found them, I swear I am. Realizing I could be small enough somewhere inside to be jealous of it, or resent it, or whatever the hell I was, it makes me sick. I hope, after a while, you can forgive me for it. That's all."

When she reached for the door, he cursed under his breath. "Wait. Just wait a minute." He grabbed a towel, rubbed it roughly over his face, his hair. "You kick the legs out from under me, I swear, like no one else. Now I have to think, I have to ask myself, what would I feel, should that family situation have been reversed? And I don't know, but it wouldn't surprise me to find some nasty little seed stuck in my belly over it."

"It was ugly and awful that I said it. That I

could say it. I wish I hadn't. Oh Jesus, Roarke, I wish I hadn't said it."

"We've both said things at one time or another we wish we hadn't. We can put that aside." He tossed the towel on a bench. "As to the rest . . ."

"I was wrong."

His brows shot up. "Either Christmas has come early, or this should be made another national holiday."

"I know when I've been an idiot. When I've been stupid enough I wish I could kick my own ass."

"You can always leave that one to me."

She didn't smile. "She came after your money, you slapped her back. It was just that simple. I made it complicated, I made it about me, and it never was."

"That's not entirely true. I slapped her a good deal harder than was necessary, because for me, it was all about you."

Her eyes stung, her throat burned. "I hate that . . . I hate that— No, no don't," she said when he took a step toward her. "I have to figure out how to get this out. I hate that *I* didn't stop this. Wasn't even close to capable of stopping it. Because I didn't, couldn't, and you did, I stomped all over you."

She sucked in a breath as the rest came to her. "Because I knew I could. Because I knew, somewhere in the stupidity, that you'd forgive me for it. You didn't go behind my back or betray any trust, or any of the things I tried to convince myself you had. You just did what needed to be done."

"Don't give me too much credit." Now he sat on the bench. "I'd like to have killed her. I think I'd have enjoyed it. But you wouldn't have cared for that, not at all. So I settled for convincing her that's just what I'd do, and very unpleasantly, should she try to put her sticky fingers on either of us again."

"I sort of wish I could've seen it. How much did she figure I was worth?"

"Does it matter?"

"I'd like to know."

"Two million. A paltry sum considering, but then, she doesn't know us, does she?" His eyes—a bold, impossible blue that saw everything she was—stayed on her face. "She doesn't know we wouldn't give her the first punt. She doesn't know there's no limit on your worth to me. It's only money, Eve. There's no price on what we have."

She went to him then, dropping into his lap, wrapping arms and legs around him.

"There," he murmured. "There we are."

She turned her face, pressed it to his throat. "What's a punt?"

"A what? Oh." He gave a baffled laugh. "It's an old word for an Irish pound."

"How do you say 'I'm sorry' in Gaelic?"

"Ah . . . *ta bron orm,*" he said. "And so am I," he added when she'd mangled it.

"Roarke. Is she still in New York?" When he said nothing, she leaned back, met his eyes. "You'd know where she is. It's what you do. I made myself feel stupid. Don't make me feel incapable on top of it."

"As of the time I left the office, she hadn't yet checked out of her hotel, nor had her son and his wife."

"Okay, then tomorrow . . . No, tomorrow's the thing. I'm not forgetting the thing, and I'm going to do . . . whatever."

And whatever the whatever was that went into preparing for a major party would be her penance for bitchy idiocy.

"Somebody'll have to tell me whatever it is I should do for the thing." She framed his face with her hands, spoke urgently. "Please don't let it be Summerset."

"There's nothing you have to do, and the thing is called a party."

"You do stuff. Coordinate stuff, and approve it, blather with the caterer and that kind of thing."

"I never blather, not even with the caterer, but if it'll make you feel better you can help supervise the decorating up in the ballroom."

"Am I going to need a list?"

"Several. Will that help with the guilt you're feeling?"

"It's a start. On Sunday, if Lombard's still here, I'm going to see her."

"Why?" Now he framed her face in turn. "Why put yourself through that, or give her any sort of an opening to stab at you again?"

"I need to make it clear to her she can't. I need to do it face-to-face. It's—and this is embarrassing enough that I'll have to hurt you if you repeat it—but it's about self-esteem. I hate being a coward, and I stuck my head in the sand on this."

"That's an ostrich."

"Whatever, I don't like being one. So, we do what we've planned to do tomorrow—because she's not worth putting on the list—and if she's still here on Sunday, I deal with her."

"We deal."

She hesitated, then nodded. "Yeah, okay. We deal." She pressed her cheek to his. "You're all sweaty."

"I used my temper constructively, as opposed to kicking my desk."

"Shut up, or I might not still feel guilty enough to offer to wash your back in the shower."

"Lips are sealed," he murmured, and pressed them to her throat.

"After." She gripped his tank, yanked it up and off. "After I screw your brains out of your ears."

"Far be it from me to dictate how you should assuage your guilt. Do you have a lot of it?"

She bit his good shoulder. "You're about to find out."

She toppled them both off the bench and onto the mat. "Well, ouch. I take it guilt doesn't bring out your gentler side."

"What it does is make me edgy." She straddled him, planted her hands on his chest. "And a little mean. And since I've already kicked my desk . . ."

She lowered down, her breasts skimming his damp chest, her nails raking lightly over his skin on their way to the waistband of his shorts. She tugged again, freed him.

Then her mouth clamped over him like a vise.

"Oh, well then." He dug his fingers into the mat. "Have at it."

His mind switched off, his vision went red, and pulsed. She used her teeth—yes, just a little bit mean—and tore the breath out of him. Muscles he'd tuned and oiled in temper began to quiver, helplessly. And a moment before his world imploded, she released him. Slicked her tongue up his belly.

He started to roll her over, but she scissored her legs, shifted her weight, and pinned him once more. Her eyes were dark gold and full of arrogance.

"I'm starting to feel a little better."

He caught his breath. "Good. Whatever I can do to help."

"I want your mouth." She crushed it under hers, using her teeth, her tongue, her lips, so his own blood pounded through him, a hundred drums.

"I love your mouth." Hers was wild on his. "I want you to do things to me with it." She dragged and pulled at her own shirt. This time when her breasts skimmed his chest it was flesh to flesh.

She let him flip her to her back, arched up to him so that his mouth, hot and ravenous for her, could take. Her stomach clenched, twisted, a fist of need and pleasure. Her breath was already going ragged when he yanked down her pants.

His hands, she thought on a fresh leap, his hands were as skilled as his mouth. And the fist in her belly tightened, tightened, then flew open in release.

Her fingers tangled in his hair, gripped all that black silk to guide him down, down to where the need was already blooming again, so full, so ripe, it took only a flick of his tongue to send her flying.

And he was with her, right with her through every breath and beat.

Now she quivered, and the heat poured off her. She was wet and wild and his. When he braced himself over her, looked down at her face, she gripped his hair again.

"Hard," she told him. "Hard and fast. Make me scream." And pulled his mouth to hers even as he drove himself into her.

He plunged, a beast on fire, and she raced with him. Her hips surged up, demanding more even as his lips muffled the scream.

They whipped each other mercilessly to the edge, and over.

She nearly had her breath back, and figured she'd recover the full use of her legs, eventually.

"Just remember, it was my fault."

He stirred. "Hmm?"

"It was my fault, so I'm the reason you just got your rocks off."

"Entirely your fault." He rolled off her, onto his back, breathed. "Bitch."

She snorted out a laugh, then linked fingers with him. "Do I still have my boots on?"

"Yes. It's quite an interesting and provocative look, particularly since your trousers are inside out and hooked on them. I was in a bit of a rush."

She braced on her elbows to take a look. "Huh. I guess I'll get them the rest of the way off, maybe take a swim."

"I believe you're scheduled to wash my back."

She glanced over. "Strangely, I'm no longer feeling guilty."

He opened one eye, brilliant and blue. "But here I am, with my feelings so bruised."

She grinned, then levered up to work off her boots. When he sat up beside her, she turned so they sat facing each other, naked, forehead to forehead.

"I'll wash your back, but it goes on the credit side of my account, to be counted the next time I'm a complete asshole."

He patted a hand on her knee. "Done," he said, then pushed up, and offered her a hand.

In a small hotel room on Tenth Avenue, Trudy Lombard studied herself in the mirror. He thought he'd scared her, and maybe he had, but that didn't mean she'd just turn tail and run like a whipped dog.

She'd *earned* that compensation for tolerating that nasty little bitch in her home, nearly six months of her. Six months of having that dirty child under her roof. Feeding and clothing her.

Now, the mighty Roarke was going to pay for the way he'd treated Trudy Lombard— make no mistake about it. It was going to cost him a lot more than two million.

She'd taken off her suit, put on her nightgown. Preparation was important, she reminded herself, and washed down a pain blocker with the good French wine she preferred.

No point in chasing the pain, she thought. No point at all. Though she didn't mind a little pain. It sharpened the senses.

She took slow, even breaths as she picked up the sock she'd filled with credits. She swung it at her own face, striking between jaw and cheekbone. Pain exploded, nausea rolled in her belly, but she gritted her teeth, struck a second time.

Woozy, she lowered herself to the floor. It hurt more than she'd bargained for, but she could take it. She could take a great deal.

Once her hands had stopped shaking, she picked up the homemade sap again, slammed it into her hip. She bit her lip to bring blood, and smashed it twice against her thigh.

Not enough, she thought, even as tears leaked out of eyes that glittered with purpose and a kind of dark pleasure. Not quite enough, as the thrill of the pain coursed through her. Every blow was money in the bank.

With a keening wail, she swung the sap into her belly, once, twice. On the third blow, her stomach revolted. She vomited in the toilet, then rolled away. And passed out cold.

There was more to it than she'd realized, Eve admitted. The house was full of people and droids, and at this point it was tough to tell which was which. It looked as though an entire forest had been purchased and re-planted in the ballroom, with another acre spreading to the terrace. Several miles of garlands, a few tons of colored balls, and enough tiny white lights to set the entire state aglow, were hung, about to be hung, waiting to be discussed where they should be hung.

There were ladders and tarps and tables and chairs, there were candles and fabrics. The guy in charge of setting up the platform for the orchestra, or band—she wasn't sure which it was—was arguing with the guy in charge of some of the miles of garland.

She hoped they came to blows. That, at least, would be her territory.

It seemed Roarke had taken her at her

word about supervising the ballroom decorations.

What had he been thinking?

Someone was always asking her what she
thought, what she wanted, if she'd prefer
this to that, or the other thing.

One of the crew had actually rushed from
the room in tears the third time Eve said she
didn't care.

Okay, she'd said she didn't give a gold-
plated crap, but it meant the same thing.

Now she had a stress headache circling
the top of her skull just waiting to clamp
down on her brain and destroy it.

She wanted to lie down. More, she
wanted her communicator to beep and
have Dispatch inform her there was a triple
homicide that needed her immediate attention.

"Had about enough?" Roarke whispered
in her ear.

Such was her state that she jumped like a
rabbit. "I'm fine. I'm good." And she broke,
spinning to him, gripping his shirt. "Where
have you *been*?"

"Why, blathering with the caterer, of
course. The truffles are spectacular."

A steely light came into her eyes. "The chocolate kind?"

"No, actually, the sort the pigs snuffle out for us." He ran an absent hand over her tousled hair while he scanned the room. "But we have the chocolate kind as well. Go, make your escape." He gave her shoulder a squeeze. "I'll take over here."

She nearly bolted. Every instinct had her out the door, running for her sanity. But it wasn't only pride, it was marriage that held her in place. "What am I, stupid? I've run ops bigger than this when lives are on the line. Just back off. Hey, you!"

Roarke watched as she strode across the floor, cop in every swagger.

"I said you!" She shoved between Garland Guy and Platform Guy before blood was spilled. "Button it," she ordered as each began to complain. "You, with the shiny stuff, put it where it belongs."

"But I—"

"You had a plan, the plan was approved. Stick with the plan and don't bother me, or I'll personally stuff all that shiny stuff up your butt. And you." She jabbed a finger in the other man's chest. "Stay out of his way, or

I'll save some shiny stuff for you. Okay, you, tall blond girl with the flowers . . ."

"Poinsettias," the tall blonde clarified with New Jersey so thick in her voice Eve could have driven on it across the river. "There were supposed to be five hundred, but there're only four hundred and ninety-six, and—"

"Deal. Finish building your . . . what the hell is this?"

"It's a poinsettia tree, but—"

"Of course, it is. If you need four more, go get four more from the poinsettia factory. Otherwise work with what you've got. And you, over there with the lights."

Roarke rocked back and forth on his heels and watched her rip through the various crews. Some of them looked a little shaky when she'd finished, but the pace of work increased considerably.

"There." She walked back to him, folded her arms. "Handled. Any problems?"

"Other than being strangely aroused, not a one. I think you've put the fear of God into them and should reward yourself with a little break." He draped an arm over her shoulders. "Come on. We'll find you a truffle."

"The chocolate kind."

"Naturally."

Hours later, or so it seemed to her, she stepped out of the bathroom. She'd done the best she could with the lip dye and the eye gunk. On the bed, waiting for her, was what looked like a long panel of dull gold. She figured it became a dress of some kind once it was on a body.

At least it wasn't fussy, she decided as she fingered the material. There were shoes of the same tone, if you could call a couple of skinny straps with an even skinnier heel shoes. She glanced at the dresser and saw he'd thought of the rest. A black case was open, and the diamonds—nothing sparkled like that but diamonds, she assumed, though they looked to be the color of champagne—formed a circle against the velvet. Another held the dangle of earrings, and still another a thick bracelet.

She picked up the panel of gold fabric, studied it, and concluded it was one of those deals you just wiggled into. Once that was done, she carried the shoes, which weren't going on her feet until zero hour,

and fumbled her way through the acces-
sories at the dresser.

The bracelet was too big, she noted.
She'd probably lose it, then someone would
pawn it and have enough money to buy a
nice little island country in the South Pacific.

"You're wearing it wrong," Roarke told her
from the doorway. "Here." He stepped in,
walked to her, elegant in formal black. He
slid the glittering triple band to just above
her elbow. "A bit of a warrior touch, suits
you."

He stepped back. "You look like a flame.
A long golden flame on a cold night."

When he gazed at her like that, things
started melting inside her, so she turned
away, studied herself in the mirror. The
dress was a column, sleek and fluid from
just over her breasts to her ankles.

"Is this dress going to stay up?"

"Until the guests leave, at any rate." He
leaned over to brush his lips over her bare
shoulder. Then he wrapped his arms around
her waist so they studied the image they
made in the glass.

"Our second Christmas together," he
said. "We've stored up a few things in the

memory box Mavis and Leonardo gave us last year."

"Yeah." She smiled at him, and had to admit the two of them looked pretty damn terrific. "We have. Maybe things'll stay quiet this year, so we can make more instead of running around after a deranged Santa."

"We can hope." The bedroom 'link beeped twice. "Our first guests are arriving. Shoes?"

"Yeah, yeah." She bent down to tug on one, narrowed her eyes at the sparkle on the strap. "Oh, my Jesus, don't tell me these are fricking diamonds on my shoes."

"All right, I won't tell you. Hustle up, there, Lieutenant. The hosts can't be fashionably late."

Diamonds on her shoes. He was a crazy man.

The crazy man threw a hell of a party—she had to give him credit. Within the hour, the ballroom was crowded with people. Lights sparkled like wine, and the music streamed through. The tables were loaded with a good deal more than pig truffles. Fancy canapés, pâtés, mousse, glossy delicacies from around the world, and beyond it.

The waitstaff was every bit as elegant as the champagne they served on silver trays. She didn't bother to count the poinsettias, but the tree looked fine to her. In fact, it looked amazing, as did the pines that dripped more light, more color. The forest she'd seen that afternoon had become a wonderland.

Yeah, the guy threw a hell of a party.

"This is so totally juiced!" Mavis Freestone rushed up, leading with her very pregnant belly. At her velocity she bumped into Eve before Eve could avoid contact. "Nobody throws a splash like you guys."

Her hair was silver tonight, in a lot of long, shaggy layers. She wore red, so snug Eve wondered that the ball of her belly didn't burst free. In concession to her condition, her silver boots had short, squat heels shaped like Christmas trees.

Her eyebrows were a curve of silver stars. Eve didn't want to ask how she'd managed that one.

"You look absolutely radiant." Roarke took her hand, then smiled at the giant of a man in silver and red at her side. "Both of you, in fact."

"We're coming to the countdown." Leonardo rubbed his big hand over Mavis's back.

"Almost at what they consider full-term. Um, what's that? Can I have some of that?" She snatched three canapés off a passing tray, popped them like candy. "So when, you know, we're there, we're going to have sex day and night. Orgasms can kick you into labor. My teddy bear can sure do orgasm."

Leonardo's wide, copper-hued face went red along the cheekbones.

"So, you're set for the classes, right?"

Eve just couldn't talk about it, couldn't think about the coaching classes she and Roarke were scheduled to take. "Hey, there's Peabody. I think she's got a truffle."

"Truffle? Chocolate? Where? Later."

"There's my clever girl," Roarke murmured. "Saving us by baiting your best friend with food. The Miras have just arrived," he added.

Before Eve could comment, he was steering her toward them.

It was going to be awkward, she knew. It

had been awkward between her and Mira since the two of them had knocked heads and sensibilities over the Icove case.

They'd both worked to keep it smooth, but there were still ripples. And Eve could feel them now as Mira glanced over and spotted her.

"We were held up." Mira kissed Roarke's cheek, smiled at Eve.

"Not literally, I hope," Roarke said as he shook Dennis's hand.

"Misplaced my tie." Dennis patted it. It was Christmas red with a pattern of little green Christmas trees running over it.

"Actually, I hid it." Mira slanted a look at her husband. "And was found out."

"I like it." Something about Dennis Mira with his dreamy eyes and mussy hair went straight to Eve's soft spot. "Festive."

"And look at you." Dennis took her hands, pulled back, wiggled his bushy eyebrows. "Glamorous."

"His idea." Eve tipped her head toward Roarke. "I'm ditching the shoes first chance."

"You look wonderful, both of you. And everything looks amazing." Mira, lovely as always in midnight blue, glanced around the ballroom. She'd done something with her hair, Eve noted. Little sparkly things glinted against the rich sable sweep.

"Let's get you a drink." Even as he spoke, a waiter magically appeared at Roarke's elbow. He lifted a glass of champagne from it for Mira. "Champagne, Dennis? Or can I offer you something stronger?"

"Stronger? Wouldn't say no."

"Come with me. I have something a little special. Ladies."

That was on purpose, Eve thought, and her neck tensed. Small talk was bad enough, and she only had a limited supply. But in the strained small-talk department, she was all but empty.

She fell back on the cliché. "So, I guess you're all ready for the holidays."

"Just about. You?"

"I don't know. I think. Listen, the food's—"

"Actually, I have something for you. I didn't bring it because I hoped you might be able to find a little time, come by the house tomorrow. For coffee."

"I . . ."

"I badly want to be friends again." Mira's eyes, a quiet blue, went misty. "I miss you. I miss you very much."

"Don't. We're friends." Or something more complicated, Eve thought, that was tangled in friendship. "I have something I have to do tomorrow, but after . . . I think I might want to talk about it. I think I might need to talk about it. After."

"Something serious." Mira touched a hand to Eve's arm, and the tension was gone. "I'll be home all day."

6

The next morning, she felt better than she'd anticipated. Her feet hurt a little because she'd never found the right moment to get rid of the shoes. But considering she hadn't hit the mattress until nearly four A.M., she was doing okay.

She couldn't say it was because she had a rare two days off in a row. Preparing for a party, giving a party, recovering from a party wasn't time off in her book. But it had kept the task she had today off her mind.

In any case, she felt better in normal clothes and a good pair of boots.

She found Roarke in his office, his feet propped on his desk as he talked on a headset. "That will do very well." He held up a finger, signalling her that he was nearly done. "I'll expect you then. Yes. Yes, I'm sure I will. Thank you."

He took off the headset, smiled at her. "Well, you look rested."

"It's nearly eleven."

"So it is. I imagine some of our guests are still in bed—a sign of a successful party."

"Pouring Peabody and McNab into one of your limos so that Mavis and Leonardo could cart them into their apartment's probably another sign. What was that all about? You don't usually use a headset at your desk."

"A quick call to Santa."

"You haven't, like, gone completely insane with the presents, right?"

His smile remained easy and mild. "So, it seemed as if you and Mira were back to normal."

Of course he'd gone insane with presents, she thought. And there was no point fighting it.

"Yeah, we're good. In fact, she wanted me to stop by today, and I was thinking maybe I would." She slid her fingers into her pockets, gave a little shrug. "Maybe talking to her about all this will put it to bed. Figuring that, you really don't have to come with me to the hotel. If they're still at the hotel."

"As of an hour ago, they were. And haven't indicated they plan to check out today. I'm going with you."

"It's really okay if you—"

"I'm going," he repeated, and swung his feet to the floor, rose. "If you want to speak with Mira alone, I'll drop you there afterward. I'll either come back for you myself and we could go have ourselves a nice meal somewhere, or I'll send a car. Are you ready now?"

No point fighting this either, she decided. Better to save all the energy for the face-to-face with Trudy. "As I'll ever be." She stepped up, put her arms around him, and squeezed. "In case I get all worked up and pissed off and forget to thank you later."

"So noted."

It wasn't a fleabag, Eve decided when she studied the façade of the hotel. In a city of five-diamond hotels, it maybe earned a half carat. It didn't run to parking, so Roarke had paid an obscene amount in a private lot a block east. But then his ride was probably worth more than the building that housed the hotel and some souvenir shop called To-kens on Ten.

It didn't run to doormen either, and what passed for its lobby was a double-wide al-cove with a counter. Behind it and a security screen was a droid clerk fashioned to re-semble a man in his forties suffering from male-pattern baldness.

He wore a tired white shirt, and as bored an expression as a droid could manage.

"Checking in? Luggage?"

"Not checking in. No luggage. Try this in-stead." Eve drew out her badge.

Bored became long-suffering. "Was there a complaint? No one filed a complaint through me. All our licenses are in order."

"I need to speak to one of your guests. Lombard, Trudy."

"Oh." He swiveled to his register comp. "Ms. Lombard has a Do Not Disturb on her room. She hasn't taken it off yet today."

Eve kept her eyes on his, tapped a finger on her badge.

"Yeah, well . . . She's in four-fifteen. Do you want me to call up, let her know you're here?"

"I think we can find four-fifteen all by our-selves."

She eyed the single elevator with some distrust, but her feet were still a little achy from her diamond slippers.

"Voice activation's broke," the desk droid called out. "You have to push for your floor."

She stepped on, pushed four. "This thing gets stuck, you can get us out, right?"

"Not to worry." Roarke took her hand. "Look at her the way you looked at the clerk, and you'll be done."

"How'd I look at the clerk?"

"Like he was nothing." He lifted their joined hands, kissed hers as the elevator groaned its way upward. The droid wouldn't have registered the nerves, Roarke thought, and he doubted Trudy would. But they were there, under the surface. "If you're up for it after Mira's, why don't we do a little shop-ping?"

"Have you lost your mind?"

"No, seriously. We'll stroll around on Fifth, look at the decorations, wander over to watch the skaters. Be New Yorkers."

She started to point out that no sane New Yorker would hassle with Fifth on a week-end this close to Christmas, much less stroll. But suddenly, it seemed like just the thing.

"Sure. Why not?"

The elevator squeaked open on four. The hall was narrow, but it was clean. A maid's cart stood outside the open door of four-twelve, and a woman—curvy, blond, mid-twenties—was knocking lightly on four-fifteen.

"Come on, Mama Tru." The woman's voice was soft as cotton. As she knocked again, she shifted from foot to foot, nervously, on simple canvas skids the same quiet blue as her pants. "We're worried about you now. Come on and open the door. Bobby'll take us out for a nice lunch."

She glanced over with eyes baby blue like her outfit, and gave Eve and Roarke an embarrassed smile. "Morning. Or afternoon by now, I expect."

"She doesn't answer?"

The woman blinked at Eve. "Um . . . No. My mother-in-law. She wasn't feeling very well yesterday. I'm sorry, is the knocking bothering you?"

"I'm Dallas. Lieutenant Eve. She probably mentioned me."

"You're Eve!" She slapped crossed hands

to her chest as her face lit up. "You're Eve. Oh, I'm so glad you came by. This is going to make her feel so much better. I'm just so happy to meet you. I'm Zana. Zana Lombard, Bobby's wife. Oh, gosh, and I'm just not fixed up like I wanted." She brushed at her hair that fell in soft, shiny waves. "You look just like you did on-screen. Mama Tru played that interview for me a couple times. I'm just so distracted I didn't recognize you. Goodness, we're like sisters, aren't we?"

She made a move—an obvious hug move—which Eve evaded by stepping to the side. "No, we're really not." This time Eve knocked, three good, strong pounds with the side of her fist. "Lombard, it's Dallas. Open up."

Zana bit her lip, twisted the silver chain she wore around her fingers. "Maybe I should get Bobby. We're down at the end of the hall. I should get Bobby."

"Why don't you give this a moment?" Roarke suggested, and drew her back gently with a hand on her arm. "I'm the lieutenant's husband."

"Oh, Lord, oh my, of course you are. I recognize you, I sure do. I'm just so confused. I'm starting to worry that something's

wrong. I know Mama Tru went to see Eve—
the lieutenant—but she wouldn't talk to us
about it. She was that upset. Then yesterday." She gripped her hands together,
twisted them. "I don't know what's going
on. I hate when everyone's upset."

"Then you'd better take a long walk," Eve
told her. She shook her head at Roarke,
then signalled to the maid who was peeking
around the corner of the open door of four-
twelve. "Open it," she ordered and flashed
her badge.

"I'm not really supposed to without permission from the desk."

"See this?" Eve waved her badge in the
air. "This is permission. You open the door,
or I break in the door. Take your pick."

"I'll get it, I'll get it." The maid hustled
over, digging her master out of her pocket.
"Sometimes people sleep late on Sundays,
you know. Sometimes they just like to sleep
in."

When she'd used the master, Eve nudged
her aside. "Stand back." She thumped
twice more on the door. "Coming in."

She wasn't sleeping. Not in that position,
not sprawled on the floor with her night-

gown hiked up to her hips and her head resting in a pool of congealed blood.

Odd to feel nothing, Eve realized as she automatically pulled her recorder from her coat pocket. Odd to feel nothing at all.

She fixed it to her lapel, engaged. "Dallas, Lieutenant Eve," she began, then Zana was wiggling around her.

"What is it? What's . . ."

The words became a gurgle, and the first screech erupted before Eve could push her aside. By the second, the maid had joined in with a kind of hysterical harmony.

"Quiet. Shut up! Roarke."

"Wonderful. Ladies . . ."

He caught Zana before she hit the floor. And the maid ran like a gazelle toward the stairs. Doors began to open here and there along the hall.

"Police." She turned, held her badge in clear view. "Go back in your rooms, please." She pinched the bridge of her nose. "I don't have my field kit."

"I have one in the car," Roarke told her, and laid Zana down on the hall carpet. "It seemed wise to store a few in various vehicles, as this sort of thing happens entirely too often."

"I'm going to need you to go get it. I'm sorry. Just leave her there." She drew out her communicator to call it in.

"What's going on? What's happening?"

"Sir, I need you to go back to your room. This is . . ."

She wouldn't have recognized him. Why should she? He'd been a blip in her life more than twenty years before. But she knew by the way he paled when he saw the woman passed out cold in the hallway, it was Bobby Lombard who had rushed out of the room at the end of the hall.

She eased the door to four-fifteen closed, and waited.

"Zana! My God, Zana!"

"She fainted. That's all. She'll be fine."

He was on his knees, clutching Zana's hand, patting it the way people do when they feel helpless.

He looked hefty, but in the way a ballplayer does, she thought. Strong and solid. His hair was the color of straw, cut short and neat. Water was beaded on it, and she could smell hotel soap. He hadn't fin-ished buttoning his shirt, and the tail was out.

She had another flash of memory. He'd

snuck her food, she remembered. She'd forgotten that, as she'd forgotten him. But sometimes he'd snuck a sandwich or crackers into her room when she was being punished.

He'd been his mother's pride and joy, and had gotten away with a great deal.

They hadn't been friends. No, they hadn't been friends. But he hadn't been unkind.

So she crouched down, laid a hand on his shoulder. "Bobby."

"What? Who . . ." His face was a sturdy kind of square, and his eyes were the blue of jeans that had faded from countless washings. She saw recognition layer over confusion.

"My God, it's Eve, isn't it? Mama's going to get a thrill. Zana, come on, honey. We had an awful lot to drink last night. Maybe she's . . . Zana, honey?"

"Bobby—"

The elevator opened, and the droid clerk came rushing out. "What happened? Who's—"

"Quiet," Eve snapped. "Not a word. Bobby, look at me. Your mother's inside. She's dead."

"What? No, she's not. God, almighty,

she's just feeling off. Sorry for herself, mostly. Sulking in there since Friday night."

"Bobby, your mother's dead. I need you to take your wife and go back to your room until I come to talk to you."

"No." His wife moaned, but he was staring at Eve now, and his breath began to hitch. "No. No. I know you're upset with her. I know you're probably not happy she came, and I tried to tell her so. But that's no reason to say something like that."

"Bobby?" With her hand on the side of her head, Zana tried to sit up. "Bobby. I must've . . . Oh, God. Oh, my God. Mama Tru! Bobby." She flung her arms around him and burst into wild sobs.

"Take her back, Bobby. You know what I do? Then you know I'm going to take care of this. I'm sorry, but I need you to go back to your room and wait for me."

"What happened?" Tears swirled into his eyes. "Did she get sick? I don't understand. I want to see Mama."

Eve got to her feet. Sometimes there was no other way. "Turn her around," she said with a nod toward Zana. "She doesn't need to see this again."

When he had, pressing Zana's face to his

shoulder, Eve eased the door open enough for him to see what he needed to.

"There's blood. There's blood." He choked and pulled himself up with his wife in his arms. "Did you do that? Did you do that to her?"

"No. I just got here, and now I'm going to do my job and find out what happened, and who did this to her. I need you to go wait for me."

"We should never have come here. I told her." He began to sob along with his wife as they helped each other back to their room.

Eve turned back. "Looks like she should've listened."

She glanced over as the elevator clunked to a stop on the floor. One of the two uniforms responding looked familiar enough to have her nod in acknowledgment.

"Bilkey, right?"

"Sir. Howzit going?"

"Not so good for her." She jutted her chin toward the open doorway. "I need you to stand by. My field kit's on the way. I was here on personal, so my . . ." She hated to say "my husband" when she was on the job. But how else did you say it? "My, ah, husband's gone back to our ride for it. My partner's being tagged. Vic's son and daughter-in-law are down the hall in four-twenty. I want them to stay there. You can start the knock-on-doors when . . ."

She trailed off as the elevator bumped to a stop again. "There's my kit," she said as Roarke stepped out. "Start knocking. Vic's Lombard, Trudy, out of Texas."

She took the kit from Roarke, opened it for a can of Seal-It. "You made good time." She coated her hands, her boots. "Might as well say it so I can say I said it. You don't have to stay for this."

"And so I can say I said it, I'll say I'll wait. Do you want help?" He eyed the can of Seal-It with some disgust.

"Better not, not in there anyway. Anyone comes out or onto the floor, you can look stern and tell them to move along."

"A boyhood dream of mine."

That got a wisp of a smile out of her before she stepped inside.

The room was standard, which meant it was bland. Dull, washed-out colors, a few cheap prints in cheaper frames on the tofu-colored walls. There was a midget-sized kitchenette, which included a self-stocked AutoChef, minifriggie, and a sink the size of a walnut. A stingy entertainment screen was across from the bed, where the sheets were rumpled and a remarkably ugly spread was shoved down, draping its green leaves and red flowers at the foot.

The carpet was green, thin, and pocked with a few burn holes. It had soaked up some of the blood.

There was a single window, green drapes pulled tight, and a narrow bath where the short beige counter was jammed with various face and body creams and lotions, medications, hair products. There were towels on the floor. Eve counted one bath, one washcloth, and two hand towels.

On the dresser—a just-up-a-level-from-cardboard affair with a mirror above—were a travel candle, a disc holder, a pair of faux pearl earrings, a fancy wrist unit, and a string of pearls that might have been the genuine deal.

She studied, recorded, then stepped to the body that lay between the bed and a faded red chair.

The face was turned toward her, those eyes filmed over the way death did. Blood had trickled and dried on the hair and skin of the temple, running there from where she could see the death blow at the back of the head.

She wore rings—a trio of silver bands on her left hand, a blue stone in an ornate silver setting on the right. The nightgown was good quality cotton, white as snow where it wasn't stained with blood. It was hiked up to the top of her thighs, and exposed bruising on both legs. The left side of her face carried a whopper that had blackened the eye.

For the record, she took out her Identipad and verified.

"Victim is identified as Lombard, Trudy. Female, Caucasian. Age fifty-eight. Vic was discovered by primary investigator, Dallas, Lieutenant Eve, at this location. The body shows bruising on both thighs as well as facial bruising."

And that was off, Eve thought, but continued.

"Cause of death appears to be a fractured skull caused by multiple blows to the back of the head. There's no weapon near the body." She took out her gauges. "Time of death is found to be one-thirty this morning."

A part of her unclenched at that. Both she

and Roarke had been at home, with a couple hundred people, at the time in question.

"Examination of the wound indicates your classic blunt instrument. There is no evidence of sexual assault. Vic's wearing rings, and there is jewelry in plain sight on the dresser. Burglary is unlikely. There's no evidence of struggle. No defensive wounds. The room is orderly. Bed's been slept in," she murmured as she re-examined the lay of the land from her crouch by the body. "So why is she over here?"

Eve rose, crossed to the window, opened the drapes. The window was half-open. "Window's open, emergency escape is easily accessible. Possibly the perpetrator entered through this route."

She turned around again, studied again. "But she wasn't running toward the door. Somebody crawls in your window, and you've got time to get out of bed, you run—for the door, maybe the bathroom. But she didn't. She was facing the window when she fell. Maybe he had a weapon, woke her, ordered her out of bed. Looking for a quick score. But he doesn't take this very nice wrist unit? He smacks her around—an activity nobody hears, or at least reports—

then bashes her over the head and leaves? It's not like that. Nothing like that."

She shook her head as she re-examined Trudy. "Bruises on the face and body are older than one-thirty this morning. Hours older. ME will verify. What were you into Trudy? What were you up to?"

She heard Peabody's voice, just the rhythm of it out in the hall, then the muffled *boing* of airskids. "Peabody, Detective Delia, now on-scene. Record on, Peabody?"

"Yes, sir."

"Check out the closet, and see if you can find her pocket 'link. I'll want the room 'link replayed."

"On that." She stepped to the body first. "Coshed, back of the head. Blunt. Classic." Her gaze came up, met Eve's. "Time of death?"

"Just after one-thirty this morning."

And Eve saw the flash of relief. "Sexual assault?" Peabody asked as she turned to the closet.

"No evidence thereof."

"She robbed?"

"It's possible her killer was after something specific, had no interest in some jewelry and a quality wrist unit."

"Or funds," Peabody added, holding up a large handbag. "Wallet's in here. Couple of credit cards, a debit, and some cash. No personal 'link or PPC. A couple of good-sized shopping bags in the closet here."

"Keep looking."

Eve moved into the bath. The sweepers would go over the room, inch by inch. But she could see quite a bit without their particular brand of magic.

She had, unfortunately, a solid working knowledge of hair gunk and face crap and body slathering stuff. The feared and dreaded Trina seemed to find a way to torture her with all of it every few weeks.

Trudy, it seemed, hadn't stinted on the products—quantity or quality. She had, by Eve's estimation, a couple grand in vanity crowded onto the bathroom counter.

The towels were still damp, Eve noted. In fact, the single washcloth was sodden. She glanced toward the tub. She'd bet the sweepers would find traces of bath products in the tub, face products on one of the towels.

So where were the missing bath towel and washcloth? Should be two of each.

She'd had a bath. Eve recalled how Trudy had enjoyed what she'd called her long soaks. If you'd disturbed her during that hour, you'd better have lopped off an appendage. Otherwise, you'd end up locked in a dark room.

Took a beating sometime yesterday, or as far back as Friday evening, Eve thought. Closes herself up, long soaks and pills. Trudy had liked pills, too, Eve remembered.

Take the edge off my nerves.

Why didn't she have Bobby or Zana tending to her? Being tended to had been another of Trudy's favorites.

Least you can do is bring me a cold drink.

You're going to eat me out of house and home, I expect you could fetch me a cup of coffee and a piece of that cake.

You're the laziest damn thing on two legs. Get your skinny butt moving and clean up around here.

Eve blew out a breath, settled herself. If Trudy had suffered in silence, there was a reason for it.

"Dallas?"

"Yeah."

"No 'link." Peabody stood at the bathroom door. "More cash in a security pack. More jewelry in pouches tucked into her clothes. Couple of transmissions, in and out, between her and either her son or her daughter-in-law. In-hotel trans. Bottle of blockers on the night table by the bed."

"Yeah, I saw that. Let's check the kitchen, see if we can determine the last time she got food."

"Nobody breaks in, kills someone, for a 'link."

"Depends what's on the 'link, doesn't it?" Eve moved to the AutoChef, hit replay.

"Chicken soup, just after eight last night. Chinese wrap about midnight. A lot of coffee on and off until seven P.M." She opened the friggie. "Wine, good stuff—about a glass and a half left in the bottle. Milk, juice—both opened—and a quart, half gone, of chocolate frozen nondairy dessert product."

She glanced at the sink and counter. "Yet there's not a bowl, glass, spoon unwashed."

"She was tidy?"

"She was lazy, but maybe she was bored enough to clean up after herself."

She heard Crime Scene arrive, took another minute. "Door's locked from the inside." Two clicks, she thought, when the maid had used her master. "Killer exited from the window. Possibly entered through same. Tourist hives like this one don't go for soundproofing. Makes you wonder why she didn't scream the place down."

She stepped out, saw not only the sweepers, but Morris, the Chief Medical Examiner.

She remembered he'd worn a suit to the party, a kind of muted blue overlaid with a faint sheen. His long, dark hair had been intricately braided and he'd knocked back a few. Enough that he'd gotten up on stage with the band at one point and wailed away on the sax.

His talents, she'd discovered, weren't limited to deciphering the dead.

Now he was in casual pants and a sweatshirt, and his hair was scooped back in a long, shiny tail. His eyes, slanted and oddly sexy, skimmed down the hallway and found her.

"Have you ever considered, just for the hell of it, taking a Sunday off?"

"Thought I was." She drew him aside. "I'm sorry to call you in, especially since I know you were up late."

"Very. In fact, I'd just gotten home when you tagged me. I have been to bed," he added with his slow smile. "Just not my own."

"Oh. Well. Here's the thing. I knew her."

"I'm sorry." He sobered. "Dallas, I'm very sorry."

"I said I knew her, not that I liked her. In fact, it's the opposite. I need you to verify time of death. I want to be sure your gauge matches mine. And I want to know, as close as you can get it, when she obtained the other injuries you're going to find."

"Of course. Can I ask—"

"Lieutenant, sorry to interrupt." Bilkey stepped beside her. "Vic's son's getting antsy."

"Tell him I'll be there in five."

"No problem. Nothing on the canvass so far. Just fyi, two rooms this floor had check-outs this morning. Got you the data on that. Room next to the scene was a no-show. Contacted the desk last night about eighteen hundred to cancel. Got the name in case you need it. You want I should get the lobby security discs?"

"Do that. Good work, Bilkey."

"All in a day's."

She turned back to Morris. "I don't want to get into it here and now. Just want to emphasize your confirmation of my time of death. I've got next of kin down the hall, and I have to deal with them. I'll fill you in on whatever's salient once you've filed your report. I'd appreciate if you'd handle all of it personally."

"Then I will."

With a nod, she signalled to Peabody. "This is bound to be messy," she began as they started down the hall.

"You want to separate them?"

"No. Not yet, anyway. Let's see how it goes."

She braced herself, and knocked on the door.

7

Odd, Eve thought, how little she remembered him. He was, essentially, the first child near her own age she'd ever known.

They'd lived in the same house for months, and it had been a series of firsts for her. The first time she'd ever lived in a house, or stayed in one place night after night with a bed of her own. The first time she'd been around another kid.

The first time she hadn't been beaten or raped.

But she could only see him vaguely the way he'd been—the pale blond hair cut short over a wide, almost chubby face.

He'd been shy, and she'd been terrified. She supposed it wasn't that odd that they hadn't bonded.

Now, here they were, in a bland hotel room with grief and death fouling the air.

"I'm sorry, Bobby. I'm very sorry about what's happened."

"I don't know what happened." His eyes were ravaged, and he clung to Zana's hand as they sat together on the side of the bed. "No one will tell us anything. My mother . . . my mother."

"Do you know why she came to New York?"

"Of course." When Zana made a little whimpering sound, Bobby took his hand from hers so he could wrap his arm tight around her shoulders. "She wanted to see you. And we haven't had a vacation in a while. She was excited about coming to New York. We've never been. And seeing you, and shopping for Christmas. Oh, God." He dropped his head onto his wife's shoulder, then just dropped it into his hands. "How could this have happened to her? Who could've done it?"

"Do you know anyone who was bothering her? Who had threatened her?"

"No. No. No."

"Well . . ." Zana bit her lip, then pressed them tight together.

"You thought of someone?" Eve asked her.

"I, well, it's just that she's got that feud going with Mrs. Dillman next door?" She knuckled tears away. "Mrs. Dillman's grandson's over there and out in the backyard all the time with that little dog he brings over, and they do carry on. Mama Tru and Mrs. Dillman had more than a few words over it. And Mrs. Dillman said she'd like to slap Mama Tru silly."

"Zana." Bobby rubbed and rubbed at his eyes. "That isn't what Eve meant."

"No, I guess not. I'm sorry. I'm so sorry. I'm just trying to help."

"What have you been doing in New York?" Eve asked. "What sort of things?"

Zana looked at Bobby, obviously expecting him to take the lead, but he just kept his head in his hands. "Um, well, we got in. It was Wednesday, and we walked around, shopped a little bit, and we went to see the show at Radio City. Bobby got tickets from a man right out on the street. They were awfully expensive."

Scalped tickets generally were, Eve thought.

"It was wonderful. I've never seen anything like it. Mama Tru said we didn't have very good seats, but I thought they were just fine. And we went and had an Italian dinner after. It was awfully nice. We came back sort of early, because it'd been a long day with all the traveling."

She began to rub a hand up and down Bobby's back as she spoke. The gold band of her wedding ring glinted dully in the poor light. "Next morning, we had breakfast in a cafe, and Mama Tru said how she was going to see you, and she wanted to go by herself this first time. So Bobby and I went to the Empire State Building, 'cause Mama Tru said she didn't want to stand in those lines anyway, and—"

"You've been doing the tourist thing," Eve interrupted, before she got more play-by-play. "Did you see anyone you knew?"

"No. You'd almost think you would, because it doesn't feel like there could be anyone left out in the rest of the world with all these people."

"How long was she gone, out on her own?"

"That day? Um." Zana went back to biting her lip, creasing her forehead as she thought. "I guess I don't know for sure, because Bobby and me didn't get back until almost four, and she was here already. She was a little upset."

Zana glanced at Bobby again, took one of his hands and squeezed it. "I guess things didn't go as well with you as she'd hoped, and she was a little upset and irritated that we weren't here when she got back."

"She was spitting mad." Bobby finally lifted his head. "It's all right to say so, Zana. She was hopping because you'd brushed her off, Eve, and she felt put upon because we weren't waiting for her. Mama could be difficult."

"Just got her feelings hurt, that's all," Zana soothed, brushing her hand over his thigh. "And you fixed it all up, like always. Bobby took her right back out, bought her a real nice pair of earrings, and we went all the way downtown for a fancy dinner. She was feeling just fine after that."

"She went out on her own the next day," Eve prompted, and Bobby's expression turned puzzled.

"That's right. Did she come to see you again? I told her to leave it alone, at least for a while. She didn't go to breakfast with us, said she was going to be lazy, then go out for some retail therapy. Shopping always made her happy. We were booked for dinner that night, but she said she didn't feel like going out. Said she was feeling tired, and she'd have something in her room. She didn't sound like herself."

"How'd she look?"

"I don't know. She was in her room. When she didn't answer the room 'link, I called on hers, and she had the video blocked. Said she was in the tub. I didn't see her. I didn't see her again after Friday morning."

"What about Saturday?"

"She called our room, about nine, I guess. Zana, you talked to her that time."

"I did. She had the video blocked again, now that I think of it. She said we should go on with whatever we wanted to do. She wanted to be on her own. Truth is, I thought she was sulking a little, and I tried to talk her into coming out with us. We were going to take one of the sky trams, and we had a ticket already for her, but she said no. Maybe she'd go walking. She wasn't feeling that well anyway. I could tell she was upset—didn't I say, Bobby? 'Your mama's irritated, I can tell by her voice.' But we let her be and went on. And that night . . . You tell it, Bobby."

"She wouldn't come to the door. I was getting a little irritated myself. She said she was fine, but still wanted to stay in, watch the screen. We went out to dinner, just the two of us."

"We had a wonderful meal, and champagne. And we . . ." She slid her eyes toward Bobby in a way that told Eve they'd done some celebrating when they'd gotten back to their room. "We, ah, slept a little late this morning. We tried to call her room, and her 'link, but she didn't answer. Finally, when Bobby was in the shower, I thought, 'Well, I'm going down there and knocking 'til she lets me in. I'm just going to make her . . .'"

She trailed off, pressed her hand to her mouth.

"And all that time. All that time . . ."

"Did you hear or see anything last night, anything unusual?"

Bobby only sighed. "It's loud here, even with the windows closed. And we'd had a bottle of champagne. We put on music when we got back, never turned it off. It was still playing when we got up this morning.

And we . . . made love when we got back last night, and again this morning."

His color came up as he spoke. "The fact is, I was annoyed with her, with my mother. She pushed to come here, and she wouldn't contact you by 'link before we came, no matter how much I talked to her about it. Then she started holing up in her room— sulking, I figured, because you weren't playing the role she wanted you to play, I guess. I didn't want Zana's trip spoiled because of that."

"Oh, honey."

"My feelings were, 'Fine, she wants to pout in there, she can stay in until we leave on Monday. I'm going to do the town with my wife.' Oh hell. Oh hell," he repeated and wrapped his arm around Zana. "I don't know why somebody'd hurt her like that. I don't understand it. Did they . . . was she—"

Eve knew the tone, knew the look in the survivor's eye. "She wasn't raped. Did she have anything of value with her?"

"She didn't bring much of her good jewelry." Zana sniffled. "Said it was asking for trouble, though she loved wearing it."

"I see you've got your window closed and locked."

Bobby glanced over. "It's noisy," he said absently. "And there's that emergency escape out there, so it's best to . . . Is that how they got in? Through her window? I told her to keep that window shut, keep it locked. I told her."

"We haven't determined that yet. I'm going to take care of this, Bobby. I'm going to do everything I can. If you need to talk to me, either of you, you can contact me at Central."

"What do we do now? What do we do?"

"Wait, and let me do my job. I'm going to need you to stay in New York, at least for the next few days."

"Yeah, okay. I . . . I'll get in touch with my partner, tell him—tell him what happened."

"What do you do?"

"Real estate. I sell real estate. Eve? Should I go with her? Should I go with Mama now?"

He was no good to anyone now, Eve thought. He and his baffled grief would only be in the way. "Why don't you give that some time? There's nothing you can do. Other people are taking care of her now. I'll let you know when there's something more."

He got to his feet. "Could I have done something? If I'd made the manager open the door last night, or this morning, could I have done something?"

And here, she thought, she could do the one thing, the single thing, that soothed. "It wouldn't have mattered."

When Eve and Peabody walked out, she drew a clear breath. "Take?"

"Comes off a decent guy. Shocky right now. So's she. One holds up 'til the other goes down. Want me to run them?"

"Yeah." Eve rubbed her hands over her face. "By the book." She watched as the morgue unit rolled out the body bag. Morris came out behind them.

"One-twenty-eight A.M. on time of death," he said. "On-scene examination indicates the fatal blow was a head wound inflicted with our old favorite—the blunt object. Nothing in the room, at my scan, matches. The other bodily injuries are older. Twenty-four hours or more. I'll get you more exact once I've got her in my house." His eyes stayed level on hers. "Is that what you wanted to hear?"

"Yeah, it is."

"I'll let you know what I know when I know it."

"Thanks." Eve walked back into the crime scene, signalled one of the sweepers. "I'm looking, particularly, for a pocket or hand 'link, her personal communication device."

"Haven't got one yet."

"Let me know when and if." She moved straight to the window, glanced back at Peabody. "We'll go down this way."

"Oh, man."

Eve ducked through and out the window, dropped lightly on the narrow evac platform. She hated heights, freaking hated them, and had to wait a moment for her stomach to stop rolling. To give her system time to adjust, she concentrated on the platform itself.

"Got blood." She hunkered down. "Nice little dribble of a trail. Over the platform." She hit the release, watched the steps jut out. "And down."

"Logical route out and away," Peabody commented. "Sweepers will get samples, and we'll know if it's the vic's."

"Yeah." Eve straightened, studied the access to other rooms on the floor.

Tricky, she decided, with the gaps, but not

impossible if you were athletic or ballsy enough. A good strong jump would do it, which she'd have preferred over the tiptoe route along the skinny spit of ledge. Which meant the killer could have come from inside or outside the hotel.

But logic said in and out the emergency route. Down and away, to ditch the weapon just about any damn where.

She looked down, breathed through her teeth as her head went light. People crawled along the sidewalk below. Four floors, she thought. She probably wouldn't pull a Tubbs if she fell, and kill some innocent pedestrian.

Then she crouched, examining a splat of pigeon dung. She cocked her head up as Peabody stepped out beside her. "See this flying rat shit."

"What a lovely pattern, abstract yet compellingly urban."

"Looks smeared to me, like somebody caught the side of it with a shoe." She poked her head back in the window. "Yo! Got some blood and some pigeon crap out here. I want it scraped up and bagged."

"We get all the class work," one of the sweepers commented.

"Mark it, Peabody," Eve ordered, then started down the zig-zagging stairs. "I want the hotel's recyclers, and any recyclers in a four-block radius, searched. We got some luck there, it being Sunday."

"Tell that to the team pawing through the garbage."

"Emergency evac makes basically every room this side of the building accessible to the other. We're going to want to take a look at the copy of the registration disc."

"No security cams in the hallways, stairways," Peabody added. "If it's an inside job, why not just go out the door when you were finished?"

"Yeah, why not? Maybe you don't know there aren't any cams." Her boots clanged on metal as she went down, and her stomach began to level out. "Maybe you're really careful and don't want to chance being seen by Mr. and Mrs. Tourist, who may be strolling in from a night on the town."

At the last platform, she hit the second release, and the short ladder rattled out. Steady now, she swung out, used the rungs, then dropped to the sidewalk.

Peabody clambered down after her.

"Couple of things," Eve began as they

skirted around to the front of the building. "Lombard went to Roarke's office on Friday to try to shake him down."

"What? *What?*"

"It needs to go in the report. It needs to be out there, up front. He met her, booted her out. End of story, but it needs to be up front. Sometime after that and several hours before she got bashed, she ran into trouble. It's easy for both Roarke and myself to account for our time and our whereabouts at the time of her death, and should be just as easy to account for the period between her leaving his office and TOD."

"Nobody's going to be looking at either of you."

Eve stopped. "I'd be looking at me if I didn't know I was alibied. I wouldn't be above smacking her in the face."

"Killing her?"

Eve shook her head. "Maybe whoever tuned her up wasn't the same person who killed her. Maybe she was working with someone, hoping to fall into easy money through Roarke. When she didn't pull it off, he or she tuned her. It's something to look at."

"All right."

"Here's the deal." She turned to Peabody and gave what she considered a statement. "We had a houseful of caterers and decorators and God knows crawling all over the house all day Saturday. All day. When Roarke has outside contractors on the premises, he keeps cams on, full. You're going to contact Feeney, request that he pick up those discs, examine the equipment, and verify we were both there, all day."

"I'll take care of it. I'm going to repeat: Nobody's going to look at you." She held up a hand before Eve could interrupt. "Neither would you, Dallas, after five minutes. A face punch, sure. You're not above it. And so what? But that was more than a punch that left her face messed up. More than a fist, and you *are* above that. She tries to shake Roarke down? Shit, she had to be bird stupid. He'd scrape her off like, well, like you'd scrape flying rat shit off your shoe. It's a nonissue. Trust me, I'm a detective."

"Been a while since you've managed to work that into a conversation."

"I've grown mature, and selective." As they rounded the corner, Peabody dipped her hands into her pockets. "He's going to have to be interviewed, you know."

"Yeah." She could see him leaning up against the side of her vehicle—where had that come from—and working on his PPC. "I know."

He looked over, spotted her. His eyebrows lifted, and he tucked his PPC away. "Out for a stroll?"

"You never know where cop work's going to take you."

"Obviously. Hello, Peabody. Recovered this morning?"

"Barely. It was a hell of a party."

"Give us a minute, will you?" Eve asked her.

"Sure. I'll go talk to people, and get those discs."

When they were alone, Eve gave her vehicle's tire a little boot. "How did this get here?"

"A bit of sleight of hand. I assumed you'd want your own."

"Yeah, you're right."

"I contacted Mira, let her know what was going on and that you'd be tied up for a while."

"Mira? Oh, right, right." She shoved a

hand through her hair. "Forgot. Thanks. What do I owe you?"

"We'll negotiate."

"I've got to ask you for one more. I need you to come down, make an official statement regarding your conversation with the victim on Friday at your office."

Something sizzled in his eyes. "Am I on your short list, Lieutenant?"

"Don't pull that. Don't." She drew a breath in, slowly. Released it, slowly. "Another investigator catches this, we're both on the short list until we clear it up. We both had motive to cause her pain, and someone caused her plenty. We're out regarding the murder. Can't kill someone in Midtown when you're partying with the chief of police in another part of town. Still, we've both got connections, and the wherewithal to hire somebody to do it."

"And we're both smart enough to have hired someone who wouldn't be quite so obvious and sloppy."

"Maybe, but sometimes obvious and sloppy is purposeful. Added to it, somebody busted up her face earlier. We need to cover that, too."

"So, you don't think I murdered her, but as for beating her up—"

"Stop it." She jabbed a finger into his chest. "Hitting me with this attitude isn't helping."

"Which attitude would you prefer I hit you with? I have several available."

"Goddamn it, Roarke."

"All right, all right." He waved a hand in dismissal. "It just pisses me off, having my wife interview me over assault."

"Well, cheer up, I won't be. Peabody'll handle it."

"Won't that be delightful?" He took her arms, turned her so they were toe-to-toe and eye-to-eye. "I want you to tell me—I want you to look at me and tell me, right now, if you believe I put hands on her."

"No." There was no hesitation. "It's not your style, and if you'd lost it enough to jump out of character, you'd have told me already. The fact is, it's my style, and I'll be putting her visit to me in my report."

He swore. "Bloody bitch is as much trouble dead as she was alive. Don't give me that look. I won't be lighting a candle for her. You would, in your way. Because for better or worse, she's yours now, and you'll stand for her because you can't do otherwise."

He continued to hold her arms, and now ran his hands lightly up and down. "I'll come with you now, and have it done."

"Crappy way to spend a Sunday."

"Wouldn't be the first," he said and opened the car door.

At Central, Peabody set up in one of the interview rooms. Her move-ments were a little jerky, and her eyes stayed down.

"Relax," Roarke advised. "I believe it's traditional for the subject to be nervous rather than the investigator."

"It's awkward. It's just a formality." Peabody looked up. "It sucks. It's a sucky formality."

"Hopefully, it'll be quick and painless for both of us."

"You ready?"

"Go ahead."

She had to clear her throat, but read the data into record. "Sir, we understand you're here voluntarily, and we appreciate your co-operation with this investigation."

"Whatever I can do . . ." He shifted his

gaze to the long mirror, to indicate he knew very well Eve was observing from the other side. "For the department."

"You were acquainted with Trudy Lombard."

"Not really. I had the occasion to meet her once, when she requested a meeting with me, at my office, this past Friday."

"Why did you agree to meet her?"

"Curiosity. I was aware that my wife was briefly in her charge many years ago."

"Ms. Lombard was Lieutenant Dallas's foster mother for a five-and-a-half-month period in 2036."

"That was my understanding."

"Were you aware that Ms. Lombard had made contact with the lieutenant at her office in this facility this past Thursday?"

"I was."

"And how would you describe the lieutenant's reaction to that contact?"

"As her business." When Peabody opened her mouth, shut it again, he shrugged. "My wife had no desire to renew the relationship. Her memory of that time was unhappy, and I believe she preferred to keep it in the past."

"But you agreed to meet with Ms. Lombard, at your office in Midtown."

"Yes, as I said, I was curious." His gaze tracked to the mirror again, and, he was sure, met Eve's. "I wondered what she wanted."

"What was it she wanted?"

"Money, naturally. Her initial pitch was to play on my sympathy, to enlist me to help her soften the lieutenant. Her claim was that my wife was mistaken in her feelings toward her, and her memory of that portion of her life."

He paused, looked at Peabody, and nearly smiled. "As the lieutenant is, as you know, rarely mistaken on such matters, I didn't find the woman's claims credible, and wasn't sympathetic. I suggested that she leave things as they were."

"But she wanted you to pay her?"

"Yes. Two million dollars was the suggestion. She would go back to Texas for that amount. She was unhappy when I informed her that I had no intention of paying her any amount, at any time."

"Did she threaten you in some way?"

"She was no threat, to me or mine. She was an irritant at worst. A kind of leech, you could say, who'd hoped to suck a bit of blood out of what was a difficult time in my wife's childhood."

"Did you consider her request for money blackmail?"

Tricky area, Roarke thought. "She may have hoped I'd see it that way—I can't say. For myself, I considered it ridiculous, and nothing that I, or the lieutenant, should concern ourselves with."

"It didn't make you angry? Somebody comes into your office, tries to hose you down? It'd tick me off."

He smiled at her, wished he could tell her she was doing a good job of it. "To be frank, Detective, I'd expected her to try me. It seemed the most logical reason for her contacting the lieutenant after all these years."

He leaned back in his chair. "Angry? No. On the contrary, I got some satisfaction out of the meeting, by letting her know, unmistakably, that there would be no payment. Now or ever."

"How did you make that clear?"

"By telling her just that. We spoke in my office for perhaps ten minutes, and I sent her on her way. I requested that my admin inform Security, to make certain she'd left the building. Oh, there's a record of her entering and exiting the building, and my office. Standard security measures. I took it upon myself to contact Captain Feeney of EDD, and ask that he personally retrieve those discs so that you have them for your files. I thought that would be best."

"Good." Peabody's eyes went wide. "That's good. Um, did you have contact with Ms. Lombard after she left your office on Friday?"

"None. The lieutenant and I spent the evening at home on Friday, and she and I hosted a large holiday party on Saturday at our home. We were quite busy throughout the day with preparations. There are also security discs for that period, as we had numerous outside contractors in our home. Captain Feeney will also retrieve those. And, of course, Saturday evening we were among more than two hundred and fifty friends, acquaintances, and business colleagues from approximately eight P.M. until after three in the morning. I'm happy to provide you with the guest list."

"We appreciate it. Did you have any physical contact with Trudy Lombard, at any time?"

His voice remained neutral, but he allowed just a hint of disgust to show on his face. "I shook her hand when we met. That was quite enough."

"Could you tell me why you and the lieutenant were at the West Side Hotel this morning?"

"We'd decided it would be best if the lieutenant spoke to Lombard face-to-face, to inform her that she—my wife—had no desire for further contact, and that neither of us intended to pay for the privilege of choice."

Peabody nodded. "Thank you. Again, we appreciate your cooperation in this matter. Interview end."

She heaved out a breath, went comically limp in her chair. "Thank God that's over."

He reached over to pat her hand. "How'd we do?"

"She'll let us know, believe me, but my take? You were forthcoming, articulate, and gave the details. You're alibied up to your gonads—Oh, sorry."

"Not a problem, I like knowing that part of my anatomy is protected." He glanced over as the door opened. "Now this one may bring out the rubber hoses. But I could learn to like it."

"Why didn't you tell me you'd contacted Feeney?" Eve demanded.

"I believe I just did."

"You could've—never mind. Peabody, let's start those runs, and do a quick check of the other guests at the hotel. I'll be a minute."

"See you later," Peabody said to Roarke.

"I'm going to—"

"Be a while." Roarke finished Eve's sentence. "I can find my way home."

"It's good you did this. Good it's done and out of the way. She could've pushed a little harder, but she got the details, and that's what counts."

"All right, then. About what you owe me? I've got my price."

She pursed her lips in thought. "We've probably got some rubber hoses in the basement somewhere."

And he laughed. "There's my girl. Go by Mira's when you're done."

"I don't know how long—"

"It won't matter. Go talk to Mira, then come home to me."

"Where else would I go?"

"The gifts? They're in the boot of your car."

"That's trunk in the U. S. of A., mick-boy."

"Right." He grabbed her arms, yanked her forward, kissed her good and hard. "I'll be waiting."

He would, she thought. She had someone waiting for her, and that was her miracle.

At her desk with an oversized mug of black coffee, Eve studied the official data on Lombard, Bobby. Not Robert, she noted. He was two years her senior, the product of a legal cohab that had dissolved when he'd been two. His father, when she did a cross-run, was listed as Gruber, John, married since 2046, and residing in Toronto.

Bobby himself had graduated from business college and been employed at Plain Deal Real Estate from that time until eighteen months earlier, when he'd gone into partnership with a Densil K. Easton to form L and E Realtors, in Copper Cove, Texas. He'd married Kline, Zana, a year later.

No criminal.

Zana was twenty-eight, originally from

Houston. No paternity listed on her record. She'd been, apparently, raised by her mother, who had died in a vehicular accident when Zana was twenty-four. She, too, had gone to a business college, and was listed as a C.P.A. One, Eve noted, who'd been employed by L and E Realtors almost from the onset.

So she moved to Copper Cove, and married the boss, Eve thought.

No criminal, no previous marriage or cohab.

Officially, they came off as what they seemed, she decided. A couple of simple, ordinary people who'd had some extreme bad luck.

Finally, she pulled up Trudy Lombard.

She skimmed over what she already knew, and lifted her eyebrows at the employment record.

She'd been a health care assistant, a receptionist in a manufacturing firm. She'd applied for professional mother status after the birth of her son, and had worked part-time—reporting an income just under the legal limit to retain that status.

Retail clerk, Eve scanned. Three different employers. Data cruncher, two employers.

Domestic coordinator? What the hell was that? Whatever it was, it hadn't lasted either.

She'd also lived in four different places, all in Texas, over a six-year period.

On the grift, Eve thought. That's what the pattern told her. Run the game, wring it dry, move on.

She'd applied for, tested for, and been approved for foster parenting. Had applied and been granted the retention of full pro-mom status under the fostering waiver—make every penny count, Eve thought. Austin area, Eve noted, for a full year, before she'd moved again, applied again, been approved again.

Fourteen months in Beaumont, then another move, another application. Another approval.

"Itchy feet? You know what, Trudy, you bitch? I don't think so. Then I came along, and look here, you pulled up stakes again three months after I went back inside. More applications, more approvals, and you just grifted your way around the big-ass state of Texas, taking the fostering fees, right up until Bobby graduated from college and your pro-mom status was up."

She leaned back, considered.

Yeah, it could work. It was a good game. You've got your license and approval, in state. So you just move from location to location, pick up more kids, more fees. Child Services, busy agency. Always understaffed, underfunded. Bet they were pleased to have an experienced woman, a pro-mom, willing to take on some charges.

Trudy had settled in one place after her professional mother status elapsed, and she'd gone out of the fostering business. Kept close to her son, Eve mused. Another handful of short-term jobs. Not a lot of income for a woman who supposedly liked to shop, and had jewelry valuable enough, reportedly, to leave home when traveling.

Interesting, Eve thought. Interesting. And she'd bet a pound of real coffee beans that she hadn't been the only child Trudy Lombard had traumatized.

8

She wished Roarke hadn't made her feel obliged to go by the Miras. She was tired, and there was still a lot of work on her plate, a lot of thinking time to put in.

Now she'd have to *visit*. Sit around, drink something, make conversation. Exchange presents. The last always made her feel stupid, and she didn't know why. People seemed to have this unstoppable need to give and receive stuff they could easily afford to go out and get for themselves anyway.

Now here she was, standing outside the pretty house in its pretty neighborhood. There was a holly wreath on the door. She knew holly when she saw it now, after her experience with the decorators. There were candles in the windows, pretty white lights glowing calm against the dark, and through one of those windows she could see the sparkle of a Christmas tree.

There would be presents under it, probably a considerable haul as Mira had grandchildren. She'd also learned that if one present wasn't enough to give a spouse for the holiday, a half dozen didn't come up to snuff for a kid.

She happened to know Peabody had already bought three—count them, three—presents for Mavis's baby, and the kid wasn't due to be born for over a month.

What the hell did you buy for a fetus, anyway? And why did nobody else think that was kind of creepy?

Roarke had shipped a damn cargo freighter of gifts to his relatives in Ireland.

And she was stalling. Just standing out in the cold and dark, stalling.

She shifted the packages under her arm, rang the bell.

It was Mira who answered moments later. Mira in her at-home wear, soft sweater, trim pants, bare feet.

"I'm so glad you came."

Before Eve could speak, she was being drawn inside, into warm, pine- and cranberry-scented air. There was music playing, something quiet and seasonal, and more candles flickering.

"Sorry it's so late."

"It doesn't matter. Come into the living room, let me take your coat."

"I've got these things. Just some things I picked up."

"Thank you. Just sit. I'm going to get you some wine."

"I don't want to hold you up from—"

"Please. Sit."

She laid the gifts on the coffee table beside a big silver bowl full of pine cones and red berries.

She'd been right about the mountain of gifts, Eve noted. There had to be a hundred packages under the tree. How many was that each? she wondered. How many of the Miras were there, anyway? They were kind of a horde. Might be almost twenty of them altogether, so . . .

She got to her feet as Dennis Mira strolled in.

"Sit, sit, sit. Charlie said you were here. Just came in to see you. Wonderful party last night."

He was wearing a cardigan. Something

about the scruffy look of it with one of its buttons dangling from a loose thread turned her heart to mush.

He smiled, and since she continued to stand, walked to stand beside her and turned that dreamy smile toward the tree. "Charlie won't go for fake. Every year I tell her we ought to buy a replica, and every year she says no. I'm always glad."

He stunned Eve by draping an arm over her shoulder, giving it a squeeze. "Nothing ever seems too bad, too hard or too sad when you've got a Christmas tree in the living room. All those presents under it, all that anticipation. Just a way of saying there's always light and hope in the world. And you're lucky enough to have a family to share it with."

Her throat had snapped shut. She found herself doing something she'd never have believed, and even as she did it, she couldn't *see* herself doing it.

She turned into him, pressed her face to his shoulder, and wept.

He didn't seem the least surprised, and only stroked and patted her back. "There now. That's all right, sweetheart. You've had a hard day."

She hitched in a breath, drew away, appalled. "I'm sorry. Jesus, I'm sorry. I don't know what's . . . I should go."

But he had her hand. However soft and sweet he appeared, he had a grip like iron. "You just sit down here. I've got a handkerchief. I think." He began patting his pockets, digging into them with that vague and baffled expression.

It settled her more than a soother. She laughed, rubbed her face dry. "That's okay. I'm fine. I'm sorry. I really need to—"

"Have some wine," Mira said, and crossed the room with a tray.

As it was obvious she'd seen the outburst, Eve's embarrassment only increased.

"I'm a little off, that's all."

"Hardly a wonder." Mira set the tray down, picked up one of the glasses. "Sit down and relax. I'd like to open my present, if that's all right."

"Oh. Yeah. Sure. Um . . ." She picked up Dennis's gift. "I came across this, thought you might be able to use it."

He beamed like a ten-year-old who'd just found a shiny red airbike under the tree. And the twinkle didn't fade when he drew out the scarf. "Look at this, Charlie. This ought to keep me warm when I take my walks."

"And it looks just like you. And, oh! Look at this." Mira lifted out the antique teapot. "It's *gorgeous*. Violets," she murmured, tracing a finger over the tiny painted flowers that twined around the white china pot. "I love violets."

She actually cooed over it, Eve realized, as some women tended to do over small, drooling babies.

"I figured you're into tea, so—"

"I love it. I absolutely love it." Mira rose, rushed over and kissed Eve on both cheeks. "Thank you."

"No problem."

"I think I'm going to try my gift out right now, have myself a little walk." Dennis rose. He walked over, bent down to Eve, tapped her chin. "You're a good girl and a smart woman. Talk to Charlie."

"I didn't mean to run him off," Eve said after Dennis left the room.

"You didn't. Dennis is as astute as he is absentminded, and he knew we needed a little time alone. Will you open your gift?" She took a box from the tray, held it out to Eve.

"It's pretty." She never knew the right thing to say, but that seemed appropriate when holding a box wrapped in silver and gold and topped by a big red bow.

She wasn't sure what it was—something round, with open scrollwork and small glittering stones. As it was on a chain her first thought was that it was some sort of necklace, though the disk was wider than her palm.

"Relax," Mira said with a laugh. "It's not jewelry. No one could compete with Roarke in that area. It's a kind of sun catcher, something you might hang at the window. In your office, I thought."

"It's pretty," Eve said again, and looking closer, made out a pattern in the scrollwork. "Celtic? Sort of like what's on my wedding ring."

"Yes. Though my daughter tells me the symbol on your ring is for protection. This one, and the stones with it, are to promote peace of mind. It's been blessed—I hope you're all right with that—by my daughter."

"Tell her I appreciate it. Thanks. I'll hang it in my office window. Maybe it'll work."

"You don't catch much of a break, do

you?" Roarke had filled Mira in on the afternoon's work.

"I don't know." She studied the disk, ran her thumb over it. "I guess I was feeling sorry for myself, before, when Dennis put his arm around me. Standing there with him, looking at the tree, the way he is, the way the house smells, and the lights. I thought, I just thought if once—just once—I'd had someone like him . . . Just once. Well, I didn't. That's all."

"No, you didn't, and that shame lies in the system. Not in you."

Eve lifted her gaze, steadied herself again. "Wherever, it's the way it was. Now Trudy Lombard's dead, and she shouldn't be. I had to have my partner interview my husband. I have to be prepared to answer personal questions, put those answers on record if they apply to the investigation. I have to remember what it was like with her, because knowing her helps me know her killer. I have to do that when, a few days ago, if you'd asked me, I could barely remember her name. I can do that," Eve said, fiercely now. "I'm good at pushing it out, shoving it down. And I *hate* when it jumps up and kicks me in the face. Because she's nothing, nothing to who I am now."

"Of course, she is. Everyone who touched your life had a part in forming it." Mira's voice was as soft as the music that wafted through the air, and as implacable as iron. "You overcame people like her. You didn't have a Dennis Mira, bless him. You didn't have the simplicity of home and family. You had obstacles and pain and horrors. And you overcame them. That's your gift, Eve, and your burden."

"I fell apart when I first saw her in my office. I just crumbled."

"Then you picked yourself up and went on."

Eve let her head fall back. Roarke had been right—again. She'd needed to come here, to say it out loud to someone she trusted. "She made me feel afraid, sick with fear. As if just by being there, she could drag me back. And it wasn't even me she cared about. If I wasn't hooked to Roarke, she wouldn't have given me a second thought. Why does that bother me?" She closed her eyes.

"Because it's hard not to matter, even to someone you dislike."

"I guess it is. She wouldn't have come here. Not much to squeeze out of a cop, unless that cop happens to be married to billions."

She opened her eyes now, gave Mira a puzzled look. "He has billions. Do you ever think of that?"

"Do you?"

"Sometimes, this kind of time, and I can't really get a handle on it. I don't even know how many zeros that is because my brain goes fuzzy. And I don't know the number that goes ahead of them because once you have all those zeros it's just ridiculous anyway. She tried to shake him down."

"Yes, he gave me the basics. I'm sure he handled it appropriately. Would you have wanted him to pay her off?"

"No." Her eyes went hot. "Not one cent out of the billions. She used to tell me I didn't have a mother or a father because I was so stupid that they'd tossed me away because I wasn't worth the trouble."

Mira lifted her wine, sipped, to give herself a chance to push back her own anger. "She should never have passed the screening. You know that."

"She was smart. I look back now, and I

see she was smart, the way you have to be to run long cons or quick scams success-fully. She played the system, figured the ins and outs. I think, well, you're the head doctor, but I think she believed her own bullshit. You have to believe the lie to live it, to make others see you the way you need to be seen."

"Very possibly," Mira agreed. "To have lived it for so long."

"She had to figure she deserved the money, had earned it. Had to believe she'd worked and sacrificed, and given me a home out of her humanitarian nature, and now, hey, how about a little something for old times' sake? She was a player," Eve said, half to herself. "She was a player, so maybe she played too deep with some-body. I don't know."

"You could pass this off. In fact, you may be asked to do so."

"I won't. I think I've got that covered. I'll call in favors if I have to, but I'm going to see it through. It's necessary."

"I agree. That surprises you?" Mira asked when Eve stared at her. "She made you feel helpless and worthless, stupid and empty. You know better than that, but you need to *feel* it, to prove it, and to do that you'll need to take an active part in resolving this. I'll say just that to Commander Whitney."

"That has weight. Thanks."

When she stepped through the door of her home, Summerset was looming like a black crow in the foyer, fat Galahad at his feet. She knew by the gleam in his beady eyes he was primed.

"I find myself surprised," he said in what she figured he considered droll tones. "You're out for several hours, yet you return—dare I say—almost fashionably dressed, with nothing torn or bloodied. A re-markable feat."

"I find myself surprised that no one's bothered to beat you into a pulpy mass just on the general principle of your ugliness. But the day's young yet, for both of us."

She whipped off her coat, dumped it on the newel post just because she could, and strutted up the stairs. The quick and habit-ual sally made her feel marginally better. It was just the thing to take Bobby's devas-tated face out of her head, at least tem-porarily.

She went straight to her office. She would set up a murder board here, set up files and create a secondary base, on the off chance Whitney vetoed both her and Mira. If she was ordered to step aside, officially, she intended to be ready to pursue the work on her own time.

She engaged her 'link to touch base with Morris.

"I'm going to come by in the morning," she told him. "Am I going to get any surprises?"

"Head blow did the job, and was incurred about thirty hours after the other injuries. While those were relatively minor in comparison, it's my opinion they were caused by the same weapon."

"Got anything on that?

"Some fibers in the head wounds. I'll be sending them over to our friend Dickhead at the lab. A weighed cloth sack would be my preliminary guess. Tox screen's come back positive for legal, over-the-counter pain meds. Standard blockers. She took one less than an hour before death, chased it with a very nice Chablis."

"Yeah, there was a bottle of that in her room, and blockers on the bed table."

"She had some soup, mostly chicken broth, and some soy noodles about eight, and some soft meat in a wrap closer to midnight. Treated herself to some chocolate frozen dessert, more wine with her late supper. She was, at time of death, nicely buzzed on wine and pills."

"Okay, thanks. I'll catch you in the morning."

"Dallas, are you interested in the fact that she's had several sculpting procedures over the last, I'd say, dozen years? Face and body, tucks and nips. Nothing major, but considerable work, and good work at that."

"Always good to know the habits of the dead. Thanks."

She ended the transmission, sat back at her desk to study the ceiling.

So she'd gotten herself roughed up sometime Friday after leaving Roarke's office. Doesn't, by their statements, tell her son or daughter-in-law, doesn't report same to the authorities. What she does, apparently, is hole up with wine and pills and easy food.

Either leaves her window unlocked, or opens the door to her killer.

Now why would she do that if the killer

had already played a tune on her the day before? Where was her fear, her anger? Where was her survival instinct?

A woman who could run a game on CPS for over a decade had damn good survival instincts.

Even if you're in some pain, why would you get buzzed alone in a hotel room when someone's hurt you, and obviously can hurt you again? Especially when you have family right down the hall.

Unless it was what was down the hall that hurt you. Possible, she thought. But if so, why stay where they could so easily get to you, hurt you again?

She glanced over as Roarke came in through his adjoining office.

"You get yourself beat up," she began, "you don't want the cops involved."

"Certainly not."

"Right, okay, I get that. You don't tell your son?"

"I don't have one to tell at the moment." He eased a hip onto the corner of her desk. "But pride might very well prevent me."

"That's guy thinking. Think like a woman."

"A stretch for me," he said with a smile. "How about you?"

"If I'm thinking like this woman, I whine ASAP to anyone who'll listen. But she doesn't, which gives me a couple of possibilities."

"One, she doesn't have to tell her son, because her son's the one who used her as a punching bag."

"That's one," she agreed. "One that's not fitting so well into my memory of their relationship. If that relationship soured since, why does she stay where he can get to her again?"

He picked up the little statue of the goddess, a symbol of mother, he thought, from her desk. He toyed with it idly as he spoke. "We both know relationships are thorny areas. It's possible that he made a habit out of knocking her about. She was used to it, and didn't consider telling anyone, or getting out of his way."

"There's the daughter-in-law. No marks on her, no typical signs of an abusive relationship there. A guy who pounds on Mommy is likely to smack the little woman around, too. It doesn't fit very well for me."

"If you bump that down the list"—he set the statue back on her desk—"what leapfrogs over it?"

"She doesn't want anyone to know. Which isn't pride, it's planning, it's precaution. She had an agenda, a personal one." And yeah, Eve thought, she liked that a lot better.

"But it doesn't explain why she drank a lot of wine, took blockers, got herself impaired."

She shuffled the close-up still of Trudy's face to the top of her pile. And took a hard look at it. "That doesn't say fear to me. She's afraid, she uses her son as a shield, she locks herself up tight, or she runs. She didn't do any of those things. Why wasn't she afraid?"

"There are some who enjoy pain."

Eve shook her head. "Yeah, there's that. But she liked being tended to. Run me a bath, get me a snack. She'd used the tub, and I got a prelim sweeper's report that tells me there was some blood in the bathroom sink, in the drain. So she washed up after she got tuned."

Missing towels, she remembered, and made another note of it.

"And she turns her back on her killer. Blow came from behind. She's not afraid."

"Someone she knows and mistakenly—as it turns out—trusts."

"You don't trust somebody who smashes your face the day before." Love them, maybe. She knew there was a kind of love that ran to that. But trust was different. "Morris thinks the same weapon was used throughout, but I'm thinking two different hands on it, two different times. You've got the run from your building security."

"A copy, yes. Feeney has the original."

"I want to see it."

He took a disc from his pocket. "Thought you might."

She plugged it in, ordered the review on the wall screen.

"I've had the whole business put on here," he said as Eve watched Trudy enter Roarke's Midtown building. She crossed the acres of marble, passed animated screens, rivers of flowers, sparkling little pools, and moved straight to the information desk that handled the offices.

That suit, she noted, had been in the closet of the hotel room. Neatly hung. The shoes had been tucked in there, too. She hadn't been wearing that outfit when she was beaten.

"Done her research," Eve mused. "No fumbling around, no looking around to get her bearings."

"She presses at information, as you see. 'No, I've no appointment, but he'll want to see me,' and so on. Look confident, look friendly, and as though you belong. She's very good."

"She got upstairs, anyway."

"They called through, got to Caro, who passed the request on to me. I had them make her wait a bit. I'm good as well. She doesn't care for it, as you can see by the way her face tightens up, but she has a seat in one of the lobby waiting areas. Unless you want to watch her twiddle her thumbs for the next bit of time, you can move forward."

Eve did, then slowed it down when a young woman approached Trudy.

"Caro, who knows the ropes, sent one of the assistants down to escort her up on one of the public elevators. Takes her round about, up to my level, through outer areas, down the skyway. A goodly hike, and when she arrives, well, she can wait a bit more. I'm a busy man, aren't I?"

"She's impressed," Eve commented.

"Who wouldn't be? All that space, the glass, the art, the people at your beck and call. Good job."

"Here you see Caro coming to get her at last, to walk her back. Then Caro goes out, shuts the doors, and we have our little chat."

Eve ran the disc forward, marked the time elapsed at twelve minutes before Trudy came hurrying out.

And there was fear, Eve noted, a hint of wildness in the eyes, a jerkiness to the walk that was nearly a trot.

"She was a bit annoyed," Roarke said with a wide, wide grin.

Eve said nothing, simply watched as Trudy was escorted down, and quickly made her way out of the building.

"Unharmed, as you see, and where she went from there, I couldn't say."

"She wasn't afraid of her killer." Eve's gaze met his. "But she was afraid of you."

He held up his hands, palms out. "Never laid a hand on her."

"You don't have to," Eve replied. "But you're clear. You had a record going inside your office. You would have."

He lifted a shoulder. "And your point?"

"You didn't offer that to Feeney, to the investigation."

"It's private."

She took a careful breath. "And if it comes to a squeeze?"

"Then I'll give it to you, and you can decide if it's needed. I said nothing to her that I'm ashamed of, but it's your privacy. It's ours, and we're bloody well entitled to it."

"If it has weight in the investigation—"

"It doesn't. Damn it, Eve, take my word and let it go. Do you think I had her done, for Christ's sake?"

"No. But I know you could have. I know a part of you could want that."

"You're wrong." He braced his hands on the desk, leaned forward until their eyes were level. And his were cold as arctic ice. "If I'd wanted her done, I'd have given myself the pleasure of seeing to it personally. That's who you married, and I've never pretended otherwise. It's for you to deal with."

He straightened, turned, started for the door.

"Roarke."

When he glanced back, she had her fingers pressed to her eyes. It tugged at his heart even as temper and pride burned at his throat.

"I know who I married." She lowered her hands, and her eyes were dark, but they were clear. "And you're right, you'd have done it yourself. The fact that you could and would do that, for me—the fact that you wouldn't, didn't do that, again for me, well, sometimes it's a hell of a jolt."

"I love you, beyond all reason. That's a hell of a jolt for me as well."

"She kept me afraid, the way I think a dog's afraid of the boot that kicks him, again and again and again. It's not even a human fear, it's more primal, it's more . . . sheer. I don't know how to say it."

"You have."

"She played on that, she used that, kept me down in the fear until there was nothing but just getting through one day to the next. And she did it without the boot. She did it by twisting what was inside me until it was all there was. Until, I swear I'd have ended myself, just to get out."

"But you ran instead. And got out, and did more than anyone could expect."

"This, all this, makes me remember too well what it was like to be nothing but fear."

The fact that her breath shuddered out told her the memory was very close to the surface. "I have to see this through, Roarke. I have to end this the way I am now. I don't think I can if you walk away from me."

He came back, took her hand, gripped it. "I never walk very far."

"Help me. Please? Will you help me?"

"What do you need?"

"I need to see the run from your office." She tightened her hand on his. "It's not mistrust of you. I need to get into her head. I need to know what she was thinking, feeling, when she left. It can't have been many hours after that she got beat up. Where did she go, who did she go to? It might help me figure it out."

"All right then, but it's not going into the file. Your word on that first."

"You've got it."

He left her to go back into his office. When he returned, he handed her a fresh disc. "There's audio as well."

With a nod, she plugged it in. Looked and listened.

She knew him, the ins and outs of him, and still, his face, his tone even more than his words, made her belly jitter.

When the run ended, she took the disc out, gave it back to him. "It's a wonder she didn't piss herself and ruin your expensive chair and carpet."

"Would've been worth it."

Eve rose, paced around the room. "She had to be working with someone. But if it was Bobby . . . nothing I have on him clicks for this. It takes a certain type to punch out your own mother. I don't like him for it. Someone else."

"She was an attractive enough woman. A lover, perhaps."

"Logical, and lovers are notorious for using fists and weapons. So, she's scared, scared bad, maybe wants to drop the whole thing and head back to Texas, and this pisses him off. She had a job to do, a part to play, and she didn't pull it off. He slaps her around to remind her what's at stake. When he comes to see her later, she's whiny, she's half-drunk. *I want to go home. I don't want to be here, I don't want to do this anymore.* And he's pissed again, and kills her."

"Logical."

Yeah, logical, she thought. But shook her head. "I don't like it. She doesn't give up that easy. Plus, while you scared her, he hurt her. Maybe she's caught between the two—fear and pain. But she's not running from either. And why kill her?" She lifted her hands. "Wait until she's calmed down. With her dead, you've got nothing."

"He lost control."

She brought the murder scene, the body, back into her head. "But he didn't. Three blows. Three deliberate blows. He loses control, he's drunk or juiced or just plain murderous, he beats the shit out of her, he smashes her face. He whales on her, but he doesn't. He just bashes the back of her head, and leaves her."

She rolled her shoulders. "I'm going to set up a board. I have to start putting this in order."

"Well then, let's have a meal first."

9

She ate because he'd nag her otherwise.
And the mechanical act of fueling the body
gave her more time to think. She had a
glass of wine, nursing it throughout the
meal. Small sips, like medicine taken reluc-
tantly.

She left the wall screen on, data scrolling
over. More pieces of the players she knew,
or knew of, thus far. Trudy herself, and
Bobby, Zana, and Bobby's partner, Densil K.
Easton.

Finances looked solid, if not spectacular,
all around. Easton had attended the same
college as Bobby, graduated with him. He
was married, one offspring.

A knuckle rap for disorderly conduct his
last year in college. Otherwise, no criminal.

Still, a good candidate if Trudy had a partner, or a lover. Who'd know the ins and outs of personal and professional data better than the son's business partner?

Easy enough to get from Texas to New York. Tell the wife you've got to make a quick trip out of town, wheel a deal.

The killer had to be good with details. Remembering to take Trudy's 'link, bringing the weapon, or using something handy, then taking it along with him.

Quick temper, though, bashing a woman's brains out with a couple of hard blows. But not rage.

Purpose.

And what was the purpose?

"Why don't you talk it through," Roarke suggested, tipped his glass toward her. "It might help."

"Just circling around it. I need to see the body again, need to talk to Bobby and his wife again, check out this business partner, Densil Easton, get a line on if the vic had any lovers or tight friends. Sweepers didn't find much. Plenty of prints. Vic's, son's, daughter-in-law's, the maid's. A couple of others that checked out as previous guests, back home and alibied at the time in question. No prints on the escape platform or ladder. Got blood there, and some smeared pigeon shit."

"Lovely."

"Little bit of blood in the drain, and I'm betting it's the vic's."

"Meaning the killer didn't wash up at the scene, and either wiped whatever he touched, or sealed up. So you'd say prepared."

"Maybe prepared, maybe somebody who knows how to seize opportunity." She was silent a long moment. "I don't feel."

"Don't feel what?"

"What I'm used to feeling. They're worried I can't be objective because I knew her, but that's not the problem. I don't feel . . . I guess it's a connection. I always feel some kind of connection. I knew her, and I don't feel anything at all. I helped scrape two men off the sidewalk a few days ago."

Tubbs—Max Lawrence in his Santa suit— and Leo Jacobs, husband and father.

"Their mothers wouldn't have recognized them," she continued. "I didn't know them, but I felt . . . I felt pity and anger. You're supposed to put that aside. It doesn't help the victims, the investigation, that pity, that anger. But it does. If I can hold on to it, just enough of it to drive me on. But I don't have it. I can't hold what I don't have."

"Why should you?"

She looked up sharply. "Because—"

"Because she's dead? Death conveniently makes her worth your pity, your anger? Why? She preyed on you, an innocent and traumatized child. And how many others, Eve? Have you thought of that?"

Her throat burned. But it was his anger heating it, she realized. Not her own. "Yes. Yes, I've thought of that. And I've also thought that because I don't feel, or can't, I should've passed on this. And I can't pass because if you can walk away, even once if you can just turn your back and walk, you've lost what made you."

"Then use something else this time." He reached over, just to brush his fingers over the back of her hand. "Your curiosity. Who, why, how? You want to know, don't you?"

"Yeah." She looked back at the screens. "Yeah, I want to know."

"Then let that be enough this time. This one time."

"I guess it's going to have to be."

• • •

So she set up her board, reviewed her notes, compiled lists, checked data. When her office 'link beeped, she checked the readout, glanced at Roarke. "It's Bobby."

She answered. "Dallas."

"Um, sorry. I'm sorry to contact you at home, and so late. It's Bobby Lombard."

"Yeah, it's all right. What's the problem?"

Other than your mother being dead, she thought, and the fact that you look one thin step up from a ghost.

"I wanted to ask, if we can move. I mean, if we can get another hotel." His hand lifted, raked through his short, sandy hair. "It's hard—it's hard to be here, right down the hall from . . . It's hard."

"You got a place in mind?"

"I . . . no. I tried a couple of places. Things are booked. Christmas. But Zana said maybe we had to stay here, and I didn't think of that, so I wanted to ask."

"Hold on." She put the 'link on wait mode. "You saw the digs they were in. You got anything comparable to that, something that has a vacancy for a few days?"

"There's always something."

"Thanks." She changed modes. "Listen, Bobby, I can have a place for you tomorrow.

I need you to hang on there tonight, and I'll have a new location for you in the morning."

"That's nice of you. It's a lot of bother. I'm not thinking so clear right now."

"You can hang on for tonight, right?"

"Yeah. Yeah." He passed his hand over his eyes. "I don't know what exactly we should do."

"Just stay there. My partner and I will come by in the morning. About eight. We need to do a follow-up, and afterward you can relocate."

"Okay. That's good. Okay. Can you tell me if you know anything about . . . if you know anything more?"

"We'll talk in the morning, Bobby."

"Yeah." His breath came out in a sigh. "In the morning. Thanks. Sorry."

"No problem."

When she disconnected, Roarke moved over behind her chair, laid his hands on her shoulders. "You have pity enough," he said quietly.

She thought she would dream, thought the nightmares would chase her in sleep, hunt her down. But they stayed shadows, never took form. Twice she woke, her body tight and tensed for the fight that didn't come. In the morning, tired and edgy, she tried to combat the fatigue with a blistering shower, with strong coffee.

In the end, she picked up her shield, shouldered on her weapon. She'd do the job, she told herself. If there was an empty place inside her, she'd just fill it with work.

Roarke walked in, already suited up for the day. Those staggering blue eyes alert, aware. Once all she'd had was the work, and those empty places.

Now she had him.

"I thought hell had frozen over during the night." She took a slug out of her second mug of coffee. "Since you weren't sitting here scanning the financials when I got up."

"Did that in my office, so hell's still a fiery pit, if that's a comfort." He tossed her a memo cube. "Took care of this from there as well. Mid-level, Big Apple Hotel. It should suit them."

"Thanks." She pushed it into her pocket as he cocked his head and studied her.

"You don't look rested."

"If I were a girl, a comment like that would piss me off. I think."

Now he smiled, moved in to touch his lips to hers. "Lucky for both of us, then." And he laid his cheek to hers, rubbed. "Nearly Christmas."

"I know, seeing as the room smells like a forest from the big-ass tree you had hauled in here."

He smiled at it over her shoulder. "You had a fine time hanging the baubles on the boughs, didn't you?"

"Yeah, that was good. I had a better time banging your brains out under them."

"That did put a nice finish on things." He eased back, smoothed his thumbs under her eyes. "I don't like seeing shadows there."

"You bought the territory, Ace. They go with it."

"I want a date with you, Lieutenant, seeing as our Sunday plans were aborted."

"I thought dates went out with the I do's. Isn't that in the marriage rule book?"

"You didn't read the fine print. Christmas Eve, barring emergencies. You and me, in the parlor. We'll open our gifts, drink a great deal of Christmas cheer, and take turns banging each other's brains out."

"Will there be cookies?"

"Without a doubt."

"I'm there. Gotta go." She pushed the coffee into his hand. "Peabody's meeting me at the crime scene." Then she grabbed his hair, gave it a yank, and gave him a hard, noisy kiss. "See you."

He was better than hot showers and real coffee for getting the system up and running, she decided. And she had one more thing left to top it off.

She jogged down the stairs, grabbed her coat from the newel post, and sent Summerset a wide, toothy smile as she swirled it on. "Figured out just what to get you for Christmas. A brand-new shiny stick for you to shove up your ass. The one you've had up there the past couple decades must be showing some wear."

She strode out to her car with the smile still on her face. She had to admit, despite a shitty night's sleep, she wasn't feeling half bad.

Peabody was stomping up and down in front of the hotel when Eve pulled up. The way she was eating up sidewalk told Eve she was either trying to walk off a few calories, cold—which didn't seem possible as she had some sort of long muffler deal wrapped about six times around her neck—or seriously pissed.

It only took one look at her partner's face to opt for door number three.

"What is that?" Eve demanded.

"What is what?"

"That thing that's strangling you. Should I call pest control?"

"It's a scarf. My grandmother wove it, sent it to me, and told me to open it now. So I did."

Eve pursed her lips, studied the length of zigzagging reds and greens. "Festive."

"It's warm, and it's pretty, and it's the fricking season, isn't it?"

"Last I checked. You want me to call that exterminator after all, for the bug crawling around in your ass, or are you getting a thrill out of it?"

"He's such a jerk. He's a total and complete asshole. What am I doing cohabbing with that moron?"

"Don't ask me. Really," Eve said holding up a hand. "Don't ask me."

"Is it my fault we're in a budget crunch? It is not," Peabody announced and jabbed a finger in Eve's face. "Is it my fault his stupid family lives in stupid Scotland? I don't *think* so. And so what if we spent a couple of measly days with my family at Thanksgiving?" The snaking scarf flew and billowed when Peabody threw up her hands. "They have the sense to live in the United States of America, don't they? Don't they?"

"I don't know," Eve said cautiously as Peabody's eyes seemed to pinwheel with passion. "There're a lot of them."

"Well, they do! And I just mention, just casually mention, that maybe we should stick around home for Christmas. You know, seeing as it's our first one as a couple—and maybe, considering his attitude, our last. Stupid fuckhead. What are you looking at?" she demanded of a man who glanced her way as he walked by. "Yeah, keep walking. Dumbass man."

"The dumbass man is an innocent bystander. One of those dumbasses we're sworn to protect and serve."

"All men are dumbasses. Every mother's son. He said I was *selfish*! He said I wasn't willing to share. Well, bullshit. Doesn't he wear my earrings? Doesn't he—"

"If he wears anything else of yours, I

really, really don't want to know about it. We're on the clock, Peabody."

"Well, I'm not selfish, and I'm not being stupid. And if it's so important to him to go roast his damn chestnuts in Scotland, then he can just go. Screw him. I don't know those people."

Tears swam now, and had Eve's stomach going on alert. "No, no, no. No. There's no crying on the job. No crying on the damn sidewalk in front of a crime scene."

"His parents, and his family. And his cousin Sheila. You know how he's always talking about her. I can't just go over there. I still have five pounds to lose, and I haven't finished doing this skin-care regimen that's supposed to shrink my pores—which are currently the circumference of moon craters. And by the time we pay for the flight, we'll be tapped for a month. We should stay home. Why can't we just stay home?"

"I don't know. I don't know. Maybe because you did the holiday thing with your half, and—"

"But he *knew* my parents. Didn't he?"

There were still tears threatening, Eve noted, but with the heat in those brown eyes, it was a wonder they didn't turn to steam.

"Didn't he meet my parents before that? He wasn't going in cold. Besides, my family's different."

She knew it was a mistake to ask, but the words just popped out of Eve's mouth. "How do you know?"

"Because they're my family. And it's not like I don't want to meet his. Eventually. But I have to go to a foreign country, and eat—I don't know—haggis or something. It's disgusting."

"Yeah, I bet the tofu surprise was a big winner over Thanksgiving."

Peabody's pinwheeling eyes went to lethal slits. "Whose side are you on?"

"Nobody's. I'm neutral. I'm—what is it— I'm Switzerland. Can we go to work now?"

"He slept on the couch," Peabody said in a trembling voice. "And he was gone when I got up this morning."

Eve heaved a huge sigh. "What time is his tour?"

"On at eight, same as me."

Eve pulled out her communicator, contacted EDD.

"Don't!" Now Peabody did the panic

dance on the sidewalk. "I don't want him to know I'm worried about him."

"Shut up. Lieutenant Dallas, Sergeant. Has Detective McNab clocked in?" When she got an affirmative, she nodded. "Thanks, that's it." She clicked off. "There, he's on the job. Like we should be."

"Bastard." Tears dried up in eyes gone hard. Her mouth tightened to the width of a scalpel blade. "Just strolls right in to work."

"Jesus. Jesus Christ. My head. My head." Eve cradled it in her hands a moment. "Okay. I was going to do this later." She dug into her pocket, pulled out a small wrapped box. "Take it now."

"My Christmas present? That's nice. But I'm not really in the mood to—"

"Open the goddamn thing or I'll kill you where you stand."

"Sir! Opening it." She ripped the paper, stuffed it hurriedly in her pocket, and pulled off the lid. "It's a key code."

"That's right. It's to the ground transpo that'll be at the airport over in that foreign country. Air transpo's been arranged, for two, on one of Roarke's private shuttles. Round trip. Merry fricking Christmas. Do what you want with it."

"I—you—one of the shuttles? Free?" Peabody's cheeks went pink as a summer rose. "And—and—and—a vehicle when we get there? It's so . . . It's so seriously mag."

"Great. Can we go now?"

"Dallas!"

"No. No. No hugs. No hugs. No. Oh, shit," she muttered as Peabody threw her arms around her and squeezed. "We're on duty, we're in public. Let me go or I swear I'll kick your ass so hard that extra five pounds you're whining about will end up in Trenton."

Peabody's response was incoherent and muffled against Eve's shoulder. "Get snot on my coat, and I'll strangle you with that scarf after I kick your ass."

"I can't believe it. I just can't believe it." Sniffling, Peabody drew back. "It's the ult. Thanks. Man. Oh boy, thanks."

"Yeah, yeah, yeah."

"I guess I've got to go now." Peabody stared down at the box. "I mean, the main part of the excuse—reason. I meant reason. The main part's flipped, so . . . Gosh."

"Whatever." She'd been feeling pretty good, Eve remembered. And now a frustration headache was circling just over the crown of her skull. "Do you think, maybe, we could go spend just a couple minutes on murder now? Will that fit into your schedule?"

"Yeah. I can shuffle it in. I'm good now. Thanks, Dallas. Really. Thanks. God, I have to go now. I actually have to go."

"Peabody," Eve said, darkly, as they entered the building. "Ice is thinning."

"I'm nearly finished obsessing. Just another minute."

The same droid manned the desk. Eve didn't bother to flash her badge, but started up the steps as Peabody muttered to herself. Something about packing, a red sweater, and five pounds.

Ignoring her, Eve checked the seal on the crime scene, found it undisturbed, then continued down the hall. "Once they're out of the room and gone, I want sweepers. Full sweep," she added. "Cover the bases."

She knocked, and seconds later Bobby opened the door. His face looked gaunt, as if grief had carved away some of the flesh. He smelled of soap, and indeed she could see the open bathroom doorway behind him, and the faint sheen of steam still on the mirror over the sink.

There was a murmur from the entertainment screen, as the on-air reporter recounted the morning's headlines.

"Come in. Ah, come in. I thought you were Zana. That maybe she'd forgotten her key."

"She's not here?"

"She went out to get some coffee, some bagels and stuff. I thought she'd be back by now. We packed last night," he said when Eve glanced at the two suitcases standing by the door. "We wanted to be ready to go. We just don't want to stay here."

"Why don't we sit down, Bobby. We can get some of this out of the way before Zana gets back."

"She should've been back by now. The message said she'd only be twenty minutes."

"Message?"

"Um . . ." He looked around the room, one hand raking distractedly through his hair. "She set a message alarm for me. She does things like that. Said she woke up early and wanted to go down to this deli she'd seen a few blocks from here, get some stuff so you'd have coffee when you got here. I don't like her being out there, alone. After what happened to Mama."

"Probably a line at the deli, that's all. She say which one?"

"I don't remember." But he went to the bed, picked up the little travel clock on the table, hit playback.

Morning, honey. Time to get up now. Your clothes for today are in the top drawer of the dresser, remember? I'm already up, don't want to wake you. I know you didn't sleep very well. I'm just running out to get some coffee and some bagels or danishes, something. Doesn't feel right to have your friend coming by and not have anything to offer. I should've stocked the AutoChef before. Sorry, honey. I'll be twenty minutes—just running to that deli a couple blocks down. Or up. I can't figure this city out. Deli Delish. I'll have coffee for you when you get out of the shower. I love you, honey.

Noting the time on the stamp, Eve flicked Peabody a glance.

"Why don't I walk out and meet her?" Peabody said. "Give her a hand."

"Have a seat, Bobby," Eve told him. "I have a few questions."

"Okay." He stared at the door Peabody

closed behind her. "I shouldn't worry. It's just that she's never been to New York. She probably turned the wrong way coming out, something like that. Got turned around, that's all."

"Peabody'll find her. Bobby, how long have you known your partner?"

"D.K.? Since college."

"So you're tight—on a personal level?"

"Yeah, sure. I was best man at his wedding, and he was at mine. Why?"

"He knew your mother then?"

"I had to tell him, had to call and tell him yesterday." When his mouth trembled, Bobby firmed it. "He's covering for me back home. Said he'd come out here if I needed him to. Don't want him to do that. Christmas coming, and he's got a family." Bobby put his head in his hands. "Nothing he can do anyway. Nothing to do."

"What kind of relationship did he have with your mother?"

"Careful." When he lifted his head, he nearly mustered a smile. "Oil and water, you know?"

"Why don't you explain it to me?"

"Well, D.K., he's what you'd call a risk-taker. I never would've gone out on my own if he hadn't nudged me. My mama, she could be a little critical of people. She didn't think we'd make it in the business, but we're doing okay."

"They didn't get along?"

"Mostly, D.K. and Marita stayed out of her way. Marita's his wife."

"Anyone else she didn't get along with?"

"Well, I guess Mama wasn't what you'd call a people person."

"How about people she did get along with, people she was close to?"

"Me and Zana. Always used to tell me she didn't need anybody but me, but she made room for Zana. She raised me on her own, you know. That was hard. She had to give up a lot to make sure I had a good home. I came first. She always told me I came first."

"I know this is hard. How about her assets? She had the house, right?"

"It's a good place. Can't have a son in the business and not have a good property. She was pretty well set. Worked hard all her life, was careful with her money. Frugal."

"You inherit."

He looked blank. "I guess. We never talked about it."

"How'd she get along with Zana?"

"Good. Things were a little rough at first. Mama—I was all she had, and she wasn't real happy about Zana right off. You know how mothers are." He caught himself, colored. "Sorry, that was stupid."

"No problem. She had a problem with you marrying Zana?"

"Just me getting married, I'd say. But Zana won her over. They get—got along fine."

"Bobby, were you aware that your mother went to see my husband on Friday afternoon?"

"Your husband? What for?"

"She wanted money. A lot of money."

He simply stared, shook his head slowly side to side. "That can't be right."

He didn't look shocked, she noted. He simply looked baffled. "Do you know who I'm married to?"

"Yeah, sure. There were all those media reports after the cloning scandal. I couldn't believe it was you, right up on the screen. I didn't even remember you at first. It's been a long time. But Mama did. She—"

"Bobby, your mother came to New York for a reason. She wanted to contact me again because I happen to be married to a man who has a lot of money. She wanted some of it."

His face remained blank, his voice slow and careful. "That's just not true. That's just not."

"It is true, and it's very likely she had an associate, and that associate killed her when there was no money given. Bet you could use a couple million dollars, Bobby."

"A couple million . . . You think I did that to Mama?" He got shakily to his feet. "That I'd hurt my own mother? A couple million dollars." His hands went to the sides of his head, squeezed. "This is crazy talk. I don't know why you'd say things like that. Somebody broke in, came in through the window, and killed my mother. He left her lying on the floor in there. You think I could do that to my own blood? To my own mother?"

She stayed where she was, kept her tone just as brisk, just as firm. "I don't think anyone broke in, Bobby. I think they came in. I think she knew them. She had other injuries, injuries she sustained hours before her death."

"What are you talking about?"

"The facial wounds, bruising elsewhere on her person, all were inflicted sometime

Friday night. Injuries you claim you knew nothing about."

"I didn't. It can't be." The words hitched and jumped out of his mouth. "She'd have told me if she was hurt. She'd have told me if somebody hurt her. For God's sake, this is just crazy."

"Someone did hurt her. Several hours after she left my husband's office, where she attempted to shake him down for two million. She left empty-handed. That tells me she was working with someone, and that someone was seriously pissed off. She walked into Roarke's office and wanted two million to go back to Texas and leave me alone. It's on record, Bobby."

There was no color left in his face. "Maybe . . . maybe she asked for a loan. Maybe she wanted to help me out, with the business. Zana and I are talking about maybe starting a family. Maybe Mama . . . I don't understand any of this. You're making it sound like Mama was—was—"

"I'm giving you the facts, Bobby." Cruelly, she thought, but the cruelty could take him off the suspect list. "I'm asking who she trusted enough, cared for enough to work with on this. The only ones you're coming up with are you and your wife."

"Me and Zana? You think one of us could've killed her? Could've left her bleeding on the floor of some hotel room? Over money? Over money that wasn't even there? Over anything?" he said and sank back onto the side of the bed.

"Why are you doing this to me?"

"Because someone left her bleeding on the floor of some hotel room, Bobby. And I think it was over money."

"Maybe your husband did it." His head shot up, and his eyes were fierce now. "Maybe he killed my mother."

"Do you think I'd be telling you any of this if there was a chance of that? If I wasn't absolutely sure, if the facts weren't rock solid on his side, what do you think I'd do? Open window, escape platform. Unknown intruder, botched break-in. Sorry for your loss, and that's that. Look at me."

She waited until he took a good long look at her face. "I could do that, Bobby. I'm a cop. I've got rank, I've got respect. I could close the door on this so nobody'd look back. But what I'm going to do is find out who killed your mother and left her lying on that floor. You can count on it."

"Why? Why do you care? You ran away from her. You took off when she was doing her best by you. You—"

"You know better, Bobby." She kept her voice low, kept it even. "You know better. You were there."

He lowered his gaze. "She had a hard time, that's all. It was hard raising a kid on her own, trying to make ends meet."

"Maybe. I'll tell you why I'm doing this, Bobby. I'm doing it for me, and maybe I'm doing it for you. For the kid who snuck me food. But I'll tell you, if I find out you're the one who killed her, I'll lock you in a cage."

He straightened; he cleared his throat. His face, his voice, were very set now. "I didn't kill my mother. I never once in my life raised a hand to her. Never once in my life. If she came for money, it was wrong. It was wrong, but she was doing it for me. I wish she'd told me. Or—or somebody made her do it. Somebody threatened her, or me, or—"

"Who?"

"I don't know." His voice cracked and shattered. "I don't know."

"Who knew you were coming to New York?"

"D.K., Marita, the people who work for us, some of the clients. God, the neighbors. We didn't keep it a secret, for God's sake."

"Make a list of everyone you can think of. We'll work from there." She rose when the door opened.

Peabody came in all but carrying a pale and shaking Zana.

"Zana. Honey." Bobby sprang off the bed, leaped to his wife's side, caught her in his arms. "What happened?"

"I don't know. A man. I don't know." Sobbing now, she threw her arms around Bobby's neck. "Oh, Bobby."

"Found her a block east," Peabody told Eve. "Looked lost, shaken up. She said a man grabbed her, forced her into a building."

"My God, Zana, honey. Did he hurt you?"

"He had a knife. He said he'd cut me if I screamed or tried to run. I was so scared. I said he could have my purse. I told him to take it.

"I don't know. I don't think . . . Oh, Bobby, he said he killed your mama."

Eve waded through the next flood of

tears, muscled Zana away from Bobby. "Sit down. Stop crying. You're not hurt."

"I think he—" With a trembling hand, she reached down the small of her back.

"Take off the coat." Eve noted the small hole in the red cloth, and the tear in the sweater Zana wore under it. There were a few spots of blood. "Superficial," Eve said, then pulled up the sweater, examined the shallow cut.

"He *stabbed* you?" Horrified, Bobby slapped at Eve's hands to get a look for himself.

"It's a scratch," Eve said.

"I don't feel very well."

When Zana's eyes started to roll back, Eve grabbed her and shook. "You're not going to faint. You're going to sit down, and you're going to tell me what happened." She pushed Zana into a chair, then shoved the woman's head between her knees. The thin silver dangles at her ears swung like bell clappers.

"Breathe. Peabody."

"On it." Already prepared, Peabody came out of the bathroom with a damp washcloth. "It really is a scratch," she said gently to Bobby. "A little antiseptic wouldn't hurt."

"In my travel kit. It's already packed." Zana's voice was weak and wavery. "In my little travel kit in the suitcase. God, can we go home? Can't we just go home?"

"You're going to make a statement. On record," Eve said and showed Zana the recorder. "You got up, went out to get coffee."

"I feel a little sick to my stomach."

"No, you don't," Eve said brutally. "You left the hotel."

"I . . . I wanted to be able to offer you something when you got here. And Bobby's hardly eaten a thing since . . . I thought I'd just run out, pick up a few things before he woke up. We didn't sleep much last night."

"Okay, you went downstairs."

"I went down, and I said good morning to the desk clerk. I know he's a droid, but still. And I went outside. It looked like a nice day, cool though. So I started buttoning up my coat as I walked. Then . . . he was just there. He had his arm around me so fast, and I could feel the point of the knife. He said if I screamed he'd ram it right into me. Just to walk, keep walking, look down, down at my feet and keep walking. I was so scared. Can I have some water?"

"I'll get it." Peabody moved into the kitch-enette.

"He walked really fast, and I was afraid I'd trip. Then he'd kill me right there." Her eyes went glassy again.

"Focus. Concentrate," Eve snapped. "What did you do?"

"Nothing." Zana shivered, hugged herself. "I said, 'You can have my purse.' But he didn't say anything. I was afraid to look up. I thought maybe I should run, but he was strong, and I was too afraid. Then he pushed open this door. It was a bar, I think. It was dark and there was nobody there, but it smelled like a bar, you know. Thank you."

She took the water in both hands, and still it slopped over the rim as she brought it to her lips. "I can't stop shaking. I thought he was going to rape me and kill me, and I couldn't do anything. But he told me to sit down, so I did, and keep my hands on the table, so I did. He said he wanted the money, and I told him to take my purse. Just take it. He said he wanted the full two mil-lion, or he'd do to me what he did to Trudy. But he'd cut me up so nobody'd even rec-ognize me when he was finished."

Tears streamed down her face, sparkled

on her lashes. "I said, 'You killed Mama Tru, you killed her?' He said he'd do worse to me, and to Bobby, if we didn't get him the money. Two million dollars. We don't have two million dollars, Bobby. I told him, my God, where are we going to get that kind of money? He said, 'Ask the cop.' And he gave me what he said was a numbered account. He made me say it back, over and over, and said if I screwed it up, if I forgot the number, he'd come find me, and he'd carve it into my ass. That's what he said. 505748711094463. 505748711094463. 505—"

"Okay, we got it. Keep going."

"He said for me to just sit there. 'You sit there, little bitch,' that's what he said." She swiped at her wet cheeks. " 'You sit there for fifteen minutes. You come out before then, I'll kill you.' And he left me there. I just sat there in the dark. Afraid to get up, afraid he'd come back. I just sat until the time was up. I didn't know where I was when I came out. I was all turned around. It was so noisy. I started to run, but my legs wouldn't run, and I couldn't find my way back. Then the detective came, and she helped me.

"I left my purse. I must've left my purse. Or maybe he took it. I didn't get the coffee."

She dissolved into tears again. Eve gave her a full minute of them, then pushed. "What did he look like, Zana?"

"I don't know. Not really. I hardly got a look. He was wearing a hat, like a ski hat, and sunshades. He was tall. I think. He had on black jeans and black boots. I kept looking down, like he said, and I saw his boots. They had laces, and they were scuffed at the toes. I kept looking at his boots. He had big feet."

"How big?"

"Bigger than Bobby's. A little bit bigger, I think."

"What color was his skin?"

"I hardly saw. White, I think. He wore black gloves. But I think he was white. I only got a glimpse, and when he took me inside, it was dark. He stayed behind me the whole time, and it was dark."

"Facial hair, any scars, marks, tattoos?"

"I didn't see any."

"His voice? Any accent?"

"He talked down in his throat, low down. I don't know." She looked piteously at Bobby. "I was so scared."

Eve pressed a little more, but the details were getting hazier.

"I'm going to have you escorted to your new location, and I'm going to put a uniformed guard on you. If you remember anything else, however slight, I want you to contact me."

"I don't understand. I don't understand any of this. Why would he kill Mama Tru? Why would he think we could give him so much money?"

Eve looked over at Bobby. Then she signalled for Peabody to arrange for the escort. "Bobby will tell you what we know."

10

To expedite the transfer, Eve personally escorted Bobby and Zana to their new location. She assigned two uniforms to canvass for the location Zana said she'd been taken, fanning out in a four-block radius from the original hotel. Rather than search the vacated room herself, she left it to Peabody and the sweepers before heading to the morgue.

At her request, Morris had Trudy waiting.

Nothing, Eve thought as she looked down at the body. There was still nothing inside her. No pity, no anger.

"What can you tell me?" Eve asked.

"Facial and bodily injuries sustained twenty-four to thirty-six hours before the head wounds. We'll get to them shortly." Morris handed her a pair of microgoggles, gestured. "Have a look here."

She stepped to the slab with him, bent to study the fatal injuries.

"Some ridges. And these circular or half-circular patterns."

"Good eye. Now let me bump it up for you." He brought the section of the skull onto his screen, magnified.

Eve shoved the goggles to the top of her head. "You said you found fibers in the head wound."

"Waiting for the labs on that."

"These patterns. Could be credits. Cloth sap filled with credits. Old-fashioned and dependable. You've got ridges, possibly from the edges, then those more circular shapes. Yeah, could be credits. Lots of them from the weight it would take to crush the skull."

She put the goggles back on, re-examined the wounds. "Three blows maybe. The first at the base—they'd be standing, vic with her back to the killer. Goes down, second blow comes from above—you've got more punch there, more velocity. And the third . . ."

She stepped back, shoving the goggles back up. "One," she said, miming a two-handed swing from her right and down.

"Two." Overhead, this time and down. "And three." Swinging, still two-handed, from the left.

She nodded. "Fits the spatter pattern. If the sap was cloth—a bag, a sock, a small pouch—you could get those imprints. No defensive wounds, so she didn't put up a fight. Taken by surprise. From behind, so she's not afraid. If the killer had another weapon—a knife, a stunner to force her to turn around—why not use it? And it'd be a quiet murder. First blow takes the vic down, she wouldn't have time to scream."

"Simple, and straightforward." Morris set his own goggles down. "Let's go back, review our previous program."

With his sealed fingers, he tapped some icons on his diagnostic comp. He wore his long, dark hair in a braid today, and the braid curled up in a loop at the nape of his neck. His suit was a deep, conservative navy, until you added the pencil-thin stripes of showy red.

"Here's our facial wound. Let's enhance it a bit."

"Similar ridged pattern. Same weapon."

"And the same on the abdomen, torso, thighs, left hip. But something interests me here. Look closely at the facial wound again."

"I'd say the attacker was close in." She paused, puzzled. "From the bruising, the angle, it looks like an uppercut." She turned to Morris, swung up toward his face, and had him blink and jerk his head back a fraction as her fist stopped a hairsbreadth from his skin.

"Let's use the program, shall we?"

She couldn't quite stop the grin. "I wouldn't have tapped you."

"Regardless." He moved back to the screen, cautiously keeping it between them. He pulled up his program, showing two figures. "Now, you see the angles and movements of the attacker, programmed to recreate the injuries we see. The facial injury indicates a left-handed blow, uppercut, as you said. It's awkward."

Eve frowned as she watched the screen. "Nobody hits like that. If it's a leftie coming at her that way, he'd've swung out, caught her here." She flicked fingers on her own cheekbone. "If he swung up, he should've caught her lower. Maybe right-handed, and he . . . no."

She turned from the screen and back to

the body. "With a fist, maybe, maybe you get bruising like that. But with a sap, you've got to swing it, even close in, you've got to lead with it."

Her brows drew together, and her eyes narrowed. Then she lifted them to Morris. "Well, for Christ's sake. She did it to herself?"

"I ran that, and got a probability in the mid-nineties. Have a look." He brought up the next program. "One figure, a two-handed swing, right taking the weight, cross-body to the face."

"Sick bitch," Eve said under her breath.

"And a motivated one. The angles of the other injuries—save the head—could all be self-inflicted. Probability hits 99.8, when we factor in the facial injuries as self."

She had to wipe away previous theories, get her head around the self-inflicted. "No defensive wounds, no sign she struggled or was restrained."

While her mind whirled, Eve put the goggles on yet again, moved back to examine every inch of the body. "The bruising on the knees, the elbows?"

"Consistent with a fall, timing coordinates with the head wounds."

"Okay, okay. Somebody clocks you in the face like this, comes at you to beat on you some more, you run, or you fall, you put your hands up to try to ward them off. Should be bruising on her forearms at least. But there isn't, because she's beating on herself. Nothing under her nails?"

"Now that you mention it . . ." Morris smiled. "A couple of fibers, under the index and ring fingers of her right hand, under the index of her left."

"They're going to be the same as what you found in the head wound." Eve closed her right fist. "Digs into the cloth, gets her courage up. Crazy bitch."

"Dallas, you said you knew her. Why would she do this?"

Eve tossed the goggles aside. She'd found her anger now, and it soaked into her bones. "So she could say someone else did. Me, maybe Roarke. Maybe go to the media with it," she said as she began to pace. "No, no, you're not going to get big fat piles of money that way. Attention, sure, and some dough, but not a bakery full. Blackmail. Figured she could go back on us. Pay up, or I go public, show people how you hurt me. But it turned back on her.

Whoever she was working with decided they didn't need her anymore. Or she got greedy, tried to cut them out."

"Takes some brass ones to try to blackmail a cop like you, or a man like Roarke." He looked back at the body. "Takes some sick need to do this to yourself for money."

"Got paid back, didn't she?" Eve said quietly. "All the way back."

Peabody took a detour. Dallas would roast her if she got wind, but she didn't intend to be long. Besides, the sweepers hadn't found anything so far in the rooms vacated.

She wasn't even sure McNab would be in-house. He could be out in the field for all she knew. Since he hadn't bothered to leave her a message.

Men were such pains in the ass, she wondered why she bothered to keep one. She'd been doing okay solo. It wasn't as if she'd gone out looking for somebody like Ian Mc-Nab.

Who would?

Now she was cohabbing, with a lease in both their names. They'd bought a new bed together—a really uptown gel. And that made it *theirs* instead of *hers,* didn't it? Which she hadn't thought about until now.

Which she wouldn't have to think about now, except he'd been such a complete dick.

And technically, he'd been the one to walk out, so he should be the one to make the first move. She hesitated, nearly jumped off the glide. But the box Dallas had given her was burning a hole in her pocket—and the idea that maybe she'd been partly to blame was burning one in her gut.

Probably just indigestion. She shouldn't have grabbed that soy dog on the corner.

She stalked into EDD, her chin jutted up. There he was, in his cube. How could you miss him when even in the rainbow hues of the division his green zip pants and yellow shirt vibrated.

She sniffed, then stomped over to jab him sharply on the shoulder twice. "I need to talk to you."

His eyes, cool and green, flicked to her face, away again. "Busy here."

The back of her neck sizzled at the dismissal. "Five minutes," she said between her teeth. "Private."

He shoved back from his station, swiveled

around fast enough to make his long tail of blond hair swing. He gave a jerk of the shoulder to indicate she should follow him, then strode off on his shiny yellow airboots.

Color, from anger and from embarrassment, rode her cheeks as she wove through the clicks and clacks of EDD. The fact that no one paused long enough to hail her or send her a wave told her McNab hadn't kept their situation to himself.

Well, neither had she. So what?

He opened the door to a small break room where two detectives were arguing in the incomprehensible terms of e-geeks. McNab simply jerked a thumb toward the door. "Need five."

The detectives took their argument and a couple of cherry fizzies out the door. One paused long enough to glance back at Peabody with a look of sympathetic understanding.

Of course, Peabody thought, the look came from a female.

McNab got himself a lime fizzy, probably color-coordinating his outfit, Peabody thought nastily. She closed the door herself as he leaned back against the short counter.

"I've got something cooking, so make it fast," he told her.

"Oh, I'll make it fast. You're not the only one who's got something cooking. If you hadn't snuck out of the apartment this morning, we could've dealt with some of this before shift."

"I didn't sneak." He took a long drink, eyeing her over the neon tube. "Not my fault you sleep like a corpse. Plus, I didn't feel like slamming up against your attitude first thing in the morning."

"My attitude?" Her voice came out in a squeak that would have mortified her if she'd noticed it. "You're the one who said I was selfish. You're the one who said I didn't care."

"I know what I said. So if this is just a re-play—"

Peabody planted her feet. For once she was happy to know she outweighed him. "You make a move to that door before I'm done, I'll flatten your bony ass."

Now temper flashed in his eyes. "Say what you've got to say, then. Odds are it'll be more than you've had to say to me for the past week."

"What're you talking about?"

"You've always got something to do." He slammed down his drink, and true to its name, lime-colored liquid fizzed over the lip. "Always got something going. Every time I try to talk to you, it's 'We'll get into it later.' You're going to dump a guy, you could have the decency to wait until after the holidays. Wouldn't fucking kill you."

"What? What? Dump you? Have you lost what little brainpower you had?"

"You've been avoiding me. Coming in late, heading out early, every damn day."

"I've been Christmas shopping, you moron." She threw her hands in the air as her voice pitched toward a shout. "I've been going to the gym. And I've been up at Mavis and Leonardo's because . . . I can't tell you why. And if I've been avoiding you, it's because all you want to talk about is going to Scotland."

"We've only got a couple of days left to—"

"I know, I know." She slapped her hands to her head and squeezed.

"I've got a line on some side work I can do, help pay for it. I just want to . . . You weren't going to dump me?"

"No, but I should. I should dump you right

on your pointy head and save myself all this aggravation." She dropped her hands, sighed. "Maybe I was avoiding you because I didn't want to talk about going to Scotland."

"You always said you wanted to go one day."

"I know what I said, but that's when I didn't think we'd ever go. Now you're pinning me to it, and I'm nervous. No, not nervous. Terrified."

"Of what?"

"Of meeting your family—all at once. Of being the one you bring home for Christmas, for God's sake."

"Jesus, Peabody, who the hell do you want me to bring home for Christmas?"

"Me, you idiot. But when you bring somebody home for Christmas, it's a big. It's a *real* big. They're all going to be looking at me and asking me questions, and I can't lose a stupid goddamn five pounds, because I'm nervous, so I eat. And I figured if we could just stay home I wouldn't have to worry about it until whenever."

He just stared at her in the baffled way men had stared at women across the ages. "You took me home for Thanksgiving."

"That's different. It *is*," she said before he could object. "You'd already met my parents, and we're Free-Agers. We feed anybody and everybody on Thanksgiving. I feel fat and clunky, and they're going to hate me."

"Dee." He only called her Dee when he was particularly tender, or especially exasperated. This, from his tone, seemed to be some of both. "It is a real big to take someone home for Christmas. You're the first I have."

"Oh, God. That just makes it worse. Or better. I don't know which." She swallowed, pressed a hand to her belly. "I think I feel sick."

"They're not going to hate you. They're going to love you because I do. I love you, She-Body." He gave her the smile, the one that made her think of little puppy dogs. "Please come home with me. I've been waiting a long time to show you off."

"Oh, wow. Oh, boy." Sentimental tears sprang to her eyes as she jumped him. His hands clamped on her ass.

"I've got to lock the door," he muttered as he bit cheerfully at her ear.

"Everybody'll know what we're doing."

"I love being the object of envy. Mmm, I missed you. Let me just—"

"Wait, wait!" She shoved back, dug into her pocket. "I forgot. God. It's our present from Dallas and Roarke."

"I'd rather have one from you right now."

"Look. You've got to look. They're giving us the trip," she said as she opened the box, showed him the cards inside. "Private shuttle, ground transpo. The works."

Since his hands dropped off her ass, she figured he was as stunned as she'd been. "Holy shit."

"All we have to do is pack," she said with a watery smile. "You don't have to take the side job, unless you want it. I'm sorry I was such a freak about this. I love you, too."

She threw her arms around him, locked lips. Then eased back with a wicked wiggle of eyebrows. "I'll lock the door."

Minutes after Eve stepped into her office to coordinate her next move, Peabody rushed in.

"I've got the initial sweeper's report on the room the Lombards vacated—nothing," Peabody said hurriedly. "Canvassing cops found the bar—one block east, two south of the hotel. Door was unlocked. Zana's purse was inside on the floor. I have a team heading there now."

"You've been busy," Eve said. "How did you manage to fit in sex?"

"Sex? I don't know what you're talking about. I bet you want coffee." She darted to the AutoChef, then whirled back. "How do you know I had sex? Do you have sex radar?"

"Your shirt's not buttoned right, and you've got a fresh hickey on your neck."

"Damn it." Peabody slapped a hand to the side of her neck. "How bad is it? Why don't you have a mirror in here?"

"Because, let's see, could it be because it's an office? You're a disgrace. Go do something about yourself before the commander—" Her interoffice 'link beeped. "Too late. Step back. Step the hell back so you're not on-screen. Christ."

Her head might have dropped in shame as she eased out of range, but a smile tugged at Peabody's mouth. "We made up."

"Can it. Dallas."

"Commander Whitney would like to see you in his office, immediately."

"On my way." She clicked off. "Give me the salient, make it fast."

"I'll come. I just need to—"

"Give me the salient, Detective. Then write your report."

"Sir. The sweepers found no evidence in the rooms vacated by Bobby and Zana to tie them to the murder under investigation. Zana Lombard's handbag was located by canvassing officers inside a bar called Hidey Hole on Ninth between Thirty-nine and Forty. The officers entered the premises when it was noted that the security was off, and the lock disengaged. The officers sealed the building, and sweepers are responding."

"Name of the owner of the bar, the owner of the building."

"I intended to obtain that information after bringing you up to date."

"Do it now. Run the names. I want the data and your written report within thirty."

Eve let the steam of temper carry her out of her office, through the bull pen, into the elevator, where for once she didn't have to use her elbows to maintain a little personal space.

Good thing, she decided. She might've broken some asshole's ribs.

Then she shut it down, turned it off. She would show Whitney nothing but control and professionalism. She'd use them, and whatever else she needed, to keep the case.

He was waiting, sitting back in his chair behind his desk. His wide, dark face showed no more than hers what was inside his head. His hair was salt and pepper, with the salt liberally dashed. There were lines carved in his face, around the eyes, around the mouth, etched there by time and, she was sure, the burden of command.

"Lieutenant, you've named yourself as primary in a homicide investigation that is now in its second day, and this office has not been so informed by you."

"Sir, the investigation came into my hands yesterday morning. Sunday morning, sir, when both of us were off duty."

He acknowledged that with a slight dip of his head. "Yet you took charge of this matter while off duty, utilizing departmental personnel, and equipment, neglecting to inform your superior."

No point in bullshit, she decided. "Yes, sir,

I did. I believed the circumstances warranted my actions, and am fully prepared to report said circumstances and actions at this time."

He lifted a hand. "In the 'better-late-than-never' category?"

"No, sir. In the 'immediate-need-to-secure-the-scene-and-gather-evidence' category. Respectfully, Commander."

"The victim was known to you."

"She was. I haven't seen or had contact with the victim for over twenty years until two days before her death, when she came to my office."

"You're entering a boggy area, Dallas."

"I don't believe so, sir. I knew the victim briefly when I was a child. Therefore—"

"You were under her care for several months when you were a child," he corrected.

Okay, she thought, screw it. "The term 'care' is inaccurate, as she gave none. I would have passed her on the street without recognizing her. There would have been no further contact between us after her visit to me this past Thursday if she had not gone to my husband's office the following day and attempted to shake him down for two million dollars."

His eyebrows winged up. "And this is not boggy territory?"

"He showed her the door. Captain Feeney has the security discs from Roarke's office, was requested to retrieve them by Roarke in order to aid this investigation. She left the same way she came in."

"Sit down, Dallas."

"Sir, I'd do better standing. I went to her hotel room Sunday morning as I felt it necessary to speak with her, to make it clear that she would not blackmail or extort funds from Roarke or myself. That neither of us were concerned regarding her threat to go to the media or the authorities with copies she claimed to have of my sealed files. At that time—"

"Did she have copies?"

"Very likely. None were found at the scene, though a disc holder was recovered. The probability is high that whoever killed her now has possession of them."

"Dr. Mira has spoken to me. She came to see me this morning, as you should have done."

"Yes, sir."

"She believes that you're capable of handling this investigation, and further that it's in your best interest to do so." His chair creaked as he shifted his weight. "I've also just spoken with the ME, so I'm not completely in the dark regarding this case. Before you give me your report, I want to know why you didn't come to me. I want it straight, Dallas."

"I felt I would be in a better position to continue as primary if the investigation was ongoing. My objectivity on the matter would be less likely called into question."

He said nothing for a long moment. "You could have come to me. Report."

He'd shaken her, and she had to struggle not to fumble, to take him through clearly from her first contact with the victim to the data Peabody had just given her.

"She self-inflicted in order to bolster her plan for blackmail. Would that be your opinion?"

"It would, given the ME's findings and the current evidence."

"Her partner or accomplice kills her, abducts the daughter-in-law, and through her continues the demand for money, using the threat of exposure of your sealed files."

"I don't believe the killer would be aware that both Roarke and I were in the company of the chief of police and security, and yourself, sir, when the murder took place. It's possible implicating one or both of us is part of the plan at this point."

"It was a good party." He smiled a little. "The numbered account is being traced?"

"Captain Feeney is taking that. With permission, I'd like Roarke to assist in that area."

"I'm surprised he isn't already."

"I haven't brought him fully up to date. It's been a busy morning, Commander."

"It's going to get busier. It'd be a mistake to keep your connection to the victim undercover. It'll come out. Better if you bring it out. Use Nadine."

Eve thought of her media connection. She'd hoped for more breathing room there, but he was right. Get it done, get it out. Get it spun. "I'll contact her right away."

"And the media liaison. Keep me informed."

"Yes, sir."

"Dismissed."

She started toward the door, stopped, and turned back. "Commander Whitney, I apologize for keeping you out of the loop. It won't happen again."

"No, it won't."

She walked out unsure if she'd been given a supportive pat on the back or a rap across the knuckles. Probably both, she decided, as she headed back to Homicide.

Peabody popped up from her desk in the bullpen the minute Eve strode in, and trotted behind her into her office.

"I have the data you requested, Lieutenant, and my report."

"Good. I don't have coffee."

"That abhorrent oversight will be corrected immediately, sir."

"If you're going to lick my boots, Peabody, try to be subtle about it."

"Was my tongue hanging out that far? I deserved the slap—I won't say it wasn't worth it, but I deserved it. McNab and I cleared the air, and straightened stuff out. He thought I was dumping him. Stupid idiot."

It was said with such affection, almost sung, that Eve just dropped her head in her hands. "If you want to wiggle out of another kick in the ass, spare me the details."

"Sorry. Coffee, sir, just the way you like it.

Would you like me to get you something from vending? My treat."

Eve lifted her head, slanted her eyes over toward Peabody. "Just how long were the two of you banging? No, no, I don't want to know. Just get me whatever, then contact Nadine. Tell her I need a meet."

"On that."

As Peabody scooted out, Eve tried Roarke on his personal 'link. She dragged a hand through her hair as she was transferred to voice mail.

"Sorry to bump into your day. There are some complications. Get back to me when you get the chance."

She shrugged her shoulders, hissed, then contacted the dreaded media liaison. With that duty done, she plugged in Peabody's data disc, began the scan as her partner came back.

"I got you a Go Bar, tide you over. Nadine's up for a meet—in fact, she said she had stuff to talk to you about, and wanted lunch."

"Lunch? Why can't she just come here?"

"She's juiced about something, Dallas. Wants you to meet her at Scentsational, at noon."

"Where?"

"Oh, it's a real hot spot. She must be able to pull fat strings to get a reservation. I've got the address. She asked me to come, too, so . . ."

"Sure, sure. Why the hell not. Just us freaking girls."

II

Though the sweeper's report on Hidey Hole told her the locks and security had been tampered with, Eve went to the scene herself and met with the owner.

His name was Roy Chancey, and he was just as pissed to be hauled out of bed as he was with the break-in.

"Probably kids. Mostly is." He scratched the paunch of his belly, yawned, and gave her a good whiff of breath that had yet to be refreshed.

"No, it wasn't kids. Give me your whereabouts between seven and nine this morning."

"In my Christing bed, where d'ya think? Don't close 'til three. Time I get locked up and hit the sheets, it's damn near four. I sleep days. Nothing out there but sun and traffic days anyway."

"You live upstairs."

" 'S'right. Got a dance studio second floor, apartments on three and four."

"Alone? You live alone, Chancey?"

" 'S'right. Look, why'd I wanna break into my own place?"

"Good question. Do you know this woman?" She showed him Trudy's ID photo.

She gave him credit for taking a good look. Cops and bartenders, Eve thought. They knew how to make people.

"Nope. She the one got pulled in here?"

"Nope. She's the one got dead a couple days ago."

"Hey, hey, hey!" His rheumy eyes finally showed some life. "Nobody got dead in my place. Some might mix it up a little now and then, but nobody gets dead."

"How about this one? You know her?" She offered Zana's ID.

"No. Jesus, she dead, too? What's the deal?"

"What time does the dance studio open?"

"Like eight. Closed on Monday, though, thank Christ. Nothing but noise otherwise."

. . .

He's not in it," Peabody said when they stepped outside.

"Nope." On the street, Eve studied the building, the ground-level door, the exterior. "Easy enough to pick out. Locks were crappy, security crappier. Minimal skill required to get in."

She scanned the pedestrian and street traffic. "Midlevel risk to get her in. Guy quick-walking with a woman, her head's down. Who pays attention? She'd drummed up a little spine, makes some noise, resists, maybe she shakes him off."

"Small-town girl, big city, dead mother-in-law." Peabody shrugged. "Not surprising she went along, especially when he gave her that little stick."

"Sloppy, though, whole thing's sloppy. Stupid on top of sloppy. And you're hitting for two million when, as far as you know, the well's a hell of a lot deeper. Chump change."

"You're jaded."

"Yeah, so?"

"No, I mean about money, if you can call two mil chump change."

"I am not." The insult went deep. "You're

in for two, then you get bloody. Stakes go up when there's blood, and you ask for more. Small-time, it's small-time. Has to be another reason he took Trudy out."

"Lover's quarrel, maybe. No honor among thieves. Maybe she was trying to cut him out."

"Yeah, greed always works."

Her 'link beeped on the way to the car. "Dallas."

"Complications?" Roarke said.

"A few." She filled him in. "You're on for ECC status if you want and can fit it in."

"I've a few things to deal with I'd rather not shift, but I'll touch base with Feeney. I should be able to work on it a bit at home this evening. In the company of my lovely wife."

Eve's shoulders automatically hunched together, particularly when she noted Peabody looking her way with fluttering eyelashes. "My day's pretty packed. I'm going to go by the lab now . . . No, shit, meet first, then lab. Gotta do some media spinning, so I'm tagging Nadine. Appreciate the assist if you manage it."

"Not a problem. Squeeze some food into your schedule."

"I'm having lunch with Nadine at some stupid place."

"Scentsational," Peabody told him, leaning over enough to get a glimpse of his face on the 'link screen.

"Well, now, the world's full of surprises. Let me know what you think of it."

It only took Eve a beat. "Yours?"

"A man's got to keep his hand in. I've a lunch meeting myself. Try the nasturtium salad. It's very nice."

"Yeah, that's going to happen. Later. That's flowers, right?" she asked Peabody when she ended transmission.

"Edible ones."

"In my world, flowers aren't on the menu."

Apparently they were in Roarke's world. They could be sampled, sipped, and sniffed, all in one elaborate setting where the tables rose up on graceful stems and bloomed in a garden of colors.

The air smelled like a meadow, which Eve assumed was supposed to be a good thing.

The floor was some sort of green glass, translucent so the flowers thriving below shimmered in a sophisticated garden. There were various levels, up trios of steps. An arbor arched over the bar, where diners could order flowery or herbal drinks as well as the more pedestrian wines.

Nadine sat at a table near a little lagoon where golden fish swam among water lilies. She'd done something to her hair, Eve noted, straightening its usual waves and fluffs so it was sleek, streaky rain angled around her face.

She looked sharper, somehow honed, suited up in pansy purple. She wore an earpiece, and spoke softly into it between sips of something very pink and very frothy.

"Gotta go. Hold everything for the next hour. Yes, everything." She tugged off the earpiece, dropped it into her purse. "Isn't this a place? I've been dying to come here."

"Your hair looks absolutely mag," Peabody told her as they sat.

"You think? First time I've taken it for a spin." In the way of women, Nadine combed her hand through the angled ends. "I'm trying it out."

A waiter, decked out in leafy green, poofed beside their table like magic. "Welcome to Scentsational, ladies. I'm Dean, and I'm your server today. Can I get you a cocktail?"

"No," Eve said even as Peabody's eyes brightened. She kept hers bland as Peabody's dimmed. "Got Pepsi?"

"Of course, madam. And for you?"

"Can I get what she's got?" Peabody gestured to Nadine's drink. "Virgin."

"Absolutely."

"Fantastic party the other night, by the way," Nadine began when the waiter went off to fill the order. "I'm still recovering. Didn't have a lot of time to talk to you then, and I didn't think it was the right time and place for what I need to talk about. So—"

"Hold that, will you? I've got something going, and I need some spin."

Nadine's eyebrows shot up. "You've got a hot one already? Why haven't I heard?"

"Female vic, skull cracked, hotel room on the West Side."

"Mmmm." Nadine shut her eyes a minute. "Yeah, I got some wind on that. Tourist, bungled break-in. What's the big?"

"I found the body. I knew her. It wasn't a burglary gone wrong."

"Let me get this down."

"No, keep it in your head. No record, not now."

"You never make it easy. All right." Nadine sat back, gestured with her glass. "Shoot."

Eve gave her the basics, quick and pointed. "The department feels it would be in the best interest of the investigation if my connection, however slight, with the victim was made known straight off. I'd appreciate some . . ." She couldn't think of the right word. ". . . I guess delicacy. I don't want big drums banging about the whole foster business."

"I won't, others might. Are you going to be prepared to deal with that?"

"Not much choice. The point is—and the point that should be banged is—a woman was murdered, police are investigating. Evidence indicates that the victim knew her assailant."

"We do a one-on-one, you can put it in your own words. Get your face out there while you do. The public hasn't forgotten the Icove business, Dallas, believe me. Seeing you, hearing you, reminds them. Oh yeah, there's that cop who busted those crazy doctors. And when I wrap the story with that tag, that's what they'll focus on more than your negligible connection to a recent murder victim."

"Maybe. Maybe." Eve paused as their drinks were served and the waiter began his litany of the day's specials and chef's recommendations.

Because the descriptions were long and rapturous—lots of "infused with" or "scented with" and "delicately swathed in"—she tuned him out and turned over Nadine's suggestion.

"Give me the pasta thing," Eve said when it was her turn to order. "How soon can you do the one-on-one?"

"I'll get a camera, do it right after lunch if we cut the meal a little short. I need to skip dessert anyway."

"All right. Good. Thanks."

"You're always good for ratings. Speaking of which, mine are currently through the stratosphere. One of the things I wanted to discuss with you. I had the front line with the Icove story—thanks—and I'm raking in the offers. Book deals, vid deals, and the big one, for me . . . Drum roll, please," she said while her face lit up. ". . . I'm getting my own show."

"Your own show!" Peabody all but

bounced on her seat. "Wow! Mega-wow! Congratulations, Nadine. This is beyond up-town."

"Thanks. A full hour weekly, and I can call my own shots. I'm going to have a staff. Je-sus, I can't get over it. My own staff, my own show." Laughing, she patted her heart. "I'm sticking with the crime beat, it's what I know and what I'm known for. We're calling it *Now*, as I'm going to deal with what's hap-pening up to the minute we air, every week. Dallas, I want you to be my first interview."

"Nadine, congrats and blah-blah. Seri-ously. But you know I hate that crap."

"It'll be great, it'll be good. You can take us into the mind of the NYPSD's hottest cop."

"Oh, shit."

"How you work, how you think, the rou-tine. The steps and stages of an investiga-tion. We'll talk about the Icove case—"

"Hasn't that horse been beaten dead yet?"

"Not as long as people are interested, and they are. I'm going to start working with a writer on the book, and the vid script. I need you to meet with her."

Eve lifted a finger, slashed it through the air. "Line drawn."

Nadine's smile was sly. "It's going to get done with or without you, Dallas. You want to make sure it's done right, don't you?"

"Who's playing you in the vid?" Peabody wanted to know, and attacked the orange blossom chicken on her plate the minute it was in front of her.

"Don't know yet. We're just getting started."

"Am I in it?"

"Sure. The young, steady detective who hunts murderers alongside her sexy, seasoned partner."

"I'm going to boot," Eve muttered, and was ignored.

"This is too frosty! Entirely. Wait 'til I tell McNab."

"Nadine, this is good for you. Another round of big congrats and all that." Eve shook her head. "But it's not the kind of thing I want to get tangled in. It's not what I do, what I am."

"Be iced if we could do some of the shoot for the show and the vid at your house. Dallas at home."

"Not in this lifetime."

Nadine grinned. "Figured as much. Think about some of it, anyway, will you? I'm not going to push it on you."

Eve sampled pasta, gave Nadine a wary look. "No?"

"No. I'll nag a little, finagle where I can, but I won't push. Here's why," she said, tapping her fork in the air. "Remember that time you saved my life? When that psycho Morse had me in the park, ready to slice me to pieces?"

"I have a vague recollection."

"This is bigger." Nadine signaled the waiter. "Another round here. So I'm not going to push," she continued. "Much. But if you could catch a juicy case mid-February when we debut, it wouldn't hurt."

"Mavis is due then," Peabody commented.

"God, that's right. Mama Mavis," Nadine added with a laugh. "Still can't get around it. You and Roarke started your coaching classes yet, Dallas?"

"Shut up. Never mention it again."

"They're dragging butt over it," Peabody told her. "Procrastinating."

"The word's 'avoiding,'" Eve corrected.

"People always want you to do stuff that's not natural."

"Childbirth's natural," Peabody put in.

"Not when I'm involved."

Going to the lab to boot some ass, Eve thought. *That* was natural. She found Dick Berenski, of the spidery fingers and egg-shaped head, at a work station, slurping coffee through his flabby lips.

"Gimme data."

"It's always 'gimme' with you cops. Always think your shit's the priority."

"Where are my fibers?"

"In the fiber department." He snorted, obviously amused with himself as he rolled on his stool to a screen, gave a few taps. "Harvo's working on it. Go hound her. She did your hair already. Out of the drains, out of both the rooms. Must not clean out the pipes in that shithole but every decade. Got the vic's, and other unidentified—for now—on crime scene. No blood traces in the drains of the second room, just the vic's on crime scene, bathroom sink. ID'd hair from vic, son of vic, daughter-in-law of vic, hotel maid, couple of former tenants already listed on your report. All the blood on crime scene was the vic's. Surprise, surprise."

"In other words you can't tell me anything I don't already know."

"Not my fault. I can only work with what you give me."

"Let me know when you've compared hair and prints from the hotel scene and the bar."

"Yeah, yeah, yeah."

"Cheery today," Peabody muttered as they headed through the glass-wall maze of the lab.

They found Harvo at her station studying the screen. Her red hair was stiff with spikes that contrasted with her pale, almost translucent skin. There were little Santas dangling from her ears.

"Yo," she said.

"That my fiber?"

"One and the same. Hair's turned in."

"Yeah, I got that from Dickhead. I thought you were the Queen of Hair, not fiber."

"Queen of Hair," Harvo agreed with a snap of her chewing gum. "Goddess of Fiber. Fact of it is, I'm just fucking brilliant."

"Good to know. What've we got?"

"Synthetic white poly with traces of elastizine. Same constitution as the particles found in the unfortunate vic's bone and gray matter. What you're looking for is either a sock or a tummy tamer. But I'd say not a girdle—not enough elastizine."

"Sock," Eve said.

"And you'd win the prize. Compared fibers to a lone white sock taken from the scene. You got your match. New sock, never worn, never washed. Still traces of gum on the lone one, from the tag, and I got me a tiny bit of plastic jammed in the toe. You know how they snap the socks together with the little plastic string?"

"Yeah, I hate those."

"Everyone does. You got to cut them apart, and who's got a knife or scissors handy when you want to wear your new socks?" Harvo snapped the gum in her mouth and circled a finger in the air. The nail was painted Christmas red with little green trees. "Freaking nobody. So you—" She fisted her hands together, twisted. "And half the time you snag the socks, or end up with a little bit of plastic inside that stabs you in the foot."

"Pisser."

"Yeah."

"How about the tag?"

"It's your lucky day—the sweepers were thorough and brought in the contents of the trash can. Came from the bathroom. I took it since I was doing the fibers anyway."

She scooted, showed Eve the tag.

"It was balled up, like you do, and a piece of it torn. Fibers stuck to the gummy side. Anyways, got it straightened out, put together, and you can see our handy bar code, and the type."

She tapped the protective shield over the evidence.

"Women's athletic socks, size seven to nine. Which is another pisser on my personal bitch list. See I wear a seven myself, and when I buy socks like this, I always got too much length in the foot. Why can't they just make them fit? We have the technology, we have the skill. We have the feet."

"That's a puzzler," Eve agreed. "Prints?"

"Vic's, tag and sock. Got another on the tag. Ran it." She bumped back to the screen. "Hitch, Jayne. Employed by Blossom Boutique on Seventh, sales clerk. I don't know, call me crazy, but I bet Jayne sold the vic a pair of socks recently."

"Nice job, Harvo."

"Yeah, I awe myself regular."

• • •

It was a simple matter to track down Jayne. She was behind the counter at the boutique ringing up sales with the focused determination of a soldier on the front lines.

The shop was jammed with customers, drawn, Eve imagined, by the big orange SALE signs on every rack, table, and wall. The noise level, punched upward by incessent holiday music, was awesome.

You could shop online, Eve thought, if you were desperate to shop. Why people insisted on pushing into retail outlets with other people who probably wanted the same merchandise, where the lines roped around in endlessly confusing misery and torture, and where the sales clerks were bitter as raw spinach, was beyond her.

When she said the same to Peabody, her partner's answer was a chipper "Because it's fun!"

To various consumers' annoyance and objections, Eve cut the line and muscled her way up front.

"Hey! I'm next."

Eve turned to the woman all but buried under piles of clothing, and held up her badge. "This means I go first. Need to talk to you, Jayne."

"What? Why? I'm busy."

"Gee, me, too. Got a back room?"

"Man. Sol? Cover register two. Back here." She thumped her way on two-inch-thick airsoles down a short corridor. "What? Listen, we were having a damn party. Parties get loud. It's Christmas, for God's sake. My across-the-hall neighbor is a primo bitch."

"Next time ask her to the party," Peabody suggested. "Hard to complain if you're part of the noise."

"I'd rather eat worm shit."

The back room was loaded with stock, boxes, bags. Jayne sat down on a stack of underwear. "Anyway, I'm off my feet for a minute. It's lunacy out there. Christmas makes people insane. And that bit about goodwill toward men? It sure as hell doesn't apply to retail."

"You sold a pair of socks to a woman sometime between Thursday and Saturday," Eve began.

Jayne ground her fist into the small of her back. "Honey, I sold a hundred pairs of socks between Thursday and Saturday."

"Lieutenant," Eve said and tapped her badge. "White athletics, size seven to nine."

Jayne dug in her pocket. She seemed to have a dozen of them between her black shirt and black pants. She pulled out a piece of hard candy, unwrapped it. Her fingernails, Eve noted, were as long as ice picks and painted like candy canes.

Yeah, Christmas made people insane.

"Oh, white athletic socks," Jayne said sourly. "That's a real tip-off."

"Take a look at a picture, see if you remember."

"I can barely remember my own face after a day like this one." The candy made rattling noises against Jayne's teeth as she played with it. But she rolled tired eyes and took the photo.

"Jeez, what are the odds? Yeah, I remember her. Talk about primo bitch. Listen," she said and sucked air through her nose. "She comes in, grabs a pair of socks. One lousy pair, complains we don't have enough help after she gets to me, and demands the sale price. Now, it's clear the socks are on sale in lots of three. Says so right on the display. One pair's nine-ninety-nine. Buy three for twenty-five-fifty. But she's squawking that she wants the socks for eight-fifty. She's done the math, and that's what she'll pay. She's got a line clear to Sixth behind her, and she's busting on me for, like, chump change."

She crunched down hard on the candy. "I'm not authorized to cut a price, and she won't budge. People are going to riot any minute, so I've got to call over the manager. Manager caves because it's just not worth the aggravation."

"When did she come in?"

"Man, it blurs together." Jayne rubbed the back of her neck. "I've been on since Wednesday. Straight seven days from hell. I get two off starting tomorrow and I'm going to sit on my ass for most of it. It was after lunch, I remember, because I thought how this asshole woman was going to make me lurch my gyro. Gyro!"

She snapped her fingers, shot her index up, leading with the festive ice pick. "Friday. Me and Fawn grabbed gyros on Friday. She had the weekend off, and I remember crabbing about it to her."

"Was she alone?"

"Who'd hang with that type? If anybody was with her, they stayed back. She strutted out by herself. I watched her go." She smiled a little. "Shot her the bird behind her back. Couple of the customers applauded."

"Have you got security discs?"

"Sure. What's this about? Somebody kick her ass? I'd've held their coat."

"Yeah, somebody did. I'd like to view the discs for Friday afternoon. We'll need to make copies."

"Wow. Okay. Gee. I'm not in trouble with this, am I?"

"No. But we'll need the discs."

Jayne shoved herself to her feet. "I gotta get the manager."

Back at her office, Eve reviewed the disc again. She drank coffee and watched Trudy walk in through the street doors. Sixteen-twenty-eight on the time stamp. Time enough to stew about the result of her visit to Roarke, Eve decided. Time enough to discuss it with a partner, or just walk around until a plan formed.

Pissed, Eve noted, when she paused, magnified Trudy's face. She could almost hear the teeth grinding together. Seething anger, not cold deliberation. Not right now, anyway. Impulse, maybe. I'll show them.

Had to look for the socks, elbow people out of her way, skirt around tables. But she found what she wanted . . . and at a bargain price.

Eve watched Trudy's teeth bare in a snarl when she yanked the socks from the display. But she frowned at the price, at the sale display, before marching over to stand in line.

Tapping her foot, glaring at the customers in line ahead of her.

Impatient. And alone.

She continued to watch, through the altercation with the clerk, Trudy looking down her nose, fisting her hands on her hips. Digging in. Turning briefly to snap something at the woman behind her in line.

Making a scene over pocket change.

Buying her own murder weapon on the cheap.

She didn't wait for a bag, didn't wait for a receipt. Just stuffed the socks in her purse and stalked out.

Eve sat back, perused the ceiling. Had to get the credits. Nobody carries enough to fill a sock around with them. And the way she'd slung the purse around didn't indicate it was weighed down.

"Computer, find and list all banks from Sixth Avenue to Tenth, between . . . Thirty-eighth and Forty-eighth.

Working . . .

Pushing up, she checked the time. Banks were closed for the day. But Trudy would have had just enough time to get to one, get herself a sackful of credits.

Check that out tomorrow. "Print out data," Eve ordered when the computer began to recite a list of banks. "Copy to file, copy to my home computer."

Acknowledged. Working . . .

She could see it. She'd have to find the bank, verify, but she could see it. Closest one to the boutique, that's the one it would be. Stride in, still steaming. Used cash if she was thinking, Eve decided. No point in having a transaction like that popping on a credit or debit report, so you use cash. And you dispose of the bank bag before you go back to the hotel.

Alone, she thought again.

Comes to the station alone, then to Roarke's office. No sign anyone's waiting for her in the lobby.

Makes a call maybe, uses her 'link once she's outside the building. No way to check that when the 'link's gone. Smart to take the 'link from the murder scene.

She paced, ordered more coffee.

Scared when she leaves Roarke. Contacts her pal, her cohort. Cries the blues. Could've cooked up the next part together.

She turned to her murder board, studied the photos of Trudy's face.

"What does it take to do that to yourself?" Eve muttered. "Plenty of motivation. Plenty of anger. But how the hell did you expect to prove you got tuned up by me or Roarke, or somebody we sicced on you?"

Back to stupid, she thought with a shake of her head. That was leading with anger, that was impulse and fury. Smarter to have gotten one or both of us out of the house on some pretext, somewhere we wouldn't be easily alibied. Stupid to assume we wouldn't have one. Sloppy.

A memory nudged at her, nearly faded

once more. Eve closed her eyes, pressed and focused.

Dark. Can't sleep. Too hungry. But the door of her room was locked from the outside. Trudy didn't like her to wander around the house—*sneaking around, getting into trouble*.

She was being punished anyway.

She'd talked to the boy across the street, a couple of his friends. Older boys. Taken a ride on one of their boards. Trudy didn't like the boy across the street, or his friends.

Hoodlums. Delinquents. Vandals. And worse. And you, nothing but a slut. Nine years old and already putting out. That's nothing new for you, is it? Get upstairs, and you can forget about supper. I don't feed trash in my house.

Shouldn't have talked to the boy. But he'd said he'd show her how to use the board, and she'd never ridden one before. They could do tricks on theirs—loops and wheelies and spins. She liked to watch them. The boy had seen her watching, and grinned at her. Motioned her over.

Shouldn't have gone—hell to pay. But he'd held that colorful board out, said she could take a breeze. He'd show her how.

And when she'd shot off on it, he'd whistled through his teeth. His friends had laughed. He'd said she had balls.

It was—she thought it was—the happiest, most liberating moment of her life at that time. She could remember, even now, the odd way the smile had fit on her face. The way her cheeks had stretched out, and the laugh that had rumbled up in her throat and hurt her chest a little. But a good hurt, like nothing she'd ever experienced.

He'd said she could go again, that she was a natural.

But Trudy had come out, came streaming out with that look on her face. That hell-to-pay look. She had yelled, screamed at Eve to get off that damn thing.

Didn't I tell you to stay in the yard. Didn't I say? Who gets the blame if you break your fool neck? You ever think of that?

She hadn't. Had only thought of the thrill of riding the board for the first time.

Trudy had screamed at the boys, too, told them she'd call the police. She knew what they were up to. *Perverts, hoodlums.* But they'd just laughed and made rude noises. The one whose board she'd ridden had called Trudy an old bitch, right to her face.

Eve had thought it was the bravest thing she'd ever seen.

He'd given Eve a quick grin, a quick wink, and told her she could have another ride whenever she shook the old bitch loose.

But she'd never ridden it again. She'd stayed away from him, and his friends.

And she'd paid for the momentary thrill with an empty gut.

Later, with stomach growling, she had stood at the window of her room. And she'd seen Trudy go out of the front door below. Had watched her take rocks and smash the windshield of her car, then the side windows. Had watched her spray paint on the hood—and made out the gleam of the letters in the dark.

OLD BITCH

Trudy had then marched across the street, had wiped the can on a rag, and then tossed it into the bushes in front of the boy's house.

She'd been smiling, a bared-teeth snarl of a smile as she'd walked back toward the house.

12

Eve had one more chore before she went off duty, and took it solo.

The hotel Roarke had provided for Bobby and Zana was a step up from the previous location. No big surprise there. Still, it was moderate, short on frills. Just the sort of place tourists or businesspeople on a budget might choose.

Security was subtle, but it was there.

She was stopped on her way across the tidy lobby before she could access the elevators.

"Excuse me, miss. Can I help you?"

The woman who tapped her shoulder had a pleasant face, an easy smile. And the faint bulge of a stunner under the armpit of her smart jacket.

"Police." Eve held up her right hand,

reached for her badge with her left. "Dallas, Lieutenant Eve. My people are in five-twelve. I'm going up to check on them and the uniform on duty."

"Lieutenant. Orders are to scan ID. So . . ."

"Good." They were her own orders, after all. "Go ahead."

The woman took out a hand scanner—jazzier than any police issue—verified. She tapped a button, brought Eve's ID photo onto the scanner's screen. Satisfied, she handed Eve her badge.

"Go ahead up, Lieutenant. Do you want me to call the uniform on duty and tell him you're on your way?"

"No. I like surprising them."

Fortunately for the uniform, he was at the door. They knew each other by sight, so rather than ask for ID, he simply sucked in his stomach, straightened his shoulders. "Lieutenant."

"Bennington. Status?"

"Quiet. All the rooms this level are occupied except five-oh-five and five-fifteen. Few people in and out—shopping bags and briefcases. Not a peep out of five-twelve since I came on shift."

"Take ten."

"Thanks, Lieutenant. I'm relieved in thirty, so I can stand until."

"Good enough." She knocked, waited while someone inside checked the security peep. Zana opened the door.

"Hi. I wasn't sure you'd be by today. Bobby's in the bedroom talking to D.K. Do you want me to get him?"

"No need." Eve stepped inside the little parlor. Roarke had provided what she supposed was termed an 'executive suite,' with a jut of kitchenette off a cozy sitting area. The bedroom was separated by a pair of pocket doors, currently shut.

"How you doing?" Eve asked.

"Better, thanks. Better." Her cheeks pinked a little. She fluffed nervously at the long waves of her sunny hair. "It occurred to me that you've mostly seen me hysterical. I'm not usually. Really."

"You had reason." Eve scanned. Privacy screens engaged. Good. Entertainment screen on some sort of girlie talk show. No wonder Bobby had the doors shut.

"Can I get you something? The kitchen's got a good supply." She smiled wanly. "No need to run out for bagels. I can get you coffee or—"

"No, that's okay."

"It's a nicer room than the other. Terrible way to get it."

"No point in being uncomfortable and uneasy."

"No. No, I guess not." She turned her wedding ring around and around on her finger. Another nervous habit, Eve thought. There was a ring with a little pink stone on her right hand, and the same pink stone, as studs, in her ears.

They matched her lip dye, Eve noted. How—and why—did women think of that kind of detail?

"I'm so glad you got my purse back. It had all my stuff, pictures and ID and this new lip dye I just bought, and . . . God." She rubbed her hands over her face. "Want to sit down?"

"For a minute. You've known Bobby and D.K. awhile."

"Since I started working for them. Bobby, he's just the sweetest thing." She sat, brushed at the thighs of her pants. "I fell right off. He's a little shy, you know, with women. D.K. was always teasing him."

"Bobby mentioned that D.K. and Trudy didn't get along."

"Oh, well." Zana's color resurfaced, just a little. "Mostly D.K. just kept his distance. Kind of a personality clash, I guess. Trudy, she'd just say what she was thinking, right out. And sometimes, well, people got a little offended."

"You didn't?"

"She's—she was—the mother of the man I love. And she raised him single-handed." Her eyes went starry. "Raised such a good man. I didn't mind her giving me advice. I've never been married before, after all, or kept a home. Anyway, Bobby knew just how to handle her."

"Did he?"

"He'd just tell me to nod and go along, then do what I wanted." Zana laughed, then covered her mouth with her hand as if to smother the sound. "That's what he did, mostly, and there was hardly ever a cross word between them."

"But there were some."

"Little spats now and then, like families have. Eve—is it all right if I call you Eve?"

"Yeah, that's fine."

"Do you think we can go home soon?" Her lips trembled before she pressed them together. "I was so excited about coming here, seeing New York, it was all I could think about. Now I just want to go home."

"At this point of the investigation, it's more convenient if you and Bobby are here."

"That's what he said." She sighed. "And he doesn't want to go home for Christmas. Says he just doesn't want to be there for it. I guess I can understand. It's just . . ." Tears shimmered in her eyes, but didn't fall. "It's selfish."

"What is?"

"It's our first Christmas married. Now we'll spend it in a hotel room. It is selfish." She sniffed back the tears, shook her head. "I shouldn't even be thinking about it with his mama . . ."

"It's natural enough."

Zana cast her guilty look toward the pocket doors. "Don't tell him I said anything. Please. He's got enough on his mind."

She got to her feet when the doors opened. "Hi, honey. Look who's here."

"Eve. Thanks for coming. I was just talking to my partner." He worked up a smile for his wife. "We closed the deal."

She slapped her hands together, bounced on her toes. "The big house?"

"The big one. D.K. got the contract and deposit from the buyer this morning."

"Oh, honey! That's just wonderful. Congratulations." She hurried around the sofa to give him a fierce hug. "You both worked so hard for that."

"Big sale," Bobby told Eve. "Hell, a white elephant we took on. We'd just about given up, when we got a nibble last week. My partner tied it up in a bow this morning."

"Back in Texas."

"Yeah. Took them through it three times over the weekend. They just wouldn't commit. Wanted to go through it again this morning, so he walked them through it again, and they finally bit. It's a big commission for us."

And put the partner out of the running, Eve decided, unless he'd found a way to be two places at once. "Congratulations."

"Mama would've been on the moon."

"Honey." Zana took his arms. "Don't be sad. She wouldn't want you to be sad. She'd be so *proud*. In fact, we're going to celebrate. I mean it." She gave him a little shake. "I'm going to order a bottle of champagne, and you're going to take a little while to relax and be proud of yourself. Will you have some with us, Eve?"

"Thanks, but I've got to go."

"I thought maybe you had some news, about my mother."

"The investigation's moving forward. That's the best I can tell you now. I'll check in with you tomorrow. If anything breaks beforehand, I'll let you know."

"Okay. Thanks. I'm glad it's you, Eve. It's easier somehow because it's you."

She could go home, Eve thought, as she muscled her way into traffic. It was more than Bobby could do at this point. She could go home where things were normal, at least by her standards.

As traffic snarled, she studied one of the bright, animated billboards, touting cut rates for holiday trips to Aruba.

Everyone wanted to be somewhere else, she decided. People from Texas, and wherever, flocked to New York. New Yorkers crawled up the highway to the Hamptons, or got on a shuttle south for some island.

Where did people on the islands go? she

wondered. Probably to some noisy, over-crowded city.

Why couldn't people just stay put?

Because they didn't, the streets and side-walks were clogged, with the airways over-head little better. And still, there wasn't any-where she'd rather be.

She drove through the gates, finally, toward the lights.

Every window was lit, candles or fes-tooned trees glittering. It looked like a paint-ing, she thought. Dark sky, rising moon, and the fanciful shapes and shadows of the house, with all those windows glowing.

She could go home.

So why was she depressed? It dragged at the base of her skull, at the pit of her belly as she parked the car, pushed herself out. She wanted to lie down, she realized, and not because she was tired. She just wanted to shut her head down for five damn min-utes.

Summerset was there, a dour skeleton amid the festive colors of the grand foyer.

"Roarke is in his office, attending to some of your business."

In her current mood, the disapproval scraped over the weight in her belly. "Nobody held a stunner to his throat," she snapped. "Which is what I dream of doing to you, night after night."

She stomped upstairs without bothering to take off her coat.

She didn't go to the office, which was petty and wrong. She knew it. But instead she went straight to the bedroom and, still in her coat, dropped facedown on the bed.

Five minutes, she thought. She was entitled to five damn minutes of solitude and quiet. If only she could shut off her head.

Seconds later, she heard the rapid pad of little feet, then the vibration of the bed as Galahad made his leap. She turned her head, stared into his bicolored eyes.

He stared back. Then did a couple of lazy circles, curled up by her head, and stared some more. She found herself trying to out-stare him, to make him blink first.

When she lost, she thought he smirked.

"Pal, if you were a cop, you'd crack suspects like walnuts."

She shifted so she could scratch his ears. With the cat purring like a souped-up engine, she watched the lights glimmer on the bedroom tree.

It was a good deal she had here, she told

herself. Big bed, pretty tree, nice cat. What was wrong with her?

She barely heard him come in, probably wouldn't have if she hadn't been listening for him.

When the mattress depressed, she turned her head again. This time she stared into eyes of wild and vivid blue.

Yeah, a pretty good deal.

"I was coming in," she murmured. "I just wanted a couple minutes."

"Headache?"

"No. I'm just . . . I don't know."

He stroked a hand over her hair. "Sad?"

"What have I got to be sad about? I've got this big-ass house. Did you see how it looks all lit up?"

"Yes." His hand moved down to the nape of her neck where some of the weight lay.

"I've got this fat cat hanging around. I think we should torment him on Christmas, make him wear some of those antler things. You know, like a reindeer."

"Undermine his dignity. Good idea."

"I've got you. The icing on my personal cake. I don't know what's wrong with me." She curled into him, burrowed into him. "I don't even care that she's dead, so what's wrong with me?"

"You're too hard on yourself, that's what's wrong with you."

She breathed him in, because it was a comfort. "I went to the morgue and looked at her. Just another body. I looked at what she did to herself, to try to screw with us. And it disgusted me. Didn't surprise me— not once I thought about it. I looked at what someone else did to her, and it was like: Well, what goes around. I'm not supposed to think that."

"What else did you do?"

"Today? Reported to Whitney. Got a little spanking there. Had lunch with Nadine to get her to spin the connection up front. Hit the lab. Followed the fabric trail to a retail outlet where Trudy bought the socks she used to make a sap. I got a list of banks between there and the hotel. Figure she had to get the credits. Check that tomorrow. Went by the bar where Zana was taken, talked to the owner. Reviewed the discs. Um . . . updated reports. Checked in on Bobby and Zana. Good security at the hotel. You've got a solid frontman in your lobby."

"Good to know."

"Then I came home. Other stuff in there, but that's the gist."

"In other words, you did your job. Whether or not you care she's dead, you did the work that will lead you to her killer."

She rolled over, stared up at the ceiling. "I've got no juice."

"What did you have for lunch?"

She gave a half laugh. "Taking my mind off my pity party? This pasta thing with some sort of herb stuff. It was good. Whatever Nadine and Peabody chowed on, they made a lot of girl yummy noises. The place was swinging, so I guess you've got a hit. Big surprise."

"The service?"

"Spooky. The waiter sort of poofs at the table out of nowhere if you even think about wanting something. Nadine's getting her own show."

"I heard about that just today. Good for her."

"And she's got vid and book deals. You in on any of that?"

"As a matter of fact."

"She wants to interview me, which maybe. And wants to do some of the vid here at the house, which is definitely no."

"Definitely."

She turned her head again to look at his face. How could one man be so beautiful, day after day? "I figured we'd line up in the same column on that."

"This is home." His hand stroked over hers, then lay, quiet and warm, over it. "It's private."

"I'm always bringing work home. Doing work here."

"As am I."

"You don't fill it with cops on top of it."

"I don't. And certainly don't plan to in the future. If I had a problem with you doing so, I'd let you know."

"I had this memory flash today."

Ah, he thought, *now we've got the root.* "Tell me."

"I was thinking about the way she'd hurt herself, gone out, bought socks for God's sake, for the sole purpose of bashing herself in the face, bruising her body. Vicious, self-destructive behavior. And I remembered this time . . ."

She told him, just as the memory had come back to her. And more, as she remembered more. That it had been hot, and she could smell grass. Strange smell to her as she'd so rarely experienced it before. One of the boys had had a disc player, and there was music jingling out.

And how the police car had slid almost silently up to the house that night. How the buttons on the cops' uniforms had glinted in the moonlight.

"They went across the street. It was late, it had to be late, because all the lights were out, everywhere. Then they came on, lights came on in the house across the street, and the boy's father came to the door. The cops went inside."

"What happened?" he asked when she went silent.

"I don't know, not for sure. I imagine the kid told them he didn't do anything. He'd been asleep. Couldn't prove it, of course. I remember the cops came out, poked around. Found the spray can. I can still see how one of them bagged it, shook his head. Stupid kid, he was probably thinking. Asshole kid.

"She went over, started shrieking. Pointing at the can, her car, their house. I just stood there and watched, and finally I couldn't watch it anymore. I got into bed. Pulled the covers over my head."

She closed her eyes. "I heard other kids talking about it in school. How he'd had to go down to the police station with his parents. I tuned it out. I didn't want to hear about it. A couple days later, Trudy was driving a new car. Nice shiny new car. I ran away not long after. I took off. I couldn't stand being there with her. I couldn't stand being there, seeing that house across the street."

She stared up at the dark window above her head. "I didn't realize until today that's the root of why I ran. I couldn't stand being there with what she'd done, and what I hadn't. He'd given me the best moment of my life, and he was in trouble. I didn't do anything to help him. I didn't say anything about what she did. I just let that kid take the rap."

"You were a child."

"That's an excuse for doing nothing to help?"

"It is, yes."

She sat up, pushed around so she could stare down at him. "The hell it is. He got dragged down to the cop shop, probably got a sheet, even if they couldn't prove he did it. His parents had to make restitution."

"Insurance."

"Oh, fuck that, Roarke."

He sat up, took her chin firmly in his hand. "You were nine years old, and scared. Now you're going to look back twenty years and blame yourself. Fuck *that,* Eve."

"I did nothing."

"And what could you have done? Gone to the police, told them you saw the woman—licensed and approved by Child Protection—deface her own car, then blame the kid across the street? They wouldn't have believed you."

"That's beside the point."

"It's not. And we both know that boy survived that bump in his childhood. He had parents, a house, friends, and enough character to offer a little girl a ride on an airboard. I imagine he survived very well. You've devoted your adult life to protecting the public, risking your life to do so. So you can bloody well stop blaming yourself for once being a frightened child and behaving as one."

"Well, hell."

"I mean it. And take off your coat. Christ Jesus, aren't you roasting?"

It wasn't often she felt— The only word she could think of was "abashed." She tugged off her coat, left it pooled around her. "You'd think a person could wallow a little in her own bed."

"It's my bed, too, and there's been quite enough wallowing. Want to try for something else?"

She picked up the cat, plopped him in her lap. "No."

"Go ahead and sulk, then, it's a step up from wallowing." He rolled off the bed. "I want some wine."

"He could've been scarred for life."

"Please."

She narrowed her eyes as he opened the liquor cabinet. "He could've become a career criminal, all because of that one frame job."

"There's a thought." He selected a nice white out of the cooler section. "Maybe you've put him away. Wouldn't that be some lovely irony?"

Her lips twitched, but she bore down on the laugh. "You could've done business with him in your nefarious past. He's probably a kingpin somewhere in Texas right now."

"And he owes it all to you." He came back to the bed with two glasses of wine, gave her one. "Better?"

"I don't know. Maybe. I'd forgotten about it, you know, the way you do even if it's all normal. And when it came back, it just rushed in with all this guilt. He was only about fourteen, fifteen. He felt sorry for me. I could see it on his face. No good deed goes unpunished," she said, toasting before she drank.

"I can find him if you want. You can see what he's up to, other than being a Texan crime lord."

"Maybe. I'll think about it."

"Meanwhile, I'd like to ask you for something."

"What?"

"I don't have any pictures of you from before we met."

It took her mind a moment to catch up with the non sequitur. "Pictures?"

"Yes, from when you were a nubile young girl, or a green rookie in uniform, which I'm hoping you'll put on again one day soon. I do love my woman in uniform. I could access older ID photos, but I'd like it more if you could find something for me."

"I guess. Maybe. Probably. Why?"

"Our lives didn't start when we met." He touched her face, just a feathering of those wonderful fingers over her skin. "Though I like to think the best of them did. I'd like to have a piece or two of you, from before."

"That's pretty sappy."

"Guilty. And if you come across any photos of yourself at, oh, around eighteen, scantily clad, so much the better."

She couldn't stop the laugh this time. "Perv."

"Again, guilty."

She took his glass, scooted over, and set both it and her own on the bedside table. She shoved the black butter of her coat carelessly onto the floor.

"I feel like doing something else."

"Oh?" He cocked his head. "Such as?"

She was quick, and she was agile. In a flashing movement, she rolled, reared up, and had her legs clamped around his waist, her hands fisted in his hair, and her mouth fused hotly to his. "Something like this," she said when she let him breathe again.

"I suppose I'll have to make the time for you."

"Damn right." She flipped open buttons on his shirt, leaned down to take a sharp nip at his jaw. "You scolded me. Counting my session with Whitney, that's the second knuckle rap I've had today."

Her hands were very busy, and by the time they reached his zipper, he was hard as steel. "I hope you didn't have the same reaction with your commander."

"He's pretty studly, if you go for the big-shouldered, careworn type. Me, I like 'em pretty." She took another nip at his ear as she overbalanced them and shoved him to his back.

The cat might have been fat, but he was also experienced, and dodged aside.

"You're so pretty. Sometimes I just want to lap you up like ice cream." She tugged his shirt open, spread her hands on his chest. "And look at this, all that flesh, all that muscle. All mine." She scraped her teeth down the center of his torso, felt him quiver. "Now that's something to make girl yummy noises over."

His hands were on her, little thrills. But he let her lead, let her set the pace. He would let her, she knew, for the moment at least. And not knowing when he might take her over was another thrill.

She yanked open her own shirt, put her hands over his to slide them up her body, close them over her breasts. And cruised on the sensation of those long, strong fingers against her. Then bowed back, eyes closed, as his hands skimmed down to unhook her trousers.

She came down to him again, bracing on her elbows. Mouth-to-mouth—long, sumptuous kisses punctuated by quick bites as her heart beat, beat, beat against his. When she offered her breast, he took it, and her breath caught, then released on a shudder.

His now, as much as he was hers. Her body was fueled for him. He rolled her over, pinned her hands to either side of her head. Her eyes were heavy with passion, dark with challenge.

"I want you naked. Lie still while I undress you."

He touched his lips to hers, then to the dent in her chin, lining little opened-mouth kisses down her throat, over her breasts, down to her belly.

He roiled her pants down her hips, exposing more flesh, then traced his tongue over the tender dip where legs met her center. She arched, shivered.

"Ssh." A soothing murmur even as he used his mouth to drive her to the edge, finally to push her over it. When she went limp, he continued down her thighs.

He tugged off her boots, let her trousers fall in a heap on top of them. Then began to work his way up, slowly, tortuously.

"Roarke."

"Look at this flesh and muscle," he said, echoing her earlier words. "All mine."

Again, her body began to churn, that outrageous and breathless pressure building and building until everything inside her burst open. She could only reach for him.

He was inside her, deep and strong. His mouth on hers, his fingers linked with hers. Tasting, feeling, holding, they flashed together.

She thought, blind with love, that, yes, she could go home.

They lay quiet for a moment, settling. He'd rolled again so her head could rest on his shoulder, her hand on his heart that was still drumming.

"I should scold you more often."

"Wouldn't make a habit of it. Might tick me off next time. I felt off all day. I was doing the job, like you said, but I felt off. Almost like I was watching myself do the job. Passive or something. That's not my rhythm. I need to tune it up."

He gave her belly a light rub. "You felt tuned to me."

"Sex'll do that. With you, anyway." She pushed herself up. "I need to start at the beginning of this, in my head. Rub off this film that's been clouding my brain, and start over."

He stretched out to reach the wine. "Then that's what you'll do."

She took a sip of the one he handed her. "What I'm going to do is take a shower and get dressed. Go over my own notes and reports from the scene, the statements. Take an hour and just line it up in my head."

"All right. I'll go back to the account, see what I can chisel out."

"Can I bounce some things off you after I line them up?"

"I'd be disappointed otherwise. Why don't we rendezvous in an hour, do that bouncing over dinner?"

"That'll work." She took his hand, squeezed. "This works."

He kissed her knuckles. "It certainly does."

13

She took her hour and went back to the beginning. She walked back through it, step by step, using the crime scene record, her own notes, the reports from the sweepers, the ME, the lab.

She listened to statements, judging inflection, expression, as much as the words themselves.

She stood in front of her board and studied each photograph, every angle.

When Roarke came in from his office, she turned to him. He acknowledged the light in her eyes with a grin and cocked brow. "Lieutenant."

"Goddamn right. I was acting like a cop, doing the cop walk, but I wasn't *feeling* like a cop. I'm back now."

"Welcome."

"Let's eat. What do you want?"

"Since you're feeling like a cop, I suppose it best be pizza."

"Hot damn. If I hadn't already rolled you, I'd probably jump you just for that."

"Put it on my account."

They sat at her desk, one on either side, with pizza and wine between them. He'd even put a tree in here, she thought. A small one, by his standards, but, by God, she liked looking at it over by the window, sprinkling light out into the dark.

"See, here's the thing," she began, "it doesn't make any sense."

"Ah." He gestured with his glass, sipped. "Glad that's cleared up."

"Seriously. Here's what you've got on the surface, when you walk cold into the scene: Dead woman, killed by multiple blows of a blunt instrument, head shots from behind. Previous bodily injuries indicating she'd been attacked and/or beaten the day before. Door locked from the inside, window not."

With a slice of pizza in one hand, she waved toward her board with the other. "Appearance, basic evidence points to intruder entering through the window, bashing her, exiting the same way. As there are no defensive wounds whatsoever, investigator would assume she probably knew her killer, or didn't believe she was in jeopardy. Now, somebody pounds on you one day, you're going to be a little concerned next time he pops around."

"Not if those initial injuries were self-inflicted."

"Yeah, but you don't know that—why would you think that—when you find the body? The killer had to be aware of at least the facial injury. It's right there. And the same weapon was used. So we go back over it, with that data, and we have the murder being set to look like she was killed by whoever tuned her up."

She took a huge bite of pizza, savored the spice. "We got the killer using the previous injuries as smoke. That's not bad. Not bad at all. It's good thinking, just like taking her 'link was good thinking."

"Exploiting the victim's greed and violent impulses."

"Yeah. But there's little things that blow that. Again, no defensive wounds. No indication she was bound when she was beaten, and no sign that she attempted, in any way, to fight back or shield herself. Doesn't wash. Then you add the angles of the bruising. Comes up self-inflicted."

"Which moves you to a different arena."

"Exactly. Then there's the crime scene itself, the position of the body, and TOD."

"Time of death."

"Yeah, somebody strange comes in the window middle of the night and you can get out of bed, you run and you scream. She didn't do either. So the killer came through the door. She let the killer in."

"The window's still viable. If indeed she and her partner were having differences, he may have chosen to come in that way rather than risk her not letting him in."

"The window was locked. That's the thing about memory. It's tricky." She took another bite of pizza, washed it down. "It's the thing about having a cop on an investigation who knew the victim—who, once that memory gets poked, clearly recalls how the victim always locked every door, every window. The world was full of thieves and rapists and bad business, according to the Bible of Trudy. Even during the day, when we were in the house, it was locked like a vault. I'd forgotten that. She's not going to leave a window unlocked in big, bad New York. It's out of character."

"She lets the killer in," he prompted. "Late-night visit."

"Yeah. Late. And she doesn't bother to put on a robe. She had one in the closet, but she doesn't bother with it and entertains her killer while wearing her nightgown."

"Indicating a certain level of intimacy. A lover?"

"Maybe. Can't dismiss it. She kept herself in tune. Face and body work. I can't remember any guys," Eve murmured, trying to look back into the past again. "It was only about six months I was there, but I don't remember any guys coming around, or her going out with any."

"From then to now would indicate a very long dry spell."

"Can't rule out a booty call," Eve continued, "but I went over the list of her possessions, everything she had in that room: no sex toys, no sexy underwear, no condoms or any shields against STDs. Still, could be a long-term relationship—I'm not finding indications, but could be. Not a partner, though. Not on equal terms."

"No?"

"She had to be in charge. She had to give the orders. She liked telling people what to do and liked watching them do it. Look at her pathology—take her employment record. Scores of jobs over the years, none lasting long. She didn't take orders, she gave them."

"So, in her mind, fostering was perfect." Roarke nodded. "She's the boss, she's in charge. Total authority."

"She'd think," Eve agreed. "She was cruising toward sixty, and no marriages on record. Only one official cohab. No, she wasn't a team player. Partnership wouldn't work for her. So maybe she tagged this individual on her 'link. *Get over here, we need to talk.* She's had some wine, some meds. Probably just enough to be floaty and full of herself."

"Another reason she might not have taken as much care as she might have otherwise."

Eve nodded. "She's relaxed, medicated. And she's figuring on squeezing you for the two million. She's cracked her own face for it. Yeah, she's full of herself. But how's she going to squeeze you when she's holed up in a hotel room?"

"I've considered that already. You were off your rhythm," he reminded her when she frowned at him. "Documented the injuries, I imagine, with a shaky, perhaps teary, account of the attack. An attack which would impli-cate either or both of us as the assailant, or— if she were more clever—which had the un-known assailant warn her that either or both of us would see she got worse unless she did what she was told."

He topped off the wine in Eve's glass. "There would be a statement that this record was made to protect herself, in the event of her untimely death. Or further in-jury. In which case the record would be sent to the media, and the authorities. This doc-umentation would be sent to me, as she'd trust me to decipher the subtext: Pay, or this goes public."

"Yeah, well." She took another slice of pizza. "Did all this considering tell you where that record might be?"

"With her killer, no doubt."

"Yeah, no doubt. So why wasn't it brought up along with the numbered ac-count during Zana's abduction? Why haven't you received a copy of the documenta-tion?"

"The killer may have assumed the record would do the talking. And may have been foolish enough to trust it to regular mail."

"See." She shook the slice at him, then bit in. "Smart, sloppy, smart, sloppy. And that doesn't work for me. There's no sloppy here. It's all smart—smart enough to try to look sloppy. Crime of passion, covering it up, little mistakes. Bigger ones. But I think . . . I'm starting to wonder if some of those mistakes are purposeful."

She looked back at the board. "Maybe I'm just circling."

"No, keep going. I like it."

"She was a difficult woman. Even her son said so. And yeah," she added, reading Roarke's expression, "I haven't eliminated him as a suspect. I'll come back to why he's not higher on my list. So you're doing grunt work for a difficult woman. You're going to get a cut, but no way you're getting half. Maybe she tells you she's going for a million, and you can have ten percent for your trouble. That's not bad for grunt work. Maybe that's the play, and she gives you the record to deliver or send."

"Sure of herself to do that," he commented.

"Yeah, and sure of her grunt. But it also takes her a step back if anything goes wrong. It all fits her profile."

"But her grunt isn't as obedient as she assumed," Roarke continued. "Instead of being a good doggy and delivering, you take a look at it first. And start thinking this is worth more."

Here was her rhythm, Eve realized. Batting it back and forth with him, seeing the steps, the pieces, the possibilities.

"Yeah. Maybe you come back, tell her you want a bigger cut. Maybe you point out they could squeeze for more than a measly million."

"That would piss her off."

"Wouldn't it." Eve smiled at him. "And she's loose. Been drinking, taking meds. Could be her tongue got away from her and it comes out she was going for two. Oops."

"Or she just flat out refuses to widen the slice of the pie."

"That's a pisser either way. And any way it plays, you're back in that room with her late Saturday night, early Sunday morning. She turns her back on you. You've got the record, you've got the weapon. You've got motive, you've got opportunity. You take her out. You bag up her 'link, her copy of the documentation, her disc files, anything else that might implicate you or help you out. You unlock the window, and you're gone."

"Now you'll get the whole pie." Roarke glanced down at the pizza between them. They'd fairly well demolished it, he noted. Hungry work.

"Then it angles back." Eve licked a little sauce from her thumb. "Bright and early Monday morning, you're right there, right on the spot to snatch Zana when she comes out. Happy coincidence for you that she's out hunting bagels on her own."

"Maybe Trudy wasn't the one with the lover."

"That's a thought, isn't it?" She inclined her head, and shoved the pizza away before she made herself sick. "Going to take a closer look at Bobby's pretty little wife."

"Not Bobby?"

"I'll go down a few layers. But the thing with matricide is it's usually uglier. More rage."

As was patricide, she thought. She'd all but swam in the blood when she'd killed her father.

As that was one memory she didn't need

or want, she focused on the now. "Then the motive's murky there. If it's the money, why not wait until she scooped it up? Then you arrange for an accident back home, and you inherit. Could've been impulse, just of the moment, but . . ."

"You've got a spot for him," Roarke said. "A soft one."

"It's not that." Or maybe part of that, she admitted. "If he was putting on a show outside that hotel room, he's wasting his talents with real estate. And I was with him when Zana had her adventure, so that means he'd have to have a partner. Or he and Zana are in this together. None of that's impossible, so we'll go down those layers. But it's not what rings for me."

He studied her face. "And something does. I can see it."

"Back to the vic. She likes to be in charge, keep people under her thumb. Like you pointed out, she didn't just take kids in for the fees. She took them in so she had sway over them, so they'd do her bidding, fear her. According to her, she kept files on them. So why would I be the first she's hit on?"

"Not a partner then. A minion."

"That's a good word, isn't it?" Eve sat back in her chair, swiveled back and forth. "Minion. Right up her alley. From the look back I already took, she always fostered females. Which plays into her being in her nightgown. Why bother with a robe when it's another woman? No need to be concerned or afraid when it's someone you bossed around when she was a kid and who, for whatever reason, is still under your control."

"Zana was abducted by a man, if we take her at her word."

"And if we do, going by this theory, there are two. Or Trudy had herself a man. I'm going to take a closer look at who she fostered."

"And I'll play with my numbers."

"Getting anywhere?"

"It's a matter of time. Feeney got a start and a warrant. Which makes it possible for me to use my office equipment without dodging around CompuGuard."

"Only half the fun for you."

"Sometimes you settle." He got to his feet. "I'll get back to it."

"Roarke. Before, what I said about bringing work home, and cops into the house. I should've added pulling you into this mix."

"I put myself into the mix quite a few times, going around you to do so." His lips curved, just a bit. "I've tried to learn to wait to be asked first."

"I ask a lot. And I haven't forgotten you were hurt, took a couple of pretty serious hits on my last two major cases because I asked you first."

"As did you," he reminded her.

"I signed up for it."

He smiled fully now—it was enough to make a woman's heart do a header—and walked around the desk to lift her hand, rub his finger over her wedding ring. "As did I. Go to work, Lieutenant."

"Okay. Okay," she repeated quietly as he walked to his own office. She turned to her computer. "Let's start earning our pay."

She brought up the list of the children Trudy had fostered, then began to pick at their lives.

One was doing her third stretch for aggravated assault. Good candidate, Eve thought, if she wasn't currently in a cage in Mobile, Alabama. She put a call through to the warden, just in case, and confirmed.

One down.

Another had been blown to bits while dancing at an underground club in Miami when a couple of lunatics stormed it. Suicide bombers, Eve recalled, protesting—with their lives, and more than a hundred others—what they considered the exploitation of women.

The next had a residence listed as Des Moines, Iowa, one current marriage on record, with employment as an elementary educator. One offspring, male. The spouse was a data cruncher. Still, they pulled in a decent living between them, Eve mused. Trudy might have dipped into the well.

Eve contacted Iowa. The woman who came on-screen looked exhausted. Banging and crashing sounded in the background. "Happy holidays. God help me. Wayne, *please,* will you keep it down for five minutes? Sorry."

"No problem. Carly Tween?"

"That's right."

"I'm Lieutenant Dallas, with New York City Police and Security."

"New York. I've got to sit down." There was a huge sigh, and the screen tipped just enough for Eve to get a glimpse of an enormously pregnant belly. Another down, she decided, but followed through.

"What's this about?"

"Trudy Lombard. Ring a bell?"

Her face changed, tightened. "Yes. She was my foster mother for several months when I was a child."

"Could you tell me the last time you had contact with her?"

"Why? *Wayne.* I mean it. Why?" she repeated.

"Ms. Lombard was murdered. I'm investigating."

"Murdered? Wait, just wait, I have to move to somewhere else. I can't hear with all this noise." There was a lot of huffing before the woman gained her feet, and the screen swayed as she waddled across what Eve saw was a family living area into a small office space. She shut the door.

"She was murdered? How?"

"Mrs. Tween, I'd like to know the last time you spoke with or had contact with Ms. Lombard."

"Am I a suspect?"

"The fact that you're not answering a routine question makes me wonder."

"I was twelve," Carly snapped. "I was under her care for eight months. My aunt was able to get custody and I went to live with her. Matter closed."

"Then why are you angry?"

"Because a New York cop is calling my home and asking me questions about a murder. I have a family. I'm eight months pregnant, for God's sake. I'm a teacher."

"And you still haven't answered my question."

"I have nothing to say about this or her. Nothing. Not without a lawyer, so leave me alone."

The screen went black. "That went well," Eve commented.

While she didn't see Carly Tween waddling her way to New York to bash Trudy's brains in, she kept her on the list.

On the next call she was switched to voice mail—two faces, two voices, both of them glowing to the point Eve wished for sunshades.

Hi! This is Pru!

And this is Alex!

We can't talk to you right now because we're on our honeymoon *in Aruba!*

They turned to each other, giggling insanely. *Catch you when we come back. If we come back.*

Apparently someone was taking advantage of those low rates to the islands, Eve thought. If Pru and Alex had tied the knot, they'd done so recently enough that the data hadn't caught up.

She confirmed with vital records in Novi, Michigan. Pru and Alex had indeed applied for a marriage license, and had put it to use the previous Saturday.

She doubted they'd detoured to New York to commit murder on their way to sun, surf, and sex.

"All right, Maxie Grant, of New L.A., let's see what you're up to. A lawyer, huh? And with your own firm. Must be doing pretty well. I'd bet Trudy would've liked a piece of that."

Factoring the time difference, she tried Maxie Grant's office number first.

It was answered on the second beep, in brisk tones, by a woman with a great deal of curly red hair around a sharply defined face. Her mossy green eyes fixed on Eve's. "Maxie Grant, what can I do for you?"

"Lieutenant Dallas, NYPSD."

"New York? You keep late hours, Lieutenant."

"You answer your own 'link, Ms. Grant."

"Entirely too often. What can I do for New
York?"

"Trudy Lombard."

The smile that curved across Maxie's face
was anything but friendly. "Tell me you're
Homicide, and the bitch is on a slab."

"That's just what I'm going to tell you."

"No shit? Well, strike up the band and
hand me a tuba. How'd she buy it?"

"I take it you weren't a fan."

"I hated her guts. I hated the atoms that
made up her guts. If you've got who did her
under wraps, I'd like to shake his hand."

"Why don't you tell me your whereabouts
from this past Saturday through Monday."

"Sure. I was right here. On the coast, I
mean. Even I don't spend every minute in
this office." She eased back in the chair,
pursed her lips in consideration. "Okay, Saturday, eight to noon, I was volunteering at
St. Agnes's. I coach girls' volleyball. Get you
a list of names to verify if you want them. Did
some Christmas shopping after, with a pal.
Spent too much, but hell, it's Christmas. Got
the pal's name, and my receipts. Party Sat-

urday night. Didn't get home 'til after two, and didn't come home alone. Sex and breakfast in bed Sunday morning. Went to the gym, hung around the house. Did some work from home Sunday night. How about some details. Did she suffer? Please tell me she suffered."

"Why don't you tell me why you'd enjoy that?"

"She made my life hell for nine months. Unless you're a total fuckup—and you don't look like one—you've got my file right there. Went into the system when I was eight, after my old man finally beat my mother to death and got his sorry ass locked up. Nobody wanted me. I got shot to that sadistic bitch. She used to make me scrub floors with a toothbrush, locked me in my room every night. Cut the power to it sometimes, just so I'd be in the dark. Told me my mother probably deserved what she got, and I'd end up the same way."

She took a deep breath, then reached for the bottle of water at her elbow, drank. "I started stealing, squirreling money away for my escape fund. Got caught. She showed the cops all these bruises on her arms, her legs. Told them I'd attacked her. I never touched the bitch. So I'm slapped in juvie. Got bad, lots of fights.

"You've seen this picture before."

"Yeah, a few times."

"I was dealing illegals by the time I was ten. Bad ass," she said with a smile that said she was ashamed of it. "In and out of kid cages until I was fifteen and a deal went south. I got cut up. Best thing that ever happened to me. There was a priest . . . This sounds very Vid of the Week, but there you go. He stuck with me, wouldn't quit. He turned me around."

"And you went into law."

"Just seemed to suit me. That sadistic bitch had me when I was eight, and I was scared. I'd watched my mother die. She used that, did her level best to ruin me. And she nearly did. I won't be sending flowers to her wake, Lieutenant. I'll be strapping on red shoes and drinking French champagne."

"When's the last time you saw her?"

"I haven't seen her, face-to-face, in four years."

"Face-to-face?"

She took another sip, slowly. "I'm a lawyer, good enough to know I should have representation. I shouldn't be talking to you. But I'm so damn happy she's dead, I'm going to walk on the wild side. Four years ago, I was working for a high-powered firm. Junior partner. I was engaged to a guy who had a solid shot at the Senate. I was pulling in a big salary, one I worked my ass off for. She shows up at my office. Where I worked, for God's sake. She's all smiles, and look at you, aren't you something. Made me sick."

Maxie took one more slug of water, then slapped the bottle down again. "I should've kicked her out, but she caught me off guard. Then she hits me with it: She's got copies of my record, all of it. The illegals, the cage time, the assaults, the thefts. It wouldn't do, would it, for that to come out? Not with me in this cushy job, in this important firm. Not with me planning my wedding to a man favored to head to East Washington."

"She blackmailed you."

"I let her. So stupid. I gave her fifty thousand. In three months, she was back for more. That's the way it works. I'm not green, I knew better. But I paid her again. Even when my relationship went down the sewer. My fault, I was so stressed, so determined not to let him know, that I torched it."

She broke off a moment, and her tone changed, softened. "I'm sorry for that. Still sorry for that. So, I paid her for two years. To the tune of a quarter mil. And I just couldn't take it anymore. I quit my job. And the next time she contacted me, I told her to go ahead. Go ahead, you bitch, do your worst. I've got nothing to lose now. Already lost it," she said quietly.

"How'd she take it?"

"She was steamed. At least I had that. She screamed and carried on like I was jabbing hot sticks in her eyes. Nice moment for me. I'd get disbarred, she said. And that's bull, of course. No firm would ever hire me again. And there she might've had something. I didn't give a cold shit. I stuck, and she went away. And now, thank the gods, she won't be back."

"You should've gone to the cops."

"Maybe. Shoulda, coulda, woulda. I played my hand. I got my own firm now, such as it is. I'm happy. I didn't kill her, but I'll offer my services pro bono to whoever did. She made me bathe in cold water, every night. Said it was good for me. Cooled hot blood."

Eve shuddered before she could stop herself. She remembered the cold baths.

"I'm going to want the names of the people who can verify your whereabouts, Maxie."

"No problem. Tell me how she bought it."

"Fractured skull, blunt instrument."

"Oh. I was hoping for something more exotic. Guess that'll have to do."

Cold, Eve thought later. Cold and brutally frank. She had to respect that.

Even better, she had her first step toward a pattern of blackmail.

She found two more. Though they didn't confirm it, she saw it in their eyes. Alibis would be checked for them, and for the two others she couldn't reach.

She got up for coffee, detoured into Roarke's office. "Any progress?"

"Continues to dead-end on me." He shoved back from the desk, obviously annoyed. "Are we sure she had the numbers right?"

"She was shook, so she may have screwed up. But she said them twice, in the sequence I gave you. No hesitation."

"I'm getting nothing. I'm going to have the computer run them, in various sequences. See what pops up. What about you?"

"I've got one confirmed blackmail. Lawyer out in California. I don't like her for the murder, but she claims she shelled out a quarter million over a couple of years before she cut Trudy off. That's a lot from one source, and I'm banking there's more. I'm also banking Trudy had herself a couple of quiet accounts, the sort she wouldn't report for taxes."

"Now that I can find easily enough."

"I've got two account numbers from the lawyer where she transferred money to Trudy. But it's been several years, and maybe Trudy shuffled funds around."

"The best way to keep the IRS from sniffing. I'll start with those, find the rest."

"When you do, if they were e-transfers, we'd be able to track them to the source."

"Child's play, and it'll give me a break from this frustration."

"Want coffee?"

"How wifely. I would, yes. Thanks."

"I was getting some for me anyway."

She heard him laugh as she started out, then she stopped by the board again. If Trudy had income from blackmail, money tucked away, just how much would Bobby inherit now?

A nice boost to his business, she imagined.

She thought briefly of the boy who'd snuck a sandwich into her room when she'd been alone and hungry. How he'd done so without a word, with the faintest of smiles and a finger to his lips.

Then she got coffee, and prepared to find out if he'd killed his own mother.

14

She was standing in a room, brilliantly lit,
drinking champagne with a group of
women. She recognized their faces. The
California lawyer was drinking right from
the bottle and doing a hip-swinging dance
in high red heels. Carly Tween was sitting
on a stool with a tall back, sipping delicately while she rubbed her enormous
belly with her free hand.

The others—the others who'd been like
her—were all chattering the way women do
at girl parties. She'd never been fluent in the
language of fashion and food and men, so
she drank the frothy wine and let the
sounds roll over her.

Everyone was duded up. She herself was
wearing the same outfit she'd donned for

the holiday party. Even in the dream—even *knowing* it was a dream—her feet ached.

Part of the room was sectioned off, and there the children they'd been sat, watching the party. Hand-me-down clothes, hungry faces, hopeless eyes—all closed off from the lights, the music, the laughter by a sheer glass wall.

Inside it, Bobby served the children sandwiches, and they ate ravenously.

She didn't belong here, not really. She wasn't one of them, not quite. And the others sent her quick, sidelong glances, and whispered behind their hands.

Still, it was she who walked first to the body that lay on the floor in the middle of the celebration. Blood stained Trudy's nightgown and congealed on the glossy floor.

"She's really not dressed for it," Maxie said, and smiled as she chugged down more champagne. "All the money she carved out of us, you'd think she could afford a nice outfit. It's a fricking party, isn't it?"

"She didn't plan to be here."

"You know what they say about plans."

She gave Eve an elbow nudge. "Loosen up. We're all family here, after all."

"My family's not here." She looked through that sheer glass, into the eyes of children. And wasn't so sure. "I've got a job to do."

"Suit yourself. Me, I'm going to get this party started." Maxie turned the bottle over, gripped the neck in both hands, and with a wild laugh smashed it against Trudy's already shattered head.

Eve leapt forward, shoved her back, but the others swarmed in. She was knocked down, kicked aside, trampled as they fell on the body like dogs.

She crawled clear, struggled to stand. And saw the children behind the glass. Cheering.

Behind them, she saw the shadow, the shape that was her father.

Told you, didn't I, little girl? Told you they'd toss you into the pit with the spiders.

"No." She jerked, struck out when someone lifted her.

"Easy now," Roarke murmured. "I've got you."

"What? What?" With her heart skittering,

she shook herself awake in his arms. "What is it?"

"You fell asleep at your desk. Small wonder as it's nearly two in the morning. You were having a nightmare."

"It wasn't . . ." She took a moment to steady herself. "It wasn't a nightmare, not really. It was just weird. Just a weird dream. I can walk."

"I like this better." Still carrying her, he stepped onto the elevator. "We'd have headed for bed sooner, but I got caught up."

"I'm fuzzy." She rubbed her face, but couldn't scrape away the fatigue. "You get anywhere?"

"What a question. Three accounts so far. I suspect there are more. Feeney can take over with it in the morning. I've some work of my own to deal with."

"What are—"

"Morning's soon enough. It's nearly here, in any case." He stepped out of the elevator, took her straight to the bed. When he started to tug down her pants, she tapped his hands aside.

"I can do that. You might get ideas."

"Even I have limits, broad though they may be."

Still, when he slid into bed with her, he drew her close to his side.

She started to nag him into giving her some of the data. And the next thing she knew, it was morning.

He was having coffee in the sitting area, with the viewing screen split between stock reports and the morning bulletins. At the moment, she didn't care about either. So she grunted what passed for a morning greeting and slogged off to the bathroom.

When she came out, she smelled bacon.

There were two plates on the table. She knew his game. He'd fill her in if and when she ate. To expedite it, she plopped down across from him, grabbed the coffee first.

"So?"

"Good morning to you, too. Such as it is. Forecast is for sleet, possibly turning to snow by midmorning."

"The fun never ends. The accounts, Roarke."

He pointed a finger at the cat, who was trying to belly over toward the food. Galahad stopped, and began scratching his ears.

"The accounts the lawyer gave you were closed. Timing coordinates with the cutoff. I found others, off shore and off planet. Numbered, of course, but with some finessing, I unearthed the certified names. Roberta True and Robin Lombardi."

"Not very imaginative."

"I don't think imagination was her strong suit. Greed certainly was. She had close to a million in each. Tracing back, I've got the lawyer's transfers. And another six figures transferred from an account under the names Thom and Carly Tween."

"Yeah, I knew she'd been scalped some."

"Also a chunk from a Marlee Peoples."

"Peoples—that's the doctor, pediatrician, in Chicago. I wasn't able to reach her yesterday."

"There's more. I made you a list. Deposits that I've found so far go back about ten years."

"Round about the time she'd have lost the pro-mom status. You got a kid in college, you keep the status until he's done, or turns twenty-four."

"A handy way to make up for the loss in income."

"But she doesn't buy a nice outfit for the party."

"Sorry?"

"Stupid dream." Eve shook her head. "Or not so. What the hell did she do with her money, anyway? Comes to New York, stays in an economy hotel."

Roarke plucked up a piece of bacon, handed it to her. "For some, it's simply the having, the accumulating. It's not what you can buy with it."

Because it was in her hand, she ate the bacon. "Well, Morris said she'd had good face and body work, so she spent some on that. Daughter-in-law stated Trudy left her better jewelry at home, so she spent some there. Personal stuff," Eve mused. "Appearance. That fits her. And maybe she invested in something. Bobby's in real estate. Could be she's got property. Something she figured to retire to when she was done bleeding her former charges."

"Does it matter?"

"I don't know. How much she had, who knew she had it, who had access. It might matter." She ate as she thought about it. "I couldn't find anything that points to Bobby or his bride. I went through financials, medical, education, criminal. But if either or both of them knew she had a couple million stashed away, and thought there was a shot at doubling that, maybe."

She toyed with it a moment. "If we can freeze the accounts, prove the funds were from illegal means . . . Might get the killer to try to follow Trudy's path to blackmail. Might piss him off, too. And eventually, through the maze of red tape, we might even get the money back where it came from."

"And justice for all."

"In a perfect world, which isn't even close to this one. But it's an angle. If money was the motive, removing the money could stir things up."

With some surprise she realized she'd finished her breakfast. She rose. "I'm going to get dressed, get started. Maybe we'll lower the visual on the security I've got on Bobby and Zana. Make it seem like it's eased up. Need some bait, is what we need."

She went to the closet, remembered what he'd said about sleet and snow, so detoured to her dresser to dig out a sweater. "It's the twenty-third, right?"

"Only two more shopping days before Christmas."

"Makes sense, lighter duty this close to the big day. Couple of out-of-towners cooped up in a hotel. They'd start whining about getting out some. So we let them. See what we can see."

At Central, she set up a briefing in one of the conference rooms. She called in Detective Baxter and Officer Trueheart, as well as Feeney, Peabody, and McNab.

She caught them up, then began to assign duties.

"Feeney, you'll continue to follow the money. I realize this isn't your top priority, so whatever time and manpower you can spare."

"Things are pretty loose. Losing a lot of my boys over the next day or two. Including this one." He jerked a thumb at McNab. "No reason I can't work their asses off until then."

"Appreciate it. I'm going to need a couple of homers," she told him. "I want small and discreet. I'm going for a warrant to use them on our two protective custodys."

"A warrant?" He scratched his fingers

into his wiry, ginger-colored hair. "You don't figure they'll grant permission?"

"I'm not going to ask for it. So I want something I can get on them without them being aware. You got something in your bag of tricks that'll give me some audio, it wouldn't hurt."

"Tricky." Considering, he rubbed his chin. "Warrant for something like that, you generally got to have some evidence points to them as suspects, or have their prior knowledge and cooperation."

She'd already worked the skirt around that one in her head. "In the opinion of the primary, the subjects are already under duress and stress. The purpose of the homers is for their own safety, as the female subject was purportedly abducted once."

"Purportedly?" Peabody repeated.

"We've only got her word on it. We're running a thin line with these two, between victims and suspects. Homers are my method of walking the line. I'm going to do a dance for the warrant. I'll call Mira in to back me up if necessary. We get them wired, and we open the cage."

She turned to Baxter. "That's where you and your partner come in. I want you out there, soft clothes, tailing them. I want to know where they go, how they look."

"You're tossing us out on the street on Christmas Eve—Eve . . . Eve." Baxter grinned. "Somebody had to say it."

"It would be you. They split up, you split up. You stay in contact with each other, and with me. This is low risk, but I don't want sloppy. They may be approached. It's unlikely they'll be harmed. Probability's in the low twenties. Let's take that down to zero and keep sharp."

"Lieutenant?" As was his habit, Trueheart raised his hand. He wasn't as green as he once was, Baxter was ripening him. But a little color rose up his throat over his uniform collar when Eve turned to him.

"If they are approached, do we move in to apprehend?"

"You observe, use your own judgment. I don't want you giving chase and losing this guy on the street. You take him if you're close enough to do so without risk. Otherwise, you follow, give me the coordinates. From all evidence, the victim was target specific. There's little risk to the populace, so let's keep it that way."

She gestured to the board, and Trudy's

picture. "Still, he did that, so we're dealing with someone who can and will kill if motivated. I want everybody home for Christmas."

She held Peabody back when the others left. "I'm going to see Mira, run this by her and get her behind me on this warrant. I've got names of former fosters. The ones I was unable to reach are marked. See what you can do with them. But first, contact Carly Tween from that list. She wouldn't talk to me. She's eight months pregnant, scared, and cranky. Use your soft sell. If you can confirm her husband's whereabouts for the murder, so much the better."

"She got a father? Brothers?"

"Shit." Eve rubbed her neck. "Can't remember. Doubtful on the father as she was in foster, but check it out."

"On that. Good luck with the warrant."

To Eve's shock and surprise, Mira's admin didn't throw herself bodily in front of the office door. Instead, she beeped through, got the okay, then gestured Eve in.

"Oh, Merry Christmas, Lieutenant, if I don't see you before."

"Ah, thanks. Same to you."

She glanced back, still baffled, as the dragon at the gates began to hum "Jingle Bells."

"You'd better do a head exam on your admin," Eve said to Mira as she shut the door. "She's suddenly perky and she's out there singing."

"The holidays do that to people. I told her to put you through at any time, unless I was in session. It's important that I keep up, not just with the progress of your investigation, but with your emotional state."

"I'm fine. I'm good. I just need—"

"Sit down, Eve."

Because Mira turned to her AutoChef, Eve rolled her eyes behind Mira's back. But she sat, dropping into one of the pretty blue scoop chairs. "I'm hitting snags and deadends on the investigation, so I'm pushing it open. I want to—"

"Have some tea."

"I really don't—"

"I know, but indulge me. I can tell you didn't get much sleep. Are you having nightmares?"

"No. Not exactly. I worked late last night." She took the tea—what choice did she have? "I dropped off for a few minutes. Had a weird dream. Nothing major."

"Tell me anyway."

She hadn't come for a session, damn it. But she knew that arguing with Mira on her own turf was like beating your head against rock.

She described the dream, shrugged. "Weird, mostly. I didn't feel threatened or out of control."

"Even when the other women stampeded you?"

"No, that just pissed me off."

"You saw yourself, as a child, through the glass."

"Yeah. Having a sandwich. I think it was ham and cheese."

"And, at the end of it, your father."

"He's always there. Can't get around it. Look, I get it. Him on one side, her on the other. Me in the middle. Then and now. I'm squeezed on this, but it's not a problem. For once, nobody's trying to kill me."

"Do you really feel that different—that distance from the others? The other women?"

"I feel different from most of the women I know. Never can figure out how I end up pals with them, when half the time they're like another species. Okay, I understood where Maxie was coming from. I know why she felt the way she did, at least initially. Somebody who screwed with her is dead. I don't feel the same way. Not like busting out the champagne. If I wanted everyone I disliked dead, the city'd be a bloodbath.

"I don't blame her, but I don't agree with her. Death isn't an answer, it's an end. And murder's a crime. That makes Trudy, whether I liked her or not, mine. Whoever ended her has to pay for it."

She hesitated a moment, then decided to finish it out, to close it off with what had just gone through her mind. "I wish I'd had the chance to say what I went there to say to her. To face her like that. More, I wish she were alive so I could help put her away for dogging those women all these years, exploiting them, taking their money and their peace of mind."

"And you can't."

"No. Life's full of disappointments."

"Cheery thought," Mira added.

"Here's a cheerier one, then: She can't take from me what I've got. I know that. She didn't. She thought she could get under me, use me. She wouldn't have. It helps knowing that. Part of what she couldn't take was what I am. What I am is the cop who's going to close this case. That's it."

"All right. What do you need from me?"

Eve told her of the plans to try for a warrant.

Mira sipped at her tea, and from the expression on her face, Eve knew she was far from convinced. "That's a shaky line, Eve."

"I'm freezing the accounts. Money's cut off. Nobody can get to them in the hotel. Sooner or later I've got to spring them. So maybe he waits until I do, until they're back in Texas. Maybe he goes after one of them there, when they're not being protected. There's no motive, at this point, to attack them. Approach, yes, but not attack. Not if money's the root."

"What else?"

"Payback, maybe. But I'm hitting dead ends there. The fact is, she could've—and probably did—piss off a lot of people we don't know about. But Zana's abduction points to money. So that's our first stop."

"I'll back you on this since I agree the physical jeopardy is low. It could be argued that their emotional state is exacerbated by being kept in the hotel, under guard. Some return of normalcy could benefit them, while aiding your investigation."

"That's good enough. I'll get on it." She rose. "Peabody and McNab are heading for Scotland tomorrow."

"Scotland? Oh, his family, of course. They must be excited."

"Peabody's running on nerves over it. His family and all that. If nothing breaks today, this is going to cool on me over the holiday. Right now, this is my best chance to keep it hot."

"Then I wish you luck. And if I don't see you, have a lovely Christmas. Both you and Roarke."

"Yeah, thanks. I've got to take care of a couple things regarding that yet."

"Ah, another last-minute shopper."

"Not exactly."

She started toward the door, then turned back and took another study. Mira wore a suit in a kind of rusty red today, and the shoes matched. Her necklace was short, thick gold with a lot of little stones sparkling in it. Multicolored, triangular shape. Her earrings were thick gold triangles.

"Something else?"

"Just a passing thought," Eve began.

"How much time and thought did it take for you to deck yourself out this morning?"

"Deck myself?" Mira looked down at herself.

"You know, to pick the outfit and the stuff, to fiddle with your hair and face. All that. So you're all put together just so."

"I'm not entirely sure that's a compliment. Probably the best part of an hour. Why?"

"Just wondering."

"Wait." Mira held up a hand before Eve opened the door. "How long did it take you?"

"Me? I don't know. Ten minutes?"

"Get out of my office," Mira said with a laugh.

Eve gave the warrant a good, solid push. It took over an hour, a lot of tap dancing, but at the end she got what she wanted.

She was told to consider it a Christmas present.

Satisfied, she headed out to the bull pen. "Suit up," she told Baxter. "Get your boy. I want you in position, at the hotel, in thirty."

"It's going to snow. Did you know it's supposed to start snowing?"

"Wear boots, then."

Ignoring his whine, she walked to Peabody's desk, got a little brushback. "I hear you, Carly."

Peabody used an earpiece on privacy mode. "You've only got one thing to worry about now, and that's your family. Having another beautiful, healthy baby boy. It's a big help to us that you cooperated. Now I want you to put it out of your mind, and go enjoy the holidays."

She listened for a moment, smiled. "Thanks. I'll be in touch when we have more information. Merry Christmas to you and your family."

Peabody pulled off the earpiece, then made a show of buffing her nails on her shirt. "I'm good."

"Did you stop short of sending her a gift? Jesus. What'd you get?"

"Husband's out of it. He was with her Saturday, in the hospital. She had false labor, and they were there several hours. I ran a secondary check on that while I had her on 'link. Pans out. No brother, no father. Only child. Jeez, Dallas, she had it rough."

"Walk and talk. We've got a warrant coming through, and I want to head up, see what toys Feeney's picked out for me."

"Mother was a junkie. Used while she was pregnant, so Carly was born an addict. She got passed around, various relatives. Too much for them to handle, too much expense, too much trouble."

They hopped on a glide, blissfully uncrowded as the holidays had everyone who could manage it copping time off.

"She's dumped in the system. Her physical problems are dealt with, but she's a hard placement. Scrawny, possible physical complications. Mother cleans up, supposedly—at least enough to get the courts to put the kid back in her care. Then she starts using again, turning tricks. Kid's ten, and it's a bad life. Mother gets popped again, but not before she uses the kid to sell a little kiddie porn on the 'net. Back in the system, and she ends up with Trudy."

"Who made things worse."

"I'll say. Made her scrub in cold water every night. And other various torments. Kid squeals, but nobody's buying. Not a mark on her. No outward signs of abuse, and it's all put down to her prior difficulties. Until she tried to off herself. Slashed her own wrists with a kitchen knife."

Eve paused long enough to breathe out. "Oh, hell."

"Said it was Bobby who found her, called an ambulance. When she woke up in the hospital, they told her she'd attacked her foster mother. She swore that was a lie, but Trudy had superficial stab wounds on her forearms."

"Bitch did it to herself."

"I'm with that. But she's back in the system again, and this time she stays in state schools until she's of age.

"She turned her life around, Dallas, you gotta admire it. Scraped it together to go to college for a degree in Elementary Ed, snagged a couple scholarships. She settled out in Iowa, said she just wanted to put it away. Close that door. Met her husband five years ago, got married."

"Then Trudy comes back."

"Parents might not like the idea of someone with her background teaching their tots, that's how Trudy put it. If she wanted to keep all that boxed up, it would cost. These aren't wealthy people, but Carly was scared. They paid. When I told her we were going to try to get the money back, she cried."

"How much did Trudy take her for?"

"Over the years, about a hundred and fifty thousand."

There was an account Roarke had opened in her name when they'd married. She'd never touched it, had never intended to do so. But, she thought now, if the system didn't do right by Carly Tween this time, she'd do it herself.

In EDD, Eve studied the homers Feeney offered. They were bigger than she'd wanted, almost thumb-sized.

"How am I supposed to get these on the subjects without them being aware?"

He gave her one of his morose scowls. "Hey, that's your part of the show. You wanted audio. You settled for a simple beacon, I get you something not much bigger than a piece of lint."

"I want audio. I'll figure it out."

"You're welcome," he muttered.

"Sorry, sorry. Jesus. You're the god of electronics. Appreciate you doing this. I know you're shorthanded."

"Might as well be doing something." He nodded toward his office door where the sounds of loud music, loud voices pressed.

"They're having a party. A quick one. I gave them an hour to blow off the steam, do the Secret Santa crap. Anybody who's not on an active's not coming in next two days."

"Cops know better than to figure crime takes holidays."

"Yeah, yeah. I got some boys on call. I'm coming in a half-day, just to round things up. Wife's making Christmas dinner, and you'd think she was cooking for the royal freaking family. Says we gotta dress for it."

"What, you generally eat naked?"

"Dress, Dallas. Like formal or some shit." His already droopy face sagged. "She got the damn idea from you."

"Me? Me?" Insult, and a little fear, jumped into her voice. "Don't hang your marital weirdness on me."

"It was the party at your place did it. Everybody all duded up and sparkly. Now she wants us all to get fancy. I gotta wear a suit in my own house. At my own table."

Because she felt guilty, Eve pulled her hands through her hair, and struggled to tug out an idea. "You could spill gravy on it right off."

His eyes brightened. "I knew I kept you around for something. The wife's gravy's lethal, too. I spill that on the suit, it'll practically eat through the lining. Hey, Merry freaking Christmas, kid."

"Back atcha."

She toted the homers out, and had to slap a hand to her cheek as a muscle twitched. Straight in her line of vision, Peabody and McNab were locked in a big, sloppy kiss, hips grinding together as they used the music as an excuse for vertical humping.

"Stop! Cease and desist, or I'm locking you both in separate cells for public lewdness."

She kept walking. When Peabody caught up, she was huffing. Eve didn't think it was the quick trot that had her breathing heavy.

"We were just—"

"Say nothing," Eve warned. "Do not speak. We're heading to the hotel. I'm going to get these wires planted, give the subjects the talk. You're going to check out the banks on the list I'm going to give you. Show them Trudy's picture. See if anyone remembers her coming in for a big bag of credits on Thursday or Friday."

"Where do you want me after?"

"I'll tag you, let you know."

She dropped Peabody off, continued to the hotel. Spotting the security, she walked over.

"I'm pulling my uniform. At least I want it to look that way. Can I plug him into one of your security areas, give him access to the cam on the fifth floor?"

"We can do that."

"I'm keeping the Lombards unapprised."

"No problem. Just send him to me when you're ready."

"Thanks." She moved to the elevator, going over the steps in her head as she rode up.

Once the uniform was given his orders, she knocked.

Bobby answered. "You've got news."

"We've had some progress. Nothing much I can tell you at this point. All right if I come in?"

"Sure, sure. Sorry. Zana's in the shower. We slept in. Not much else to do."

"I want to talk to you about that," Eve began. "Why don't you go in and tell Zana I'm here."

"Oh. Okay. Be right back."

"No rush."

The minute he went into the bedroom, Eve hurried to the closet by the door. The tidy state of the suite told her these were people who put things in their place. She found their coats where she expected.

She took out the two homers, slid one under the collar of each coat, secured them, then engaged. There were two jackets as well, and she considered.

It was cold, she thought. They were from Texas. They'd wear the coats.

She glanced toward the bedroom doorway. "Feeney, if you read, beep my communicator."

When the beep sounded, she closed the closet door, stepped away. Moments later, Bobby came out.

"She'll be done in a minute."

"I guess the two of you are getting antsy, stuck in here."

"Maybe." He smiled a little. "I can do some work from here. And I've been making arrangements. For my mother. Zana's been a big help. I don't know what I'd do without her, don't know how I managed before she came along. Lousy Christmas for her. I thought maybe I could order a little tree. Or something."

"I'm going to clear you to go out."

"Out?" He looked toward the windows as if they were prison bars. "Really? You think it's safe, after what happened?"

"I think the chances of you being approached or accosted, especially while you're together, are pretty low. Basically, Bobby, I can't keep the two of you holed up like this as material witnesses when you didn't see anything in the first place. If you've thought of anything else, remembered anything, that might help."

"I've gone over it and over it. Not doing a lot of sleeping since . . . since it happened. I don't understand why my mother would've gone to you for money. She's—she was— pretty well set. And I'm doing good. Good enough, and better now that we closed that big deal. Somebody must've pushed her to do it. But I don't know who'd do that. I don't know why."

"Get out, clear your head a little bit. Maybe something will come to you." If not, Eve thought, she was going to bring them both in, formal interview. Hit them with the facts, she decided, straight out. See what shakes.

"We could—" He broke off when Zana stepped out.

She was dressed in a white sweater and trim pants with tiny brown and white checks. Eve noted she'd taken the time to put on some lip dye, a little cheek color.

"I'm sorry I kept you waiting. We're getting a late start today."

"It's okay. How're you feeling?"

"All right. It's all starting to seem like some long, strange dream."

"Eve said we can go out for a while," Bobby told her.

"Really. But . . ." As he had, Zana glanced toward the window, bit her lip. "But what if . . . He could be watching."

"I'll be with you." Bobby walked over, put an arm around her. "We'll go out, buy a little tree. We might get some real snow."

"I'd really like that, if you're sure." She looked back at Eve. "I guess we're both going a little stir-crazy."

"Take your 'link," Eve advised. "I'll check in with you now and then." She headed for the door, stopped. "It's pretty cold. You'll want to dress warm if you're going to be walking around."

As she headed for the elevator, she pulled out her communicator again. "Peabody, status."

"Two blocks west. Got what we were looking for, first stop."

"Meet me in front of the hotel."

"Are we a go?"

"We're a go," Eve said. She switched over to Baxter. "We're in place. You have the signals."

"That's affirmative."

"Give them some room. Let's see how they spend their day."

On the street, she took a look around. If Trudy's killer had tracked them to the new location—and anything was possible— where would he wait and watch? There were always places. A restaurant, another hotel room, even the street for a period of time.

But those chances were slim. Tracking them wouldn't have been a cinch. That would take skill, smarts, and luck. Finding a spot to watch for a couple of days would take a great deal of patience.

And for what purpose? Money, if money

was the object, would only come through them if she paid it out. Smarter, simpler, to try the direct blackmail route.

Smarter, simpler, to try to shake her rather than the victim's daughter-in-law.

She leaned on her car as she waited for Peabody. If money was the motive for murder, why wasn't the killer pushing harder for a payoff?

Peabody hiked up, rosy-cheeked from the cold and the walk.

"What if the money's the beard?"

"Whose beard?"

"*The* beard, Peabody. I keep circling back to payback instead of payoff. It just slides in better. But if it's payback, why do you wait until she's in New York, coming after me? Why do you smash her head in after she's made contact? Why don't you wait until you see if she gets the dough first? Or you take her out at her home base, easier to make it look accidental."

"Maybe the killer lives here. In New York. Maybe she was playing two at once."

"Maybe. But so far, I've got nobody who's local popping out of her file. If it was impulse, why hang around trying to threaten

Zana into coughing up money she doesn't have?"

"Because now you're greedy."

"Yeah, greed's usually good." But it wasn't gelling for her.

She got in the car. She didn't want to be loitering out front when and if the Lombards came out.

"What did you find out?" she asked Peabody.

"National Bank, a block from the boutique. One of the tellers made her photo straight off. She was in right before they closed, Friday afternoon. Wanted two hundred single-dollar credits. Snippy about it, so says the teller. Wanted them loose. No bag, no rolls. Just dumped them into her purse. Oh, they want a warrant before they turn over any security discs."

"Get one. Let's tie up all the threads."

"Where are we heading?"

"Back to the murder scene. I've run re-enactments on the comp. I want to try it on the spot." She dug out her homer, stuck it on the dash. "Baxter and Trueheart can handle the shadow, but we'll keep an eye on them anyway."

"Haven't moved yet," Peabody observed.

"They will."

Eve took a second-level street slot at the West Side Hotel. "How could there be anything left in the city to buy?" She clambered down, scowling at the masses of people. "What more could they possibly want?"

"Speaking for myself, I want lots and lots. Piles of boxes with big shiny bows. And if McNab didn't spring for something shiny, I'll have to hurt him. Maybe we'll get that snow." She sniffed the air like a hound. "Smells like it."

"How can you smell anything in this city but city?"

"I got a prime nose. I can scent soy dogs grilling. And there they are, down the block. I'm sort of going to miss being here for Christmas. I mean, it's exciting—scary, too—going to Scotland, but it's not New York."

Inside, the same droid worked the desk. "Hey!" He signaled. "When you gonna unseal the room?"

"When justice is served."

"Manager's busting me on it. We got reservations. Full house next week for New Year's Eve."

"He's got a problem with my crime scene,

tell him to contact me. I'll tell him what he can do for New Year's."

She checked her homer on the way up. "They're moving. Baxter?" she said into the communicator. "They're coming out."

"We've got them. Got audio. They're talking about heading over to Fifth, window shopping. Looking for a tabletop tree for the room."

"I can hear them. I'm tuning down the audio. Tag me if there's anything I should know."

"They're stepping out. My youthful companion and I will be taking a stroll. And we're out."

Eve pocketed her communicator, took out her master to break the seal. A woman opened the door across the hall a crack.

"Are you the police?"

"Yes, ma'am." Eve drew out her badge.

"Somebody said a woman was killed in that room, just a few days ago."

"There was an incident. There's no reason for you to be concerned."

"Easy for you to say. Larry! Larry, I *told* you there was a murder. The cops are right here." She poked her head back out. "He wants to get his vid cam. Get something we can show the kids tomorrow."

Larry, busting with smiles as he pushed the door open, led with the camera. "Hi! You think maybe you could put your hand on your weapon, maybe hold up your badge. Look tough. The kids're going to love it."

"Now's not really a good time, Larry."

"It'll only take a minute. You going in? Great! I can just get a quick shot of the inside. Is there still blood?"

"What, are you twelve? Put that thing down, go back in your room before I arrest you for being dirt stupid."

"Great! Great! Keep going."

"Jesus Christ, where do people come from? What dark hole vomits them out into my face? Peabody."

"Sir, I'm going to have to ask you to go back inside now. This is a police investigation." She lowered her voice as she moved to block his view. "You don't want to tick her off. Trust me."

"Can you say your name? Like this is Officer Smith, ordering you to cease and desist."

"It's detective, and, sir, you will have to cease and desist before—"

Eve simply stepped forward, wrenched the little camera out of his hand.

"Hey!"

"If you don't want me to drop it, and have it somehow end up under my boot, you're going to go back inside."

"Larry, give it a rest." The woman elbowed him back. "I'll take it."

"I got some good stuff on there," Larry said as his wife nudged him back inside. "You can't buy this kind of stuff." The door finally shut after him.

Eve glanced back. She knew damn well Larry had that damn camera up to the security peep. She broke the seal on room 415, jerked a thumb at Peabody. She kept the door open just enough for her partner to squeeze through, then followed. Closed it. Locked it.

"Asshole." Eve scanned the room, shook off the incident in the hall. "She comes in Friday, worked up. Got herself a new plan. Following a pattern we've established. Doesn't mind hurting herself or her property to pin it on someone else. Complicate their lives. Pay them back. She's laid in some supplies. We'll check some of the markets. Harder to pin that down, though. But she's going to have some supplies. The wine, soup, easy food."

"She's already planning how to take care of herself once she's hurt. Blockers, then," Peabody added. "Some soothers."

"If she didn't travel with enough, yeah. We'll check that, too. Bet she has a drink first. Yeah. A big gulp of wine maybe. Maybe some solid food. Thinking, working it out."

Eve walked the room as she imagined it. "Does she call her killer? I don't know, I don't know. Why? This is her deal. She's in charge. And she's hot. She's plenty steamed."

"Have to be gritting down to do that to herself."

"She thinks how it's going to play out. How it's going to make Roarke scramble. Thinks he can brush her off? Well, she'll show him. Rips the socks apart. Pulls off the tag, balls it up, tosses it and pulls the pair apart. Tosses the spare, floor, dresser. Fills the one with the credits. Checks the weight. Maybe takes a blocker first, gets ahead of the pain."

Eve strode to the bathroom. "In here. You'd do it in here, in case the pain makes you sick. Don't want to puke on the floor. Who's going to clean it up?"

Eve stepped to the sink, looked into the mirror. "Takes a good look. She's paid good money to keep her face in tune. But that's all right, that's okay. There'll be more. And there's no way that son of a bitch is going to get away with treating her that way. He doesn't know who he's dealing with."

Eve brought her fist up hard, right below the chin. Fast enough, violently enough to make Peabody jolt behind her.

"Jeez, I could almost feel it."

"Saw stars. Pain grinds right down into the gut. Dizzy, half sick. Gotta do the rest, gotta do it while you've still got the courage, and the strength." She mimed the blows, imagined them. Tipped forward, gripped the sink as if for support.

"They got her prints off the sink? Where?"

Peabody pulled out her PCC, called up the file. "Pretty much where your hand is. Good imprints—all four fingers and thumb, left hand."

"Yeah, cause she's still holding the sap in her right, had to grab hold to stay upright. Good grip, good prints. Got to bleed a little, from the face."

She turned, reached out for a washcloth. "Should be two of these. She takes one, holds it to her face, maybe dampens it first. So we get a little of her blood in the sink. But the cloth's not here when we find her."

"Killer took it? Why?"

"To keep the illusion she was beaten. Trudy takes the cloth, probably puts some ice in it, just to cool her face. None of her clothes had blood on them, except for the nightgown. Most likely she wore it while she clocked herself. Don't want to mess up a nice outfit. Besides, she's going to want to lie down for a while anyway. Sleep off the pain."

"It still doesn't make sense."

"Call up the list of her belongings. Is there a vid cam?"

"Hold on." Peabody shoved at her hair, then found the file. "No cam, but . . . hey. There's a disc for one. Unused. It was in her purse."

"Tourists don't come to New York without a vid cam. Just like our pal, Larry. And she used recordings before. Sleeps it off, first. Has to have her wits about her when she documents her injuries. Sets the stage, works up some tears, some shakes. Puts the finger on Roarke, or me. Or both of us."

Eve looked toward the bed, could picture Trudy sitting there, her face battered, tears streaming. "*'This is what they did to me. I'm afraid for my life.'* All she has to do is get a copy of it delivered to one of us. Have to have some subtext on the recording. 'I don't know what to do. Should I go to the police? But *she's* the police. God help me,' blah-blah. 'He's so rich, so powerful. What will happen if I take this recording to the media. Will I be safe?'"

"Figuring you'd read between the lines."

"And when we contact her, she'll insist one of us come here. No 'link conversations that can be turned around on her. Face-to-face. Give me the money, or I ruin you. But it doesn't get that far."

"Because her delivery boy took her out."

"Had to come in the door. I just don't buy the window, not with this scenario. Security's not heavy here. Anybody wants to walk in, they walk in. Or he could've been staying at the hotel. Keep him close that way, under her thumb that way. At her beck and call. We'll run the registration list again, go deeper there. Find a connection. Better if your minion's close by. She tells him to come up."

"She couldn't be feeling her best, even with the blockers, the alcohol."

"No, and she'd want to be able to complain to somebody. Fix me a drink. Get me some soup. Maybe bitching—if she'd sent the disc with him—why we hadn't jumped already. What's taking us so long? Maybe she slips about the amount she's going to demand, or maybe she just pushes the wrong button. But she's not concerned. Pacing around in her nightgown. She's there."

Eve pointed so that Peabody would assume Trudy's position. "Back to him. He picks up the sap, takes her down. Rug burns on the heels of her hand. Get down, Peabody."

"Cops have no dignity." Peabody went down on her knees, shot her hands out as if catching herself.

"And again, from above. One more to make sure. Blood. Had to get some blood on him. Now he's got to figure it out, cover his tracks. Take the weapon, take the 'link, take the camera. Record would be on the hard drive, if anyone decided to look. Make sure. Washcloth, towel, sock. Anything with her blood on it. Wrap everything up in a towel. Go out the window. Leave the window open. Logic says the killer came in that way."

By the window now, Eve looked out. "Down and gone, no problem. Or . . ." She studied the distance to the window of the next room, the emergency platform. "Next room was empty. Maybe . . ."

She turned back. "Let's have the sweepers take a look next door. I want those drains checked for blood. Bring them in now. I'll go down and deal with the desk droid."

He wasn't happy about it. The room was occupied, and moving guests generally made them unhappy.

"They'll be a lot unhappier if they're in there while my crime scene team's tearing up the room. You'll be a lot unhappier if I go through the trouble of getting a warrant to shut down this establishment until my investigation is closed."

That did the trick. While she waited, she checked in with Baxter.

"What's the status?"

"They're making up for lost time. I think

we've walked five fricking miles. And it's spitting some wet snow."

"So button up. What are they doing?"

"Shopping mostly. Just bought a little tree after looking at all the little trees in the borough of Manhattan. They're talking about heading back, thank the tiny baby Jesus. If anyone's tailing them but me and my faithful sidekick, I'm a monkey."

"Stick with them."

"Like glue."

In Midtown, Baxter shoved his communicator back in his coat pocket. On his earpiece he heard Zana talk about lunch. Should they buy some dogs and stay out a while longer? Or go drop off their things, have lunch at the hotel?

"Hotel," he mumbled. "Go to the hotel. The one with a nice warm coffee shop across the street."

Trueheart shrugged. "It's nice being out. Being able to see all the decorations. The snow just adds."

"You kill me, kid. It's thirty degrees, windy, and this snow is more like sleet. The sidewalks are jammed, and we're walking the soles of our shoes thin. Shit. Damn it. They're going for the dogs."

"And glide-cart coffee." Now Trueheart shook his head. "They'll be sorry."

"And now she's window-shopping. Typical female. He's got to haul the bags, buy the dogs, juggle it all so she can sigh over a bunch of sparklers they'll never be able to afford."

"If they're blackmailers they can."

Baxter gave Trueheart a look of pride and approval. "Now that's the kind of cynicism I like to hear. Take the point, move on the cart once he's got his dogs. Order up a couple. It's crowded. Hard to keep a visual going. I'll hang back in case she talks him into going in the store."

Baxter eased right, toward the buildings, and caught a glimpse of Zana looking over her shoulder, smiling as Bobby came over, balancing food and packages.

"I'm sorry, honey!" She laughed, took one of the bags, one of the dogs. "I shouldn't have left you with all that. I just wanted a peek."

"You want to go in?"

She laughed again. "I can hear the pain in your voice. No, I just wanted to look. I wish I'd thought to wear a hat, though. My ears are cold."

"We can go back, or we can buy a hat."

She beamed at him. "I'd really like to stay out just a little while more. There's a place across the street."

"The one we walked by to get to this side of the street?"

"I know, I know," she said with a giggle. "But they had hats and scarves. On sale. You could use a hat, too, honey. Maybe a nice warm scarf. And I just can't face that hotel room again right now, Bobby. I feel like I've been let out of prison or something."

"I know. I guess I feel the same way." He shifted the bag holding their tree. "We'll go buy hats. Then we could walk over, watch the skaters, get another look at the big tree."

"That'd be just perfect. What makes a soy dog taste so good when it's cooked outside on a cart in New York? I swear you can't get a real grilled dog anywhere on the planet outside of New York."

"Pretty damn good," he agreed around a bite of it. "Especially if you don't think about what's in it."

Her laugh was light and blissfully happy. "Let's not!"

When they got to the corner, squeezed in by the crowd, he managed another bite. "I didn't know I was so hungry. Should've gotten two."

They made it to the curb. He started to step out, when Zana gasped. His fingers closed over her arm like a vise.

"I spilled my coffee, that's all. Damn."

"You burned?"

"No. No." She brushed at the stain on her coat with her hand. "Just clumsy. I got bumped a little. Gosh, I hope this doesn't stain. Oh, now we missed the light, too."

"There's no hurry."

"Tell that to everyone else," she murmured. "People weren't pushing so much, I wouldn't have coffee on my coat."

"We'll get something and—"

He pitched forward, straight into the path of an oncoming cab.

The bag he held went flying. The last thing he heard before he hit the pavement was Zana's screams and the shrill shriek of brakes.

While Eve waited for the room to be cleared and the sweepers to arrive, she ran a check on Trudy's debit and credit statements. The charges and withdrawals had just been put through. Spent a few bucks on Friday at the drugstore, she noted. Time stamp confirmed that that came after the socks, after the bank.

Lining up your ducks.

Market, too.

What happened to the bags?

As she was working out a theory, her communicator beeped.

"Dallas."

"We've got a problem." Baxter's face held none of its usual sarcasm. "Male subject's been hit by a cab, corner of Fifth and Forty-second."

"Well, Jesus Christ. How bad?"

"Don't know. MTs are on-scene. Wife's hysterical. They were on the sidewalk, waiting for the light. I had them on audio, Trueheart had a reasonable visual. But the corner was packed. He only got a look at the guy doing a header into the street. He got clipped pretty good, Dallas, I know that. Damn near run over. I got the cabbie here."

"Have some uniforms take him down to Central until we can get his statement. Stick with the subjects. Where are they taking him?"

"ER at Boyd Health Center. Straight shot down Fifth."

"I'll meet you there. One of you go in the ambulance with him. I don't want either of them out of your sight until I'm there."

"You got that. Jesus, Dallas. Guy was eating a dog, drinking bad coffee. Then he just flew. MTs are giving the wife something to calm her down."

"Make sure she's coherent. Damn it, Baxter, I don't want her put out."

"Let me get on that. I'm out."

She whirled toward the door, pulling it open just as Peabody pushed from the other side. "Sweepers are heading up."

"We'll get them started. We've got to go. Bobby's heading to the hospital. Hit by a cab."

"Hit by—what the hell—"

"Don't ask, I can't tell you. Let's just get this moving, and get there."

She went in hot, dodging clogged traffic as her sirens blasted. And doing her best to ignore quick, sharp pinches of guilt.

Had she put Bobby in a position to be

hurt? Two cops on him, a homer with audio. Still not enough?

"Could just be an accident." Peabody tried not to whimper as they threaded between a van and a cab with a layer of cheap paint to spare. "People, especially out-of-towners, have road accidents in New York every day. Step out too far, don't look where they're going. Gawking at the buildings instead of watching the lights."

"There's no point in hurting him. No point." She rapped her fist on the wheel. "What does it get you? Roarke's not going to cough up two mil because some guy he doesn't know is in the path. Why should he? Why would he? It serves no purpose to hurt Bobby."

"You said Baxter reported he was eating and drinking, at the curb. He gets bumped, or slips. It's sleeting, things are slippery. Dallas, sometimes things just happen. Sometimes it's just bad luck."

"Not this time. No bullshit coincidence." Her voice was fierce and furious. "We missed it, that's all. We missed something, someone, and now we've got a witness in Emergency."

"It's not your fault."

"I made the call, so it's on me. You make copies of the recording. Get a copy shot down to the lab. I want to be able to hear everything, every voice."

She pulled up to the emergency entrance. "Park it," she ordered, jumping out. "I need to get in there."

She strode to the doors, through.

It was the usual place of pain. Victims waiting to be heard, to be helped. The sick slumped in chairs. The healthy waiting impatiently for whoever they'd come with to be treated, released, admitted.

She spotted Trueheart, somehow younger in a sweatshirt and jeans. He sat close to Zana, holding her hand, murmuring to her as she wept.

"Eve! Eve!" Zana jumped up, threw herself into Eve's arms. "Bobby. Oh, my God. It's all my fault. Bobby's hurt. He's hurt so bad. I don't know—"

"Stop." Eve pulled back, gave Zana one brisk shake. "How bad is he hurt?"

"They didn't say, they won't tell me. He was bleeding. His head. His head, and his leg. He was unconscious." Tears spurted. "I heard them say concussion, and something broken, and maybe—"

"Okay, what happened?"

"I just don't know." Now she sank back

into the chair. "We were just waiting for the light. We'd gotten some soy dogs and coffee. It was cold, but it felt so good to get out. And I said I wanted to buy a hat, and they were across the street. Then I spilled my coffee, so we missed the light and couldn't go. We were waiting and he just fell. Or slipped. I just don't know. I tried to grab his coat. I got my hand on it. I think I did."

She stared down at her hand. Eve noted the light bandage. "What happened to your hand?"

"I spilled the coffee. It splashed all over when I grabbed for him. Burned my hand a little. I started to fall. I think. Somebody pulled me back. But Bobby . . ."

Zana wrapped her arms around her waist and rocked. "The cab hit him. It tried to stop, but it was too quick, and it hit him, and then he flew back, and fell. So hard."

"Where is he?" She looked at Trueheart.

"They took him to Treatment Room Two. Baxter's on the door."

"Zana, stay here. Trueheart, stand by."

She strode through the waiting area, straight by a nurse who called out for her to stop, and swung right when she saw Baxter at a pair of double swinging doors.

"Goddamn it, Dallas. We were ten feet away. One on either side."

"Wife thinks he slipped."

"Yeah, yeah, maybe. What are the odds? They're working on him. Arm's broken, that's for certain. Maybe the hip, too. Head took a hard crack. I couldn't tell how bad, and the MTs wouldn't say."

Eve rubbed her hands over her face. "You get any sense somebody helped him in front of that cab?"

"Second-guessing myself now. We had a good tail on them, good observation. But it's insane out there, Dallas. You know how it is this time of year. Sidewalk is a sea of people, and everybody's either in an all-fired hurry, or they're gawking and taking vids. You got street thieves making more this holiday week than they do in six regular months. If I had to swear nobody got by us, I couldn't. The thing is . . ."

"What?"

"Just before, she spilled coffee on herself. Said she got bumped. And I got this little tingle, started moving in a little. Then our guy's airborne."

"Fuck."

15

Eve sent Baxter back to stand with True-heart, then paced in front of the treatment room doors as the sharp scents and harried sounds washed over her.

She hated hospitals, health centers, emergency treatment centers. Places, she thought, full of sickness and pain. Of death and misery.

Of waiting.

Had she put Bobby here? Had her need to push things forward put him in harm's way? A personal need, she thought now. She wanted to slam the door on this part of her past, lock it away again. Not only for her own peace of mind, she admitted, but to prove she could. Because of that, she'd taken a risk—a calculated one, but a risk nonetheless.

And Bobby Lombard was paying the price.

Or was it just some ridiculous accident? Slippery, crowded streets, people in a hurry, bumping, pushing. Accidents happened every day. Hell, every hour. It could be just that simple.

But she couldn't buy it. If she ran it through a probability program and it came up one hundred percent, she still wouldn't buy it.

He was unconscious, broken and bloody, and she'd sent him out so she could sniff the air for a killer.

It could be him, even now, it could be Bobby who'd done murder. People killed their mothers. A lifetime of tension, irritation, or worse, and something snapped inside them. Like a bone, she thought, and they killed.

She'd killed. It hadn't been only the bone in her arm that had snapped in that awful room in Dallas. Her mind had snapped, too, and the knife had gone into him. Over and over again. She could remember that now, remember the blood, the smell of it—harsh and raw—the feel of it wet and warm on her hands, her face.

She remembered the pain of that broken bone, even now through the mists of time. And the howling—his and hers—as she killed him.

People said that sound was inhuman, but they were wrong. It was essentially human. Elementally human.

She pressed the heels of her hands to her eyes.

God, she hated hospitals. Hated remembering waking in one, with so much of herself—such as it was—gone. Evaporated.

The smell of her own fear. Strangers hovering over her. *What's your name? What happened to you? Where do you live?*

How could she know? And if she'd remembered, if her mind hadn't closed up and hidden away, how could she have told them?

They'd hurt her to heal her. She remembered that, too. Setting the bone, repairing the tears and scars inside her from the repeated rapes. But they'd never found those secrets behind the wall her mind had built.

They'd never known that the child in the hospital bed had killed like a mad thing. And howled like a human.

"Dallas."

She jerked herself back, but didn't turn. "I don't know anything yet."

Peabody simply stepped up beside her. Through the porthole of glass, Eve could see the emergency team working on Bobby. Why, she wondered, did places like this have glass? Why did they want people to see what they did in those rooms?

Hurting to heal.

Wasn't it bad enough imagining without actually seeing the splash of blood, the beep of machines?

"Go back and check with Baxter," Eve said. "I want whatever witness statements he has. Names of the wits. I want to verify the cabbie's license. Then send him and Trueheart back. I want that record into the lab. You stay with Zana. See what else you can get out of her for now."

"Should we get uniforms for his room? For when they finish in there?"

"Yeah." Think positive, Eve decided. He'd be moved to a room, and not the morgue.

Alone, she watched, made herself watch. And wondered what the girl she'd been—lying in a room so much like the one beyond the glass—had to do with what was happening now.

One of the med team rushed out. Eve grabbed her arm. "What's his status?"

"Holding. The doctor will give you more information. Family members need to stay in Waiting."

"I'm not family." Eve reached for her badge. "Your patient is a material witness in a homicide. I need to know if he's going to make it."

"It looks good. He's lucky. If getting hit by a cab a couple days before Christmas counts as luck. Got some broken bones, contusions, lacerations. Some internal bleeding we've stopped. He's stabilized, but the head trauma's the main concern. You're going to need to talk to the attending."

"His wife's in Waiting, with my partner. She needs to be updated."

"Go ahead."

"I've got a material witness on that table in there. I'm at the door."

Irritation flashed over the nurse's face, then she brushed a hand through the air. "Okay, okay. I'll take care of it."

Eve stood by. She heard the rush and confusion of the ER behind her, the beeps

and the pages, the clop of feet with somewhere urgent to go.

At some point someone began to call out
"Merry Christmas!" in slurred, drunken
tones, laughing and singing as he was
carted off. There was weeping, wailing, as a
woman was hurried down the hall on a gur-
ney. An orderly streamed by with a bucket
that smelled of vomit.

Someone tapped her shoulder, and she
turned, only to have home-made brew and
poor dental hygiene waft into her face. The
man responsible wore a filthy Santa suit with
a white beard hanging off one ear.

"Merry Christmas! Want a present? Got a
present for you right here!"

He grabbed his crotch, and flipped out
his penis. At some more sober yet equally
crazed time, he'd painted it up like a candy
cane.

Eve studied the red and white stripes.

"Gee, that looks delicious, but I don't
have anything for you. Wait, yes, I do."

His wide grin faded when she held up her
badge.

"Aw, c'mon."

"The reason I don't haul you in for lewd
and lascivious behavior, for indecent expo-

sure—though, hey, nice paint job—and for possibly having the foulest breath on or off planet, is I'm busy. If I decide I'm not busy enough, you're going to be spending Christmas in the tank. So blow."

"Aw, c'mon."

"And put that thing away before you scare some kid."

"Santa, there you are." The nurse who'd come out earlier rolled her eyes at Eve, then got a good grip on Santa's arm. "Let's go over here."

"Want a present? I got a present for you right here."

"Yeah, yeah. That's all I want for Christmas."

Eve turned back as the doors opened. She grabbed the closest pair of scrubs.

"What's his status?"

"You the wife?"

"No, I'm the cop."

"Cab versus man, cab usually wins. But he's stable." The doctor veed his fingers, slid them up his nose to rub the inside corners of his eyes. "Broken arm, fractured hip, bruised kidney. Head trauma's the worst of it. But barring complications, he should do. He got off lucky."

"Need to talk to him."

"He's loaded up. We've got him stabilized. Going to send him up for some tests.
Couple hours, maybe, things go right, he'll
be able to hold a conversation." Curiosity
washed over the fatigue in his eyes. "Don't
I know you? The cop, right? I've worked my
magic on you before."

"Dallas. Probably."

"Yeah, Dallas. You get around. Look, I
need to talk to the wife."

"Fine. I'm going to put a man on him. I
don't want anyone talking to him but me until I clear it."

"What's the deal?"

"Material witness. I'm Homicide."

"Oh, yeah. Yeah! Icove case. Crazy bastards. Well, your material witness should live
to sing. I'm that good."

She shifted, watching as they wheeled
Bobby out. He'd left some of his skin on the
street, she noted. What was left was white
as bone. When they cut back the drugs, he
was going to hurt like a son of a bitch, but
he was breathing on his own.

"I'm going up with him, until the uniform
reports."

"Suit yourself. Just stay out of the way.

Happy holidays and so forth," the doctor added as he headed toward the waiting area.

Eve stood outside again, another floor, another door, while they ran their scanners and diagnostics. And while she waited, the elevators opened. Zana rushed out, Peabody on her heels.

"The doctor said he was going to be okay." Tears had tracked through Zana's makeup, leaving their trail. She grabbed Eve's hands, squeezed.

"He's going to be okay. They're just running some tests. I was afraid . . . I was afraid—" Her voice hitched. "I don't know what I would've done. I just don't know."

"I want you to tell me what happened."

"I told the detective. I told her I—"

"I want you to tell me. Hold on."

She walked to the uniformed officer as he got off the elevator. "Subject is Bobby Lombard. Material witness, homicide. I want you with him every step. You check the room they put him in, you check ID on everyone— I mean everyone—who attempts access.

He grunts the wrong way, I want to hear about it. Understood?"

"Yes, sir."

Satisfied, she went back to Zana. "Okay, we're going to find a place, have a seat. I want everything. Every detail."

"Okay, but . . . I just don't understand any of this." She chewed her lip, looking over her shoulder at the doors while Eve hauled her away. "Can't I just stay, wait until—"

"We're not going far." She hailed a nurse simply by holding up her badge.

"Good," he said. "I'm under arrest. That means I can sit down for five minutes."

"I need your break room."

"I have a vague recollection of the break room. Chairs, a table, coffee. Down there, make a left. Oh hell, you need a key card. Security's getting to be a bitch. I'll take you."

He led the way, keyed them in, then stuck his head in. "Okay, I smelled the coffee. It's not all bad." He headed off down the hall.

"Sit down, Zana," Eve told her.

"I've just got to move around. I can't sit still."

"I get that. Go over what happened."

"Just like I told you before. Like I told the detective."

"Repeat it."

As she did, Eve picked apart the details. "You got bumped, spilled coffee."

"On my coat." Zana picked up the coat she'd tossed in a chair. "It wasn't this bad. The first time. More spilled when Bobby . . . God, I can still see it."

"Was it a bump or a push?"

"Oh, I don't know. A bump, I guess. So many people. In part of my head I was thinking it was so exciting. Being out, the crowds, the windows, the noise. We had the soy dogs, and the packages. We should've gone back. I know Bobby wanted to. But—"

"You didn't. Did Bobby say anything? Did you see anything, before he fell?"

"No . . . I was fussing with my coat, looking down and thinking how I hoped it would come out. I think he held a hand out, like he was going to take the coffee so I could deal with the stain. Then he was falling. I—I grabbed for him," she managed, as her voice began to break. "Then the horn, and the squealing. It was horrible."

Her shoulders shook as she dropped her face in her hands. Peabody stepped up with a cup of water. Zana took a sip and a couple of shuddering breaths. "People stopped to help. Everyone says how New Yorkers are cold and kind of mean, but they're not. People were nice, they were good. They tried to help. The police came up. The ones who came with us. Bobby was bleeding, and he wouldn't wake up. The MTs came. Do you think they'll let me see him soon?"

"I'll check." Peabody turned toward the door, stopped. "Do you want some coffee?"

"I don't think I'll ever drink another cup." Zana dug in her pocket, pulled out a tissue. And buried her face in it.

Eve left her there, stepped out with Peabody.

"I didn't get any more out of her either," Peabody began. "She's clueless about the fact that it may have been a deliberate attack."

"We'll see what Bobby says. The record?"

"Baxter was taking it to the lab personally and I got the homers off the coats."

"Good thinking."

"I've got his list of wits, and copies of statements taken on-scene. The cabbie's holding at Central. His license is valid. Been hacking for six years. Few traffic bumps. Nothing major."

"Head down there now. Get his initial statement, and his particulars for follow-up. Spring him. Write it up, copy to me, copy to Whitney." Eve checked the time. "Shit. Nothing more to be done. I'm sticking here until I interview Bobby. Get it wrapped back at the house, then go home. Merry Christmas."

"You sure? I can wait until you report in."

"No point. If there's anything, I'll let you know. Finish packing, go to Scotland. Drink . . . what is it?"

"Wassail. I think it's wassail, especially over there. Okay, thanks. But I'll consider myself on call until the shuttle takes off tomorrow.

"Merry Christmas, Dallas."

Maybe, she thought, and looked back toward the break room as Peabody walked away. But some people were going to have the crappiest of holidays.

She waited an hour while Bobby was tested, transferred, and set up in a room. When she walked in, he turned his head, tried to focus with glassy eyes that were rimmed with red. "Zana?" he said in a voice slurred with drugs.

"It's Dallas. Zana's fine. She'll be here in a minute."

"They said . . ." He licked his lips. "I got hit by a cab."

"Yeah. So how'd that happen?"

"I dunno. It's mixed up. I feel really weird."

"It's the meds. The doctor says you're going to be fine. Got some broken bones, and took a good crack on the head. Concussion. You were waiting for the light. To cross the street."

"Waiting for the light." He closed his bruised eyes. "Packed in on the corner like, what is it, sardines. Lots of noise. Zana made a noise. Scared me."

"What kind of noise?"

He looked up at her. "Like, ah . . ." He sucked in his breath. "Sorta. But she just spilled some coffee. Coffee and dogs and bags. Arms loaded. Gonna get a hat."

"Stick with me here, Bobby," she said as his eyes fluttered closed again. "What happened then?"

"I . . . she gave me that smile. I remember that smile—like, 'Oops, look what I did now.' And I dunno, I dunno. I heard her scream. I heard people yelling, and horns blasting. I hit something. They said it hit me, but I hit, and I don't remember until I woke up here."

"You slip?"

"Musta. All those people."

"Did you see anyone? Did anyone say anything to you?"

"Can't remember. Feel weird, out of myself."

His skin was whiter than the sheets that covered him, so that the bruises and scrapes seemed to jump out—and slapped straight into her guilt.

Still, she pressed. "You'd been shopping. You bought a tree."

"We had the tree. Cheer ourselves up some. What happened to the tree?" His eyes rolled, then refocused on her. "Is this really happening? Wish I was home. Just wish I was home. Where's Zana?"

Useless now, Eve decided. She was wasting her time and his energy. "I'll get her."

Eve stepped out. Zana stood in the corridor, wringing her hands. "Can I go in?

Please. I'm not going to upset him. I've got myself settled down. I just want to see him."

"Yeah, go on in."

Zana straightened her shoulders, put a smile on her face. Eve watched her go in, heard her say, in cheerful tones, "Why, just look at you! You got some way of getting out of buying me a hat."

While she waited, she tried the lab. Bitched when she was informed she couldn't have what she wanted until the twenty-sixth. Apparently Christmas over-rode even her wrath.

She might not be able to make a dent there, but Central was another matter. From there, she ordered up uniforms in rotation to stick with Zana at the hotel, with Bobby at the hospital, twenty-four hours.

"Yes," she snapped. "That includes Christmas."

Irritated, she tagged Roarke. "I'm going to be late."

"Aren't you cheerful. What are you doing in the hospital?"

"It's not me. Fill you in later. Things have just gone to shit, so I have to shovel it clear before I clock out."

"I have a considerable amount to clear

myself in order to take time off. Why don't I meet you somewhere for dinner? Get back to me when you've made a path."

"Yeah, okay. Maybe." She glanced over as Zana came out. "Gotta go. Later."

"He's tired," Zana said, "but he was joking with me. Said how he was off soy dogs for life. Thanks for staying. It helped to have somebody here I know."

"I'll take you back to the hotel."

"Maybe I could stay with Bobby. I could sleep in the chair by his bed."

"You'll both do better if you're rested. I'll have a black-and-white bring you back in the morning."

"I could take a cab."

"Let's take precautions now. Just to be on the safe side. I'll put a cop back on the hotel."

"Why?"

"Just a precaution."

Zana's hand shot out, gripped Eve's arm. "You think somebody hurt Bobby? You think this was deliberate?"

Her voice rose several octaves on the question, and her fingers dug through to skin.

"There's nothing to substantiate that. I'd

just rather be cautious. You need to pick up anything for back at the hotel, we'll get it on the way."

"He slipped. He just slipped, that's all," Zana said definitively. "You're just being cautious. You're just taking care of us."

"That's right."

"Could we see if they have a store, like a gift shop here? I could get Bobby some flowers. Maybe they even have a little tree. We bought one today, but I think it got smashed."

"Sure, no problem."

She fought back impatience, went downstairs, into the gift shop. Waited, wandered, while Zana appeared to agonize over the right flowers, and the display of scrawny tabletop trees.

Then there was the matter of a gift card, which meant more agonizing.

It took thirty minutes to accomplish what Eve figured she could have done in thirty seconds. But there was color back in Zana's cheeks as she was assured the flowers and tree would be delivered upstairs within the hour.

"He'll like seeing them when he wakes up," Zana said as they walked outside. With the wind biting, she buttoned her stained coat. "You don't think the flowers are too fussy? Too female? It's so hard to pick out flowers for a man."

What the hell did she know about it? "He'll like them."

"Gosh, it's cold. And it's snowing again." Zana paused to look up at the sky. "Maybe we'll have a white Christmas. That'd be something. It hardly ever snows where we are in Texas, and if it does, it usually melts before you can blink. First time I saw snow, I didn't know what to think. How about you?"

"It was a long time ago." Outside the window in another nasty little hotel room. Chicago, maybe. "I don't remember."

"I remember making a snowball, and how cold it was on my hands." Zana looked down at them, then tucked them in her pockets out of the chill. "And when you looked outside in the morning, if it had snowed at night, everything looked so white and clean."

She waited by the car while Eve unlocked the doors. "You know how your stomach would get all tied up with excitement, because maybe there'd be no school that day?"

"Not really."

"I'm just babbling, don't mind me. Happens when I'm nervous. I guess you're all ready for Christmas."

"Mostly." Eve maneuvered into traffic, resigned herself to small talk.

"Bobby wanted to have his mama's memorial before the end of the year." As if she couldn't keep her hands still, Zana twisted the top button of her coat. "I don't know if we can do that, now that he's hurt. He thought—we thought—it'd be good to do it before. So we'd start off the new year without all that sorrow. Are we going to be able to go home soon?"

Couldn't keep them, Eve thought. Could stall, but couldn't reasonably demand they stay in New York once Bobby was cleared for travel. "We'll see what the doctors say."

"I don't think we'll ever come back here." Zana looked out the side window. "Too much has happened. Too many bad memories. I guess I'll probably never see you again either, after we go."

She was silent a moment. "If you find out

who killed Mama Tru, will Bobby have to come back?"

"I'd say that depends."

Eve went into the hotel, up to the room to satisfy herself nothing had been disturbed. She asked for and received a copy of lobby security, posted her man, and escaped.

She went back to Central and found two gaily wrapped boxes on her desk. A glance at the cards told her they were from Peabody and McNab. One for her, one for Roarke.

Unable to drum up enough Christmas spirit to open hers, she set them aside to work. She wrote her report, read Peabody's, and signed off on it.

For the next half hour, she sat in the relative quiet, studied her murder board, her notes, and let it all circle.

Before she left, she hung the prism Mira had given her.

Maybe it would help.

She left it shimmering dully against the dark window as she pulled out her 'link, tucked the presents under her arm, and left the office.

"I'm clear."

"What are you hungry for?" Roarke asked her.

"That's a loaded question." She held up a hand, acknowledging Baxter, and stopped. "Let's keep it simple."

"Just as I thought. Sophia's," he told her, and rattled off an address. "Thirty minutes."

"That'll work. If you get there first, order a really, really big bottle of wine. Big. Pour me a tumbler full."

"Should be an interesting evening. I'll see you soon, Lieutenant."

She pocketed her 'link, turned to Baxter.

"Don't suppose I could tag along, share that really, really big bottle."

"I'm not sharing."

"In that case, can I have a minute? Private?"

"All right." She walked back to her office, called for lights. "I'll spring for coffee if you want it, but that's my best offer."

"I'll take it." He went to the AutoChef himself. He was still wearing his soft clothes, Eve noted. Light gray sweater, dark gray pants. He'd gotten some blood—Bobby's blood, she imagined—on the pants.

"I don't know what to think," he told her. "Maybe I was too loose. Maybe I'm just fucking losing it. I've gone over it in my head. I wrote it up. I still don't know."

He took out the coffee, turned. "I let the kid take point. Not blaming him, it was my call. I sent him down for dogs, for Christ's sake. Figured they were just getting theirs, and it put him in a decent position. And screw it, Dallas, I was hungry."

She knew guilt when she saw it, and at the moment, it was like looking in a mirror. "You want me to ream you for it? I've got some left."

"Maybe." He scowled into the coffee, then downed some. "I'm listening to them, and there's nothing. Just chatter. Can't get a full visual, but he's tall enough I can see the back of his head, his profile when he turns to her. I moved forward when she spilled the coffee, then I relaxed again. If they're at noon, Trueheart's at ten o'clock. I'm at three. Then she's screaming in my ear."

Eve sat on the edge of her desk. "No vibe?"

"None. Blimps are blasting overhead. One of those street-corner Santas ringing his damn bell. People are streaming by, or crowding in to get the light."

He drank more coffee. "I pushed in, soon as she screamed. I didn't see anybody take off. Bastard could've stood there. Could be one of the wits, far as I know. Or he could've just melted back. It was a freaking parade on Fifth today. And some people slipped, tumbled."

Her head came up, lips pursed. "Before or after?"

"Before, during, after. Putting it back, I see this woman—red coat, big blonde 'do. She slips a little. Right in back of where Zana was standing. That'd be the initial bump. Spilled coffee. I can see the male sub turn. I hear him ask her what happened. Anxious. Then he relaxes when she says she got coffee on her coat. So do I. Then he pitches forward. Chaos ensues."

"So maybe we're both beating ourselves up because the guy lost his footing."

"Coincidences are hooey."

"Hooey." At least she got a short laugh out of it. "Yeah, they are. So we'll run the record backward and forward. He's tucked up. Nobody's getting near him. So's she. We'll run it when the damn lab stops playing Christmas carols. No point slapping ourselves, or me slapping you, until we know if this is the one in a million that actually is coincidence."

"If I screwed this up, I need to know."

She smiled thinly. "On that, Baxter, I can promise you. I'll let you know."

16

Roarke watched her come in, his tall, lanky cop in the rather spectacular black leather coat. Her eyes were tired, the stress showing in them even as he noted the way she scoped the room.

Cops were cops, he knew, 24/7. She'd be able to tell him, should he ask, how many were in the booth at the opposite corner, what they were wearing, possibly what they were eating. And she'd be able to do so with her back to them.

Fascinating.

She checked her coat, brushed off the waiter who must have offered to escort her to their table. And crossed the restaurant alone, in that long, loose stride he loved.

"Lieutenant," he said, rising to greet her, "you make a picture."

"A picture of what?"

"Confidence and authority. Very sexy." He kissed her lightly, then gestured to the wine he'd poured when he'd seen her come in. "It's not a tumbler, but you can consider it a bottomless glass."

"Appreciate it." She took a good slug. "Crappy day."

"So I gathered. Why don't we order, then you can tell me about it?"

She glanced up at the waiter who materialized at her side. "I want spaghetti and meatballs, with the red sauce. You got that here?"

"Of course, madam. And to start?"

She lifted her wine. "I've started."

"Insalada mista," Roarke told him. "Two. And I'll have the chicken Parmesan." He dipped some bread in the herbed oil already on the table, handed it to her. "Sop some of that wine up, why don't you?"

She stuffed the bread in her mouth.

"Describe the waiter for me."

"What? Why?"

"It's entertaining. Go ahead." And it would settle her down, he thought.

She shrugged, took another good swallow of wine. "Caucasian male, mid-thirties.

Wearing black pants, white shirt, black loafer-style shoes. Five eight, a hundred and fifty. Brown and brown. Smooth complexion. Full bottom lip, long nose with a good-sized hook to it. Crooked eye-tooth on the left. Straight, thick eyebrows. Bronx accent, but he's working on losing it. Small stud, right earlobe—some kind of blue stone. Thick silver band, ring finger, left hand. Gay. He's probably got a spouse."

"Gay?"

"Yeah, he checked you out, not me. So?"

"So. As I said, entertaining. What went wrong today?"

"What didn't?" she answered, and told him.

The salads arrived before she'd finished, so she stabbed at hers.

"So, that's where I'm at. Can't beat up Baxter or Trueheart, because—as far as I can see—they did the job. Wouldn't have been a job if I hadn't worked it."

"Which means you beat up on yourself. What's the point, Eve? If he was pushed, where does it come from? Where's the gain?"

"You can go back to money. Trudy was pretty well set, and he's doing okay. Or you go back to revenge. He was there, living in the house, her blood relation, when she was fostering."

"He brought you food," Roarke reminded her. "You wouldn't have been the only one he'd done that for."

"Probably not. But he didn't stand up. Maybe somebody figures he should have."

"Do you?"

She stabbed more salad, drank more wine. "No. Blood's thicker, and so's self-preservation. I don't blame him for anything. But he was a kid when I was there, just another kid. He was older before she gave up fostering. Someone could figure he should pay, too."

"His silence makes him an accessory?"

"Something like that. And damn it, it would be easier to erase them at home, wouldn't it? Yeah, you got a strange city, more people, so that's a plus. But you'd be able to scope their routines more back in Texas. Which takes me back, at least part of the way, to impulse."

"Have you considered Bobby's pretty new wife?"

"Yeah, and still am. Maybe she wasn't as tolerant of her mother-in-law as she claims.

From my side, it would take a hell of a lot of tolerance. So she sees an opportunity, takes it. Get rid of Mama Tru, and put the money in Bobby's pocket. Then, hey, why not ditch the middle man? He's out, I'm in. Could she be stupid enough to think I wouldn't look at her for it?"

"When you look, what do you see?"

"Nothing that pops up and screams 'I'm a murderer,' not on evidence, not on her record. But she's a little too sweet and sissy for me."

He smiled a little. "Can girls be sissies?"

"In my world. All that pink and pastel and 'Mama Tru.'" Eve stuffed more bread in her mouth. "Cries if you look at her."

"Well now, you've a dead mother-in-law, an abduction, and a husband in the hospital. Seems a few tears are justified."

Eve just drummed her fingers. "There's nothing in her record that leans toward this. I don't see anyone marrying Bobby for money—just not enough of it, even if she'd known about Trudy's dirty little nest egg."

"A million or so makes a comfortable life in some circles," he reminded her.

"Now you sound like Peabody. I'm not jaded about money," she muttered. "But marrying somebody to get your hands on it, when you're going to have to off him, and his mother. It's a big stretch. And I don't see how she could have known, beforehand, that Trudy had dough stashed here and there."

"A connection to one of the women who'd been blackmailed?" he suggested.

She had to give him credit. He thought like a cop, something he'd wince over if she mentioned it. "Yeah, that was a thought. I did some digging, trying to see if I could find something there. Nothing, so far anyway. I read the witness reports, and two say she grabbed for him, tried to grab his arm as he went into the street. Just like she said."

"But you still wonder."

"Yeah, you gotta wonder. She's the one, on the spot, for both incidents. She's the one connected to both victims. And at this point, she's the one who stands to gain the most if money is the motive."

"So you have guards on her, as much to keep track of her as for her protection."

"Can't do much more until the twenty-sixth. Lab won't push, half my men are out or their minds are. There's no immediate danger to the populace, so I can't get the lab to push. Even the sweepers didn't get back to me on the results from the room next to my scene. Christmas is bogging me down."

"Bah, humbug."

"I get that," she said and pointed a finger at him. "I turned down a candy cane today."

She told him about drunken Santa while their entrees were served.

"You meet the most interesting group of people in your line of work."

"Yeah, it's what you'd call eclectic." Put it away, she told herself. Put the day away and remember you have a life. "So, you got things squared away in your world."

"More or less." He poured them both more wine. "A bit of business tomorrow, but I'm closing the office at noon. There are a few little details I want to see to at home."

"Details." She eyed him as she wound pasta around her fork. "What else could there be? You importing reindeer?"

"Ah, if only I'd thought of it sooner. No, just a bit of this and that." He brushed a hand over hers. "Our Christmas Eve was interrupted last year, if you recall."

"I recall." She'd never forget the manic drive to get to Peabody, and the terror of wondering if they'd be too late. "She'll be in Scotland this time. Have to take care of herself."

"She contacted me today, she and Mc-Nab, to thank me. She was surprised, and touched—both of them were—when I told them it had been your idea."

"You didn't have to do that."

"It *was* your idea."

"It's your shuttle." She squirmed a little.

"It's interesting that you have as difficult a time giving gifts as you do receiving them."

"That's because you always go overboard." Frowning at him, she stabbed a meatball. "You went overboard, didn't you?"

"Are you fishing for a hint?"

"No. Maybe. No," she decided. "You just love stringing me along, seeing as you're such a smart ass."

"What a thing to say. You might end up with a lump of coal in your stocking."

"Few thousand years, I'll have a diamond, so . . . What was she going to do with the money?"

He sat back, smiled. The cop was back.

"Tuck it away? For what? She had funds tucked. Didn't live high because she didn't want anyone to know. But she had her pretty baubles, locked up so she could look at them. Had jewelry insured," she told him. "I got the paperwork on that. Over a quarter mil in sparkles. And she had her tune-ups. But that's all piddly. Because the money was coming in in what you could call dribbles. But this was her big score. Big, fat lump sum, she's figuring on. Must've had a plan for some of it."

"Property, perhaps. Or a trip. Art, jewelry."

"Got jewelry, and can't wear it too much outside her own house. People would get ideas. But if she planned to relocate . . . I've got to check, see if she had a valid passport. When she got it, or renewed it. She's got Bobby, but he's grown up now, married now. Not so much at her beck and call. That's a pisser."

"A new home, a new location. Somewhere she can live in the manner she deserves to live. A staff of some kind."

"Need someone to boss around, sure. This isn't the kind of stake you just put in a bank somewhere. Especially since—you can put money on it—she planned to keep tapping you. Can't stick around good old Texas, where people know you. You're freaking rich now. Gotta enjoy it."

"What does that tell you regarding the investigation? If you find she'd made inquiries about a property, or travel, what does it give you besides busywork?"

"Busywork's underrated. Maybe she let something slip, to Bobby, to Zana, to someone else. Maybe we use Peabody's favorite—there's a hot young lover out there, someone she had by the short hairs, or someone who got greedy. Can circle back to revenge. One of her former charges is keeping tabs on her, or is being used by her, and gets wind she's got a big deal going."

She nudged her plate aside. "I want to play this angle. You finished?"

"Nearly. No dessert?"

"I'm fine as is."

"They have gelato." His grin was quick, brilliant. "Chocolate."

"Bastard." She fought her inner war, her weakness. "You think we can get it to go?"

It was interesting, Eve decided, when you looked in a direction that didn't seem relevant. The little pieces that shuffled down.

Maybe not into the puzzle yet, but waiting for you to find the fit.

"Her passport's current." She scooped up the decadent delight of rich chocolate. "Had one for twelve years. And she traveled. Funny nobody mentioned that. Spain, Italy, France. She liked Europe, but there's Rio, and Belize, and Bimini. Exotic locales."

"Nothing off planet?" he asked.

"Nothing she used this passport for. I'm betting she liked sticking to terra firma. Off planet takes a lot of time, and a lot of money. And while she traveled, she was in and out—with few exceptions—in a few days. Longest I find here's ten days in Italy. Went in through Florence. And had another trip there, one day, the week before she came to New York."

"Maybe a weakness for Tuscany," Roarke suggested.

"Quick trips, though." She drummed her fingers, ate more gelato. "Could be she made them on the q.t. Didn't tell her son. I've got to go back, find out if she traveled alone or with a companion."

She studied the data. "Had a reason for going back to Italy right before she came here to make her score. Looking over there, you bet your ass. Thinking she might like to find herself a villa."

"It would take some time, but I could find out if she made inquiries about property with a realtor over there."

"She'd know something about the ins and out, wouldn't she, with a son in the business."

She sat back, sighed. "So here's one way. She's looking to relocate, plop herself down to live the high life after she skins you."

"I object to the term. No one skins me."

"Yeah, but she doesn't get that. Time to start enjoying her hard-earned nest egg. Deck herself out in all those glitters she's been paying insurance premiums for. Time to kick up her heels. Got herself in tune for it. She's tapped out a couple of her income sources, but they're finite anyway. She hits the jackpot, and she can move on. Retire."

"What does she tell her family?"

Think like her, Eve ordered herself. It wasn't so hard to do. "Her son's replaced her with a wife. Ungrateful bastard. Doesn't have to tell him a damn thing. If she intended to tell him, you can bet she's got something worked out: She won the lottery, got some inheritance, something out of the blue. But she doesn't need Bobby anymore because she's got someone on her string, someone who can do the grunt work when she needs it. They should be with her in New York, just in case."

She rolled her shoulders. "Or she's going to shake her minion off, hire somebody fresh when she relocates. Who do you know in that area of Italy who handles real estate, could give us a hand with this?"

"One or two people. However, it's after one in the morning there."

"Oh, right." She scowled at the clock. "I hate the whole time difference crap. It's irritating. Okay, that waits until the morning."

"I hate to remind you, tomorrow's Christmas Eve. We're unlikely to find offices open, particularly in Europe where they believe in taking holidays. I can pull strings, but unless this is urgent, I hate to push this into someone's holiday."

"See, see"—she waved her spoon—"Christmas is bogging me down. It can wait, it can wait," she repeated. "More important to find out if she had a travel companion. It could just be the one little mistake. One little detail that moves this along."

"Then I'll help you with that."

"What I want is to plug in all her flights."

"All?"

"Yeah, all. Then we're going to run the manifest through, each one, see if any dupe names pop. Or any name on my case file list." She licked ice cream off her finger. "And yeah, I'm aware the transpo company offices are closed. Lazy bastards. And that accessing passenger information generally requires authorization."

He smiled, easily. "I didn't say a thing."

"I'm just looking is all I'm doing. And if anything pops, then I'll backtrack, go through channels. But I'm sick to fucking death of running in place."

"Still said nothing."

"But you're thinking it."

"What I'm thinking is you need to move. I want your chair."

"Why?"

"If I'm going to get this data, and we both know I can access it faster than you, I want the chair and the desk. Why don't you deal with those dishes?"

She grumbled, but got up. "You're lucky I've got some holiday spirit and didn't clock you for the 'deal with those dishes' crack."

"Ho, ho, ho." He sat in her place and rolled up his sleeves. "Coffee'd be nice."

"Thin ice, Ace. Cracking under your expensive shoes."

"And a cookie. You ate most of my gelato."

"Did not," she called from the kitchen. Well, yes, she had, but that was beside the point.

Still, she wanted coffee herself, so she could as easily get two mugs. To amuse herself she got out a single minicookie, barely the size of her thumb. She put it and his mug on a plate.

"I guess the least I can do is get you coffee and a cookie when you're putting the time in for me." She came up behind him, leaned down to plant a wifely kiss on the top of his head.

Then she set the plate down. He glanced over at it, then up at her. "That's cold, Eve. Even for you."

"I know. And fun, too. What've you got?"

"I'm accessing her account, to determine what transportation company she used for her trips. When I have that, I'll do a search on the dates that coordinate for her passport. Then I'll get your manifests, and run a

search there. I think that deserves a bleeding cookie."

"Like this one." From behind her back she
pulled a decorated sugar cookie. Whatever
else she could say about Summerset, and
there was plenty, the man could bake.

"That's more like it. Now why don't you
come and sit on my lap?"

"Just get the data, pal. I know it's insult-
ing to ask, but are you going to have any
trouble with CompuGuard on this?"

"I'm ignoring that as you provided the
cookie."

She left him to it, set up at her auxiliary
comp.

What, she wondered, did other married
couples do after dinner? Hang and watch
screen maybe, or go to their separate areas
and fiddle with their hobbies or work. Talk
on the 'link to pals or family. Have people
over.

They did some of that. Sometimes.
Roarke had gotten her hooked on vids, especially the old black-and-whites from the
early and mid-twentieth century. There were
nights, here and there, they whiled away a
couple hours that way—the way, she imagined, most considered normal.

If it was normal to while away a couple hours in a home theater bigger—certainly lusher—than most of the public ones.

Before Roarke had come into her life, she'd spent most nights alone, going over notes, gnawing at a case. Unless Mavis had pried her out for fun and games. She couldn't have imagined herself like this, socked in with someone. So in tune with someone despite some of their elemental differences.

Now she couldn't imagine it any other way.

With marriage on her mind, she moved to Bobby and Zana. They hadn't been married long, so the assumption would be they'd spend a good deal of their time together. They worked together, lived together. Traveled, as least on this fatal trip, together.

Her search turned up a passport for Bobby. The last stamp four years earlier. Australia. A couple of other, earlier trips, each spaced about a year apart. One to Portugal, one to London.

Vacations, she decided. Annual jaunts. But nothing that required a passport since Australia.

Other travel, maybe. Starting a new business—maybe shorter, cheaper trips.

No passport for Zana, maiden name or married. Well, a lot of people never left the country. She hadn't herself, before Roarke.

But she sat back, considered. Wouldn't Bobby want to take his new bride on some big trip? Honeymoon, whatever. Show her some part of the world, especially one he'd traveled to and enjoyed.

That was one of Roarke's deals, anyway. Let me show you the world.

Of course, maybe they hadn't had the time, or wanted to spend the money. Not yet. Maybe he'd decided to start with New York once the idea was popped by his mother. It made sense enough.

But it was something to wonder about.

She poked at the other fosters again, looking for some connection, some click. One in a cage, one dead, she thought.

But what if—

"Got your manifests here."

Distracted, she glanced over. "Already?"

"One day you'll afford me the awe I so richly deserve."

"You're rich enough to afford your own awe. What about matches?"

"If you're in a hurry, you take half." He tapped keys. "There. Transferring to you. Handle it from there?"

"I know how to do a search and match," she muttered, and set it up to run. She swiveled around to look at him. "I've got these two long shots. Just plucking out of the air. One of the fosters is in a cage. Assaults, mostly. No family, no known associates in particular. Nothing in her jacket to indicate any real smarts, or connections. But maybe Trudy tried to hit her up along the line. So this career violent tendency decides to get back some of her own. Works a deal with somebody who's close, or can get close to the mark. Take her out—got your revenge—make some money while you're at it."

"How would this person know Trudy was going to New York now, with the idea of shaking us down, and be able to put this kill together so quickly?"

"The kill's of the moment. I still say that. Could've had the shill in place already. And yeah, I know it's a long one. But I'm going to have another chat with the warden after Christmas. Maybe reach out to her last arresting officer."

"And the other shot in the dark?"

"One of the fosters worked as a dancer in that club that was bombed a few years ago. Miami. Remember, a couple of bonzos got through the door, protesting sin or something. Things went wrong and the boomers blew. Took out over a hundred and fifty people."

"I don't remember, sorry. Before you, I can't say I paid as much attention to that sort of thing." But he stopped what he was doing, considered it. "So she survived?"

"No. At least she's listed among the dead. But it was an underground club, and they run loose. Explosions, body parts flying. Blood, terror, confusion."

"I get the picture, thanks." He sat back, walking his mind along the path she was taking. "So, she somehow survives, is misidentified, and lives to plot Trudy's eventual demise?"

"It's an angle," Eve said stubbornly. "There are others. Somebody close to her comes back on Trudy. Revenge again. A lover or a close friend. I can talk to some of the survivors anyway, some of the people she worked with. Maybe get a clearer picture of her at least."

She got up to pace. "And there's this other thing going through my head. Did Trudy ever catch Bobby sneaking food to one of the girls? If so, what did she do about it? To her, to him. Or later, when he was older, did he ever get in contact with one of them? Or did one of them ever approach him? He never said anything about that. Easiest way to get to Trudy, it seems to me, would be through him."

"You're back to Zana."

"Yeah."

"Try this. What is it about Zana Lombard that keeps you circling back?"

"Well, like I said, she cries a lot."

"Eve."

"It's irritating. But beyond that personal annoyance, she's on the spot, both incidents. She's the only one who saw her alleged abductor."

"Why make up a story like that? It only brings her to the foreground. Wouldn't she prefer to stay in the back?"

She rose to walk over, study her murder board. "Criminals are always complicating things, saying or doing more than they should. Even the smart ones. Add ego. Look what I pulled off, but nobody knows.

Nobody can say, 'Wow, that was pretty damn clever of you. Let me buy you a drink.'"

He lifted his eyebrows. "You think she did it."

She drew a line with her finger from the photograph of Trudy, to Bobby, to Zana. A very handy triangle, she decided. Neat and tidy.

"I've thought she did it since I opened the door and found Trudy dead."

He turned in the chair now, studying her face. "Kept that one close to the vest, didn't you?"

"No need to get pissy."

"I never get pissy." He rose, deciding it was time for a brandy. "I do, occasionally, become irked. Such as now. Why didn't you say earlier?"

"Because every time I circled around her, she's come up clean. I've got no facts, no data, no evidence, no clear motive."

She stepped closer to Zana's photo. Big blue eyes, wavy blond hair. The guileless milkmaid, whatever the hell a milkmaid was.

"I've run probabilities on her, and they come up low. Even my head tells me it's not her. It's my gut saying otherwise."

"You generally trust your gut."

"This is different, because my gut's already involved because of my connection to the victim." She walked away from the board, back to her auxiliary station. "And the suspect on the top of my gut list hasn't given me any solid reason to have her there. Her actions and reactions, her statements, her behavior are pretty much what they should be under the circumstances. But I look at her, and I think: It ought to be you."

"And Bobby?"

"Could be working with her. One or both of them knew what Trudy was up to. One or both of them seduces the other, uses sex, love, money—all of the above."

She stopped, pulled the fresh scene photos of Bobby's injuries out of her file, and moved over to tack them to her board.

"But this, the incident that landed him in the hospital, doesn't fit with that. I made sure I saw him before she did. He gave no sign she'd pulled a double-cross on him. They were wired on their walk around the city, and Baxter's oral indicated they talked about shopping and lunch. Nothing about Trudy, nothing about any plot or plan. It just doesn't *feel* like him, doesn't feel like team-work. But—"

"You're afraid your memory of him colors your instincts."

"Maybe. I need to push the pieces around some more."

Task completed. There are no matches in the manifest with files currently on record . . .

"Well, that was a bust," Eve complained. "We can try name combinations, look for aliases."

"I'll set it up."

Eve poured more coffee, waiting until his back was turned to avoid a caffeine lecture. "You're married to someone—and you work with them, live with them, sleep with them—don't you figure you'd get an inkling if they were stringing you? I mean, day after day, night after night. The stringer's got to make a slip sometime and put the stringee on guard."

"You've heard the expression 'love is blind.'"

"I think it's bullshit. Lust dazzles, sure, at least for the short term. But love clears the vision. You see better, sharper, because you feel more than you did before."

His lips curved as he stepped to her, touched her hair, her face. "That, I think, is the most romantic thing I've ever heard come out of your mouth."

"It's not romantic, it's—"

"Hush." He laid his lips on hers briefly. "Let me enjoy it. You have a point, but love can also cause you to see things as you prefer to see them, as you want them to be. And you haven't factored in—if we stick with your gut, and she's responsible—that she may love him. Part of her motive might have been to free him from what she saw as a destructive, even dangerous influence."

"Now who's being romantic? If I put her in as the killer, then she pushed her husband in front of a cab a few hours ago. No way— if she did Trudy—that was an accident, a coincidence."

"You have me on that one."

"No, what I have is nothing. I've got one material witness/suspect in the hospital. Another in a hotel room, under watch. I have no evidence that points to either of them, or anyone else at this time. I need to pick at it, that's all. Shuffle things up and keep picking at it."

She thought of the recording, and Roarke's skill, his fancy computer lab. She could ask him to work it for her, put in the time.

Not right, not fair. Not starting so late.

"Guess we'll pack it in for now. Check the results of that last run in the morning."

"That suits me. What about a swim first? Work out the kinks."

"Yeah, that'd be good." She started for the elevator with him, then narrowed her eyes. "Is this some ploy to get me wet and naked?"

"Love certainly doesn't blind you, Lieutenant. You see right through me."

It wasn't snow for Christmas Eve, but another bout of nasty, freezing rain that made gleeful skittering sounds against the windows. It would, Eve thought in disgust, coat the streets and sidewalks and give the city employees who were on a shift another excuse to blow the day off.

She was tempted, nearly, to join them. She could drag on a sweatshirt and work from home, avoid the ice rink of the streets. Stay warm and comfortable. It was sheer contrariness that had her preparing to go in.

Knowing that didn't bother her a bit.

"You have everything you need here," Roarke reminded her.

"Don't." She shouldered on her weapon harness. "Don't have Feeney, for one. Don't have Mira. And I'm going to try to snag her long enough to get a profile on Zana and Bobby. Don't have whoever's bad luck has them in the lab today. And I want to go by the hotel, the hospital, do follow-ups there."

"Perhaps you haven't heard." He stretched out his legs to enjoy another cup of coffee. "There's a marvelous invention called the telelink. Some, as we have here, are also equipped for holo-conferences."

"Not the same." She pulled a jacket over her weapon. "You sticking home today?"

"If I said I was?"

"You'd be lying. You're going in, same as me, finishing things up personally. Going to let your staff go early, you softie, but you're heading in."

"I'll stay if you do."

"I'm going, and so are you." But she walked over, framed his face, and kissed him. "See you in a few hours."

"Well, have a care, will you? The roads are bound to be treacherous."

"So's a chemi-head with a lead bat, but I've handled those."

"Figuring as much, I had one of the all-terrains brought around." He lifted a brow when she frowned. "I'll be using one myself, so you've no argument there."

"Fine, okay." She glanced at the time. "Well, while you've got your worrywart on, maybe you could check with the shuttle, see if Peabody got off okay."

"Already did, they're in the air and already out of the weather. Wear your gloves," he called out as she went through the door.

"Such a nag," she mumbled under her breath.

But she was grateful for them, and the thin, soft fur lining that had somehow found its way into her coat. How did he manage that stuff?

Whatever was spitting out of the sky felt like nasty little needle pricks as cold as Mars. She climbed into the muscular vehicle, found its efficient heater already running. The man missed nothing. It was almost spooky.

Even warm, and in a vehicle with the traction and power of a jet tank, she had an ugly fight on her hands all the way downtown. Where before she'd cursed people who ditched work for an extended holiday as lazy wimps, now she cursed them for not staying the hell home. Or for driving a vehicle that couldn't handle the icy roads.

Twice she came upon fender benders, felt

obliged to stop and get out, determine if
there were injuries before calling it in to Traffic.

When traffic stalled, again, she imagined
what it would be like just to roll over the cars
in her path. The tank she was in could handle it, she thought.

When she arrived at Central, she calculated that more than twenty percent of the
slots on her level were empty.

One of the detectives hailed her when she
walked into Homicide.

"Slader, aren't you on graveyard?"

"Yes, sir. Caught one a couple hours before end of tour. Got the guy in the cooler.
Vic's his brother, who was visiting from out
of town for the holidays. Ends up with a broken neck at the bottom of the stairs. Guy in
the cooler has some swank place over on
Park. Vic's a loser, no fixed address, no vis-
ible means of employment."

"He get helped down the steps?"

"Oh, yeah." Slader's smile was thin and
wry. "Guy claims the brother was stoned—
and we'll get the tox on that—but he did
have some Juice on him. Suspect said he
was in bed, heard the noise of the fall, and
found his brother at the bottom of the steps.

Thing is, he apparently didn't think we'd notice the vic's facial bruises, or hoped we put them off on the fall. But seeing as our guy's got scraped knuckles, and a split lip, we're figuring otherwise."

Eve scratched the back of her neck. People, she thought, could be unbelievably stupid. "You work him toward the self-defense or accidental angle?"

"Yeah, but he's sticking to his story. He's an exec for an ad company. Figure he doesn't want to get his name on-screen. We're going to go at him again after he sweats a little more. Guy broke down and cried twice, but he's not moving off the story. Thing is, Lieutenant, we're into overtime."

"Keep at him, get it wrapped. I'll clear the OT. Half the damn squad's out. I'm not passing it off. He call for a lawyer?"

"Not yet."

"You run into a wall, tag me. Otherwise, just put it to bed."

She left her coat in her office after skimming the waiting paperwork and what had accumulated overnight. It bred, she thought as she headed to EDD, like rabbits.

For once, the walls of EDD weren't

bouncing with voices, music, or electronic chatter. There were a handful of detectives in cubes or at desks, and some of the machines humped away, but it was, for this division, eerily quiet.

"Crime could run rampant with the number of cops at home hanging their damn Christmas stockings."

Feeney looked up. "Things are mostly quiet."

"That's what happens before things blow up," she said darkly. "Things get mostly quiet."

"You're cheerful. Here's something that's going to put a kink in your hose."

"You still haven't pinned down the account."

"I haven't pinned down the account, because there is no account. Not with those numbers, in that order."

"Maybe she mixed up the numbers. If you do a random search, utilizing the numbers in any order, then—"

"You're going to stand there, tell me how to do e-work?"

She blew out a breath, dropped into his visitor's chair. "No."

"Thing is, we got too many numbers. At

least one extra. So you run a random, taking out any number, or numbers, what you've got, Dallas, is a hell of a lot of accounts."

"Well, shit" was the best she could think of.

"No way to pin it. I can pin the random accounts, but it's going to take time if you want all of them. 'Cause what you're doing this way, is pulling rabbits out of hats."

She drummed her fingers on her thigh. "I'll take them when you get them. Start cross-referencing."

He gave her one of his hangdog looks. "Gonna be a headache of major proportions. Thing is, Dallas, you're getting the data from a woman who was under duress and stress. No telling if she got the numbers she gave you right in the first place."

"Why didn't he make her record them? Write them down. Have some way of being sure she got them right? He's got two million on the line, and he trusts the memory of a terrified woman?"

"People are stupid more than half the time."

It was God's truth, to her mind, but it wasn't helping her. "He's smart enough, allegedly, to kill, remember the details to cover himself for the murder, get out and away undetected. He's smart enough, allegedly, to be on the spot in order to get another woman into a closed establishment, without anyone they passed noticing the abduction. He leaves no trace there either. But he flubs up the main deal? He screws up on what we would be led to believe was the motive for murder? You buy that, Feeney?"

"Well, you put it that way, I'll save my money." He pulled on his bottom lip. "You think she made it up?"

"I think it's a possibility that needs to be explored. You know, it doesn't put a kink in my hose so much as it adds weight to a theory I've been working on."

"Want to walk it by me? Got time, got coffee."

He'd trained her, she thought. She could remember countless times they'd talked through a case, picking over, niggling over the details over bad food and worse coffee.

He'd taught her how to think, how to see, and most of all how to feel an investigation.

"Wouldn't mind, but I don't see why I should have to suffer through that sludge you call coffee. Figure maybe you could share the holiday token I brought you."

She tossed a gift bag on his desk, and watched his eyes light up like Christmas morning. "That coffee in there? The real deal?"

"No point in bringing you the fake stuff if I'm going to be drinking it."

"Hot damn! Thanks. Hey, close the door, will you? Don't want anybody getting wind while I set this up. Jesus, I'm going to have to put a lock on my AC, or my boys will be swarming in here like locusts."

Once the door was safely shut, he moved to the AutoChef to begin the homey tasks of loading and programming. "You know, the wife's trying to stick me with decaf at home. Might as well drink tap water, you ask me. But this . . ."

He took a long, deep inhale through his nose. "This is prime." He turned his head, sent her a quick grin. "Got a couple of doughnuts in here. Logged 'em in as pea soup so the boys don't get wise."

"Smart." She thought of her travails with the candy thief who continually unearthed her office stash. She might give Feeney's method a shot.

"So what do you got pointing to the female wit?"

She ran it through for him while he dealt with the coffee, shared his doughnuts.

He listened, sipping his coffee, taking an occasional generous bite out of the glazed doughnut. Sugary crumbs dotted his shirt. "Probability's going to favor the son, if it's a family job. Blood kills quicker. Could be he brought the wife into it, pressured her. Hey, guess what, honey? I just killed Mom. So I need you to say I was in here with you, sleeping like a baby."

"Could've gone that way."

"But woman on woman, that's another hot button." He gestured with the last of his doughnut, then popped it in his mouth. "In-laws add to it. Sick and tired of you interfering, you old bat. Then she throws herself on the son. Oh, my God, there was a terrible accident. You have to help me."

"Doesn't explain the scam, the supposed abduction, or Bobby in the hospital."

"Yeah, it could. You got one or both of your suspects either wanting nothing to do with the scam, or wanting all the cupcakes. The abduction is frills. Maybe just frills. That'd be on her. Trying to put a bow on it.

Maybe it goes back, Dallas, like you think. Shit happens when you're a kid, it sticks with you."

She said nothing to that, and he stared into his coffee. Each let the subject of her own childhood slide away.

"You've got to get something on her—or him. Something you can use to put the pressure on. You've got yourself an onion."

"I've got a what?"

"An onion. You've gotta start peeling away the layers."

An onion, Eve thought. Leave it to Feeney.

But it had given her a fresh idea.

She headed to Mira's, caught Mira's admin at her desk, dealing with busywork while Christmas carols played on low. "How's her schedule today?"

"It's very light. We're closing the office at noon until start of business hours on the twenty-sixth. She's with another officer now." The admin checked her watch. "Nearly done. She has another appointment in fifteen minutes, then she's fairly well clear."

"I could use a minute with her between appointments. I can wait."

"All right, but I hope you don't plan to add to her schedule. She and her husband have plans."

"I won't keep her," Eve began, then stepped back as another cop came out of the office.

"Just a minute." The admin held up a finger, got up to walk to Mira's door herself. "Doctor, Lieutenant Dallas is here. She'd like a moment."

"Of course." Mira got up from her desk as Eve entered. "I didn't expect to see you again until after the holidays."

"Need a favor. I'm looking for a profile, maybe even just an impression of a suspect."

"On the Lombard matter."

"Yeah. I'm looking at the daughter-in-law."

"Oh?" Mira sat, leaned back while Eve ran quickly through her angle.

"What I'd like is for you to go with me to her hotel, or the hospital. I don't know yet where she'll be in an hour. I'm going to try to corner her at the hotel first. I know you've got plans. I can run you home myself after."

"I suppose I could—"

"Good. Great." Eve backed toward the door before Mira changed her mind. "I'll come back and get you in an hour. I'm going to set it up."

She hurried out, using her 'link to connect with Zana's room at the hotel.

"I'm swinging by in about an hour," Eve told her.

"Oh. I was hoping to go to the hospital. I just called, and they said Bobby was still sleeping, but—"

"I'll make sure you get there." Eve waited a beat. "How's his condition?"

"Stable. They said he was stable. But they want to keep him another twenty-four hours at least. Observation. And we need to make some arrangements here before they'll release him. I need to get a wheel-chair, and these medications, and—"

"Why don't you start arrangements for what you need from there? That way you'll be set for him tomorrow. I'll have a uniform take you to the hospital, get you home."

"Well, all right, I guess. Since he's asleep anyway."

"Good. I'll be there in an hour."

She headed back to her office to write up

an update for her commander. Halfway through, Slader stuck his head in the door.

"Got him wrapped, Lieutenant."

"The brother? You got a confession?"

"Junkie brother comes home, see, and the other guy's waiting for him. He's found out some stuff's missing from the apartment. His pricey wrist unit, some electronics, that kind of deal. Gonna confront his brother, kick him out. Brother comes in late, stoned to the eyeballs."

"You got the tox to substantiate?"

"Yeah. Vic had enough shit in him to fly all the way to Pluto and back. Looks like he pawned the shit he took from his brother to buy the stuff. Guy tells him to take a hike, and they get into it. Now our guy says the dead brother threw the first punch. Maybe yes, maybe no."

Slader shrugged. "But there're swings on both sides. Asshole brother takes a header down the stairs, snaps his neck. Other guy panics, tries to set it up like he'd been in bed and the dead brother just took a tumble. We can squeeze him maybe on Man Two, but the PA doesn't like it. Guy's willing to cop to Man Three. So that's how we're doing it."

"Good enough. Make sure the dead guy's

the one who pawned the merchandise. Check that before you sign off on the deal."

"Partner's doing that now. Checks out, we're clearing it. Stupid bastard—the live brother—could've saved himself a lot of time and trouble he'd just copped to the fight. People just like lying to cops."

Truer words, Eve mused as another thought occurred. Layers. Yeah, she might try peeling one.

In the garage, Mira studied the all-terrain. "This can't be your city issue."

"No. Roarke. Icy roads." Eve shrugged as she climbed in. "This thing would probably transverse the Arctic Circle, so he's satisfied I can navigate New York in it."

"Well, I feel better in it." Mira settled in. "I imagine there's so little he can control regarding your safety, he pushes on the things he can."

"Yeah, I get that."

"Dennis made noises about me staying home today." Mira adjusted the softly patterned scarf around her neck. "I ended up having to arrange for a driver to satisfy him. It's nice to have someone who'll worry."

"You think?" Eve glanced over as she reversed. "Maybe," she decided. "Maybe it is. But it's hard to know you're always worrying them."

"It used to annoy me."

"Really?"

"Charlie, he'd say, why do you take such chances, dealing with people who revel in that kind of darkness? If you're inside them, don't you see they can get inside you?" She smiled a little, stretching out her legs luxuriously in the warmth. "We went around that one, and variations on the theme, quite a bit when I took the position with the department."

"You had fights? You and Mr. Mira?"

"We're married, of course we had fights. Have them. He may seem easygoing, but he's got a mile-wide stubborn streak in him. I love it."

She brushed her hair back as she turned her head to look at Eve. "I imagine we've had a few bouts that could compete with the rounds you and Roarke have. But they bought the package, didn't they? Yours and mine, just as we bought theirs. So we find ways of dealing, of making it work. So you drive this big machine on a nasty day. Which, by the way, is a very sexy ride."

Eve had to grin. "It is, isn't it? So, how soon did the two of you bump heads?"

"Oh, God, we went at each other over buying our first sofa for our first apartment. You would have thought it was the most vital purchase we'd ever make. We ended up buying nothing for nearly a month because neither of us would give in. Then we settled on something completely different, opened a bottle of wine, and made very enthusiastic love on it."

"It's stress, right? Mostly stress and figuring each other out. People who haven't been hooked up long, they're starry-eyed, sure, and spend a lot of time boinking like bunnies, but they snipe at each other over little stuff. And you add major stress, and there ends up being some tension."

"Generally speaking. Specifically speaking about the Lombards, I'd be surprised if there haven't been some difficulties over the last several days. But often, most often, people tend to keep those private battles private."

"But they show, especially to a trained observer. And these two look smooth as glass. She's like the poster girl for wifely behavior. It just hits me wrong." She shifted in her seat. "I know I'm not much in the wifely department, but it makes me want to take another sniff at her. Going out for coffee and bagels, the morning after your mother-in-law's been bludgeoned to death? Come on."

"It's not unusual to do something basic, something everyday, to compensate for trauma."

"Well, how about tapping room service, then? Sure, it was an economy hotel, but it ran to room service."

"Devil's advocate," Mira said, holding up a hand. "She's not used to that sort of thing, more used to doing the food shopping and preparation. I agree, it would've been simpler and more sensible under the circumstances, but it's difficult to see that as suspicious behavior."

"It's more the ball of it. Of her. She does everything just so. Like she's got some checklist. Okay, turn on the tears. Now be brave, bite your lip, turn the guileless, supportive look on your husband. But don't forget your makeup and hair. There's a certain vanity in there that doesn't click with the rest of her."

"You don't like her."

"You know, I don't." Stopped at a light, Eve tapped her fingers on the wheel. Naked fingers, she realized. She'd forgotten her gloves back at Central. "And there's no reason not to like her, on the surface. So it's my gut telling me she's off. Something about her is off, that's all. And maybe I'm just full of shit, maybe I'm reaching. So your impression's going to weigh."

"But no pressure," Mira murmured.

"I'm telling her I'm bringing you along to counsel," Eve continued as she parked. "Just to offer a hand since she's had a couple of tough blows back-to-back."

"And she'll believe that?"

Eve smiled thinly. "She's not the only one who can put on a show. You want to be careful getting out. That sidewalk's going to be slick."

"It's nice," Mira said easily, "to have someone worry."

Vaguely embarrassed, Eve waited until the street was clear to climb out. Inside, she nodded toward security, then logged Mira in. "Any movement upstairs?" she asked the woman on duty.

"None reported."

"She order any food?" At the security woman's raised brow, Eve spoke casually. "Just want to make sure she's taking care of herself. Also, if my men have been hitting room service, I need to keep tabs for the budget."

"I can check on that for you."

"Thanks." She moved to the elevator, got on with Mira. "Just want to see how well she's taking care of herself," she said to answer Mira's unspoken question. "Be interesting to see what she's been eating."

She acknowledged her man on the door. "I want transportation for the witness to and from the hospital, but I want a delay. I don't want her leaving for thirty minutes after I do. Got that?"

"Yes, sir."

Eve knocked, waited. Zana opened the door with a quick, tremulous smile. "I'm so glad you're here. I just talked with Bobby's nurse, and she said he's awake, so . . . Oh." She stopped when she spotted Mira. "I'm sorry. Hello."

"Zana, this is Dr. Mira. She's a friend of mine."

"Oh, well, it's nice to meet you. Please come in. I can, uh, get some coffee?"

"That's all right, I'll take care of that in a minute. Dr. Mira's a counselor. I thought, under the circumstances, you might want to talk to someone. Maybe Bobby, too. Mira's the best," Eve added with a smile, laying a hand on Mira's shoulder to make it seem more friendly than official. "She's helped me a lot with . . . issues."

"I don't know what to say. Thanks so much for thinking of me, of us."

"You've been through some hard knocks. Survivors of violence don't always understand the full extent of the stress they're under. Talking to me, well, even though Bobby and I go back, you're still talking to a cop. But if you think it's out of line, then—"

"No, God. It's so thoughtful of you. I've just been wandering around here, most of the night. No one to talk to. I've never talked to a counselor before. I don't know where to start."

"Why don't we sit down?" Mira suggested. "Your husband's condition has improved?"

"Yes. They said he'll need to stay in the hospital another day, maybe two, then we can go to out-patient status. I don't really understand all the medical terms."

"I can help you with that, too."

"Look, I'll be in the kitchen. I'll get the coffee, get out of the way."

"I don't mind if you stay," Zana told Eve. "You know everything."

"I'll get the coffee anyway, give you a minute."

Eve moved across the room, into the narrow alcove. And gee, she thought, if she pushed the wrong buttons on an unfamiliar AC unit, who could argue?

She could hear Zana's voice, the thickness in it of suppressed tears. Oh, you're good, she decided. But I'm better.

She ran a quick scan, replaying orders over the last twenty-four hours.

Cheese, raspberries, popcorn—extra butter. Bet somebody watched vids last night, Eve thought. And a hearty breakfast this morning: Ham omelette, toast, coffee, and orange juice.

She programmed for coffee, then eased open the minifriggie. Bottle of red wine, she noted. Maybe two glasses left in it. Soft drinks. Frozen nondairy dessert, double chocolate—half gone.

Trauma and tragedy didn't seem to be affecting Zana's appetite.

When she came back with the coffee, Zana was mopping at her face with a tissue. "It's just one thing after the next," she told Mira. "I can't find my balance, I guess. We were coming here to have fun. Bobby wanted to treat me to a trip, to somewhere exciting I'd never been. Part of my Christmas present since his mama was so hot to come, you know. To talk to Eve, after all the years. And then, everything's been so awful."

She began to shred the tissue so pieces of it fell like snow into her lap. "Poor Bobby, he's been trying to be so strong, and now he's hurt. I just want to make it easier on him. Somehow."

"I'm sure you are, just by being there for him. Still, it's important that you look after yourself as well, and let yourself grieve for a woman you were close to. To go through that process, Zana. And to get rest, keep your health."

"I can't even think of myself right now. How can I?"

"I understand. It's human to put ourselves to one side at times of crisis. Especially for women to do so," Mira added and gave Zana's hand a pat. "Bobby will need you, emotionally and physically in the days and weeks to come. It's difficult—thank you, Eve—it's difficult to lose a parent, any family member. But to lose one through violent means adds another layer, even more stress and grief. You've both had a shock, several in fact. I hope when you're able to go back to Texas, you'll find someone there to talk to. I can certainly give you a list of recommendations for counselors in your area."

"I'd so appreciate that. I wouldn't even know where to start. I've never talked to a counselor before."

"You didn't go to grief counseling when your mother died?" Eve asked.

"Oh, no. I didn't even think about it. It's just not the kind of thing I was raised to think about, I guess. I just . . . I don't know, went on, I guess. But this is different, I can see that. And I want to do what's best for Bobby."

"Then you will."

"If I could have a minute, Zana. We're having trouble with the numbers you gave us. The ones your abductor made you memorize."

"I don't understand."

"We're not finding anything with those numbers. Actually, there are too many numbers. Do you think you could've gotten them mixed up, or added some?"

"Oh, I don't know." Her hands fluttered up from her lap. "I was so sure. I kept repeating them over and over, like he said to. I even said them in my head after . . . after he left. But I was so scared. What should we do? What can I do?"

"We could try hypnosis." Eve took a sip of coffee, met Mira's eyes over the cup. "That's another reason I brought Dr. Mira by today, so you could meet her, feel comfortable with her if we went this route. Dr. Mira often assists the department with this kind of thing."

"It could be helpful." Mira picked up the ball. "We could, under hypnosis, take you back to the abduction, take you through it, while making certain you feel safe and secure."

"Oh, I don't know. I just don't know. Hypnosis." She reached up, tangling her fingers in the trio of thin gold chains she wore around her neck. "I don't know. The idea scares me some. I need to think about it. It's hard right now to think of anything but Bobby."

"It would be a way to help us find whoever killed Bobby's mother." Eve pressed a little harder. "And knowing the person responsible has been identified, apprehended, and will pay for what was done helps the healing process. Dr. Mira?"

"Yes, that's very true. Why don't I send you some information so you can see how this is approached? Help you understand the process a little better."

"That'd be okay, I guess. But gosh, I don't know. Just the thought of going through that again, even in my mind. It really scares me. I'm not strong like you," she said to Eve. "I'm just ordinary."

"Ordinary people do extraordinary things, every day." But Mira smiled, rose. "I'll get you that information, Zana, and I'd be happy to talk with you again, if you think I can help."

"Thank you so very much. Thank you. Both of you." Zana got to her feet, held out both her hands to Eve. "It means a lot to know you're working so hard for us."

"I'll be in touch. I'll arrange for transportation to the hospital. Someone will call up when it's here. I'm going to try to get by to see Bobby, but if I don't make it, give him my best."

"I will."

Eve waited until they were on the elevator. "What's your take?"

"I don't know how helpful I'm going to be to you. Her actions and reactions are well within the expected range. Her responses plausible. I will say that—with your voice niggling in my ear—they were a bit too text-book. But the textbook was written simply because of these actions and reactions to trauma and violence."

"She balked at hypnosis."

"So do you," Mira pointed out. "It's often the first reaction to the suggestion."

"Me going under isn't going to help find a killer. If she'd agreed to it, I'd've lost a million-dollar bet with myself. She had popcorn last night."

"Comfort food."

"And a bottle of wine's in there, nearly empty."

"I'd be surprised if she hadn't had a few drinks."

"You're right," Eve said irritably. "You're not being helpful. She had herself a big, fat breakfast, and I'm betting she hit room service for a nice meal last night."

"Not everyone goes off food with stress. People often use food as comfort, often overeating, in fact, to compensate. It can swing either way, Eve. We both know what you've got is instinct, and no evidence. Not even circumstantial at this point."

"Shit. See if I give you a ride home next time."

Eve got off the elevator, headed straight for security. "Have you got those room service orders?"

"I do. Nothing from your men. Our guest ordered roast chicken with new potatoes and carrots. She also had a starter of crab salad, and ended with key lime pie. A bottle of merlot went with that, as well as a bottle of spring water."

"Good appetite," Eve commented.

"Yeah. Sounds like she's working to keep her strength up."

Eve heard the cynicism, appreciated it. "I'm going to want a record of any calls she made on the room 'link."

"I thought you would. Three outgoing.

One to the hospital last evening, two to the hospital this morning. No incoming."

"Okay. Thanks."

Eve strode out. "God*damn* if somebody lolls around drinking wine and eating pie when her husband's racked up in the hospital. Would you?"

"No. And neither would you. But eating pie isn't a crime, and I can't tell you it's out of the normal scope of reactions."

"How come she didn't contact Bobby's pal and partner to tell him Bobby was hurt?"

"She might very well have done so, on her personal 'link."

"Yeah, we'll check that. I'm betting she didn't. Didn't get in touch because she didn't want him heading out here, or keeping her tied up talking out the details, buzzing her back for updates. She wanted a little alone time with her fucking pie."

Mira laughed out loud before she could cough it away, and earned a scowl. "I'm sorry. I know it's not funny, it was just such an image. You want a profile, I'll give you one."

She got back in the car, strapped in. "The subject is a young, inexperienced woman, who appears used to—and amenable to—

being told what she should do. She looks to her husband to make decisions, while she deals with the more domestic areas. This is her comfort zone. She enjoys attention while having a tendency to be skittish and shy. She has an orderly, tidy, and, I would say, submissive nature."

"Or she's slipped that persona on like a skin-suit."

"Yes, or, if you're right, Eve, this is a very clever, very calculating woman. One who would be willing to subvert her own nature for a considerable length of time in order to reach her goal. She's been married to this man for several months, which brings them into a very intimate relationship every day. She knew and worked for him before that, was courted by him. Maintaining a pose contrary to her nature would be a very impressive feat."

"I'm prepared to be impressed. I'm not pushing aside other possibilities, other suspects," she added. "I'm just adding her in."

And keeping her at the top of my list, Eve thought.

18

Bobby was sitting up in bed when Eve stepped into his room. His eyes were closed, and the entertainment unit was set, she assumed, for a book on disc. In any case, there were voices spilling out of it in what seemed to be an intense and passionate argument.

If he was sleeping, he didn't need to hear it. If he wasn't, she needed his attention. So she stepped closer to the unit. "Pause program," she ordered.

In the sudden silence Bobby stirred, opened his eyes.

"Zana? Oh, Eve. I must've nodded off. Sort of listening to a book. Crappy book," he added with an attempt at a smile. "The nurse told me Zana was coming in soon."

"I just left her a little while ago. I'm having

a couple of uniforms drive her to and from. It's nasty outside."

"Yeah." He looked out the window, his expression brooding.

"So. How're you feeling?"

"I don't know. Clumsy, stupid, annoyed to be here. Sorry for myself."

"You're entitled."

"Yeah, that's what myself's telling me. The flowers, the tree. It's nice."

He gestured toward the little fake pine decorated with miniature Santas. To Eve's mind, it looked like the jolly old elf had been hanged, multiple times, in effigy.

"Zana told me you helped pick them out."

"Not really. I was just there."

"She thinks of stuff like that. Little things like that. This is a really, really shitty Christmas for her."

"For you, too. It sucks out loud, Bobby, and I'm going to add to it by asking you if you've thought of anything else, remembered anything. About what happened to your mother, about what happened to you."

"Nothing. Sorry. And I've had a lot of time to think, lying here like an idiot who can't cross the damn street." He let out a sigh, lifted the hand of his good arm, then let it fall. "A lot of time to think, about what you said, about what you said my mother did. Wanted to do. She really asked for money?"

Eve moved closer to the bed so she could stand at its side and watch his face. "How much shit can you take?"

He closed his eyes briefly. When he opened them again, she hoped what she saw in them was strength. "I might as well get it all dumped on me. I've got nothing better to do."

"Your mother had several numbered accounts, which were fed by funds she extorted from women she'd fostered as children."

"Oh, God. Oh, my God. There has to be a mistake, some kind of mix-up, misunderstanding."

"I have statements from two of these women that verify that your mother contacted them, threatened to expose their juvenile records unless they paid the amounts she demanded."

She watched the blows land on his already battered face, until he was staring at her, not with disbelief or shock, but with the focused concentration of a man fighting pain.

"Statements," he repeated. "Two of them."

"There're going to be more, Bobby, when it's done. She also informed my husband that she had copies of my files and would sell them to interested media sources unless he paid her. She's been blackmailing former charges for a number of years."

"They were just kids," he said under his breath. "We were all just kids."

"It's possible she used one of her former fosters to aid her in her attempt to blackmail me, through Roarke, and was killed by this individual."

"I would never have let her do without. Whenever she wanted something I did what I could to get it for her. Why would she do this? I know what you're thinking," he said, and looked beyond her, toward the window again. "I understand what you're thinking. You think she used and mistreated you when you were in her care, when you were a kid. So why not use and mistreat you now?"

"Am I wrong, Bobby? Is something wrong with my memory?"

His breath shuddered out softly. "No. She used to say, used to tell me that you—the kids she took in—were lucky to have someone offer them a decent home. Care enough to take them, to teach them manners and discipline and respect. That's what she said it was when she locked you up. Conse- quences for unacceptable behavior. Things would be a lot worse if you were on the streets."

"Did you buy that, Bobby?"

"I don't know. Maybe some. She never hurt me." He turned his head now, met Eve's eyes. "She never treated me that way. She said it was because I did what I was told. But I didn't, not always. If she caught me, she'd usually laugh and say, 'Boys will be boys.' It was the girls she . . . I don't know why. Something inside her. She hated her mother. Used to tell me we were lucky to be rid of the old bitch. Maybe—I don't know—maybe her mother did those things to her. It's a cycle, right? Isn't that what they say about abuse? It's a cycle."

"Yeah, it often is." Maybe that comforted him, she thought. "What about you, Bobby? Did you cycle around, take care of your mother? She must've been a hardship on you. New wife, new business, and here's this demanding woman, prying into your life. A demanding woman with a big pile of money stashed away."

His eyes filmed over for a moment. Tears he blinked away. "I don't blame you for saying it, thinking it. And you can put on record that I'll take a Truth Test. I'll take one voluntarily, as soon as you can arrange it. I want you to find who hurt her."

He took a long breath. "I loved my mother, Eve. I don't know if you can understand, but even knowing what she was, what she did, I loved her. If I'd known what she was doing, I'd have found a way to make it stop. To make her give the money back, and stop. That's what I want to do. Give the money back. You have to help me get the money back to the people she took it from. Maybe it won't make it right, but I don't know what else to do."

"Yeah, I can help you with that. How would you have made her stop, Bobby?"

"I don't know. She'd listen to me. If she knew I was really upset, she'd listen to me." Now he sighed a little. "Or pretend to. I don't know anymore. I don't know how to tell Zana all this. I don't know how to tell her this is true. She's already been through so much."

"She was tight with your mother."

"They got along. Zana gets along with everyone. She made a real effort with my mother—it takes one." He tried another smile.

"You know, women get tight in a certain way. When they do, they tend to tell each other things they might not tell a man. Could it be your mother told Zana about what she was doing?"

"Not possible." He tried to sit up straighter, as if to emphasize his point, and cursed the restriction of his broken arm. "Zana's . . . she's scrupulous. I don't know anyone as intrinsically honest. She might not have argued with my mother about it, but she'd have been horrified, and she'd have told me. We don't have secrets."

People said that, Eve knew. But how did they know the other party didn't have secrets? How did they know there'd been full disclosure?

"Zana the type to keep her word?"

His face was full of love. "Probably cut off a finger before she'd break it."

"Then she'd be in a tough spot if she'd given your mother her word not to tell you, or anyone."

He opened his mouth, closed it, and Eve could see him wrestling with this new possibility. "I don't know how she'd have dealt with it. But she'd have told me, at least after my mother was killed. She'd never have kept that to herself. I wonder where she is." His fingers began to tug at the sheet. "I thought she'd be here by now."

"I'll check in a minute, make sure she's on her way. They say when they're springing you?"

"Not before tomorrow, but I'm pushing for that. I want to salvage something of Christmas. It's our first, probably told you that. At least I bought a couple of things here, so Zana will have something to open. Man, this—how did you put it? Oh, yeah, this sucks out loud."

Reaching into the pocket of her coat, Eve brought out a little bag. "Thought you might like these. Cookies," she said as she put the bag in his good hand. "I figure they might not run to Christmas cookies around here."

"Appreciate it." He peeked inside, nearly smiled again. "Really. The food's fairly crappy around here."

He'd brought her food once, and now

she'd returned the favor. She thought that made them even, or wanted to think it.

Eve checked with her uniforms, assured Bobby his wife would be there shortly.

Then she let it all shuffle around in her mind during the long, ugly drive uptown.

Her pocket 'link signalled, causing her to fumble a moment as she interfaced it with the unfamiliar system on the all-terrain so her hands stayed free to fight the fight. "Dallas, and this better be good because I'm stuck in lousy traffic."

"I'm not!" Peabody's voice shot out thrills and excitement completely in contrast with the icy rain. On the dash screen, her face glowed like a damn candle. "I'm in Scotland, and it's snowing. It's snowing in big, fat, mag flakes."

"Yippee."

"Aw, don't be that way. I just had to tell you we're here, and it's so beyond frosty. The McNabs have this amazing house, kinda like a really big cottage, and there's a river and mountains. McNab's dad has a burr."

"Well, why doesn't he pull it out?"

"No, no, the accent. It's total. And they

like me, Dallas. I mean, they just slathered, like, all over me."

"Again, I repeat: Yippee."

"I don't know why I was so nervous and freaky. It's just piles of fun on top of more. The shuttle ride was so uptown, and then, wow, the scenery is so completely mag. It's like a vid or something, and—"

"Peabody, I'm glad you're having a good time. Seriously. But I'm trying to get home here, so I can grab a little Christmas cheer myself."

"Sorry, sorry. Wait, first, did you get the presents I left on your desk?"

"Yeah, thanks."

"Oh." Peabody's face went through several expressions, ending on a pout. "You're welcome."

"We didn't open them yet."

"Oh! Oh, okay." The pout turned into a nervous grin. "You want to wait until tomorrow. I just wondered. So, well . . . Anything I should know on the case?"

"Nothing that can't wait until you get back. Go eat some—what is it—haggis."

"I might. I've already had a really big whiskey, and it's dancing in my head. But I don't care! It's Christmas. And last year you and I were mad at each other, and now we're not. I love you, Dallas, and Roarke, and every bony inch of McNab. And his cousin Sheila. Merry Christmas, Dallas."

"Yeah, you bet." She cut off before Peabody could get started again. But she was smiling as she rolled through the gates toward home.

The house was lit as if it were night, and an icy mist rolled over the ground, sparkled just a little in the lights. She could see trees shimmering, candles glowing, and heard the patter of that cold, hard rain on the roof of her vehicle.

She stopped, just stopped in the middle of the drive. Just to look, and to think, and remember. Inside was warmth, fires burning with the crackle of real wood. Everything in her life had somehow navigated her here. Whatever the horrors had been, the pain and blood, whatever dogged her dreams like a hound, had brought her here. She believed that.

She had this because she'd survived the other. She had this because he'd been waiting on the other side of the road. Navigating his own trenches.

She had home, where the candles were lit

and the fires were burning. It was good, she thought, to take a moment to remember that, and to know, whatever else she faced, this was here.

And if she couldn't just enjoy it for twenty-four hours, what was the point?

She dashed into the house, shook rain from her hair. For once, Summerset wasn't lurking in the foyer, but even as she tugged off her coat, Roarke strolled out of the parlor.

"And there you are."

"Later than I thought, sorry."

"I only got in a few minutes ago myself. Summerset and I are having a drink by the fire. Come, sit down."

"Oh, well." Summerset. They'd have to be civil to each other. It was like a holiday law. "I have to take care of something first." She concealed a small bag behind her back. "Need a few minutes."

"Secrets." He wandered over to kiss her. And to peek over her shoulder. She shifted, poked a finger in his belly.

"Cut it out. I'll be down in a minute."

He watched her go up, then walked back into the parlor to sit by the fire with Summerset and enjoy his Irish coffee. "She's smuggling in some last-minute gift."

"Ah. I'll garage the vehicle she no doubt left out in this weather, in a moment."

"Of course. And as much as I believe the two of you enjoy your mutual sniping, we might try a moratorium on that until Boxing Day."

Summerset lifted a shoulder. "You look relaxed."

"And so I am."

"There was a time, not that long ago, when you'd have been out hounding some deal right up until the last moment. At which time, you'd have been off with the woman of the moment. Christmas in Saint Moritz or Fiji. Wherever your whim took you. But not here."

"No, not here." Roarke picked up one of the little frosted cookies Summerset had arranged on a glossy red dish. "Because, I realize now, here would have made it impossible for me not to understand I was alone. Lonely. Despite all the women, the deals, the people, the parties, what have you. I was alone because there was no one who mattered enough to keep me here."

He sipped his coffee, watched the flames.

"You gave me my life. You did," he insisted when Summerset made a protesting sound. "And I worked—in my fashion—to build this place. I asked you to tend it for me. You've never let me down. But I needed her. The one thing, the only thing that could make this place home."

"She's not what I'd have chosen for you."

"Oh." With a half-laugh, Roarke bit into the cookie. "That I know."

"But she's right for you. The one for you." His smile was slow. "Despite, or maybe due to, her many flaws."

"I imagine she thinks somewhat the same about you."

When he heard her coming, Roarke glanced back. She'd taken off her weapon, changed her boots for skids. She took a package to the tree, placed it there with the others.

He saw the expression on her face as she scanned the piles he'd stacked. Consternation, bafflement, and a kind of resignation that amused him.

"Why do you do this?" She demanded with a wave at the gifts.

"It's a sickness."

"I'll say."

"We're having Irish in our coffee."

"If that means whiskey, I'll pass. I don't know why you want to muck up perfectly good coffee that way."

"Just another sickness. I'll pour you some wine."

"I'll get it myself. Peabody tagged me on the way home. She's not only safe and sound in Scotland, she was half-piss-faced and insane with delight. She loves you, by the way, and me, and McNab's bony ass— and even his cousin Sheila." She gave Summerset a small smile. "She didn't mention you, but I'm sure it was an oversight."

She sat down, stretched out her legs. "That's one present that hit the mark, big time. You clear everything you needed to clear?"

"I did," Roarke told her. "You?"

"No, but screw it. I tried to get the lab and got a recording of 'Jingle Bell Rock.' Why don't songs like that ever die? Now it's stuck in my head."

The cat deserted Summerset to jump into her lap, complain loudly, and knead his claws into her thighs.

"He's trying you." Roarke gestured with his cup. "He wants the cookies, and got nowhere with me or Summerset in that area."

"Well, you can forget it, Fatso." She lifted him, went nose-to-nose. "But I've got something for you." She dumped him, then went to the tree, pawed around, and came up with a gift bag.

She dug out a pair of feline-sized antlers, and a toy mouse.

"He's much too dignified to wear those, or bat about some ridiculous toy," Summerset protested.

Eve just snorted.

"Catnip." She held the mouse up by the tail in front of Galahad's face. "Yeah, that's right," she said as Galahad reared up on his hind legs and grabbed the mouse with his front claws. "Zeus for cats."

"And you, a duly designated officer of the law," Roarke said, "dealing."

"I've got my sources." While the cat rolled deliriously with his new toy, Eve stuck the antlers in place. "Okay, you look really stupid, so this is only for tonight. We humans have to get our kicks somewhere."

"Is he trying to eat it," Roarke wondered, "or make love to it?"

"I don't want to think that hard about it.

But he's not thinking about cookies anymore."

She sat again, propped her feet on Roarke's lap. And when Roarke ran an absent hand up her calf, Summerset took it as his cue.

"I've prepared something simple for dinner, assuming you'd enjoy having it in here. I'm having mine with some friends in the city."

"You have friends?" nearly popped out of Eve's mouth, but Roarke squeezed her ankle in anticipation.

"Everything is in the kitchen unit."

"Enjoy your evening, then."

"I will, and you, too."

Another ankle squeeze had Eve wincing. "Um, yeah. Merry."

When they were alone, she shoved at Roarke's arm. "Take it easy, will you? I was going to say something."

"I know very well what you were going to say. We're having peace on our particular square of Earth until Boxing Day."

"Fine, I can do it if he can. Besides, I plan to get really drunk."

"Why don't I help you out with that?" He rose, and poured her more wine.

"What about you?"

"I'll have some, but I think one of us has to keep his wits. That cat is stoned," he commented, glancing down at the floor where Galahad rubbed himself lasciviously over the mouse.

"Well, seeing as he's fixed, he can't ever have sex. I just figured he should have a little thrill for the holiday. I'm counting on getting some thrills myself."

Roarke lifted a brow. "I can help you with that, too."

"Maybe I was talking about cookies."

He dropped onto the couch, full-length beside her. And fastened his mouth on hers.

"Not drunk yet," she murmured.

"Not done yet, either."

"You gotta close those doors if you're going to start fooling around. He may be going out, but the spirit of Summerset haunts these halls."

"I'm simply kissing my wife." He propped them both up, long- ways, so that they could watch the fire, sip wine. And neck.

"Nice." She took a breath, breathed him, and let every cell in her body relax. "I may not leave this room, hell, this couch, until after Christmas."

"We'll have to take turns getting provisions. Feeding ourselves and the fire."

"Okay. You first."

He laughed, brushed his lips over her hair. "You smell delicious." He sniffed down to her neck. "You've put something on."

"I can take a minute now and then."

"And it's appreciated."

"Did you get in touch with your people in Ireland?"

"I did, yes. It appeared to be a madhouse of baking and babies, which suits them very well. They wish you a happy Christmas."

"You're okay, not being over there?"

"I'm exactly where I want to be." He turned her face up to his, met her lips. "Exactly. And you need more wine."

"Already got a buzz going."

"Likely because you didn't have lunch."

"Oh, yeah, I knew I forgot something." She took the wine he poured. "After I get plowed, and make love to every square inch of you, I'll eat a ton."

Since he was up, he went over, closed the parlor doors.

From the sofa, Eve grinned. "Come over here, and start unwrapping me."

Amused, aroused, he sat at her feet.

"Why don't I start down here?" he suggested, and slipped off her shoes. Then he pressed his thumbs to her arch, made her purr.

"Good spot." She closed her eyes, drank a little more wine. "Tell you what, later, you can get plowed and I'll do you."

"Someone has the Christmas spirit." He kissed a bracelet around her ankles.

"You can't avoid it, it's winging around out there left and right." Lovely little sensations shimmered up her legs. "You can dodge, but eventually it beans you."

She opened one eye when he unhooked her trousers. "Quick work."

"Want slow?"

"Hell, no." She grinned, reared up and grabbed him, spilling wine on both of them. "Uh-oh."

"Now look what you've done. We'll have to get out of these clothes. Hands up," he said, and tugged her sweater over her head. "Here." He handed her back her wine, put both her hands on the bowl of the glass. "Mind that now."

"Prolly had enough."

"I haven't."

He stripped her, then himself. He took the

glass from her, upending it so drops scattered over her breasts, her torso.

She looked down, looked up. "Uh-oh," she said again and laughed.

He licked wine and flesh, letting the combination go to his head while she moved and moaned under him. She arched up, a trembling bridge, when his hands roamed over her.

Then she locked around him, arms, legs. And rolled hard. She plopped on top of him, giggling. "Ouch."

"Easy for you to say." She'd stolen his breath in more ways than one. To pay her back he rolled her over. With lips and fingers he tickled her into shrieks, aroused her into gasps.

She was riding on foolishness and passion, a giddy combination with the wine flowing through her. When he was inside her, still laughing breathlessly, she chained her arms around his neck.

"Merry Christmas," she managed. "Oh, God." She came on a gasping laugh, then dragged him with her.

"Merry Christmas," he said and shot her over, one last time.

She lay, all but cross-eyed, staring up at

the tree. "Jesus, talk about putting a bow on it."

Later, at his insistence, she opened her first gift. So she'd be comfortable, he'd said. It was hard to be otherwise in the long cashmere robe of forest green.

They ate by the fire, washing down Summerset's *simple* lobster with champagne. When he asked about the case, she shook her head. She wouldn't bring it into this. She was—they were—entitled to one night where blood and death stayed locked outside their world. A world where they sat like children, cross-legged under a tree, ripping at colored paper.

"The Universe According to Roarke?" He read the label on a cased disc.

"Feeney helped me put it together. Okay, Feeney mostly put it together, but I came up with the concept. It'll go for holo or comp."

She reached up for another cookie. She was making herself half-sick with sugar, but what was Christmas for? "Personalized game, and what you do is start out at the bottom. Pretty much wits only. Then you can earn money, arms, land. Build stuff, fight wars. You can pull in other people—we're all in there. And take on famous foes and stuff.

You can cheat, steal, barter, and bloody. But there are a lot of traps, so you can end up broke, destitute, in a cage or tortured by your enemies. Or you can end up ruling the known universe. The graphics are very chilly."

"You're in here?"

"Yeah."

"How can I lose?"

"It's tough. Feeney's had it up and running for a couple weeks and said he couldn't get by level twelve. It's pissing him off. Anyway, I figured since you don't get to steal in real life anymore, you'd get a kick out of virtual."

"The best present is having a woman who knows me." He leaned over to kiss her, tasted wine and sugar cookies. "Thanks. Your turn."

"I've already opened a million." Which, she thought, ran the gamut from the sparkly to the silly, the sumptuous to the sexy.

"Nearly done. This one."

She tugged the ribbon from the box he gave her, and though he winced, draped it around his neck. Inside was a magnifying glass with a silver handle.

"It's old," he told her. "I thought, 'What's a detective without a magnifying glass?'"

"It's great." She held up her hand, studied it through the glass, then grinning, shifted closer to Roarke, peered at him through it. "Jeez. You're even prettier." Then she turned it on the snoring cat. "You're not. Thanks."

When he tapped a finger to his lips, she pretended to sigh before she leaned over to kiss him.

"Here, do this one, it sort of fits." She pushed a box at him while she played with the glass. "If I'd had one of these when I was a kid, I'd've driven people crazy."

"Rather the point of toys and tools." He glanced up, found himself being inspected again. He tossed a bow at her. "Here, see what you make of that."

He opened the box, gently took out the pocket watch inside. "Eve, this is wonderful."

"It's old, too. I know how you rev on old stuff. And I figured you could put it on a shelf somewhere with all the other old stuff. It was already engraved," she added when he opened it. "But I thought . . ."

" 'Time stops.' " He said it quietly, then just looked at her with those stunning blue eyes.

"I thought, yeah, it does." She reached for his hand. "It does."

He gathered her in, pressing his lips to her throat, her cheek, just holding on. "It's a treasure. So are you."

"This is good," she murmured. Not the things, she thought, and knew he understood. But the sharing of them. The being. "I love you. I'm really getting the hang of it."

He laughed, kissed her again, then drew away. "You've one more."

It had to be more jewelry, she noted from the size of the box. The man just loved draping her in sparkles. Her first thought when she opened the box was that they not only sparkled, they could blind you like the sun.

The earrings were diamond drops—three perfect round stones in graduated sizes that dripped from a cluster of more diamonds that formed the petals of a brilliant flower.

"Wowzer," she said. When he only smiled, it hit her. "Big Jack's diamonds, from the Forty-seventh Street heist. The ones we recovered."

"After they'd stayed hidden away nearly half a century."

"These were impounded."

"I didn't steal them." He laughed, held up his game disc. "Remember? Only virtually these days. I negotiated, and acquired them through completely legal means. They deserve the light. They deserve you. Without you, they might still be shut up in a child's toy. Without you, Lieutenant, Chad Dix wouldn't be celebrating Christmas right now."

"You had them made for me." That touched her, most of all. She picked up the magnifying glass. "Let's check them out," she said, and pretended to inspect the gems. "Nice job."

"You can think of them as medals."

"A lot jazzier than any medals the department hands out." She put them on, knowing it would please him. Seeing the way it did.

"They suit you."

"Glitters like these would work on anybody." But she wrapped her arms around him, snuggled in. "Knowing where they came from, why you had them made for me, that means a lot. I—"

She jerked back, eyes wide. "You bought them all, didn't you?"

He cocked his head. "Well, aren't you greedy."

"No, but you are. You bought them all. I *know* it."

He smoothed a finger down the dent in her chin. "I think we need more champagne. You're entirely too sober."

She started to speak again, then buttoned it. The man was entitled to spend his money as he liked. And he was right about one thing. Big Jack's diamonds deserved better than a departmental vault.

"There's one more under there," he noticed as he started to rise. "The one you brought in today."

"Oh. Right." Part of her had hoped he'd forget that one. "Yeah, well, it's nothing much. No big."

"I'm greedy, remember? Hand it over."

"Okay, sure." She stretched out for it, dumped it in his lap. "I'll get the champagne."

He grabbed her arm before she could get up. "Just hold on a minute, until I see what I have here." He shoved aside tissue paper, drew it out, and said only, "Oh."

She struggled not to squirm. "You said you wanted a picture, you know, like from before."

"Oh," he repeated, and the expression on

his face had color rising up her neck. "Look at you." His eyes moved from image to woman, so full of pleasure, of surprise, of love, her throat went tight.

"I just dug it out, and picked up a frame."

"When was it taken?"

"Right after I went into the Academy. This girl I hung with a little, she was always taking pictures. I was trying to study, and she—"

"Your hair."

She shifted, a little uncomfortable. In the picture she was sitting at a desk, discs piled around her. She wore a dull gray Police Academy sweatshirt. Her hair was long, pulled back in a tail.

"Yeah, I used to wear it long back then. Figured it was less trouble because I could just tie it back out of my way. Then in hand-to-hand training, my opponent grabbed it, yanked, and took me down. I lopped it off."

"Look at your eyes. Cop's eyes even then. Hardly more than a child, and you knew."

"I knew if she didn't get that camera out of my face so I could study, I was going to clock her."

He laughed, took her hand, but remained

riveted on the photograph. "What happened to her?"

"She washed out, made it about a month. She was okay. She just wasn't—"

"A cop," he finished. "Thank you for this. It's so exactly what I wanted."

She leaned her head on his shoulder, let the lights of the tree dazzle her and thought, *Who needs champagne?*

19

She woke, thought she woke, in the brilliantly lit room with the glass wall. She was wearing her diamonds, and the cashmere robe. There was a towering pine in the corner, rising up to the ceiling. The ornaments draping its arching boughs, she saw, were corpses. Hundreds of bodies hung, covered with blood red as Christmas.

All the women, only women, were gathered around it.

"Not very celebratory," Maxie, the lawyer, said, and gave Eve a little elbow poke. "But you've got to make do, right? How many of those are yours?"

She didn't need the magnifying glass weighing down her pocket to identify the faces, the bodies, the dead. "All of them."

"That's a little greedy, don't you think?"

Maxie turned, nodded toward the body splayed in the center of the room. "She hasn't been put up yet."

"No, she can't go up yet. She isn't finished."

"Looks done to me. But here." She tossed Eve a white sock weighed with credits. "Go ahead."

"That's not the answer."

"Maybe you just haven't asked the right question."

She found herself in the glass room with the children. The child she'd been sat on the floor and looked up at her with tired eyes.

"I don't have any presents. I don't care."

"You can have this." Eve crouched down, held out her badge. "You'll need it."

"She has all the presents."

Eve looked through the glass and saw that gifts were piled now around the body. "Lot of good they'll do her now."

"It's one of us, you know."

Eve glanced back, studied the room full of little girls. Then looked into her own eyes. "Yes, I know."

"What will you do?"

"Take the one who did it away. That's

what happens when you kill someone. You have to pay. There has to be payment."

The girl she'd been held up her hands, and they were smeared with blood. "Am I going, too?"

"No." And she felt it, even in the dream she knew was a dream, she felt the ache in her belly. "No," she said again, "it's different for you."

"But I can't get out."

"You will one day." She looked back through the glass, frowned. "Weren't there more presents a minute ago?"

"People steal." The child hooked the bloodied badge on her shirt. "People are just no damn good."

Eve woke with a hard jolt, the dream already fading. It was weird, she thought, to have dreams where you talked to yourself.

And the tree. She remembered the tree with the bodies draped like morbid tinsel. To comfort herself she turned, studied the tree in the window. She ran a hand over the sheet beside her, found it cool.

It didn't surprise her that Roarke was up before her, or that he'd been up long enough for the sheets to lose his warmth.

But it did give her a shock to see that it was nearly eleven in the morning.

She started to roll out of her own side, and saw the blinking memo cube on the nightstand. She switched in on, heard his voice.

"Morning, darling Eve. I'm in the game room. Come play with me."

It made her smile. "Such a sap," she murmured.

She showered, dressed, grabbed coffee, then headed down. Proving, she decided, she was a sap, too.

He had the main screen engaged, and it gave her yet another jolt to see herself up there, in a pitched and bloody battle. Why she was wielding a sword instead of a blaster, she couldn't say.

He fought back-to-back with her, as he had, she remembered, in reality. And there was Peabody, wounded, but still game. But what the hell was her partner wearing?

More important, what was *she* wearing. It looked like some soft of leather deal more suited for S and M than swordplay.

Iced, she decided, when she lopped off her opponent's head. Moments later,

Roarke dispatched his, and the comp announced he'd reached Level Eight.

"I'm good," she announced and crossed to him.

"You are. And so am I."

She nodded at the paused screen. "What's up with the outfits?"

"Feeney added costume options. I've had an entertaining hour fiddling with wardrobe as well as taking over most of Europe and North America. How'd you sleep?"

"Okay. Weird dream again. I can probably blame it on champagne, and the chocolate soufflé I pigged out on at two in the morning."

"Why don't you stretch out here with me? This game's programmed for multiple players. You can try to invade my territories."

"Maybe later." She ran an absent hand over his hair. "I've got this dream on my brain. Sometimes they're supposed to mean stuff, right? There's something in there. I'm not asking the right question," she murmured. "What's the right question?"

Playtime, he decided, was over for now.

"Why don't we have a little brunch? You can talk it through."

"No, go ahead and play the game. I'm good with coffee."

"I slept in myself, didn't get up until about nine."

"Has anyone looked outside, checked to see if the world is still spinning on its axis?"

"At which time," he continued dryly, "I had a workout—I had soufflé, too. Then, before I came down here to enjoy one of my gifts, I worked about an hour in my office."

She studied him over the rim of her cup. "You worked."

"I did."

"On Christmas morning."

"Guilty."

She lowered the cup, grinned hugely. "We're really sick people, aren't we?"

"I prefer thinking we're very healthy individuals who know what suits us best." He rose, lithe as a cat in black jeans and sweater. "And what would suit us, I believe, is something light, up in the solarium where we can lord it over the city while you talk through your latest weird dream."

"You know what I said last night?"

"Drunk or sober?"

"Either. I said I loved you. Still do."

They had fresh fruit at the top of the

house, looking through the glass at a sky that decided to give New York a break and coast over it bright and blue.

She didn't argue with his notion that as it was Christmas they should have mimosas.

"You gave her—you, that is—your badge."

"I don't know why exactly. Mira'd probably have interpretations and all that shrink stuff. I guess it was what I wanted most. Or would, eventually, want most."

"The tree ornaments are easy enough."

"Yeah, even I can get that. They're dead, so they're mine. But Trudy wasn't up there."

"Because you haven't finished with her. You can't put her up with the others—I won't say 'aside' because you never put them aside. You won't put her up until you've closed the case."

"This lawyer keeps showing up. She's not in it. I know she's not, but she's the one I talked to. Both times."

"She's the one you understand best, I'd say. She was up-front with you on her feelings toward Trudy, didn't quibble about them. And she fought back, eventually."

He offered her a raspberry. "She stood up, as you would."

"One of us. I knew it, or the kid did."

"A cop even then, in some part of you."

"She also knew people mostly aren't any damn good." She said it lightly, tried another raspberry. Then sat up straight. "Wait a minute, wait a minute. The presents. Let me think."

She pushed out of the chair, roamed the solarium with its potted trees, musical fountain.

"Presents and greed and Christmas and shopping. She bought stuff. I know Trudy bought stuff before she hit on either of us. I went through her credits and debits. She went on a fast, hard spree."

"And?"

"Bags in her room, shopping bags. I've got the stuff in inventory, but I never checked all the contents, one by one, with the accounts. She didn't buy anything like, you know, diamonds. Clothes, some perfume, shoes. She wasn't killed for new shoes, so I didn't go through it all, do a checklist. Just a quick skim. Some of it wasn't there, but she had some shipped from stores. I checked that. But I didn't go through it all, every piece."

"Why would you?"

"Greed, envy, coveting. Women are all the time, 'Oooh, I love your outfit, your shoes, those earrings.' Whatever." She circled a hand in the air when he laughed. "They went shopping together, the three of them, when they got in. Zana knew what she bought. Some of the stuff got shipped. Why would we bother to make sure some damn shirt made it to Texas? Gives her open season, doesn't it?"

She whirled back. "She's vain, under it. Always puts herself together. I bet Trudy bought some nice things for herself, and they're close enough to the same size. Who's going to know if her killer helped herself to a couple of things she liked best? Bobby's not going to notice. Men don't. Present company excepted."

"And you get that from dreaming about a corpse surrounded by presents."

"I get that because I'm groping. And I don't know, maybe my subconscious is working something out. The thing is, it fits with my sense of her, of Zana. Opportunistic. If she took something, if I can prove she had something from the room . . . it's still wild circumstantial evidence any PD in his first week could blow holes in, but it's something to needle her with."

She sat again. "She was one of us," Eve continued. "And we didn't get the good stuff. Handouts, hand-me-downs. Crumbs from the table when everyone else is having a big, fat slab of cake."

"Baby."

"I don't care about that." She rubbed her hand over his shoulder. "Never really did. But I'm betting she does, and did. Opportunity." She closed her eyes, sipped the mimosa without thinking. "Here in New York—big, bad city where anything can happen to anybody. Mark's running a scam that just makes it easier. It's like she's putting herself on a platter. Weapon's right there, easily used, easily disposed of. Gotta go out the window, but that's no trouble. Room next-door is empty. She had to wash up somewhere, and it wasn't in her own room or Trudy's. Had to be there, in the empty room."

She pushed up again. "Shit, shit. She stowed the weapon there, her bloody clothes, the towels. It's perfect—opportunity again. Stow the stuff, go back to your own room clean, where Bobby's sleeping.

He'd never know the difference. And who's right on the spot the next morning, knocking on a dead woman's door?"

"Then you walk in."

"Yeah, she's not expecting that, but she adjusts. She's quick and she's smart. Patient, too. Ducks out the next morning, gets the stuff from the empty room. She could've ditched it anywhere, any recycler from the hotel to the bar where she staged the abduction, left her purse to add a flourish. Gone now. Son of a bitch. We didn't canvass that far, not for the weapon or bloody clothes."

"Keep going," he said when she paused. "I'm fascinated."

"It's speculation, that's all it is. But it feels right." For the first time since the beginning, it felt exactly right. "Now she has the cops out looking for some guy, and chasing down an account that doesn't exist. Gives her time. Now she's a victim. She's got Trudy's discs. The case files, and the record Trudy made of her injuries."

Yes, she could see it, Eve thought. Gather stuff up, take what you need, what you want, don't leave any trace of yourself behind.

"Does she keep the discs? Hard to toss away that kind of opportunity for a future date. You could try the squeeze down the road."

"She didn't squeeze now, when it's ripe for it," Roarke pointed out. "Anonymous delivery of a copy of the recording—if it exists—an account number and instructions."

"It's too ripe. Yeah, too hot. Why push her luck? She needs time to think that angle through. Is it worth taking on a cop and a guy with your resources? Maybe not. Maybe later. But if she's smart, and she is, she checks, sees if we're alibied tight for the times in questions. And we were. Could've hired somebody to do it, back to that, but she's going to think if that's going to fly. If we're going to pay big piles of money over it or tough it out. More, go after her with a vengeance."

She paused. "Waiting's smarter. Isn't that what you'd do? It's what I'd do."

"I'd have destroyed the camera and the discs. Anything that tied me to that room. If it could be tracked to me, I'm in a cage." Roarke poured coffee for both of them. "Not worth it, especially not when I'm going to rake in whatever Trudy's socked away."

"There's that. Of course, you'd get it all if Bobby's gone. More important, if he has an accident, fatal or otherwise, the cops're going to investigate, looking for that invisible man again. Meanwhile, you play it like it was an accident altogether. Gee, it had to be an accident, and it's all my fault for making him go shopping. I spilled my coffee. Boo-hoo."

He had to laugh. "You really dislike her."

"From the get. Just one of those itches between the shoulder blades." She moved them now as if to relieve it. "Now you've got Bobby in the hospital, and everyone—including him—is all there. So you're center, just where you deserve to be. Taken a backseat to that bitch long enough, haven't you?"

She looked back at him. Jeans and a sweater today, she thought. Day off, easy does it. Well, hell. "Listen, I'm going to ask, and it's crappy to ask, but I'm going to. The record from the tail. I'll be lucky to get them on it tomorrow. If I could just hear it clean, individual voices, tones, separate the sounds."

"Computer lab."

"Look, I'll make it up to you."

"How? And be specific."

"I'll play that game with you. Holo-mode."

"There's a start."

"I'll wear the getup."

"Really?" He expanded the word, lascivi-ously. "And to the victor will go the spoils?"

"Which would be me."

"It's medieval at the moment. You'll have to call me Sir Roarke."

"Oh, step back."

He laughed. "That may be going too far. We'll see how it goes." He pushed to his feet. "Where's the disc?"

"I'll get it. I'll start on the shopping spree. Thanks. Really."

He handed her the coffee so she could take it with her. "How else would we spend our Christmas afternoon?"

She went to work, happy, she realized, to be back at it. With a hot pot of coffee and reams of data. Whatever she found, or didn't, this angle was going to mean inter-viewing sales clerks. Which meant the hor-ror of going into retail establishments on the day after Christmas when everyone and their mothers would be in them exchanging gifts, looking for bargains, arguing about credit.

Trudy'd done pretty well for herself, Eve decided. Six pair of shoes in one spot. Jesus, what was it with people and shoes? Shipped all but two pairs home. Well, she was never going to wear them.

She cross-checked her inventory list, and came up with six pairs.

And here were three handbags from the same shop. Two sent home, one taken with customer. When she checked her list, she smiled.

"Yeah, I bet it was hard to resist a six-hundred-dollar purse. Six bills." She shook her head. "Just to lug stuff around in, most of which no rational human being has a need to lug anywhere. Let's see what else you helped yourself to."

Before she could continue, Roarke beeped on the house 'link.

"I've got this for you, Lieutenant."

"What? Already? It's only been about a half hour."

"I believe it was mentioned before: I'm good."

"On my way, and I seriously overpaid for this service."

"Pay to play," he said and clicked off.

She found him in the lab where he'd set

up a group of units to handle individual commands. "This way," he told her, "you can ask for any mix you want, or a combination. I've also got her voiceprint, in case you want to try to match it at some point."

"Might be handy. Let's just run it through as it was first. I haven't taken the time to listen to it all the way through."

Now she did, hearing the gaggle of voices. Her own, Baxter's, Trueheart's. Checks and rechecks. Zana's, Bobby's discussing where they might go. The rustling as they donned their outdoor gear.

I'm so glad we're getting out. It'll do us both good. Zana.

Hasn't been much of a trip for you. Bobby.

Oh, now, honey, don't worry about me. I just want you to try to put all this awful business aside for just a couple hours. We've got each other, remember. That's what counts.

They went out with Zana chattering about Christmas trees.

She heard New York as they went outside. Horns, voices, air blimps, the unmistakable belching of a maxibus. It was all a backdrop for more chatter. The weather, the buildings, the traffic, the shops. Interspersed were Baxter and Trueheart, commenting on direction, making small talk.

Man, you see the rack on that one? God is a man, and he's on my side. Baxter.

God might be a woman, sir, deliberately tempting you with what you can't have. Trueheart.

"Not bad, kid," Eve mumbled. "God, you could die of boredom listening to this crap. 'Oooh, look at this, honey. Oh, my goodness,' blah, blah, blah."

"Do you want to move forward?" Roarke asked her.

"No. We'll stick it out."

She drank coffee, and stuck, through the incessant shopping for and purchasing of a table tree, the extra ornaments. The giggles when Bobby made her turn around and close her eyes while he bought her a pair of earrings. Then the cooing about not opening them until Christmas.

"This may make me sick."

They discussed lunch. Should they do this, do that?

"Jesus, do something! Tourists," she said. "They kill me."

More giggles, she thought, more excitement over soy dogs. Over a tube of fake meat, Eve thought in disgust, then straightened in her chair.

"Wait, stop. Run that back. The bit she just said."

"If we must, but rhapsodizing about the menu of a glide-cart is a bit much, even for me."

"No listen, listen to what she says. How she says it."

What makes a soy dog taste so good when it's cooked outside on a cart in New York? I swear you can't get a real grilled dog anywhere on the planet outside of New York.

"Stop record. How does she know that?" Eve demanded. "She doesn't say, 'I bet there's no place.' Or, 'I've never tasted a damn dog that tastes like . . .' whatever. She makes a statement: 'You can't get.'" Nostalgic, knowing. Not the statement, not the tone of a woman having her first corner dog in Manhattan—which is what she said it was, what decided them on the cart. Oh, gee, I've never had one before, it'd be fun. Bitch is lying."

"I won't argue, but it could easily have been a slip of the tongue."

"Could, but isn't. Resume play."

She listened, talk of hats, scarves, of just a little longer. Have to cross the street. Spilled coffee. Concern, just a hint of fear in his voice, the relief.

Now screams, shouts, horns, brakes. Sobbing.

Jesus, Jesus, somebody call an ambulance. Lady, don't move him, don't try to move him.

Now Baxter moving in, moving fast, identifying himself, dealing with the mess.

"Okay, what I want is just the two of them. No background noises, from the time they get the dogs until Baxter's on-scene."

Roarke set it up, hit play.

Conversation again, easy, breezy. Indulgent on his part, Eve thought. Then the little gasp, his immediate response. Irritation in her voice. Then the screams.

"His," Eve ordered, from the coffee spill on.

She watched the graphic readout as well—breathing, volume, tone. "There, there, did you hear it?"

"Breath sucked in. Expected as he's falling into the street."

"A second before. An instant. Maybe a

slip, sure, but maybe a push, too. Now hers. Same sequence."

She leaned forward, and she saw it, heard it. "Deep breath in. Quick, fast. Just a second before the record shows his. Then that little hesitation before she squeaks his name, starts screaming."

Eve's gaze was flat and hard. "She helped him into the street. I'd bet on it. Opportunity. Of the moment again. Let's go through the background voices, the noises, individually—that same sequence. See if anything else pops out."

It was tedious, but she listened to every variant before she was satisfied.

"It's building up," she stated coldly. "Building for me. Can't charge her. The PA'd laugh me out of his office, if I got this past Whitney. But I know what I know. Now it's how to make it stick to her."

"He loves her."

"What?"

"He loves her," Roarke repeated. "You can hear it in his voice. It's going to level him, Eve. This on top of his mother. If you're right, and I have to believe you are, it's going to take him out at the knees."

"I'm sorry. But better he take a shot than be duped every day by a murderer."

She couldn't—wouldn't—think how this would hurt him. Not now, not yet.

"I didn't get far on my checklist, but I've already found one handbag missing. I'll get a full description of it, and anything else that doesn't check, tomorrow. We're going to find them in Zana's possession. I'm bringing her into Interview. That's where I'll get her on this. Interview. I've got no proof, scattered piles of circumstantial. So it's going to be me against her in the box, and that's where I'll turn it."

He was studying her face as she spoke. "You have, on occasion, commented that I can be scary. So, Lieutenant, can you."

She smiled, hard and thin. "You're damn right."

20

She started the morning poking, prodding, bitching, and bellowing at the lab. She thought about bribing, and had courtside Knicks tickets as backup. But fear brought her quicker results.

The minute it started to signal, Eve leapt toward her comp. "Computer, display incoming data on-screen, and produce hard copy."

Acknowledged. Working . . .

She skimmed, then punched a fist into her palm. "Got you, bitch."

"I'll take that as good news." Roarke leaned on the jamb of the door between their offices. "Let me say first that the unfortunate lab tech is going to need therapy. Possibly years of therapy."

"It lit up." She had to hold herself back from doing a victory dance. "Blood on the bedroom carpet, bathroom floor, shower of the empty room at the time in question. They haven't typed it yet, but it's going to be Trudy's."

"Congratulations."

"Haven't bagged her yet, but I will. Even better than the blood, so much better—neither Zana nor Housekeeping did what you could call a thorough cleaning job. I've got a *print* on the inside windowsill. And it's hers. Another on the door leading to the hall."

"Pays to be thorough, or in her case, it doesn't pay not to be."

"Yeah, you got that. Didn't think that far ahead. Didn't think we'd look there. Why bother when she'd left that nice blood trail leading down the emergency escape?"

"And now?"

"Now I dodge the laser stream of hassling with store clerks the day after Christmas." Now she did do a quick dance. "The prints are going to be enough to get me a search warrant. Enough for me to bring her into Interview. I just want to check on a couple other things first, settle on my initial approach."

"Busy day for you."

"I'm ready for one. I'm going to start out here, where it's quiet. Peabody's not due in for a few hours anyway."

"I'll leave you to it. I need to go." But he crossed to her first, cupped her chin to kiss her. "It was nice having you to myself for a couple of days."

"Nice being had."

"Remember that, because I'm going to wheedle you into a few days away. Sun, sand, sea."

"That doesn't sound like a hardship."

"Why don't you mark down January second, then. We'll make it work."

"Okay."

He started out, stopped at the door. "Eve? Will you ask her why? Does it matter?"

"I'll ask. It always matters."

Alone, she brought up the data and images on all former fosters. Once again, she looked for any connection between them. A school, a job, a case worker, a teacher. But there was only Trudy at the core of it.

"One dead," she said softly. "Everyone else alive and accounted for."

So she worked with the dead.

Ralston, Marnie, mother deceased, father unknown. Just, she thought, as Zana's records listed her mother deceased, with father unknown. It was smart to keep data close to the truth when switching IDs.

She ordered Marnie's files on-screen.

Diverse juvenile record, Eve noted. Shoplifting, petty thefts, vandalism, malicious mischief, possession. Raised those stakes to grand theft auto at the tender age of fifteen.

Psychiatric eval claimed recalcitrant, pathological liar with sociopathic tendencies. Strong IQ.

She read the psychiatrist's notes.

Subject is extremely bright, clever. Enjoys pitching her wits against authority. She is an organized thinker who excels at becoming what she believes is most expedient to her goals.

"That's my girl," Eve murmured.

While she can and does appear cooperative for periods of time, this has

*proved to be a deliberate and con-
scious adjustment of behavior. Though
she understands right from wrong, she
chooses whatever course she believes
will gain her the most, i.e., attention,
privileges. Her need to deceive is
twofold: One, for gain. Two, to illustrate
her superiority over those in authority,
which would be rooted in her history of
abuse and neglect.*

"Yeah, maybe. Or maybe she just likes lying." People like lying to cops, she remembered. For some, it was almost knee-jerk.

Eve brought up the history, including the
medical.

Broken hand, broken nose, contusions,
lacerations. Black eyes, concussions. All of
which, according to reports—medical, police, child protection—were eventually hung
on the mother. Mother did time, kid was
tossed into the system. Landed in Trudy's
lap.

But those injuries had been suffered before the psychiatric report. Before the worst
of the criminal offenses. And Marnie Ralston
had spent nearly a year with Trudy from the
age of twelve to thirteen.

Ran away, eluded authorities for nearly two years before the pop on GTA. Yeah, yeah, clever girl. A young girl had to be smart, resourceful, and just plain lucky to last on the streets that long.

And when they'd snapped her up, the clever girl—despite the shrink's findings— was placed in another foster home. Ran off weeks later, and stayed underground until turning eighteen.

Kept out of trouble—or off the radar, Eve noted. Several short-term employments. Stripping, dancing, club work, bar work.

Then, according to the records, *boom*.

"I just don't think so."

Eve brought up the last known ID image of Marnie Ralston, split-screened it with Zana's. Brown hair on Marnie, worn short and straight, she mused. And there was a hard look to her, a kind of edge that said she'd been there and done it, and wouldn't mind doing it all again.

She toyed with the idea of calling in Yancy or another police artist, but decided to fiddle awhile on her own.

"Computer, magnify eyes only, both images."

When the task was complete, she sat

back, studied. The eye color was nearly the same—and any variant could be attributed to fluctuations in the imaging, or the subject's enhancements. The shape was different. Downturned on Marnie, wide, more rounded on Zana's.

She tried the eyebrows—more of an arch on Zana's. The nose—more narrow, slight uptilt.

Was it reaching, she thought, to see those changes as improvements? The sort a vain woman might pay for if she believed they'd make her more attractive? Especially one who might want to change her appearance for other reasons?

But when she tried the mouths, her own curved up. "Oh, now, I guess you liked your lips. Computer, run comparison of current images. Are they a match?"

Working . . . Current images are a match.

"Changed your hair, your eyes, your nose. Planed down the cheeks, but you left your mouth alone. Put on a few pounds," she said aloud as she checked height and weight. "Softened yourself up. But you couldn't do anything about your height."

She wrote it up, exactly as she saw it, listed all supporting evidence. She was going personally to the PA, to a judge, and pressing for the warrants.

Her 'link signalled on her way down the steps. "Dallas, talk fast."

"Hey, I'm back, I'm here. You're not. We had—"

"Contact the PA's office," she interrupted Peabody's cheerful greeting. "Get Reo if you can. She's their golden girl right now."

"What—"

"I need a consult ASAP, and their recommendation for a judge who'll be most apt to sign a couple of warrants."

"For who? For what?"

"For Zana. Search of the hotel room, her belongings. Suspicion of murder, suspicion of attempted murder. That'll start the ball."

"Zana? But—"

"Do it, Peabody." She grabbed her coat from the newel post, swung it on as she walked by Summerset. "I'll run the game for the PA. You want to catch up, read the reports I sent to your desk unit. I've got to run this by the commander. I'm on my way in."

"Jeez, every time I take a day off, something happens."

"Get it moving. I want her in Interview this morning."

She disconnected. Her car was, like her coat, already waiting. At the moment, she decided she was just juiced enough to be grateful for Summerset's annoying efficiency.

Her blood was up. Maybe it was running hotter than it should, but she'd analyze that later. Right now she knew she was on track. She'd have surprise on her side; something she thought she could use with an opponent like Zana. Like Marnie, she corrected. It was time to start thinking of her by that name.

She was going to close this down, then it would be over. Something she would set aside and forget. Trudy Lombard and all those awful months, locked away again where they belonged.

And when it was done, she thought, as she slid into traffic, sure, she'd take a few days off with Roarke. Go to their island, run around naked as monkeys, screw each other brainless in the sand. Grab some sun and surf and gear up for the long, cold winter to come.

Her 'link signalled again. "Dallas, what?"

"Hey, hi! Did you have a magolicious Christmas?"

"Mavis." Eve had to switch her mind, do a mental one-eighty. "Yeah, yeah. Listen, I'm heading to work. Why don't I tag you later?"

"Okay, no prob. Just mostly wanted to be sure you and Roarke remember the coaching classes. Coming up in a couple weeks."

"No, I remember." The horror of it was etched on her mind like laser art on glass.

"Leonardo and I can go with you, if you want. Have some dinner or whatever after."

"Um. Sure. Sure. Ah, isn't this a little early for you to be awake?"

"Baby gets me up early. I guess it's good practice. Look, look what my honey pie made me with his own two hands!"

She held up some sort of short, footed thing—a kind of miniature skinsuit, Eve decided, in bloody-murder red with a lot of silver hearts and squiggles on it.

"Yeah. Wow."

"Because the baby'll be here before Valentine's Day. We're getting so close. What do you think of Berry?"

"What kind of berry?"

"No, for a name, because the baby will be like our sweet little berry, and it could go for a boy or a girl."

"Fine, as long as it doesn't mind being called Blueberry or Huckleberry or Boysenberry once it hits school-age."

"Oh, yeah. Ick. Well, we'll keep thinking. Catch you later."

Imagining an enormous piece of fruit with eyes and legs inside her friend's belly, Eve shuddered. To get rid of it, she contacted Whitney's office.

"Commander," she began when she was put through, "I've had a break in the Lombard homicide."

She took the elevator straight up from the garage, taking on the body jam for the sake of speed. She wanted to move now, move fast. It must've shown on her face, as Peabody jumped up from her desk the minute Eve came into the bull pen.

"Sir. Reo's on her way. I shot her the data, up to current, so she'd have a sense before you spoke with her. Aw, you're wearing the sweater I made you."

534   J. D. ROBB

Baffled for a moment, Eve looked down. She'd been too distracted that morning to pay attention to something like wardrobe. But saw now she was wearing Peabody's sweater.

"Ah . . . it's warm, but light. I like it. It's . . . You made it?"

"Yeah. Both of them—Roarke's, too. And I made this really mag jacket for McNab. Worked on that up at Mavis's, so he wouldn't catch on. Been awhile since I did any serious weaving."

She reached out to fiddle with Eve's sleeve. "McNab sprang for the material, and we worked on the colors together. It looks good."

Momentarily baffled, Eve looked down at the sweater, soft and warm and in shades of heathery blue. "It's great." She didn't think anyone had ever made her a sweater, or much of anything else for that matter. Leonardo didn't count, she decided. It was his business.

"It's really great," she added. "Thanks."

"We wanted to do something unique, you know? Because you guys are. And personal. So I'm glad you like it."

"I do." Or did now that she knew it was

Peabody's own work. Before that, it had just been a sweater.

"Baxter, Trueheart. With me." She headed into her office. It was too small for the four of them, but she didn't want to take time to book a conference room.

"I'm working on warrants. Zana Lombard."

"The Texas housewife?" Baxter interrupted.

"The Texas housewife, who I believe I can prove was once fostered by Trudy Lombard. Who changed her identity for the purpose— at least in part—of ingratiating herself with the victim's son in order to exact revenge on the mother. I want this bumping, so when those warrants come through, I'm having the subject escorted here. Ostensibly to go over her statements, update her, blah, blah. Once her hotel room's clear, I want you in there. Here's what I'm looking for."

She took out a disc. "Descriptions here of a handbag, perfume, a sweater, and some enhancements purchased by the victim. I think Zana, who is in actuality one Marnie Ralston, helped herself to them after she killed Trudy Lombard. Find them, and let me know when you do.

536 J. D. ROBB

"Peabody."

"We're rolling."

"Contact the investigators of the Miami bombing. Club Zed, spring of 2055. Data's in the file. I want to know exactly how body was ID'd. Exactly. Send Reo through when she gets here."

"She pushed him into the street," Baxter said. "That's why we didn't see anybody tailing them, didn't see anyone approach. She did it herself."

"That's what I get." She saw, too, both relief and anger wash over his face. "And what happened there's on me because I didn't see that step. Find those goods, and anything else that puts her with Trudy the night of the murder."

She shoved them out, shut her door. Sitting at her desk, she took a moment to smooth herself out, then contacted Zana at the hotel.

"Hey, sorry. I woke you up."

"It's okay. I'm not sleeping very well. Gosh, it's after nine." She rubbed her eyes like a child. "I think Bobby's going to get out of the hospital this afternoon. It may not be until tomorrow, but I'm hoping for today.

They're going to call me, so I can have everything ready for him."

"That's good news."

"The best. We had a really nice Christmas." She said it, Eve noted, with the tone of a brave little wife, making the best of the bad. "I hope you did, too."

"Yeah, really nice. Listen, Zana, I hate to put you out, but I need to go over some things with you for reports. Paperwork, routine red tape that got bogged down with the holidays. It would really help me out if you could come down here. I'm buried under it. I can have you driven down."

"Oh . . . well, it's just that if Bobby needs me . . ."

"You've got some time before they release him, even if it's today. And you'll be downtown, nearer the hospital. Tell you what, if there's anything you need to pick up, I'll have the uniforms take you around. Then give you a hand getting Bobby home."

"Really? I could really use the help."

"I'll try to get clear here, give you a hand myself."

"I don't know what I'd have done without you the last few days." Those big blue eyes went predictably damp. "It'll take me a little while to get dressed and everything."

"No rush. I've got things I've got to get out of the way first. I'll just have the uniforms bring you down when you're ready. How's that?"

"Okay."

At the knock on her door, Eve sighed. "Gotta go. It's crazed around here this morning."

"I can't even imagine it. I'll be down as soon as I can."

"Yeah, you will," Eve muttered when she cut transmission. "Come on in. Reo." She nodded at the curvy blond APA. "My Christmas was great, yours was, too. Blah, blah, blah, let's get down to it."

"Nice sweater, blah, blah, blah. Everything you've got is circumstantial and speculative. We can't charge, much less prosecute."

"I'll get more. I need the warrants first."

"I can wrangle the search. Items missing from victim's room, victim's daughter-in-law's prints, as well as the blood and the prints in the room next door. Getting the match on the mouth is good, it'll give it a nice push, but it's still in that speculative area. A pair of lips aren't solid ID."

"I'll get more," Eve repeated. "I'm getting more. Get me the search and seizure. I've got her coming in for Interview. I know how to work her."

"You're going to need a confession to lock this up."

Eve smiled. "I'm going to get one."

"Sounds like something I'll want to watch. I'll get the search warrant. Bring her in."

When it was done, she rounded up Baxter and Trueheart. "She's on her way in. Go in, find me what I need. When you're back here with it, give me a beep on my communicator. When I'm ready, I'll send Peabody out for it."

"She seemed so normal," Trueheart commented. "Nice, too."

"Bet she thinks she is. But that's for Mira," who was someone else Eve wanted to bring in.

She called Mira's office, plowed her way through the admin. "I need you in Observation, Interview Room A."

"Now?"

"In twenty. I'm bringing Zana Lombard in. I believe she's actually Marnie Ralston, who assumed a new identity in order to get inside the Lombard household. I'm sending you my report now. I've got the PA's office moving with me. I need you on this."

"I'll do what I can to shuffle things around."

That would have to do, Eve decided. She made a few more contacts, then sat back, cleared her mind.

"Dallas?" Peabody stepped to the office door. "They're bringing her up."

"Okay. It's showtime."

She went out, met Zana and her escorts in the busy corridor outside her division.

Dressed for it, Eve thought. If she wasn't mistaken—and she was getting good at bull's-eyeing wardrobe—Zana was wearing a light blue cashmere crew neck, with floral embroidery on the cuffs. And that matched the description of one of Trudy's purchases.

Ballsy, Eve decided. Smug.

"I really appreciate you coming down. Things are wonky with the holidays."

"After everything you've done for me and Bobby, it's the least I can do. I talked to him right before I left, told him you were going to try to help me bring him back to the hotel from the hospital."

"We'll try to make that happen. Listen, I'm going to use one of the rooms to finish this up. It'll be more comfortable than my office. You want something? Really bad coffee, vending drink?"

Zana looked around the busy corridors like a tourist at a street fair. "Oh, I wouldn't mind a fizzy, any flavor but lemon."

"Peabody? Would you take care of that? I'm going to take Zana into A."

"Sure, no problem."

Eve shifted the file folder as she walked. "Paperwork's a killer," she said casually. "And mostly a pain in the ass, but we want to have all the t's crossed on this, so you and Bobby can get back home."

"We are getting anxious. Work's really piled up, and Bobby wants to get back to it. Plus, I guess we're just not big-city types."

She walked into the room after Eve opened the door, then hesitated. "Oh, is this an interview room, like you see on the cop shows on-screen?"

"Yeah. Most efficient way to go through the statements. You okay with that?"

"Oh, I guess. Actually, it's kind of exciting. I've never been in a police station before."

"We'll sign off on Bobby's statements at the hotel, seeing as he's injured. But we can get yours out of the way, start moving you back toward Texas. Have a seat."

"Have you brought many criminals in here?"

"My share."

"I don't know how you do it. Did you always want to?"

"As long as I can remember." Eve sat across the table from her, slouched back. "I guess Trudy's part of that."

"I don't understand."

"That lack of control I felt when I was with her. Being defenseless. It was a pretty rough time for me."

Zana lowered her eyes. "Bobby told me she wasn't very nice to you. And now, here you are, working so hard to find out who killed her. It's . . ."

"Ironic? That's crossed my mind." She glanced over as Peabody stepped in.

"Got you a cherry," she told Zana. "Tube of Pepsi for you, Dallas."

"I love cherry, thanks." Zana accepted the tube, and a straw. "What do we do now?"

"To keep everything official—and part of the formality, Zana, is my former relationship with Trudy—I'm going to read out the Revised Miranda."

"Oh. Oh, well, gee."

"It's for your protection, and mine," Eve explained. "If this case ends up in the cold file—"

"Cold file?"

"Unsolved." Eve shook her head. "It's tough to realize that may be what happens. But if it does, it's better all around if we have everything very official."

"Well, okay."

"I'm going to set the record." Eve read off the time, the date, the names of those in the room, the case file, then recited the Revised Miranda. "Do you understand your rights and obligations in this matter?"

"Yes. Boy, I'm a little nervous."

"Relax, it won't take long. You are married to Bobby Lombard, the son of the victim, Trudy Lombard. Correct?"

"Yes. We've been married nearly seven months."

"You were well acquainted with the victim."

"Oh, yes. I worked for Bobby and his

partner before Bobby and I got married. I got to know Mama Tru. That's what I called her. Um, well, after Bobby and I got married, that's what I called her."

"And your relationship with her was friendly."

"Yes, it was. Am I doing this right?" she added in a whisper.

"You're doing fine. The victim was, according to your previous statements and statements on record from others, a difficult woman."

"Well . . . she could be, I guess you could call it demanding, but I didn't mind so much. I lost my own mother, so Mama Tru and Bobby are my only family." She stared at the wall, blinked her eyes. "It's just me and Bobby now."

"You've stated you moved to Copper Cove, Texas, looking for employment, sometime after the death of your mother."

"And after I finished business school. I wanted a fresh start." Her lips curved. "And I found my Bobby."

"You had never met the victim or her son before that time."

"No. I guess it was fate. You know how you see somebody, and you just know?"

Eve thought of Roarke, of the way their eyes had met at a funeral. "Yeah, I do."

"It was like that for me and Bobby. D.K., um, Densil K. Easton, Bobby's partner, used to say every time we talked to each other, little hearts flew out of our mouths."

"Sweet. Whose idea was it to come to New York at this time?"

"Um, well, Mama Tru's. She wanted to talk to you. She'd seen you on media reports, about that cloning business, and recognized you."

"Who selected the hotel where you were staying at the time of her death?"

"She did. I guess that's just awful when you think about it. She picked the place where she died."

"We could call that ironic, too. At the time of the murder, you and Bobby were in the room across the hall and three doors down from the victim's."

"Um, gee. I know we were across the hall. I don't remember how many doors down, but that sounds right."

"And at the time of the murder, you and Bobby were in your room."

"Yes. We'd gone out to dinner, Mama Tru said she wasn't up for it. And we got a bottle of wine. After we got back, we . . ." She blushed prettily. "Well, we stayed in the room all night. I went down in the morning, to her room, because she wasn't answering the 'link. I thought maybe she was sick, or a little irritated with us for going out on the town. Then you came, and—and you found her."

She lowered her eyes again, worked up a few tears, Eve noted. "It was awful, just so awful. She was lying there, and the blood . . . You went in. I don't know how you can do that. It must be so hard, being a policewoman."

"Has its moments." Eve opened her file, pushed through some hard copies as if checking facts. "I've got my time line here. I'm just going to read through it, on record, and see if you concur."

While she did, Zana got busy biting her lip. "That sounds right."

"Good, good, now let's see what else we need to go over. Nice sweater, by the way."

Zana preened, looked down. "Thanks. I just liked the color so much."

"Goes with your eyes, doesn't it? Trudy's were green. Wouldn't have looked nearly as good on her."

Zana blinked. "I guess not."

There was a knock on the door. Feeney stepped in. Right on schedule, Eve thought. He held a pocket 'link, bagged for evidence, keeping his hand over it so that it couldn't be clearly seen. "Dallas? Need a minute."

"Sure. Peabody, go ahead and go over the events and time line of the Monday after the murder." Eve rose, walked over to Feeney while Peabody took the ball.

"How long you want me to stand here jawing?" he said under his breath.

"Just glance over at the suspect." Eve did the same, over her shoulder. Then, taking Feeney's arm, drew him out of the room. "Let's give her a minute to think about that. You're sure this is the same type registered to the victim."

"Yep, make, model, color."

"Good. She'd have gotten just enough of a look for that to register. Appreciate it."

"Could've sent one of my boys down with it, you know."

"You look more official and scary." Since she wanted Zana to sweat another minute, Eve dipped her hands in her pockets. "So how'd it go yesterday? Fancy dress dinner."

"Had one of my grandsons tip the gravy

boat. He's a good kid, and we got a nice bond." He smiled wide. "Plus I paid him twenty. Worth it. See, the wife can't get too pissed at the kid, and I got to lose the suit. That was a winner, Dallas. Appreciate it."

"Happy to help." Her communicator beeped. "Dallas."

"Baxter. Couldn't find the sweater, but—"

"She's wearing it."

"No shit? Cocky little bitch. But we've got the handbag, the perfume, and the enhancements. Also—and you're going to love this—since the warrant included communications and electronics, I had Trueheart take a look at her 'link log. We've got her scanning about flights to Bali. She's got a hold on a reservation on one, under the name Marnie Zane, next month. Single. One way. Out of New York, not Texas."

"Isn't that interesting? I'm sending Peabody out for the bag, and other items. Nice work, Baxter."

"Me and the kid had to make up for botching the tail."

"Got her in a corner, Dallas," Feeney commented when she clicked off.

"Yeah, but I want her in a cage."

She stepped back into the room, her expression sober. "Detective Peabody, I need you to retrieve some items from Detective Baxter."

"Yes, sir. We've completed the Monday time line."

"Okay." Eve sat as Peabody went out. "Zana, did you communicate, by 'link, with the victim at any time on the day of her death?"

"With Mama Tru? On that Saturday? She called our room, told us she wanted to stay in."

Eve laid the 'link on the table briefly, put the file over it. "Did you have further 'link communication with her, later that evening?"

"Ah, I can't really remember." She nibbled on her thumbnail. "It's all sort of muddled."

"I can refresh you on that. There were more communications from her 'link to yours. You had a conversation with her, Zana. One you didn't tell me about during your previous statements."

"I guess maybe I did." She looked warily at the folder. "It's hard to remember all the times we talked, especially after everything that's gone on." She offered Eve a guileless smile. "Is it important?"

"Yeah, a little bit important."

"Gosh, I'm sorry. I was so upset, and it's hard to remember everything."

"It doesn't seem like it should be so hard to remember going to her room that night, the night of her murder. She must've looked pretty memorable with her face all busted up."

"I didn't see her. I—"

"Yes, you did." Eve nudged the folder aside so there was nothing between them. "You went down to her room that night while Bobby was asleep. That's how you got that sweater you're wearing, one she bought on the Thursday before her death."

"She gave me the sweater." Tears swam, but Eve swore she saw a light of amusement behind them. "She bought it for me, an early Christmas present."

"That's a pile of bullshit, and we both know it. She didn't give you anything. Not the sweater . . ." She looked over at Peabody who'd brought in another evidence bag. "Not that purse, the perfume, the lip dye, and eye gunk. But you had to figure they wouldn't do her any good, seeing as she was dead. Why shouldn't you enjoy them? Why shouldn't you have it all?"

Eve leaned forward. "She was a stone bitch, you and I both know it. You just seized an opportunity. That's something you're good at. Have always been good at, haven't you? Marnie."

21

It was in her eyes, just for an instant. Not just shock, Eve thought, but excitement. Then they rounded again, innocent and wholesome as a baby's.

"I don't understand what you're saying. I don't want to be here anymore." The lips she'd liked too much to change trembled. "I want Bobby."

"Did you ever?" Eve wondered. "Or was he just handy? But we'll get to that. You're going to want to drop the act now, Marnie. We'll both be happier, as I can't imagine you found someone as boring as Zana fun to cart around."

Marnie sniffled pitifully. "You're being so mean."

"Yeah, I get that way when somebody lies to me. You've been having some fun with that. But you also got a little sloppy in the room next to Trudy's, where you cleaned up. Left some blood. Better, left your prints."

Eve rose, walked around the table to lean over Marnie's shoulder. She caught the subtle floral scent and wondered if Marnie had dabbed on Trudy's new perfume that morning. How she'd felt spritzing on a dead woman's choice.

Probably just fine, Eve decided. Probably giggled while she sprayed.

"You did a good job on the identity switch," she said quietly. "But it's never perfect. Then there's Trudy's 'link. Little things, Marnie, it's always the little things that trip you up. You just couldn't resist lifting a few things from her. You've got sticky fingers, always did."

She reached over, flipped open the file on the table, exposed the split-screen photos she'd generated, along with Marnie Ralston's data and criminal record.

"Busy, busy girl. That's what I saw in you, I think, the first minute, outside Trudy's room. The busy, busy girl inside the housewife."

"You didn't see anything," Marnie said under her breath.

"Didn't I? Well, in any case, you shouldn't have kept the perfume, Marnie, shouldn't have taken that pretty sweater, or that really nice purse."

"She gave me those. Mama Tru—"

"That's crap, and see now you're lying stupid. Smarter, smarter if you worked up those tears again and told me you took them, just couldn't help yourself. You're so ashamed. You and I both know Trudy never gave anybody a damn thing."

"She loved me." Marnie covered her face with her hands and wept. "She loved me."

"More crap," Eve said easily. "More lying stupid. The problem is you ran into a cop who knew her, who remembers her. You didn't count on me showing up that morning before you finished setting things up, cleaning things up. You didn't count on me heading the investigation."

She gave Marnie a pat on the shoulder, then eased a hip on the table. "What were the odds of that?" Eve glanced over at Peabody. "I mean, really."

"Nobody could've figured that one," Peabody agreed. "And it's a really great purse. Shame to let it go to waste. You know what I think, Lieutenant? I think she overplayed it with that faked abduction. She'd've been smarter to stay in the background. But she just couldn't resist grabbing a little spotlight."

"I think you're right. You like being in the shine, don't you, Marnie? All those years you had to play the game. Cops, Child Protection, Trudy. Busted out awhile, got your own back. Never enough. But you're smart. Opportunity plants a boot in your ass, you know how to turn around and grab it."

"You're just making things up because you don't know what happened."

"But I do know. I admire you, Marnie, I have to say. All the planning, all the playacting. You really know how to pull it off. Of course, she walked right into it. Coming here, going after me. Then following her old pattern of messing herself up so she could blame somebody else. It might've taken you months more of being the good little wife, the sweet little daughter-in-law, before you could wrap it up. Come on, Marnie." She leaned forward. "You know you want to tell me. Who'd understand better than somebody who'd been through it? She make you take those cold baths every night? Scrub up after her? How many times did she lock you in the dark, tell you that you were nothing?"

"What do you care what happened to her?" Marnie said softly.

"Who says I do?"

"I don't think you have anything. Those things?" She gestured to the evidence bag. "Mama Tru gave them to me. She loved me."

"She never loved a soul on or off planet but herself. But maybe you can swing that with a jury. You think, Peabody?"

Peabody pursed her lips as if considering. "She's got a shot, especially if she turns on the waterworks. But when you put them with the rest, chances drop sharply. You know, Lieutenant, there's the case for lying in wait—the big picture. Assuming a false identity—not a big hit, but added up." Peabody lifted a shoulder. "Assuming it's for the purposes of murder. Man, you give the jury that, the fact that she married the victim's son just to get in position to kill her former foster mother. 'Cause that's fricking cold. Then factor in the money, murder for gain. She's looking at life, off-planet facility. Hard time."

Peabody looked at Marnie. "Maybe you

can convince us the actual murder was un-premeditated. Maybe you could make a case of self-defense for yourself. While you've got our sympathy."

"Maybe I should call a lawyer."

"Fine." Eve pushed off the table. "No skin off mine, 'cause I've got you. You spring the lawyer, Marnie, that's your right. Once you do, it cuts deep into my sympathy and ad-miration. You got a name?" Eve asked eas-ily. "Or do you want court-appointed?"

"Wait. Just wait." Marnie picked up her fizzy, sipped. When she sat it down again, the guilelessness was replaced by calcula-tion. "What if I tell you she was going to rake you to the bone, you and your man? I stopped her. That's got to be worth some-thing."

"Sure it is. We'll talk about that." Eve sat back down. "But you're going to want to lay it out for me. Why don't we start at the be-ginning?"

"Why not? God knows I'm sick to death of Zana, you hit on that one. You got my sheet, there. Juvie, the works?"

"Yeah."

"It doesn't tell the whole story. You know

how that goes. I got kicked around, since I was a kid."

"I saw your medicals. You had it rough."

"I learned to kick back. I looked after myself, because nobody else was going to." In disgust, she shoved the remainder of the fizzy aside. "Can I get some coffee? Black."

"Sure, I'll take care of it." Peabody walked to the door, slipped out.

"The system blows," Marnie continued. "Beats me to hell and back how you can work for it, after what it did to you."

Eve kept her gaze level. "I like being in charge."

"Yeah, yeah, I get that. Got yourself a badge, that frosty weapon. Kick some ass regular. I can see how that could work for you, how you get some of your own back."

"Let's talk about you."

"My favorite subject. So, they finally get me clear of my bitch of a mother, and what do they do? Dump me with Trudy. First, I figure, Hey, I can work this. Nice house, nice things, do-gooder and her boy. But she's worse than my mother. You know."

"I know."

"She was strong. I was puny back then, and she was strong. Cold baths every night—every fucking night—like it was her religion. Locked up in my room every night afterward. I didn't mind that, it was quiet. Plenty of time to think."

Peabody came in with the coffee, set it on the table.

"You know, she put something in my food once to make me sick after I took a pair of her earrings?" Marnie sipped the coffee, made a face. "Been awhile since I've been in a cop shop. You guys still can't come up with decent coffee."

"We suffer in our fight against crime," Peabody said dryly, and made Marnie laugh.

"Good one. Back to me. So, the second time the bitch caught me, she cut my hair off. I had nice hair. Wore it shorter back then, but it was nice."

She lifted a hand to it, shook it back. "She cut it off to the scalp—like, I don't know, I was some kind of war criminal or something. Then she told the social worker I'd done it to myself. Nobody did a damn thing about it. That's when I knew there'd be payback. One day, somehow. She cut my damn hair off."

Eve allowed herself a trickle of sympathy. "You ran away."

"Yeah. Thought about setting the house on fire, with her inside, but that wouldn't've been smart. They'd come after me harder if I'd done that."

And the trickle went dry. "Arson, murder, yeah, they'd've come after you hard."

"Anyway, I was young. Plenty of time for payback. But they came after me anyway. You cops ever think about just letting somebody be?"

She shook her head, took another sip of coffee.

"You got away from her when you were thirteen. That's half a lifetime ago for you, Marnie. Long time to hold a grudge."

Marnie's voice was as bitter as the coffee. "What good's a grudge if you don't hold it? She told me I was a whore. Born a whore, die a whore. That I was ugly, useless. That I was nothing. Every day I was with her, she told me. She wanted new living room furniture, so she busted it up, said I did it. The state wrote her a check and put me on restriction. She made my life hell for damn near a year."

"You waited a long time to pay her back for it."

"I had other things to do. Kept my eye on her, though, just in case opportunity knocked. Then it did."

"The night of the bombing in Miami."

"Sometimes fate just drops it in your lap, what can I say? I was sick that night, got somebody to cover for me. Nobody gave a shit, joint like that. Had to give her my ID and pass code so she could get in the back, into my locker for costumes. Then I hear about it on-screen. Place is blown up, nearly everybody's dead, and in pieces. Well, Jesus, lucky break for me, wasn't it? I'd gone in, I'd be in pieces. Shook me up, let me tell you. Really made me think."

"And you thought, 'Why not be someone else?' "

"Well, here's the thing. I owed a little money here and there. Can't pay if I'm dead. I took the dead friend's ID, what money we had between us, and lit out. She had a nice stash."

"You got a name on her?"

"Who? Oh, shit, what was her name? Rosie, yeah. Rosie O'Hara. Why?"

"She might have next of kin looking for her."

"Doubt it. She was a street LC with a funk

habit." She dismissed the woman who'd died in her place as callously as she'd dismissed the coffee. "Her ID wasn't going to hold me long, so I knew I needed to ditch it, get fresh. That's when I came up with the idea for Zana. It's not so hard to get fresh ID and data if you know where to go, whose palm to grease. Had some work done, face work. Off the books. Good investment, the way I looked at it. Especially when I checked out Bobby."

"Nice-looking guy, single, ambitious."

"All that, and still tight with Mama. I wasn't figuring on killing her, let's get that straight." She lifted both hands, pointed the index fingers across at Eve. "Let's get that real clear. None of this 'lying in wait' crap. I just figured on stealing her boy, then making her life a misery, like she'd done to me. Maybe getting a nice nest egg out of it."

"Just a long con," Eve supplied.

"That's right. Bobby was easy. He's not a bad guy all in all. Boring, but he's okay. Plus he's got some moves in the sheets. And Trudy?"

Marnie sat back, grinning ear-to-ear. "She was a pleasure. Figured she had a new slave, meek little Zana. Oh, Mama Tru, I'd be happy to do that for you. You got dirty work needs doing, I'm your girl. Then I get the big surprise. She's got money tucked away. Pretty big money, too, so why shouldn't I get some of it? I've got the run of her house, seeing as I'm her little helper. She's got good stuff in there, stuff that costs. Now where's this coming from? Just takes a little research, a little detecting. Blackmail. I can turn the tables on her with this. Just need a little time, need to figure it all out."

Propping an elbow on the table, Marnie set her chin on her fist. "I was looking for the best way to siphon off some of the money, then expose her. They'd lock her up, like she'd locked me up."

Enjoying this, Eve thought, enjoying every minute of this.

"Then she sees you on that media report, and gets all worked up about going to New York. I was going to wrap this up in shiny paper, drop it right in your lap. Then I'd stand back, big wide eyes, horrified that my husband's mother turned out to be a black- mailer. I'd be laughing my ass off."

"A good plan," Eve acknowledged, "but opportunity jumped out at you again."

"If you'd fallen in, it would've turned out differently. You want to think about that," Marnie said, and gestured with her drink. "I figured you'd pay her off, or at least take a couple days to think it over. Then I'd come to you, all dewy-eyed and upset, tell you what I'd found out about my darling husband's mama."

Marnie nudged the coffee aside. "You and me, we'd both have gotten something out of that. Every kid she ever screwed with would've gotten something out of that. But you pissed her off good. Roarke? He shot her through the ozone. She was going to make you pay, and pay big. That's all she could think about. Somebody screwed with her, she'd do anything to screw them back, and bigger. You saw what she did to herself."

"Yeah. Yeah, I did."

"Not the first time, like you said. You ask me, that woman had some serious issues. She'd already bunged herself up good when she called me. Not Bobby—he wouldn't put up with what she wanted to do. He'd have stopped her, or tried. But me? Her sweet, biddable daughter-in-law? She knew she could count on me, she knew she could bully me. It wasn't much of a stretch to act stunned when I went into her room. Her face was a freaking mess. You know what she told me? You want to know?"

"I'm riveted," Eve answered.

"She said you'd done it."

Eve sat back, as if stunned. "Really?"

"Oh, yeah, she put it on thick. Look what she did to me. After I took her in, gave her a home. And she's a policewoman! So I played the part right back. Oh, my, oh, gosh. We have to get you to the hospital, tell Bobby, call the police! But she lays it out. No, no, no. A cop did this, and she's married to a powerful man. She's afraid for her life, see? So she gets me to make the recording. For protection, she says, and I see just how she's wheeling it. It's all there, subtle-like. If you don't do the right thing, she'll send a copy of the recording to the media, to the mayor, the chief of police. They'll know everything. I'm supposed to make a copy—so she keeps the original— and hand-carry it to you at Cop Central. No telling Bobby. She makes me swear."

Laughing, Marnie swiped a finger over her heart. "So I make her some soup, and I put a nice tranq in it, add some wine. And she's out. Could've killed her then, you know. You want to think about that, too."

"I'm thinking about it."

"I searched the room, found the sap she'd made. Found a copy of the file she had on you, too. Interesting stuff. I took all of it. She called me later, but I said I couldn't talk. Bobby was right there. I'd call her when we got back from dinner, after he was asleep. She didn't care much for that, let me tell you. Well, you got the 'link right there, so you've heard."

"She pushed you," Eve prompted. "Trudy didn't like being told to wait."

"Nope. But I'm like, Oh, let me tell Bobby. We won't go out, we'll come down and take care of you. I know she won't go for that, so she takes another pill, and I go out on the town. Long night for me, but God! It was fun. Just bat my eyes, ask Bobby if we can have champagne, and he pulls out all the stops in his middle-class way. I'm so juiced, you know?"

She drew breath in her nose, letting her head fall back, closing her eyes as she re-lived it. "Lay him just right when we get back, give him a little something extra to make him sleep. Then I go on down the hall to have my talk with Trudy."

"You took the weapon with you?"

"Sure. Not to use it," she added quickly. "Get that straight. I'm putting that on record. What I figured was I'd show it to her, stay in character at least awhile. What have you done? You lied to me! I'm going to tell Bobby. I'm going to the police!"

Marnie laid her hands on her belly and laughed. "God! You should've seen her face. She never expected it. So, she slapped me. Told me I was hysterical, and slapped me. Said I was going to do just what she told me, and no back talk. If I wanted to keep my cozy nest, I'd shut my mouth and do what she said. Otherwise I'd be out on my ass, she'd see to it."

Her face was grim now, and full of hate. "She said I was *nothing,* just like she did when I was a kid. 'You're nothing,' she said, 'and you'd better remember who's in charge.' Then she turned her back on me. I still had the sap in my hand. I didn't think about it, didn't even think. It just happened. I let her have it good. And she went down, right down to her knees, and I let her have it again. Nothing in my life ever felt better. Who was nothing now?"

She held up her coffee. "Hey, can I get another? It's crap, but it gives you a buzz."

"Sure." Eve signaled to Peabody, then rose herself to get water from the jug kept in the room.

"I didn't plan it," Marnie continued. "But sometimes you can't stick to the plan. You got anybody behind the mirror?"

Eve studied her own reflection. "Does it matter?"

"Just like knowing if I have an audience. I didn't murder her. I just lost my head for a minute. She slapped me, right across the face."

"Open palm," Eve murmured, remembering. "Quick sting, not hard enough to leave a mark. She was good at it."

"She liked pain. Liked to give it, liked to get it." Marnie scooted around in the chair, facing Eve so their eyes met in the mirror in a gesture of intimacy.

Inside Eve, something twisted. She understood what it was to find a weapon in her hand, and to use it. Blindly, ferociously.

"She was one of those S and M types, without the kick of sex," Marnie went on.

"That's what I think. She was one sick bitch. But I didn't set out to kill her. I didn't even get a chance to tell her who I was. Watch her face when I did. Too damn bad. I used to dream about doing that."

"That must've been a disappointment." Eve turned back as Peabody came in with fresh coffee, kept her face neutral. "You had to think fast after it was done."

"Thought about just running. But I kept my head. Probably shouldn't have taken the sweater and stuff." Marnie glanced down at the sweater, smiled. "But I couldn't resist. Should've waited, gotten them later. But it was spur of the moment."

"You knew the room next door was empty."

"Yeah. The maid mentioned it. Thought we might want to take that room so we could be next door to each other. No, thank you. The window wasn't locked on it, otherwise I'd have had to clean up on the escape platform, change, and walk around, go in the front. Crappy hotel, crappy security. Didn't figure anyone would look next door. I left a trail leading down the escape. Open window, dead woman, blood trail. I was careful."

"Not half bad," Eve agreed. "You shouldn't have pushed it. You should've let Bobby find her."

"It was more fun the way I did it. You've got to get in a few kicks. You could've knocked me over with a feather when you and Roarke showed, though. Last people I expected to see come knocking on the old bitch's door. Had to improvise."

"You must've sweated some, having to leave the 'link, the weapon, the bloody towels next door while we went over the scene."

"Some, yeah. But I figured if you found them, you still didn't have reason to look at me. The business the next day was a little insurance. I get the stuff, head out, dump everything in different recyclers while I walk around, find the right spot. I used to live in New York. I knew that bar."

"I knew that."

Marnie snorted. "Come on."

"You slipped up with the dogs, made the wrong comment. I had a homer on both of you that day. A little insurance for me."

Marnie's face went blank, then there was a snap of irritation before she shrugged. "Bobby slipped."

"You're in it this far, Marnie, and you're going to get points for cooperating. Don't start bullshitting me now. Trudy's dead, and she's got all that money. Bobby's sitting between you and it. Boring Bobby."

"You think this was about money? Money's a little icing, but it's not the cake. It's payback. She deserved it, you know damn well she deserved it. Bobby's an idiot, but he's okay. If I gave him a little nudge, it was impulse, that's all. Just a little something to keep you looking for the invisible man. And I tried to pull him back. I got witnesses."

She sulked over her coffee. "Tally it up, why don't you? You've got one dead blackmailer. And she hit me first. I destroyed the discs of the recording she had me make. All of them: I destroyed the copies of your file— as a favor. If I was after money, I could've come after you with them. But I didn't, 'cause the way I saw it, she put us in the same boat back then. I could've waited, and screwed with Bobby when we were back in Texas. I've got nothing but time."

"But you aren't going back to Texas. Bali, isn't it?"

A smile glimmered again. "I'm thinking

about it. A lot of people she screwed with are going to be glad I took care of her. You ought to thank me. She messed with us, Dallas. Preyed on and played with us. You know it. You know she got what she deserved. We come from the same place, you and me. You'd have done the same thing."

Eve thought of the way their eyes had met in the mirror. What she'd seen in Marnie's. What she'd seen in her own. "That's how you figure it."

"That's how it is. I'm not going down for this. Not when it comes out what she was, what she did. Assault, maybe. I do a couple years for that and the ID gambit. But murder? You can't make that stick."

"Watch me." Eve pushed to her feet. "Marnie Ralston, you're under arrest for the murder of Trudy Lombard. Further charges are attempted murder of Bobby Lombard. We'll toss in the ID fraud, giving false statements to the police. You'll do more than a couple years, Marnie. You've got my word on it."

"Oh, cut the crap," Marnie insisted. "Turn off the record, shove your partner out so it's just you and me. Then tell me how you really feel."

"I can tell you how I feel, Marnie, on or off record."

"You're glad she's dead."

"You're wrong." What had clutched inside of her loosened. Because Marnie was wrong. Completely. "If it was up to me, she'd be in a cage, the same as you'll be. She'd be in a cage for what she did to me, to you, to every kid she ever abused, to every woman she ever exploited. That's justice."

"That's *bullshit*."

"No, that's the job," Eve corrected. "But you didn't leave it up to me. You picked up that sap, and you cracked her skull open."

"I didn't plan it—"

"Maybe you didn't," Eve interrupted. "But you didn't stop there. While she was lying there, bleeding, you stole from her. To get to that point, the point where you could exact your revenge, you used an innocent man. You left the bed where you'd made love with him, and killed his mother. Then you watched him grieve. You put him in the hospital, for kicks, for a little insurance. You did to him what she tried to do to us. You made him nothing. If I could, I'd send you over for that alone."

She braced her hands on the table, leaned over so their faces were close. "I'm not like you, Marnie. You're pathetic, taking and ruining lives for something that's over."

There were tears now, real ones, angry ones, glimmering in Marnie's eyes. "It's never over."

"Well, you'll have a long time to think about that. Twenty-five to life, I'd say. I'm nothing like you," Eve repeated. "I'm the cop. And I'm going to give myself the pleasure of taking you down to booking personally."

"You're a hypocrite. You're a liar and a hypocrite."

"You can think that, but I'll be sleeping in my own bed tonight. And I'm going to sleep really well."

She took Marnie's arm, pulled her to her feet. Pulling out her restraints, she snapped them on Marnie's wrists. "Peabody, finish up here, will you?"

"I'll be out in six months," Marnie said when Eve escorted her into the hall.

"Keep dreaming."

"And Bobby'll pay for my lawyers. She deserved it. Say it! She deserved it. You hated her, just as much as I did."

"You just piss me off," Eve said wearily. "You robbed me of the chance to face her down, to do my job and see she paid for everything she'd done."

"I want a lawyer. I want a psych eval."

"You'll get both." Eve nudged her into an elevator, headed down to booking.

When she was back in her office, Mira came in, closed the door.

"You did a good job in Interview."

"I got lucky. Her ego was on my side."

"And you recognized that. She didn't recognize you."

"She wasn't off by much. I've killed, and I know I've got the violence in me that makes me capable of it. Then. Now. But murder's got a different face. I don't see that in my mirror.

"Thing is," she added, "she won't see it in hers, either."

"But you'll see the truth. She won't. I know it wasn't easy for you, to do what you did. To do it from the start of this. How do you feel?"

"I've got to go to the hospital and tell that poor son of a bitch what she did, and why.

I've got to go there and break his heart, leave that scar on him. I could feel a hell of a lot better."

"Do you want me to go with you?"

"He's going to need something, somebody, after. It'll be up to him. But I think I have to do this, just the two of us. I think I owe him that. What do you think if I contacted the partner, they seem to be tight. Tell him to get his ass up here."

"I think Bobby's lucky to have you looking out for him."

"Friends give you a cushion for the fall, even when you think you don't need or want one. I appreciate you stopping by here, to see if I needed one. I'm okay."

"Then I'll let you finish."

An hour later Eve was sitting beside Bobby's hospital bed, helpless and miserable as tears tracked down his cheeks.

"There has to be a mistake. You've made a mistake."

"There's not. I haven't. And I'm sorry, but I don't know how else to tell you but straight out. She used you. She planned it. Parts of it maybe since she was thirteen. She claims she didn't plan to kill your mother, and that may be true. It was of the moment. It always looked that way, so it could be that way. But beyond that, Bobby, and I know it's a punch in the face, she planned, she covered up, she used. She wasn't the woman she pretended to be. That woman never existed."

"She—she just isn't capable . . ."

"Zana Kline Lombard wasn't capable. Marnie Ralston was and is. She confessed, Bobby, she walked me through it."

"But we were married, all these months. We lived together. I know her."

"You know what she wanted you to know. She's a pro, a manipulator with a sheet as long as my arm. Bobby. Look at me, Bobby. You were raised by a manipulative woman, primed to be taken by another."

"What does that make me?" His hand fisted, punched lightly on the bed. "What the hell does all that make me?"

"A target. But you don't have to keep being one. She's going to try to play you. She's going to cry and apologize and tell you things like she started all this before she really knew you, that she fell for you on the way. She'll say that part was never a lie. She'll say things like she did this for you.

She'll have all the right words. Don't be a target for her again."

"I love her."

"You love smoke. That's all she is." Impatient, a cinder of anger burning in her belly, Eve got to her feet. "You'll do what you do. I can't stop you. But I'm saying that you deserve better. I figure it took guts for a twelve-year-old kid to sneak me food, to try to make things a little easier for me. It's going to take guts for you to face what you're going to have to face. I'll make it easier for you if I can."

"My mother's dead. My wife's in prison, charged with her murder. With maybe trying to kill me. For God's sake, how can you make it easier?"

"I guess I can't."

"I need to talk to Zana. I want to see her."

Eve nodded. "Yeah, fine. You're free to go down for visitation once they spring you."

"There'll be an explanation. You'll see."

You won't, she decided. *Maybe you can't.* "Good luck, Bobby."

She went home, hating that she'd closed a case and still carried a sense of discouragement, of failure. The man would be manipulated. Maybe the system would as well.

She'd closed the case, but it wasn't over. Sometimes, she thought, they never were.

She walked in, glanced at Summerset. "Let's just keep this moratorium going another few hours. I'm too damn tired to screw around with you."

She went straight to the bedroom. And there he was, stripped to the waist, pulling a T-shirt out of a drawer.

"Lieutenant. I don't have to ask you about your day. It's all over your face. She slipped through?"

"No, I got her. Full confession, for what it's worth. PA's going with Murder Two on Trudy, reckless endangerment on Bobby. She'll go over, and for a long time."

He pulled on the shirt as he crossed to her. "What is it?"

"I just left the hospital. Told Bobby."

"You would do that yourself," Roarke murmured, and touched her hair. "How horrible was it?"

"As much as it gets. He doesn't believe it, or part of him does. You could see part of him knew I was giving it to him straight. It's more he *won't* see it, won't accept it. He's going to go down there, talk to her. She claimed he'd end up paying for her lawyers, and you know, she's going to be right."

Roarke slid his arms around her. "Love. Who can argue with it?"

"He's a victim." She dropped her forehead to his. "And one I can't reach."

"He's a grown man, making his own decisions. Not helpless, Eve." He tipped her face up. "You did your job."

"I did my job. So what am I bitching about? It didn't tie up the way I wanted. That's the breaks. Nice that you're here, though. Good that you're here."

She turned, wandered over toward the tree.

"What else?"

"She said we were alike. We're not, I know we're not. But there's a piece of me like her, and that piece knows how she could pick up that sap and whale away. There's a piece of me that understands that."

"Eve, if you didn't have that piece, didn't understand why some use it and you don't, you wouldn't be such a damn good cop."

Weight simply slid off her shoulders as she turned and looked at him. "Yeah. Yeah.

You're right. I knew there was a reason I kept you around."

She walked back to him, tugged on the sleeve of his T-shirt. "What's this for, ace?"

"I thought I'd grab a workout, but my wife got home earlier than expected."

"I could use one myself. Burn off some of this annoyance." She stepped back to remove her weapon harness, then angled her head. "If you found out I'd been putting on a sham, that I'd hooked you just to get to your bottomless vault of moolah, what would you do about it?"

He gave her that wicked smile, that bolt of blue from the eyes. "Why now, darling Eve, I'd kick your sorry ass, then invest a great deal of that moolah in making the rest of your life bloody hell."

More weight lifted, and she grinned at him. "Yeah, that's what I thought. I'm a very lucky woman."

She tossed her weapon on the chair, dropped her badge beside it. Then she reached for his hand, linked fingers, and for a little while, put the job away.